INTO THE DARK

Wincing, Eachann cradled his broken arm and looked at Dubric. "Yer him, ain't ye? Lord Dubric hisself."

"Yes. What brings a battered goose farmer to my castle?"

Eachann looked up at Dien before returning his pained gaze to Dubric. "The dark, m'lord. T'was the dark."

"That's the same thing he's been telling me," Dien said, drawing his cloak higher over the boy's shoulders. "The fall rattled his brains."

Dubric knelt stiffly before them, his knee resting beside steaming vomit. "Why the dark, Eachann? What happened in the dark?"

"The dark, it took another one," Eachann said. "This time it was one I knew."

THREADS
OF
MALICE

†

Tamara Siler Jones

BANTAM BOOKS

THREADS OF MALICE
A Bantam Spectra Book / November 2005

Published by Bantam Dell
A Division of Random House, Inc.
New York, New York

Bantam Books, the rooster colophon, Spectra, and the portrayal of
a boxed "s" are trademarks of Random House, Inc.

ISBN-13: 978-0-553-58710-4
ISBN-10: 0-553-58710-2

Printed in the United States of America
Published simultaneously in Canada

www.bantamdell.com

OPM 10 9 8 7 6 5 4 3 2 1

ACKNOWLEDGMENTS

I would like to thank my writer buddies Gail Brookhart, Catherine Darensbourg, Johnny B. Drako, Andrew Heward, C. E. Murphy, June Drexler Robertson, Wen Spencer, Linda Sprinkle, and Cassandra Ward for enduring me while I wrote this story. Also Joe and Gay Haldeman, Holly Lisle, and Lynn Viehl for being accessible, inspirational, and answering my endless questions. Additional thanks to my editor, the amazing Juliet Ulman, and my agent, William Reiss, for, well, everything.

Thank you to Ashford Handicrafts (www.ashford.co.nz) for letting me use their weaving pattern in a gruesome way.

Special thanks to Meg Godwin, website manager, and her sister, Sam Godwin. It's Sam's hard work that ensures that my narrative is clean, and she rocks, too.

Love and appreciation to my husband, daughter, and extended family. I would have lost my way long ago without them.

And, last, I'd like to thank Joshua Rode, his wife, Tracy, and their kids. Josh lit the way and believed in me, even before I believed in myself. I am and will always be his faithful grasshopper.

Josh, this book is for you.

For Joshua Rode
He put my hand on the light switch.
It's all his fault.
Remember that.

Lives weave upon the warp of family. The strength of those base threads enhances the weft or snarl against it, producing a beautiful cloth or useless rags.

Calladiere Bebhinn
From a speech given at Waterford Castle
Tenth moon, 2217

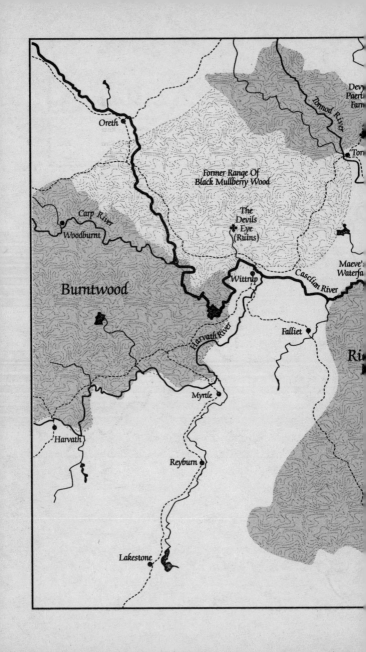

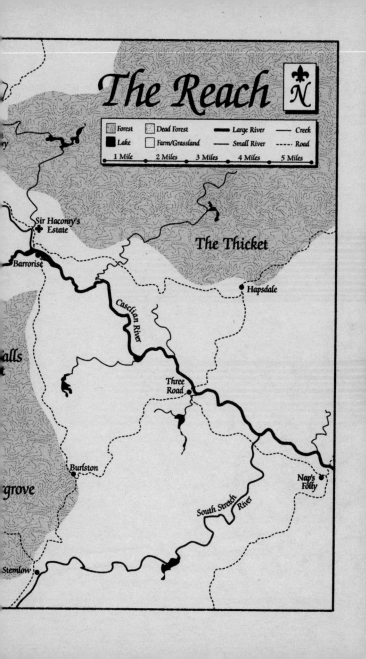

PART 1
SPIN

CHAPTER

I

✝

Braoin saw strings.

They streamed from somewhere above, dangling before his eyes. Black and shining in reflected firelight, they rustled in the slightest breeze and hung before him, just out of reach.

Not that he could move his hands to try to touch them. He felt like immovable sludge, thick and heavy and still. He lay on his belly, his head balanced upright on his chin, his muscles lax and uncooperative. He blinked and time strung away from him, fading to a dark river.

When he dragged his eyes open again the black strings had disappeared and his view had changed.

His head rested on its side and he stared at his right hand—at least it looked like his right hand, with paint on his knuckles as he remembered, but it lay slumped on a board like a dead slab of meat. Beyond it he saw only shifting darkness. He took a breath, determined to stay awake, and tried to move his fingers. One finger, the smallest, twitched, but the rest remained still.

Goddess, I've never been this drunk, he thought, letting his eyes fall closed again as he tried to think. He remembered eating supper with his aunt's family, but he'd had to leave before sunset, had to get home early because . . .

The dark! His eyes blinked open. His paint-stained right hand and his bare wrist and forearm lay still; there was no reaction when he tried again to move his fingers. He could not lift his head nor move his legs, which hung free beneath his hips. His nude upper body lay chest-down on a hard, scratchy surface, his arms were bare, and his back and shoulders felt cold. Braoin could tell from the breeze on his toes and testicles that he no longer wore his boots, or his pants.

No, no, no! Desperate to move, he forced a twitch through his dead fingers. A spasm gripped his hand, flipping it off the board like a fish out of a bucket.

"Waking, eh," a man's voice whispered from the dark. "Was afeared of that. Quit yer kicking if ye know what's good for ye."

"Let me go, please," Braoin said, his tongue thick. It sounded like "Eh ee ogh, eeh."

A sigh. "Talking ain't gonna make it no better." Fingers gripped Braoin's left ankle, then pain sliced around it, holding it fast, as the man tied him tight.

Braoin pleaded in nonsense syllables while the man moved on to fasten his right foot.

"Shh. He's coming."

Something moved far behind Braoin, something big and lumbering. "Don't talk to it," a second voice said with a low, threatening growl.

A mumbled apology, then Braoin heard steps hurry away.

He heard nothing for a long time, nothing but the rhythmic rush of blood in his ears. Try as he might, he could not move, and he saw only a long length of board leading into the dark.

A thick-bellied man in black robes walked into

Braoin's line of sight. He reached down and lifted Braoin's escaped hand, slamming it on the board.

Braoin swallowed and tried to plead, but only terrified guttural whines escaped his throat.

Fat fingers wrapped black twine around the board and Braoin's wrist, holding his hand still and tying it tight. The man muttered a curse then walked toward Braoin's head.

Braoin cried out and tried to shake his head. *Please, I'll do anything. I just want to go home.*

The man grabbed Braoin's hair and yanked his head, wrenching it upright. "No, please." Braoin scrunched his eyes shut.

"Quiet! We're not allowed to play here." The man moved to the left, tying that hand as well, then he leaned close and whispered, dragging a finger up Braoin's bare arm, "Soon, though. I do so love to play, especially with lads like you. And I have the perfect place. Quiet and . . ." the fingertip moved across his bare shoulders and gouged into his spine as it scratched down toward his buttocks, ". . . private. Just you and me and the dark."

Held tight, Braoin prayed. He looked at the curtain of shining black strings hanging over the dais before him, and noticed slippered feet poking through. "Please," he said in his garbled, dead-tongue voice, raising his eyes and struggling to see the observer sitting above him. "Please let me go. I don't want to die. For Goddess' sake, I'm only seventee—"

The man slipped black twine around Braoin's neck and pulled, wrenching Braoin's head up and back. "Behold the master," he said, tightening the vise around Braoin's throat. "May he judge you worthy."

Braoin saw above the strings, above the slippered

feet, until he could see his silent observer: a desiccated, nearly skeletal corpse holding a whip. Its long,
dead teeth were gleaming and yellow and it grinned at
Braoin while he was dragged into unconsciousness.

Dubric Byerly sat at his desk, his thoughts churning.
An open letter lay before him from the mother of a
member of the castle staff. After the murders the previous moon, her distraught daughter, the castle's morning cook, had journeyed home to fetch her family.
Once there, in the dead of night, she had killed her
children, then herself. The grieving grandmother
wanted to know what had happened. What had drawn
her beloved daughter to such despair. Why her daughter had killed herself. Why her son-in-law had done
such terrible things.

These were not questions Dubric could answer.

He settled his mind and wrote a letter of condo-
lence, expressing deep and heartfelt regret for the loss
and offering to pay a stipend to ease the financial burden it wrought.

That done, he sealed the letter, set it aside for deliv-
ery, then sipped his tea.

The door burst open and Dubric started as Lars ran
into the office. Gawky and tall as any lad on the cusp of
manhood, Lars had cheeks that were flushed an urgent
purple and his straw-colored hair was unkempt and
windblown like a tousled halo. He smelled of mud and
horse manure.

"Sir! We've received a messenger from the northern
reach."

"What is it?" Dubric asked, standing.

Lars held Dubric's gaze. "A murder, sir, at least I believe that's what he's saying. He rode all night and he's terrified."

Not again, Dubric thought, groaning. Gathering his cloak, he followed Lars from the office.

By the time they reached the stables, Dubric had slopped a fair share of mud upon his boots and trousers. Flavin, the stable master, waited outside the door, crushing his hat in his hands. "The lad's nigh about spent," he said. "And his mule . . . I'll do what I can, but I ain't holding out hope, sir. Mules ain't meant to run like that. I've got Goudin walking her, but I can't tend her further 'til she cools."

Dubric nodded grimly and Lars opened the stable door for him.

Dubric's squire, Dien, knelt near an open stall door, holding a filthy, bleeding boy as the lad splattered Dien's boots and the straw on the ground with tendrils of vomit. Dien cradled the boy as if he could protect the lad from the horrors he had come to tell.

Dubric hurried toward them with Lars close behind. "What happened?"

"Not sure yet, sir," Dien said, patting the boy gently on the back as the retching eased. "Eachann hit his head and he's not making much sense. Someone killed, best as I can tell, from the northern reach. Beyond that, your guess is as good as mine. He's insisting he talk to you."

The stable door opened again and Otlee, Dubric's youngest page, ran through with physician Rolle behind him.

"Fetch him some water," Dubric said to Otlee.

"Yessir!" Otlee bobbed a quick bow and ran out of the stable.

Dubric approached the boy slowly, leaving Rolle plenty of room to work. "How old are you, son?"

The boy winced at the physician's touch. "Thirteen summers, m'lord, give er take. Never paid much 'tention."

"And your name is Eachann?"

"Yessir, I—" He grimaced, lurching away from the physician. "Cripes! Ye ain't gotta kill me, I'm a'ready half there!"

Dubric offered a consoling smile. "You were saying?"

"Geese, m'lord. I tends 'em." The physician touched Eachann's bleeding shoulder and the boy yelped again.

The physician grasped the boy's chin, holding him still while moving a finger in front of the boy's eyes. "As well as a variety of contusions, he has a dislocated shoulder, a broken ulna . . ." the finger dropped and Rolle leaned close to look into his patient's eyes, "and a concussion, apparently." He stood, sighing. "I do believe he will survive questioning, but please, get him bathed and into a warm bed as soon as possible. You have no business keeping him here in a stable."

Rolle gathered his things. "Send a runner to inform me when he's settled so I can set the arm and give him something for the pain. Until then, I leave him to your care."

"Thank you," Dubric said as Rolle walked past.

Wincing, Eachann cradled his broken arm and looked at Dubric. "Yer him, ain't ye? Lord Dubric hisself."

"Yes. What brings a battered goose farmer to my castle?"

Eachann looked up at Dien before returning his pained gaze to Dubric. "The dark, m'lord. T'was the dark."

"That's the same thing he's been telling me," Dien said, drawing his cloak higher over the boy's shoulders. "The fall rattled his brain."

Dubric knelt stiffly before them, his knee resting beside steaming vomit. "Why the dark, Eachann? What happened in the dark?"

"The dark, it took another one," Eachann said. "This time it was one I knew."

Dubric watched the boy's fingers clench into the fine wool of Dien's cloak, crushing it. "What do you mean the dark took another one? Who? Why did you come for me, and not an official messenger?"

"There's another gone, and yesterday they found someone, dead, spit up'n the river near Barrorise. My pa said someone hadta ride, I hadta ride, hadta get to the castle, to tell Lord Dubric about the dark. No matter how scared I was, I hadta tell. We ain't go no one else."

"You said another. How many have been taken by the dark?"

Eachann shuddered. "I dunno. Some. Lots. I hear stories 'bout the dark, how it's taking us, but it ain't never took no one I knew, nor spit one back b'fore."

Dubric rocked back, resting his weight on his heels. "Who was the latest taken?"

"Neighbor. Missus Maeve's boy. Name's Braoin."

Dien paled, holding Eachann closer. "No. Oh, Goddess, no."

Dubric looked at Dien. "You know this Braoin?"

Dien smoothed the boy's blood-stiffened hair. "Yes, sir. He's my wife's cousin, her aunt's son. Good lad, never one to cause trouble. Sarea and the girls have been there a phase helping her folks get ready for the planting festival. I never should have sent them alone."

Dubric stood, gently taking Eachann from Dien. "Lars, gather my things, find Otlee, and get ready to ride. Dien, tell Rolle I am taking Eachann to my suite. Meet me here in half a bell."

His two most trusted men nodded their acceptance and followed Dubric from the stable. As he helped the boy to the castle, the wind picked up. The air smelled like rain.

The gray sky had darkened when four grim riders crossed into the Reach. Spattered with mud and drenched from incessant drizzle, they rode into the village of Stemlow and drew their mounts to the golden warmth of a tavern.

"Otlee, bring the map," Dubric said as he tied his horse.

He entered the tavern first, his nose wrinkling at the stench of cheap tobacco. Farmers and laborers looked up, their suspicious glances taking in his official garments and ready sword. The lone barmaid, a scrawny woman with a pox-scarred face, slopped a drink over her hand as she stared at him, and the barkeep paled before returning to his duties.

Many patrons turned away when Dien's dark bulk filled the doorway. "Guess they don't get many travelers," he muttered.

Dubric pulled back the hood of his cloak. "Likely not. If memory serves, this village is little more than a mark on the map." He led his men to an empty table far from the welcome heat of the fire, maneuvering between groups of grumbling men.

The barmaid followed them with a pitcher of ale and four tankards.

"Tea for the boy, and four bowls of whatever is hot," Dubric said.

"Rabbit an' dumplin's, m'lord," she replied. He nodded and she hurried off, leaving them in peace.

"Let us see where we are." Dubric spread Otlee's map on the table. He looked to Dien. "Your family is in Tormod?"

"A couple of miles north, sir," Dien said. "At Sarea's parents' farm. But her aunt Maeve lives in Falliet."

Dubric tapped both points on the map, Tormod almost due north along a road curving slightly to the northeast, Falliet closer but northwest. "We cannot reach both tonight. The road through Falliet pulls too far west, surely two bells' extra ride."

"Yes, sir." Dien frowned at the map. "Nearly three bells more with two rivers forded along that route. The road through Barrorise and its bridge give a far quicker ride. To Tormod, at least."

Lars wiped ale foam from his lips. "So what do we do?"

"We separate." Dubric returned the map to Otlee. "Dien must see to his family, whereas I must investigate the death without delay."

The barmaid brought Otlee his tea. "Beggin' yer pardon, m'lord, but I overheard ye talkin'. The boys maybe oughta stay here if they can. 'Tis not safe up north."

Dubric noted her thin, worn hands, ragged apron, and earnest worry. "You have heard of the death in Falliet?"

"Pah," she said, rocking back and rubbing her arms as if she felt a sudden chill. " 'Tain't just Falliet, but most all the Reach. Us'n Bendas are the only ones to not lose younguns, far as I know. We hear the stories, m'lord, and keep 'em dear."

Dubric sipped his ale, grateful for the warmth filling his belly. "What stories?"

" 'Tis the towns along the rivers sufferin' so, m'lord. Somethin's happenin' with the dark an' the water. Kiddies disappear in the rain er headin' to the well, an' Goddess knows ain't no child allowed to go fishin' no more, even in broad daylight. Atro the peddler done come through here a phase er two back. He said he saw the dark reach out an' take a boy, an' the boy never even screamed. Was there, then he was gone. 'Tain't safe fer yer boys, m'lord. Not on a rainy night like this."

Lars regarded her over his mug of ale and said nothing. Otlee held the map case in his thin, ink-stained hands and sat a little taller. "I'm not afraid."

"Mayhap ye oughta be." The barmaid glanced over her shoulder to the bar. Waving an affirmation, she turned back to Dubric. "We don't let rooms, m'lord, but I can tell Earl to give ye one, if 'n ye want. His daughter got hitched last moon an' her room's still empty. Be tight sleepin', but the boys'd be safe."

Dien drained his ale as the woman walked away. "You and the lads can stay here till morning, sir, but I have to get to my family. If the shit up north is so bad they know about it in this piss-pot village, I need to protect my girls."

"I'll go with you," Lars said. He took a long drink and set his tankard on the table.

Dien frowned at him and shook his head. "Maybe you'd better stay here. We don't know what we're up against yet."

The barmaid appeared with their food. Ever hungry, Lars reached for a bowl and started in. "I'm not afraid, and two swords are better than one, especially for protecting your family."

"I can protect my own family, pup," Dien said, scowling into his bowl. "Besides, Dubric will need you. You're better off helping him."

Otlee beamed at Lars. "We don't both need to go with Dubric. I can do most everything myself. It's mostly just taking notes."

Dien picked at his food. "Maybe neither of you should go, not if children are being taken. I've half a mind to send you both back to the castle."

Dubric let them argue, their voices fading as he ate. *Missing children suggests slavers. Mines? Textiles? Why only the Reach? What is the connection with water? And what about the one found dead? An escapee, or something else?* His thoughts shifted and the spoon in his hand trembled.

He knew what awaited him on the dark road ahead, and he knew he had no choice but to face it. It was his curse to bear, and a burden he would face, no matter the pain.

He took a sip of ale, washing the tang of dread and disgust from his mouth. "No one is staying behind. Otlee, you ride with me. Lars, you ride with Dien. We are leaving as soon as we finish."

The matter settled, the others finished eating while Dubric returned to his worries. He sighed and poked at his rabbit. His eyes hurt already.

In a night turning rapidly colder, they crossed an unnamed creek without incident and bade one another farewell at the crossroads. Dien and Lars rode to the east while Dubric and Otlee continued north. The drizzle was speckled with sleet, which chilled Dubric's hands through his gloves and stiffened his knuckles until he could no longer feel the reins.

Otlee rode beside him, silent and watchful, one hand guiding his horse and the other resting on the hilt of his shortsword.

Dubric unclenched one hand, opening and closing his pained fingers to loosen them. "I do not believe there is anything to fear."

"I know, sir. I'm just cold." Otlee turned, his face barely visible from beneath his cloak. "Is there an inn in Falliet? I'd hate to have to make camp in this."

"As would I," Dubric said. "Never you worry. Whether there is an inn or not, we will sleep somewhere warm and dry. You have my word."

Otlee drew his cloak tighter across his narrow shoulders. "Thank you, sir."

They rode past farms standing far from the road with warm lights twinkling from their windows. Dubric saw livestock and stone fences and an occasional clump of trees, but no other riders, no people at all.

Not that I could blame them, Dubric thought, flexing his fingers again. *What a miserable night.*

A cold thread of pain sliced behind Dubric's eyes and he winced as a ghost appeared in the road.

Dubric shook his head and pulled on the reins, startled at the boy's face. Slender and fair, with familiar features, the ghost limped toward him. Slashed across his face, chest, belly, and throat, the boy dripped from more wounds than Dubric wanted to count. "Lars?" he whispered, swallowing past the dread in his throat.

"Sir?" Otlee asked, but Dubric waved him off, letting out his breath in sudden relief.

Despite the resemblance, Dubric realized that the ghost was not Lars; he was smaller, twisted, and lame.

A boy of perhaps nine or ten summers. Most assuredly not his senior page, praise the King, nor seventeen-summers-old Braoin. This ghost moved freely and seemed aware and autonomous, like all ghosts who had been dead a long time. Dubric guessed he had been dead for several seasons, at least, and certainly not recently pulled from the river.

"It is nothing," Dubric said, urging his horse forward. The boy fell in alongside, shuffling in a jerky gait. *One dead boy will not be impossible to endure,* Dubric thought, glancing down at the crippled ghost. It grinned at him with cheerful innocence, completely lacking in mental faculties. Dubric smiled back, as tolerant as he would be of any dim-witted child. Slavers would have had little use for such a lad. A tragedy, but not unexpected.

Sudden, frigid pain slammed behind his eyes. He gasped at the familiar and hated chill, reaching desperately for his horse's mane before he fell from the saddle. A score or more ghosts slid all at once from the wet dark all around him, blocking the road and reaching for his cloak, his horse, his soul. All young, all male, they wailed silently and grasped at him, some dripping spectral blood onto the muddy road. Their vaporous touch passed through his arms and legs, leaving only icy trails behind. *So many, so sudden,* he thought, struggling to breathe past the pain filling his head. *Why all together and not one at a time? And all boys. By the King, what have I dragged the lads into? Slavers would not kill so many boys.* Unlike the crippled ghost, or any other ghost he had seen before, these were faint images, transparent and filmy.

His horse shied, lurching to a halt and rearing back,

its forehooves leaving the muddy ground. One ghost reached for its bridle and it backed away, snorting.

"Sir!" Otlee called from beyond the murky green horrors. Dubric could not see the lad past the chaos of the ghosts.

The lame ghost resembling Lars hobbled toward Dubric, pushing past taller, older, more vaporous boys. Still wearing his mindless grin, he stared into Dubric's eyes. He reached for the saddle, his frigid fingers grazing along the leather to clench around Dubric's ankle, and he pulled himself up.

"No!" Dubric hollered, lurching away and kicking at the spectre climbing up him. The crippled boy fell to the mud and faded away. Dubric rubbed furiously at his eyes and most of the other ghosts disappeared, leaving only two ghosts blocking the road.

One of the remaining pair, a wiry lad of perhaps fifteen, paced across the road and seemed oblivious to Dubric's presence. Sludge oozed from a flattened gash behind his right temple, and dripped from his crushed and mangled ear. The other, slender built with a shadow of beard sprouting on his chin, remained rooted where he stood. Naked, he silently screamed at the sky with his hands clenched beside his hips. Spectral blood dribbled down the inside of one leg and pooled at his feet. *By the King, what is happening?*

"Sir?"

Dubric blinked, shaking his pounding head. Both ghosts remained, screaming and bleeding onto the muddy road. He rubbed his eyes, but the damned things refused to leave.

"Sir!"

Dubric felt a tug at his arm. *Boys, all boys. What have I done? Lars! Otlee! No, please no.* Cold, wet fingers wrapped around his wrist, demanding he turn to look, insisting he pay them notice, while the two boys before him bled in an endless stream of spectral gore.

Snarling, he wrenched his hand away and lashed out, striking at the apparition that dared to cling to him, but he hit wet flesh and drenched woolen cloak, not the icy mist of a ghost.

Otlee yelped and fell away, disappearing into the dark.

Panting, Dubric blinked, wiping his eyes with a shaking hand as his horse danced away. *By the King, what have I done?* "Otlee?"

No answer, only rain and sleet and bleeding ghosts.

"Otlee!" Dubric scrambled from his horse and fell to his knees, cursing the Goddess for plaguing him, cursing her again for his mistake. All the while his head throbbed, and shimmery green wisps tugged at the edges of his vision.

He crawled toward Otlee's horse, to the still form beneath its feet. Dubric's fingers clenched in the frigid mud, sending shards of pain up his arthritic knuckles as he pulled himself forward.

Otlee's horse, dark and dripping wet, stood over the boy. Its forehoof stomped once beside the lad's head.

"I am sorry, so sorry," Dubric said, crawling.

Steam puffed from the beast's nose, and the same hoof pawed at the road. *So cold, so wet, and I promised the lad, I swore for King's sake, that he would have a warm, dry bed, not this damned mud!*

The hood of Dubric's cloak fell back and icy water dripped down his spine, chilling him to the core. The pawing hoof stopped, settling a step beyond Otlee's head. Dubric inched forward, watching the horse as he

...ached for Otlee. The beast's head dropped, warming Dubric's face with a snort.

"Do not die, lad," he said, maneuvering between muddy hooves. "That is a direct order. Do not disobey me, do you hear me?"

His hands shaking, he felt along the back of Otlee's neck—all the vertebrae remained in place, praise the King—before rolling the boy onto his back.

Otlee gasped at the movement, moaning, and drew his legs toward his chest. Dubric felt the horse's steamy breath warm the back of his neck, and he hurried to check Otlee for injuries. All his bones felt straight and strong and his heart beat a steady rhythm—but he was so small, with no fat to keep him warm.

Dubric slipped his fingers behind Otlee's head and he paused, his throat clenching. He touched the warm and tacky swelling, gently feeling the damage with his fingers. Otlee moaned in reply.

"Stay with me," Dubric said, lifting Otlee as he crawled from beneath the horse. "We cannot be far from Falliet. I will find help and you will be all right. I swear on my life, you will be all right."

Dubric staggered to his feet, Otlee limp in his arms. The ghosts did not seem to notice. Dubric wrapped his cloak around Otlee and climbed onto the saddle. Cradling the little boy, he urged his horse into a canter and hurried as fast as he dared. He hoped Otlee's horse would follow.

Dubric's horse shied as it moved through the pacing ghost, but he gripped the reins in one stiff hand and continued on, ignoring the chill soaking through him. Otlee twitched then fell still, slack and cold against Dubric's chest, and Dubric kicked his horse to a gallop.

* * *

Dien and Lars crossed the Casclian River bridge at Barrorise and continued north along the road following the Tormod River.

Just past the bridge, Dien reined his gelding in and dismounted. "Do you see that, pup?"

Lars heeled his mare backwards then slid off the saddle. "I don't see anything but rain and mud."

"Then you need to look closer." Dien led his horse to the edge of the road and knelt.

Lars came to stand beside him. "Seems wide for a fishing trail."

A wide swath of dead grass and weeds had been trampled in a careening path to the riverbank, and rainwater flowed down through a pair of deep gouges in the mud. Dien stood, squinting, and pulled his sword. "Let's take a look."

Lars peered down to the river. "It's probably nothing."

Descending, Dien grabbed a sapling to keep his balance. "Didn't that boy this morning say they found someone's body just north of Barrorise?"

Lars turned to inch sideways down the treacherous bank. "You think they found him down here?"

Dien reached the bottom and looked up at Lars. "Someone dragged this tangle onto the bank. It didn't get here on its own."

Lars leapt the last bit, landing in the rocks beside Dien. A vicious pile of branches and brambles lay high upon the bank, gouging into the mud incline beside them. A strip of cloth hung from a broken branch and flapped damply in the wind. "Somebody tore their shirt," Lars said, pulling it free. "It's silk."

"Maybe it was Bray's, but I doubt he could afford silk. Not many folks around here can." Dien squinted at the diamond-patterned fabric. "I don't recognize it, but that doesn't mean a lot."

Lars reached into his pocket for a small cotton evidence bag, one of the basic supplies Dubric insisted they carry at all times. "Probably someone else's, but it won't hurt to keep it." The scrap of cloth tucked away, he walked along the bank, examining the rocks and mud. "Between the rain, the river, and the dark, we're not going to see much."

Dien stretched, looking up to the sky. "No, I suppose not." Rain clouds moved overhead, but glints of stars peeked through. "And what was here is probably washed away."

Lars crouched at the river's edge and reached into the frigid water. "Not everything." Something stood in the water, breaking through the surface and sparkling in a moonlit circle against wet blackness. He pulled a bottle from the muck and stood, giving it to Dien. "Someone have a celebration?"

"Or a wake," Dien said. He tilted it in the moonlight, then sniffed it. "Whiskey, it smells like. It hasn't been in the river long. Less than a bell, I'd say."

Lars wiped his hands on his trousers. "Eachann came to the castle this morning, after riding all night. The body was found, what, yesterday?"

"Yep. Give me another sack. Someone came down here tonight."

"In the rain," Lars said, tossing Dien a bag. He reached for a bush on the bank and hoisted himself up. "I'm going to check the road."

"Be careful. I'm right behind you."

Lars continued to climb. He scrambled to the road

and checked in both directions, looking for tracks or broken weeds, but the rain had smoothed the mud and flattened most of the growth. He heard Dien climb the bank. "Cart tracks, I think," Lars called out, "but it's hard to tell. If so, they're heading north. Nothing's south of the horses."

"You sure about that, pup?" Dien asked, packing the bottle in his saddlebags. Grasping the horses' reins, he led them to Lars.

"Not sure at all," Lars replied, kneeling beside a curve gouged into the grasses. "Everything's washed away. But I think he turned around here. Look."

While the rain had leveled the road, the gouge in the grassy edge remained, opened to the mud like a wound.

Lars pointed up the road to a sprawling, brightly lit manor. "Who lives there? Would they have seen anything?"

Dien scowled and tossed Lars his reins. "That's Sir Haconry's estate. He doesn't see anything except . . ." Grimacing, Dien shook his head and mounted his horse. "Never mind. Promise me you'll stay clear of him."

"Sure," Lars said, climbing onto his horse. "Whatever you say. I won't go near the place."

His head pounding like the tide against the stones of Waterford bay, Dubric reached the village of Falliet. Two shops, a church, and a handful of homes clustered around a cleared scrap of land and a wider stretch of road. Stemlow had been a teeming city in comparison.

Dubric guided his horse to the closest building, a shop with a house attached to the back. Light shone from within, warm and beckoning, praise the King.

Even the poorest fire would be better than freezing rain.

Cradling Otlee close, he slid from his horse and hurried to the door, leaving the horses standing untied in the mud. Both ghosts followed, their weight dragging at the back of his eyes, but he clenched his chattering teeth and kept his back to them.

With Otlee balanced against his shoulder, he banged on the door with his free hand. "Open this door in the name of Lord Brushgar and the province of Faldorrah!"

Hurried footsteps, then the door eased open, bringing with it a rush of light and heated air.

A woman motioned him in with a hopeful look upon her finely boned face. "Thank the Goddess," she said. "Eachann found help. Please, please come in. You must be freezing."

Dubric brushed past her. "I need a light, a basin of clean water, bandages, and a bed, and I need them immediately."

"Why?" she asked. "Has something—" She peeled back the drenched cloak and winced as she looked upon Otlee. "Here, this way," she said, leading him past racks of fabric and clothing.

In the next room, a pair of harnessed looms held vigil across from each other, and a partially completed tapestry stood in its stretchers along the far wall. Light from the woman's candle flickered across the fabric and heddles, shining on strands of thread. A cat hissed from a bobbin-filled shelf, its eyes reflecting flashes of gold.

Dubric's host beckoned him from the shop into her home, a tidy dwelling with upholstered chairs and pillows and woven rugs. She led him farther in, beyond a small but immaculate kitchen to a closed door. "It's my son's room, but he won't mind," she said, pausing long enough to light a lamp. "Take what you need. I'll fetch the water and bandages."

"Thank you." Dubric pulled back the quilted coverlet and laid Otlee upon the bed, gently removing the sodden cloaks with shaking hands. "Your linens," he muttered at the smear of blood on the pristine pillowcase.

"Never you mind about that now," the woman said. She appeared at his elbow with a basin of water and a clean rag. "Here, let me get that." She dampened the rag and wiped Otlee's face, rinsed the mud from the cloth, then began to clean the wound. "I've got a good selection of men's garments in the shop and a kettle of water warming. Help yourself to them before you catch your death. I'll tend your grandson until you return."

Dubric swallowed his guilt and choked out, "He . . . he is not my grandson."

"I'll tend him anyway. Go on now. You're doing no one any good dripping all over my floor."

"Mama?" Otlee murmured, his eyelids flickering.

"Not your mama," she whispered, caressing his brow. "Lie still now. You're going to be fine."

Dubric staggered to his feet, slogging through the incredible cold that threatened to overtake him.

Otlee winced, pushing the woman away without opening his eyes. "It hurts."

She dampened the rag again and shooed Dubric toward the door. "I know, darling, but we'll make it all better. You'll see. Shh now and let me tend it." She stroked Otlee's cheek with one hand and mopped the wound with the other, whispering soothing words all the while.

Dubric lurched to the hall to find the pair of ghosts waiting for him. He closed his eyes and stumbled through them, his muscles threatening to stiffen. Shivering, the ghosts following, he staggered to the fabric shop. He grabbed a beautifully woven wool blanket and tugged it over his shoulders, but it did little to ease his chill.

His vision turned cloudy but he blinked the haze away, reaching for a rack of trousers, then tunics. He leaned in a corner, his fingers struggling to undo the buttons of his shirt. They were stiff and frozen, filled with arthritic pain, and uncooperative. The ghosts continued to stare at him, but he turned his head, his teeth clattering through a muttered curse. He had released one button and nearly had another free when his legs buckled. He fell to the floor, shaking, and stared at the stationary ghost's bare feet. After a moment, they shimmered and faded with Dubric into the dark.

CHAPTER

2

†

Jesscea Saworth sat near the window, trying to read from a worn book. Even the castle with its drafts and nobles and protocol was better than being stuck at her grandparents' making hats for the planting festival. Try as she might to think about the promise of the coming spring—she would be fourteen summers old soon, old enough to attend the spring faires and old enough to dance—her thoughts returned to Braoin. She sighed and the book sagged in her hands.

She'd heard the adults whispering that Braoin had not come home. According to her grandmother, no one had seen Bray since the day before yesterday, since he'd left their farm, and now . . .

Rain beat against the glass in a ceaseless rattle and she hoped it wouldn't turn to snow. She licked her parched lips and raised her eyes, braving a glance into the night. *Such a horrible night, and Braoin had not come home.*

Jess tucked her feet beneath her and tried to read again, but the words blurred as if washed away by the rain and the same horrid thought repeated in her mind.

Braoin had not come home.

He never would. She knew it deep in her heart. Somehow they all knew. Even little Alyson, only six summers old, knew that Braoin would never come home again. The dark had eaten him and would never give him back.

A shadow moved across the window on the other side of the curtain. The patter of the rain on the glass silenced for a moment, then began again as the shadow moved away. She closed the book. "Something's on the porch," she said. She stared at the door, her heart pounding.

Jess's mother, Sarea, stopped nursing the baby and shoved away from the table. "Take your sister," she said, handing the infant to Fynbelle.

Grandpapa's dog, a wizened ratter nearly as decrepit as he, growled, raising its head from its paws. Sarea reached for the fireplace poker, her face reflected in the small mantel mirror. "You sure, Jess?" she asked, her voice dangerous and low.

"Yes, Mam."

Footsteps rumbled against the porch floor and Jess stifled a squeak as Sarea pulled her from the chair. The dog barked, but didn't move from its warm place by the fire.

"It's coming for us!" Grandpapa wailed. "We're doomed, doomed!"

"Be quiet!" Grandmama said. "Ye'll scare the children."

Kialyn, the eldest at sixteen summers, squealed as she came in from the washroom and ran, dripping soapy hair flying, to huddle with Grandmama.

"Quiet!" Sarea snapped.

Aly scrambled over to them, ducking under Grandmama's bony elbow while Fyn cowered in the corner with their baby sister, her straight blond hair hanging over their faces like a curtain.

The family stared at the door. Kia and Aly struggled to get closer to Grandmama, leaving Jess to either run to her grandfather or stand alone.

She took a breath, clenched her fists, and straightened her spine while her heartbeats slammed loud as thunder in her ears.

"It's the dark, come to take us to its belly!" Grandpapa yelled. "We're dead, our bones sucked dry—"

"Please, Papa, not now!" Sarea said.

Silence stretched into a twirling strand, knotted only by their harsh, uneven breathing. Jess took a single step toward her mother just as a pound trembled the door.

"Sarea?" Grandmama asked, her fingers clenching into her granddaughters' backs. "Who is it?"

"It's the dark, you twit!" Grandpapa tittered. "It's come for us at last!"

Sarea strode to the door. "Keep quiet!" Holding the iron poker like a sword, she unlocked the door and snatched it open.

Fyn squealed, Kia and Aly whimpered, but Jess remained stoic. The first thing she saw through the open door that night was her father's relieved face, his eyes piercing and blue.

And the second was Lars, smiling at her.

Lars sat alone and nursed a hot cup of tea. The girls had gone to bed, but he'd refused to leave, choosing to remain nearby while the adults talked.

Dien, Sarea, and Sarea's mother, Lissea, spoke of Braoin's disappearance in low voices, but Devyn, Sarea's father, stared at Lars as if his muddy boots had tracked in plague.

"What I want to know," Devyn said, looking over his shoulder and licking tea-stained spittle from his lips, "is what that rich boy is doing here, spreading his filth again."

"Dev!" Lissea said, narrowing her eyes and lowering her voice. "Lars is a noble, an' a guest—"

"Guest, my pockmarked ass! He's come to corrupt my granddaughters!" Devyn stood, shaking his finger at Lars. "It's bad enough my daughter married a castle peacock, but I'll not stand for my granddaughters to be taken in by the devilish charms of him or his kind."

Dien rubbed his forehead and muttered under his breath while everyone else stared at Devyn.

Tottering on his feet, Devyn knocked aside his chair. A dark vein throbbed beside his left eye as he stared at Lars. "I know you, skulking bastard, and I know what you're plotting. You're not welcome here and neither are those lecherous thoughts! Overdressed, misbegotten, bastard boys in my barn! Rabbits and wasps! After what you did? How dare you darken my door? I'll not have the likes of you near my granddaughters!"

Dien pushed aside his tea. "Think of me what you will, but Lars won't harm anyone, least of all the girls."

Spit flecked Devyn's chin and madness floated on his breath from beyond his missing teeth. He smelled of rot with an underlying metallic tang, like tainted meat on a rusty spoon. "Pah! He wants to crawl up their skirts and rut like a beast. I've seen it before."

Lars stood in a burst of fury, his hands balling into fists and his face reddening, but he held his tongue.

Dien continued to stare at Devyn's scrawny back. "Do you know where Braoin is?" he asked, his voice barely louder than Devyn's rancid breath.

"How the peg should I know? The bastard calf ain't

mine. I done told them," Devyn said, falling into Lars's chair. "I haven't seen him for days." The old man's hand trembled in fluttering jerks and his left cheek twitched. "Days," he muttered, looking at Lars with sudden yearning. "Days gone by. Days and nights. Days of cider and violets." He winked at Lissea, his hands still fluttering. "Do you remember those days? The days of cider and violets?"

Lissea hurried to her husband and grasped his thick hand in her thin one. It stilled beneath her touch. "Yes, dear, I do."

"Sorry, pup," Dien muttered, shifting in his chair. "He has his moments."

"It's all right," Lars said, suppressing a shudder. He'd never considered that madness had its own scent, and he hoped he'd never taste it on his own breath or smell it on his skin.

"Is it suppertime yet?" Devyn asked, standing. "I'm hungry."

"Sure, Papa," Sarea said. She offered Lars a sorry smile and stood. "I'll fetch it right away."

"Who are you? Do I know you? When did we get a serving girl? How can I afford another one?"

Lars saw a pained shine in Sarea's eyes as she turned away.

"That's Sarea," Lissea said, leading Dev back to the table. "Ye remember Sarea, don't ye?"

"Nonsense. Sarea's been sent to bed. I saw her reading right over there, just before." His hand shaking, he pointed at the settee near the window. "I saw her! I did! I know I did!"

Lissea's voice remained patient and calm. "That's Jesscea, yer granddaughter. Sarea's grown up."

He blinked. "She is? Where is she? Where's my

daughter? Where's our son? How can I sell hats without my son?"

"I'm here, Papa. You go on and eat now." Sarea set a bowl of soup and a buttered bit of bread before him.

"But Stuart! Where's Stuart?" Dev glared at Lars. "That's not Stuart! He's far too old. Isn't he?"

"Stuart's gone," Lissea said with a sigh.

"Gone to the dark, yes, I remember. Dammit, woman, I'm not daft." He slopped soup into his mouth then dropped the spoon. It clattered away, leaving a splatter of broth on the table. He stared at the spilled broth and dragged a finger through it, drawing a butterfly.

As Lars watched, anxious, Devyn's hand twitched like a dying fish and he sat up straighter, his rheumy eyes glancing to the windows. "For Goddess' sake, it's dark already. Time for bed."

"Night, Papa." Sarea pulled a kerchief from her pocket and wiped at her nose.

"Night," he replied, and the tremor in his left cheek twisted his smile into a grimace. "I remember the night I became a man. Now if only I could remember her name." He stood, nudging Lars with his elbow. "Who was she? You introduced us, remember?" He blinked, leaned close, then pushed a single finger against Lars's chest. "Stuart? Is it you?"

"Sorry, milord," Lissea whispered to Lars as she ushered Devyn from the table. "He's had a long day."

Resisting the urge to commit Devyn's episode to his notes, Lars nodded. "Good night."

Devyn waved and shuffled off, one hand trailing against the wall for balance.

"I'm sorry," Sarea said, cleaning up Devyn's mess. "He shouldn't have said those things."

Lars dismissed the apology with a shake of his head. "He shouldn't have forgotten you, either. That's a far worse crime than what he said about me."

Sarea hung her head, dishes clattering into the washbasin. "It grows worse every time we visit. I don't know how Mother manages."

"Because I promised to. He's still my husband," Lissea said as she strode into the kitchen and poured a fresh cup of tea. Gaunt, with coarse, tight features, she looked shrunken and homely in comparison to her robust and beautiful daughter and grandchildren. Lars thought she was downright diminutive beside her son-in-law, but most people were.

"The offer stands, Liss," Dien said.

"I can't leave him, not now. Wouldn't be right. Who'd take care of him?" She sat and looked to Lars and Dien, folding her bony hands together with the barest twitch as evidence of her strain. She seemed to steel herself for bad news. "What can we do to find Braoin?"

Dien pulled a notebook from the pack beside his chair. "I barely knew the lad, so you need to tell us about him. Anything you can think of, good or bad or perfectly normal. What was he like? What did he do? Who were his friends?"

Sarea fell into her chair. "You speak as if he's dead."

Dien glanced at Lars before looking at her. "He may be, but we don't know who was pulled from the river, so hope isn't lost. If he's still alive, we'll do whatever we can to bring him home."

Sarea frowned and reached for Dien's hand.

Lars pulled a sack from his pocket and opened it. "We found a bit of cloth on the way here. Silk. Could it be from Braoin's clothes?"

He laid the damp strip on the table in front of Sarea and her mother. Lissea shook her head, refusing to touch it, but Sarea lifted the cloth. "I don't think so," she said, holding it in the light. Red diamonds shimmered on a black field. "Bray's mother, Maeve, is a weaver, and she makes all of his clothes. He wouldn't have any silk."

Lars retrieved the fabric and tucked it away again while Dien asked, "A barmaid told us that children have gone missing before. What can you tell us about that?"

Sarea looked at her mother. Lissea sat still and composed in her chair, streaks of white in her brilliant red hair shining like silver threads in a tapestry. The corner of her mouth trembled and she stared at her hands. "Children grow up. Some run off."

"Yes, but the barmaid said the dark was eating them."

The sigh that escaped from her sounded like wind whispering through the branches of a dead cottonwood. "They're just gone, disappearin' at night, the rumors say."

Dien asked, "How long has this been happening? A couple of moons? Less?"

"Two, maybe three summers. I ain't sure—"

Lissea jumped as Dien swore. "Two or three summers? Dammit, Liss! Why weren't we notified earlier?"

Her poised demeanor faltered and unease shadowed her face. "Surely Constable Sherrod told Sir Haconry. Folks used to say help would come from the castle. But after so many gone, folks lose hope."

Dien's hand curled into a fist. "Liss, I swear we'd never heard of missing children! We would have come, I would have come! All these times we've come to visit, you've said nothing!"

"I knew my family was safe at the castle. I wouldn't burden you with such stories, not when you're here with the children."

"Dammit, Mother, that's his job," Sarea said, standing. She picked up Devyn's overturned chair from the floor. "I can't believe you stood by, knowing something was—"

"Missus Paerth?" Lars said softly, drawing her eyes to him. "I swear on my soul that every Faldorrahn life is important to us. If we'd known, we'd have come."

"Not you, pup," Dien said, "nor my girls. None of you have any business being here. I'm escorting you back home come daybreak."

"Why?" Lars asked. "I took the same oath you did. Faldorrah first. I've every right and reason to be here."

"You might've convinced Dubric that you're safe—hell, you nearly convinced me—but that doesn't change a thing. Children are being taken—"

Lars kept his voice low and even despite the anger pounding in him. "I'm not a child. I don't think I've ever been a child. I may be young, I'll readily admit that, but I'm no child. And you're not my father."

Dien snarled, his face reddening, "Don't you be throwing that in my face! I love you as if you were my own. You know that."

"It doesn't give you the right to decide my life for me, or the right to make me disregard my duty."

"I have a responsibility to keep you safe."

Sarea slammed her hand on the table. "Stop it! This isn't the time or place for fighting like a pair of roosters. You both care very deeply for each other, we all know that."

She turned to her husband and said, "All I've heard for summers is how mature and responsible Lars is, how dependable, and every time he gets perfect marks you strut around like you've gotten them yourself. And you," she said, shifting her angry gaze to Lars, "when you broke your arm last spring, who did you call for? Who taught you to hunt? Who holds your head when you're puking and sick?"

Lars winced at the guilty bile in his mouth. He nodded and mumbled, "I'm sorry."

"So stop it. You both know damn well Dubric makes the orders and you two follow. The Planting Festival's in a few days and we have to help sell hats, so we're all staying here, like it or not. If you want to know the truth, I feel much better having both of you guarding the girls. There are no two men I know of that I trust more to watch over my daughters, and they're far safer right here with the two of you than with me on the road alone."

She huffed and resumed washing dishes. "Figure out who's doing this and catch the bastard. That's what you're both trained to do, isn't it?"

Lars and Dien stared at each other over the table. "You'll stay," Dien said at last, "but you'll do what I tell you, at least until Dubric says otherwise."

"Fair enough," Lars agreed. "And I'll protect the girls, with my life if need be."

Dien sighed and gripped his teacup, enclosing it inside his massive fist. "Let's hope it doesn't come to that."

Braoin woke, spluttering away the water dripping on his face. He hung by his wrists and ankles in the dark, suspended faceup over Goddess knew what, Goddess knew where. He heard rain on a roof above him, but he had no idea if he hung in a shed or a barn or a home, or even an outhouse. Judging by the stench, he gauged the later option most likely, but the air stank like no outhouse he had ever been in, heavy and rancid and damply vile. Whatever it was, it badly needed repairs, judging from the trickles dribbling over him. He felt freezing cold, pain throbbed from places he did not want to contemplate, and a foulness polluted his agony-filled mouth. He ran his tongue over his teeth and winced. All his incisors were missing, leaving raw and bleeding gums behind.

What in the seven hells happened while I was unconscious? He struggled against his binds and swung in the dark, the movement setting his stomach roiling. He retched, turning his head to vomit, and bitter acid dribbled from his mouth to land somewhere below.

He spat, then took a breath and tried to release one hand. *I have to keep my wits to get out of here. If I stay, I'll die.*

After swallowing a mouthful of rainwater, he flexed one arm, hoping to release the strain on the other, but as he did his body swung to the side and maintained tension to both wrists. No matter what he tried, no matter what he did, his weight remained hanging from both wrists and ankles. He could not gain slack anywhere.

He hung silently, struggling to think his way out of his binds. Exhausted and lulled by the sound of the rain, he dozed, but his eyes snapped open when he heard a metallic scrape somewhere near his head.

Clank, creak, bang, and a door opened, bringing a gust of fresh, cold air. He saw upside-down rain and nighttime sky and a distant light. Light enough to see by, praise the Goddess! A post stood near his shoulder, and dirt waited perhaps three lengths below him, crawling with tiny worms and fat, winged insects.

Braoin found a sense of space, the presence of something normal and within understanding. He hung in a barn or large shed much like the one behind his home. If so, the thin cording at his wrists and ankles must be tied to beams. If the ground was three lengths down, then the beams were six or seven lengths up, at most. Could he climb that far? Was it possible?

As he turned his hands to grasp the cord, a shadow blocked the door, the silhouette of a man.

"Let me go," Braoin begged despite his throbbing mouth, and he released his grip. He swung and the man's shadow darkened his face then slipped away, dark then light, dark, light. His stomach lurched and he hoped he would not vomit again. "Please," he choked out, gagging against the spasm in his throat and belly. "I'll do anything, if you just let me go."

The man laughed and entered, bringing with him the warm scents of meat and old whiskey. "You offer me nothing."

No! "Please, I won't say anything. Just please, let me go."

The shadow moved closer and Braoin heard something drag across the floor.

"Hungry, little cur?"

Braoin shook his head and resumed swaying, but the shadow snapped out and grasped a cord. Diffuse light shone on the edges of the man's body, shimmering on a wet cloak and the bare skin of an outstretched arm, but Braoin could not see his face or any other definite feature.

"You're going to eat, nosey little rabbit," the man said. "I need to keep you alive." Braoin clenched his teeth but hot, hard fingers wrenched his mouth open, slipping between his torn and tattered gums. Before he could twist away, the man stuffed his mouth full of congealed stew.

Braoin gagged, struggling between coughing and swallowing. The man held Braoin's mouth closed until he quieted, then wrenched it open again for another mouthful of slime.

Braoin fought, but he had no choice. Seven mouthfuls forced their way through his throat to his belly while dribbles of cold broth ran up his nose and stung his eyes.

"Thirsty?" the man asked. Braoin saw an empty bowl roll on the ground toward the door; its clotted remnants looked like black blood in the dim light.

Braoin heard cloth shift. "No," he choked out.

"Yes, you are," the man said, grabbing Braoin by the ears and hair. "Now drink, you bastard. Drink."

Braoin fought against the intrusion into his mouth, but his struggles only served to encourage his tormentor. He struggled, smearing both himself and the man with stew, but the assault continued. In the end, with his nose full of thick broth and his mouth filling with far worse fluid, Braoin drank.

The man left soon after, slamming and locking the door behind him. Alone in the dark, Braoin retched and fell into an exhausted sleep while dripping rainwater rinsed the stain and shame from his battered face.

CHAPTER

3

✝

Jess poofed hair from her eyes as she reached for the rolling pin. The air smelled of cinnamon and sizzling sausage, Grandmama had her hands full with baby Cailin, and Lars lurked nearby, watching everything as if he couldn't believe his eyes, or his ears.

Kia had spent the morning batting her eyes at Lars and arguing with Fyn. Fyn wanted to go home, Kia wanted to stay, and neither would let the other be. Verbal barbs had turned to jabs and pushes, but there were no injuries, at least not yet. Thankfully, they had left the kitchen and taken their fights and flirtations somewhere out of the way.

Her parents were talking outside, and that meant trouble. Jess rolled the scone dough and wished they'd come back in. She didn't care if they stayed to help sell hats or not ("Think of the taxes! Dammit, Dien, how are my folks going to pay their taxes, let alone eat for the next set of seasons?" her mother argued right outside the window), but Jess had eggs to cook for nine and the thought of all those yolks worried her.

She flipped the sausages then sliced the dough, sprinkling each wedge with cinnamon and sugar, but she kept glancing at the basket of eggs. Fresh eggs. She had fetched them herself that morning.

A basket full of shells to crack perfectly. Yolks she had to keep whole, whites to flip without breaking.

Goddess, I hate cooking eggs.

She opened the stove and nudged the wood with the tip of her knife, leveling the pile of coals. She slipped the pan of scones in to cook and wiped her hands. Grandpapa's little dog sat at her feet, his tail wagging hopefully.

Maybe I should just scramble them?

Aly giggled and squealed, closely followed by Lars growling. Paddle in hand, Jess dodged out of the way as Aly zipped past with Lars slavering on her heels. He caught her when she reached the rug and they rolled to the floor, laughing and tickling.

Jess sighed and removed the sausages from the pan. That done, she cracked an egg on the skillet. It landed perfectly in the grease and started sizzling. She reached for another and looked up, out the window, to see a cart coming up the lane.

"The carpenter's here," she called out.

Lars grinned at her and extricated himself from Aly's tickles. "I'll tell your dad."

"Thanks," Jess said, cracking the second egg. She watched Lars move toward the door, feigning injury and falling to the floor as Aly jumped on him. Laughing, he rolled to his feet and carried her over his shoulder like a sack of grain. Out the door they went, into the golden morning, and Jess wished she could follow them.

But she had eggs to cook, dammit. She reached for another, then paused when she saw the skillet. The egg she had cracked while Lars carried Aly away sizzled and spluttered like the one beside it, but the yolk was flecked and streaked with blood. Much more blood than a speck left by a rooster.

Grimacing, she slid the paddle beneath it and carried the nasty thing to the dog's dish. It lay there, staring like a bleeding golden eye. Queasy, she returned to her cooking, her back to the bloody mess.

Goddess, what a beautiful morning! Whistling, Lars walked to the barn and shooed a cluster of chickens from his path. He'd woken to conversation and a hot breakfast, surrounded by the mundane quarrels and warmth of a family. Parents, siblings, even grandparents all together under one roof, the very thing he had spent a lifetime wishing for. He had remained out of the way, observing but not interfering in their morning rituals, basking in the moment, the easy wonder of home and kinship. Aly had played with him, and let him tie her shoes.

The carpenter, a broad man with a wind-tanned face, nodded in greeting. "Lad!" he called, walking to Lars. "May I have a moment of your time?"

"Okay."

The carpenter looked him over, top to bottom, and offered his hand. "I'm Jak the carpenter, lad, and I'm in need of a good back for simple labor. Steady work, not the occasional odd job the folks here could provide."

Lars shook his head and smiled. "Thanks, but I'm not interested. I already have a job." He walked past Jak and on to the barn. Four young men labored on the barn roof, pulling off rotted roofing. Lars squinted against the sun and waved at them, but they paid him no heed.

The barn door stood ajar, welcoming him in with the

warm aroma of animals and hay. As he slipped inside, a flock of swallows startled and fluttered from the beams. Stalls and pens for livestock and storage paraded into the dark. Straw-dusted dirt floor lay between the rows, and a high window let patchy sunlight shine upon thick-hewn beams and posts. Far ahead, his horse nickered.

Seeking a pitchfork, he rummaged near the door, searching through the tool-filled stalls and along the rack of hoes and scythes. A few lengths away, in a roomy slat-walled pen, a very pregnant black ewe bleated, begging to be petted or fed. Ignorant of sheep, he wasn't certain which she desired most so he scratched her ears while feeding her a handful of oats. Afterward, he closed the pen door, making certain to latch it, and rubbed his grimy hands on his shirt.

"Who's there?!" Devyn called from the dim depths of the barn.

Lars jumped. *Guess I'm not alone after all.* "Just me. Lars." He climbed onto a stack of bales to look behind it. No pitchfork. "I've come to clean the stalls and feed the horses. Where would I find a pitchfork?"

Devyn shuffled into the light and squinted at Lars. He held a partially woven straw hat in his gnarled hands, the straw poking out in all directions like a bundle of thin, pale knives.

"Don't you know where they are, boy? Rabbits and wasps! They're always in the same blasted place. How many times do I have to tell you?" He turned down a crosswise aisle. Lars jumped off the bales and followed. Up ahead, two ancient pitchforks leaned against the main support post like a pair of old soldiers waiting to be called to action.

Devyn frowned and pointed at the pitchforks. "Right

here, Stuart, same as always. Don't you ever listen?" He wandered off, muttering, "Damn, boy, some days I think you've got sand b'tween you ears."

"Sir, I'm not—"

Devyn lurched around and took a step back, the hat falling to the ground. "Who are you? What are you doing in my barn?"

"I'm Lars," he said, kneeling to retrieve the fallen hat. "A page, from Castle Faldorrah. I came with Dien last night, during the storm. Remember?"

"Pah!" Devyn snatched the hat away, and the rough straw sliced Lars's fingers. "Dien ain't been here and Sarea's about to drive me batty pining over him. Take my word for it, boy, her heart's already taken. You're wasting your time."

"Yessir." Lars took a step away from the old man and winced at the stinging cuts on his right hand. "I will keep that in mind, sir. Thank you."

Devyn shuffled past, muttering about randy young idiots. Lars waited until Dev was out of sight before he grasped a pitchfork.

Grimy black thread was tangled around two of the tines; a broken twig and a scrap of ancient fabric were caught in the snarl. Lars pulled the tangle loose and let it drop at his feet. He kicked the snarl away, unsure why the sight of the strange black lump made him uneasy.

Dubric smelled bacon. He rolled onto his back, grunting at the stiffness in his legs, and dragged an arm over his eyes to block out the light.

Still groggy, his mind wandered of its own accord. When had he last smelled bacon as he woke? A long time ago, during the best time of his life. Before Oriana had died. Before everything had changed.

He felt the presence of ghosts throbbing behind his eyes and he sighed, throwing back the covers. Gasping, he yanked them back again.

By the King, he had never in all of his days slept naked!

He grimaced and sat on the edge of the bed, taking care to keep his privates covered, and rubbed his eyes. He opened them and recoiled in horror, seeing Lars's ghostly green face grinning nearly nose to nose with him. His heart settled as he realized that it was the crippled ghost, not his page. It climbed on the bed and sat beside him, bouncing as any child would. Dubric wondered how long ago the child had died. Many summers, surely, to be so corporeal.

He and the ghost sat upon the edge of a worn, four-posted bed carved from sturdy, unstained pine. The coverlet he clutched around his waist was frothy lavender and cream. A chair in the corner faced them, a gray tabby curled upon its pillow. Lacy woven curtains had been drawn back to reveal a morning sky, and cracks and patches marred the cream-painted walls.

The woman bustled in with a plate of griddle cakes and bacon. "About time you woke. I'd have sent for the surgeon to check you, if I had anyone to send."

Dubric drew the blankets closer, covering his exposed skin from mid-chest to his shins. He had no idea if the crooked frown on her face illustrated humor or concern. "Where are my trousers?"

"Drying." She handed him the plate and sat on the pillowed chair, pushing aside the cat. "I told Eachann's father that he delivered the message and is safe at the castle. He is, isn't he?"

"Yes. He hurt his arm in a fall from his mule, but he will be fine." Breakfast smelled and looked delightful, but instead of eating, Dubric asked, "How is Otlee?"

"Resting."

They stared at each other and the moment stretched before them. Dubric took a breath. Two ghosts lingered near her, one screaming in the doorway, the other pacing in the hall. The ghost boy slid down and crawled on the floor after the cat. Dubric wished all three would wander off so he could think.

While the cat hissed and ran under the bed, the woman stared at Dubric's hands. "Your ring . . . that symbol . . . Do you often strike children in your care?"

Dubric set the plate upon the bed without taking his eyes from her. The idea of bacon suddenly turned his stomach.

She swallowed and raised her eyes to his. "I asked you a question, milord, and I intend to have you answer it."

"No, I do not," he said, smoothing the blanket and drawing it to the pits of his arms. He felt cold fingers tweak the hair on the top of his foot and he jumped. *By the King, she has me trapped, and he's tormenting me.*

"And yet you struck this one. His cheek bears the mark from your ring. Its leaf is carved into his skin, for Goddess' sake."

At the mention of the Goddess, Dubric's hands clenched. His ring suddenly felt heavy and hot with the duty and burden it wrought, much as it had the day his father had given it to him. "I did not intend to harm him. It was an accident, I assure you."

She stood. "How am I supposed to believe that?"

"Because it is true. You have my word." He eased

his feet back, out of reach of the ghost's cold, pinching fingers.

She took a step closer, then another, her eyes needling through him. "What proof can you give?"

"None. I swear I love that boy as if he were my own. When I saw what I had done it ate at my soul. I would give anything to have never harmed him, even my own life, but the past cannot be undone."

Dubric paused, closing his eyes as Oriana's face danced through his memory. By the King, he missed her so, even after all this time. Forty-six summers of loneliness had withered him, yet he loved her as if he had last seen her moments ago. When he opened his eyes again, he said, "No matter how we may wish, no matter to the price we pay or the extent we atone, the past can never be undone."

The woman's hands opened and her head tilted. "If you love the boy, why did you strike him? Why with such force and anger?"

The pacing ghost continued its endless journey, but the other no longer stood naked and screaming. He now wore the fitted garments of a scribe and stared at Dubric from just behind the woman. Dubric wondered how long ago he had died. How long before he was able to choose his own form. A few days? A phase? A moon?

Dubric swallowed, pulling his eyes from the ghosts. "My past plagues me, milady. At that moment I did not know my own mind, and I am repentant for the harm I caused the lad."

The cat gave him a baleful glare and the woman's hands clenched again. "Your past? Your past haunted you on a dismal rainy night, removed you of your senses, and forced you to hit a child? Absurd! Perhaps I should summon the authorities so you may explain it to them."

"I am the authorities," he said. "As a duly appointed emissary of Lord Brushgar, I demand that you fetch my trousers this instant so I may see to my page."

She crossed her arms over her chest. "No."

"Madam, do you have any idea who I am?"

"In his sleep, the boy talked about Lord Dubric Byerly, Lord Brushgar's sheriff. I assumed it was you."

"Castellan," he corrected, grinding his teeth as the ghost boy tugged on the blanket. "As such, I insist, nay, demand, you heed my instructions and fetch—"

"Lord Dubric would not strike a child. If you are indeed he, what excuse could you have?"

He lurched to his feet, holding the blanket at his waist. "The Goddess-damned ghosts swarmed me and I thought Otlee was one of them! Now fetch my trousers!"

She took a step back, nearly tripping over the cat, then fell into the chair. "Ghosts? What ghosts?"

Dubric sighed, rubbing his aching eyes with his free hand. *Curse my temper to the seven hells. What have I done?* He strode to the open door, keeping the blanket between him and his hostess, and closed it in the face of the unmoving, staring ghost. "You are not to speak of this, do you understand? I am fatigued, concerned, and had a weak moment. Nothing more. But I swear to you, upon my very life, I did not intend to harm Otlee."

She looked up at him, fear creeping into her hazel eyes. "But how? Why?"

Where are my trousers? "I see the restless souls of those wrongfully killed within the scope of my care. Last night a score or more set upon me without warning. In the madness I struck out, trying to escape them, but Otlee, not the spectres, met my hand. I did not realize he was amongst them until it was too late. Please, milady, you must believe me. I never, ever, meant to harm the lad, only to escape the damned ghosts."

She pressed herself against the back of the chair, and her mouth worked noiselessly before she stammered, "You . . . you're telling the truth. I'll . . . I'll get your pants."

She slid away and around him, hurrying through the door. The ghost boy chased the cat from the room.

Slowed by his aching joints, Dubric staggered to the bed and fell upon it, tucking the blanket around him. *Damn fool. How could you let the secret slip?*

When the woman returned, she had Dubric's clothes crushed to her chest. Pale and shaking, she handed him his clothes and stepped back to stand by the door.

"Thank you," he said. Although still damp, the garments had dried enough for him to endure them, and all traces of mud and filth had been removed.

The woman reached behind her to close the door with a trembling hand, keeping her back against it. "I need to know," she said, scrunching her eyes and turning her face away. "Do you see the ghost of my son?"

Dubric nearly dropped his clothes. "Your son is missing?"

She stared at the hinge, her cheek trembling. "Three days now. He went to see my niece, Sarea, and the girls, but never came home. Someone found a body in the river the day before last, and I'm afraid . . ." She turned her head to look at Dubric but remained pressed against the door. "Do you see him? Is my Braoin dead?"

By the King, she is Sarea's aunt. Now if I could only remember her name. "I do not know, milady."

She fell to her knees. "How can you not know? Tell me, please! Do you see the ghost of my son?"

Dubric kept his attention on her as he drew his trousers under the coverlet. "I cannot know if I see your son, for I have never met him. Both ghosts are strangers to me."

Her eyes shone and her blotchy, pale skin highlighted the structure of her finely boned skull. "You said you saw a score or more."

"Yes, milady." His feet fumbled into the legs of his trousers and he dragged them to his knees. "A score or more set upon me in the road, but two currently remain. The rest have departed to their favorite haunts, wherever they may be."

"Was one about my height, dark hair and eyes, with the form of a grown man, yet not filled in? He's thin and wiry, but the muscles will come, I can tell."

Dubric's breath caught in his throat. A slender, almost scrawny build on a grown man's frame, having approached full height but not yet begun on the girth. Like both remaining ghosts, and most he had seen on the road. The culprit or culprits preferred boys who were not quite men, somehow capturing and killing them. Young men like Lars. *By the King, what have I done?*

"Oh, Goddess, you see him!"

Dubric silently cursed the Goddess and yanked the trousers over his hips. "I do not know if I see him or not. One is dark-haired and slight of build, but the other is fair-skinned and freckled, with curly hair." Dubric pulled the lacings tight and stood, tossing aside the blanket and reaching for his shirt. Undergarments could wait until later. He stared at the dark-haired ghost as he drew the chilly shirt on. "Does your son sport a short beard? Have a scar upon the back of his left hand?"

Air fell out of her in a rush. "No, Braoin's clean shaven, with the hands of an artist. He has a scar near his spine, though, from when he was a child."

Dubric knelt before her. "Then I do not see his ghost."

She wiped her eyes. "So there's hope?"

"Yes, milady, hope remains." He grasped her hand, finding the tips of her fingers rough and worn. "I will need help to track and catch whoever is preying upon the Reach."

She let him draw her to her feet. "I'll do whatever I can."

"First, though, milady, I would like to know your name."

She blushed, bringing color to her face once again, and looked barely thirty instead of the forty summers he had guessed her age to be. "Maeve Duncannon, milord." She released his hand and dropped into a shaky curtsy.

"Thank you, Madam Duncannon, for taking in a strange man and a boy during a storm. We appreciate it more than you can possibly realize."

Her eyes grew oddly flat. "Just Maeve, milord. Please."

"As you wish." He bowed slightly and added, "Please, allow me to reimburse you for your hospitality."

"It's not necessary, milord. I am not a pauper, and I have ample room and plenty of food. Besides, there are few inns in the Reach. I cannot allow you or that child to sleep in someone's barn, go cold and hungry." She smiled sadly and lowered her head before looking back up to him. "If you save my son and find the man responsible, I will be forever in your debt. The least I can do is assure you have hot food and a place to sleep."

"Thank you, milady." Dubric reached into his pocket for his notebook, but found it empty. "Did you find a notebook among my belongings? A battered, old, leather-bound tome?"

"Oh, yes," she said. She opened the door and he followed her through. "When I cleaned your garments I found an unusual assortment of effects. I put yours in one box, and the boy's in another." She glanced at him over her shoulder as they walked down the hall. "He has a penchant for feathers. I pulled several from his pockets; some were quite beautiful. Lachesis kept trying to play with them, but I put them away. They're safe."

They reached the kitchen, and Maeve motioned Dubric to a pair of closed boxes on her table. The cat sat upon one, cleaning itself. "Lachesis! Get down!" she said, shooing the cat away. Dubric did not see the ghost boy anywhere.

Maeve gave Dubric an apologetic frown. "The horses would barely let me lead them, let alone get close enough to tend. The saddles are still on their backs."

"That is not unexpected." Dubric picked up his notebook and sighed. The pages were drenched.

Maeve pulled two cups from a narrow cupboard in the corner. "I thought about hanging all four books near the fire to dry, but I had no idea what they contained. If they were diaries, I'd never have forgiven myself for the intrusion."

He opened the notebook and ruffled the pages, splattering his fingers with droplets. "Four? Begging your pardon, milady, but I carry only one."

She set a pot of tea to steep and glanced at him. "The boy carried three."

"Did he?" Curious, Dubric lifted the lid to Otlee's box and peered inside. Three pocket-size books lay amongst an assortment of coins and feathers, as did a worn pencil, a page's file, a pair of keys, and a library token. Dubric shook his head—Clintte the castle librarian would seethe if a borrowed book had been ruined—and closed the box. "Where is he?"

"This way." She led him from the kitchen to a closed door across from where he had slept. "I'll be in the kitchen if you need me." She slipped away, down the hall again.

Dubric closed his eyes to the pair of ghosts. The latch felt cold as he grasped it and opened the door.

Otlee lay propped upon pillows, with a shallow basin tucked between his arm and his waist. He slept, his breathing sounding steady and strong, but the air smelled vaguely of vomit. Dubric approached the bed and winced when he saw Otlee's face. A leaf-shaped mark cut into his cheek, and the surrounding bruise stained the boy's face from his cheekbone to his chin. Other bruises darkened his eye sockets, and he had a bandage wrapped around his head. The ghost boy stood in the corner, picking his nose.

"Oh, lad, I am so sorry." Dubric sat upon the edge of the bed and touched Otlee's brow.

Otlee's eyelids flickered and he yawned. "Sir? What are you doing here?" Wincing, he sat and stretched, peering at Dubric through bleary eyes. "Did I oversleep? Why didn't my mum wake me? Why does my head hurt?"

"Look at my finger," Dubric said, holding his index finger before Otlee's eyes. As soon as Otlee focused on it, Dubric moved his finger upward, then to the left. The ghost boy mimicked Dubric.

Otlee yawned again, watching Dubric's finger, then his eyes grew wide. He glanced around the room. "Where are we, sir? What happened?"

Dubric moved his finger closer to Otlee's bruised face, nearly touching his nose. Otlee's eyes tracked the movement without error. "There was an accident and you hit your head. We found shelter in someone's home. How many fingers am I holding up?"

"Three. Two. Four. An accident?"

Dubric leaned close and gently tilted Otlee's head, checking his eyes, ears, and neck. "What is the last thing you remember?"

"Crossing a rusty old river bridge. There was a man with a pack pony and a little black dog crossing, too, going the other direction. The dog was terrified of our horses."

By the King, they had passed the man and dog the previous afternoon, barely halfway through their journey. "You remember nothing since then?"

"No, sir, not really. Vague things. A fence made of old gears. Being cold. You seeing something in the rain. A woman tending my head. What happened?"

"Dien and Lars journeyed to Tormod, to Dien's family, while you and I continued to Falliet." Dubric clenched his hands, pushing past the shame. "While on the road, in the dark and in the rain, I became confused, beset by memories and my own demons. You tried to help me, but in my confusion I struck you and you fell. I am sorry."

Otlee leaned back, startled. "You . . . hit me?"

"Yes. I did not intend to, I swear."

Panic edged into Otlee's eyes and voice. "But you hit

me? You? Sir, how can that be possible? I've never seen you hit anyone, least of all a page."

"I did not know my own mind, I swear upon my life. It will never happen again."

Otlee nodded, staring at his hands. "Yes, sir."

Dubric sighed and rubbed his eyes. The older ghosts flickered and dissipated like smoke, but the solid, crippled ghost remained. "Do you think you can walk?"

"Yes, sir, I believe so."

"And are you strong enough to work?"

Otlee raised his eyes again and nodded. "Yes, sir."

Dubric grasped Otlee's shoulder and met the boy's gaze. "Good. We have much to do today." He paused, then added, "If I ever seem out of my head again, acting like I have gone mad, do not touch me. Please, I beg of you, do not touch me."

"It's that coldness, isn't it? It follows you sometimes. I've seen how you hate it, and you usually send Lars and me away when it's near."

A wry smile teased Dubric's mouth. Otlee was an observant boy. "Coldness, yes. That is as good of a description as any, and yes, you lads should not be forced to endure it."

"It's here, isn't it, sir? Here in the Reach?"

The ghosts returned. "Get dressed," Dubric said, standing. "Once you have eaten, we need to get to work."

CHAPTER

4

†

Lars finished sweeping the porch and leaned the broom beside the door. Two more goats and Jess would be done with the day's milking, then she would join her sisters making hats. Lost in quietly watching her, Lars felt a rap on the back of his head.

"Put your fool eyes back in your skull, boy." Devyn tottered off the porch, every breath a wheeze of metallic stink. "Ain't you never seen a goat before?" He took a few stumbling steps, shook his head, then turned back to the house. "I had a rope round here somewhere. You seen it, boy? Or'd you steal it?"

"Sorry, sir," Lars replied. "I haven't seen a rope."

"Damn." Up the porch again. "Mama! There's a dead bug in Stuart! It's red as blood!"

Lars gently placed an arm over Devyn's shoulders and tried to usher him to the door. "Would you like a nice cup of tea, sir? I'm sure we can get one fixed up just the way you like it."

The old man lurched into a sudden turn, his hand whipping out to encircle Lars's wrist. "Damn right I killed them! After what they'd done!" He pulled Lars close, nose to nose in a cloud of stink. "I shoved them up their asses! I should have snapped off their heads while I was at it! Bastards deserved it, every last bit! I'm

54

glad I killed them, damn you! Why won't you give me any peace?"

Lissea bustled through the door with Sarea close behind her. "Papa! Let him go!" Lissea said, reaching for Devyn.

Devyn shoved Lars away and sent him sprawling to the porch floor. "Rabbits and wasps! Damn golden bastard sons of whores! Just because you're rich, you puss-stinking ungrateful rabbit! I saw what you did in my barn. My boy, my Stuart! Think you can get away with what you did? What your daddy did? What did you do with Stuart? You're trying to trick me!"

Devyn shoved Lissea away, knocking her aside. He grabbed the broom from beside the door and spun it so the straw pointed up and the handle pointed directly at Lars. "I'll cram this frigging thing so deep it'll spout out your ears! Burn in hell, you filthy goat!"

"Papa, no!" Sarea screamed, reaching for the broom handle. Jess ran up the steps and stood between Devyn and Lars.

Goddess, he's insane! Lars scuttled back, but Dien came running from the yard and pinned Devyn against the wall. The broom clattered away.

"He didn't do it, Dev. He's not involved."

"Yes, he is!" Devyn said, his face reddening. "The wood colt did it! Why won't anyone believe me!"

"What in the seven hells is a wood colt?" Lars asked.

Dien paused, panting, and he lowered his head. "It means your parents aren't married. That you don't know who your father is."

Lars stood slowly and backed away, watching Devyn. "My parents are married. They're Bostra and Jhandra Hargrove. You're mistaking me for someone else, sir."

Dien nodded. "You hear that, Dev? He's Lord Hargrove's son. Like we told you."

Frantic, Dev looked from face to face, his wife, his daughter, his granddaughters. "He did it! It's him! He's coming! He's here!" He looked to Lars and pleaded, "Stuart, tell them!"

Jess said, "Lars wouldn't hurt anyone."

Devyn stared at Jess. "Keep the boy from him, Maeve! He's death! He'll kill your boy like he did mine!"

Jess paled. "Do you know something about Braoin?"

"Misbegotten bastards, rabbits and wasps, every one! In my home, in my barn!" He lowered his head and sobbed, snot and spittle dripping from his face.

"What brought that on?" Dien asked as Lissea led Devyn into the house.

Lars tried to settle his heart. "I don't know. Something about goats and rope and red bugs. I tried to get him to come in for a cup of tea, but he snapped."

Dien ran his hand over his head and muttered, "Dammit to the seven hells. I thought I was done with this shit."

Lars glanced at Jess, then said to Dien, "You know what he's talking about. Don't you?"

Dien frowned. "Stuart was Dev's son—Sarea's little brother. He died a long time ago when he was just a little boy. Now every young man Dev sees is either Stuart or the 'wood colt bastard' he thinks was responsible. It's just craziness, pup, nothing more. Go on and get back to work. The sooner we finish the hats, the sooner we can go home."

"Where did they find the body?" Dubric asked Maeve as he spread the map out on the table. They had retrieved it from Otlee's saddlebags, rolled tightly, safe and dry.

"Along the Tormod River, just north of Barrorise," she said. "The area surgeon's office is in town, so they likely took it to him."

Dubric tapped his finger on Barrorise. Rivers created a near-direct connection between Falliet and Barrorise, but there was no road between them. The closest route would take them northwest through Wittrup, then north to Tormod, then southeast again to Barrorise, nearly three times farther than a crow would fly.

And the saddles and tack were drenched.

"Otlee, can you walk to Tormod?"

"Yes, sir. I can." The crippled ghost nodded, too.

"Tormod?" Maeve squinted at the map. "I thought we were going to Barrorise?"

"We are, but my men have other horses in Tormod. We merely need to walk that far."

"We can go directly to Barrorise from here. There's a footpath along the river." Maeve touched the map. "It's steep and rocky, and I wouldn't want to ride over it, but it's wide enough to walk. I lead Erline down the path several times a moon."

"Erline?"

"My jenny. She's far more surefooted than your big horses."

Dubric rolled the map, returning it to its case and brushing off the ghost's assistance. He saw no other ghosts, but he felt them, a score or more, their weight lingering behind his eyes. "Then please lead the way, milady." Beside him, Otlee checked his sword and tidied his uniform.

She led them from the house and to the back pasture, past dozens of sheep and one curious and disappointed donkey. The ground rose before them, pasture turning to trees, and she led them up and into the woods, to a narrow, slippery path. Dubric trudged behind her, feeling his ghosts' weight in every step, and the crippled boy ambled beside him, happy as could be. Dubric wondered who would murder such a child.

Brambles grew close, tugging at their cloaks, and the path turned then fell down a steep bank to a burbling creek. They continued across the creek and along its shore through mud and silt and outcroppings, and eventually found themselves looking down at a waterfall. A flat-decked barge worked its way downriver, listing slightly from side to side.

"It is beautiful," Dubric said, watching the barge float away. Farmland and pasture flowed over shallow, rolling hills across the river. From this vantage point he could see for miles to the north, past pasture to old, burnt ruins, as well as a good distance up and down the river.

Maeve smiled. "You should see it in summer, when the river is quiet and blue. A pair of eagles nest beside the waterfall."

He turned and looked up at the trees and rocky hillside stretching above him. The ghost did the same. Even with bare branches this early in spring, Dubric could not see the top of the hill through the brambles. "What is behind us?"

"Acres of stick-bushes and hawthorn and osage, mostly." She picked her way onto a narrow ledge, ducking under a twisted branch. "I've heard that morels grow there in spring, but I've never known anyone face the thorns to get them." She pointed at a series of cracks in the path ahead. "Be careful here. The lime-

stone split a couple of summers ago and it's shifty footing."

The ground did indeed shift beneath Dubric's feet
and he had to grasp a branch for balance as fist-size
rocks crumbled off and rolled away, crashing through
the thicket below. Dubric and his companions continued on, losing sight of the river to thicket and bramble,
but never losing its urgent rush in their ears.

The path widened and led downward, the limestone
and mud giving way to sharp, skittery shards of black
shale. Thorny thicket remained above them, but only
the steep bank and skeletons of sparse weeds separated
them from the river. Otlee stumbled and fell on a loose
clump of rocks, cutting his palm and banging his knees.
Dubric helped him upright while the ghost boy kicked
the offending rock in the river. After pronouncing Otlee
sound, they continued along Maeve's treacherous path.

Eventually, the path flattened and became an effort-
less hike, easing into a brush-speckled patch of grasses
running alongside the riverbank. Starlings chirruped
their early spring song and frothy clouds floated in the
brilliant sky. Without warning, the pressure and pain in
Dubric's head disappeared, leaving only one whispered
weight of a ghost behind. Dubric stumbled forward
and fell to his knees, soaking them in the mud.

"Sir?" Otlee asked. "Are you all right?"

"I tripped," he muttered, lurching to his feet again
while the ghost boy peered worriedly at him. A line of
trees a furlong or so ahead stood sentinel to the
meadow. Two deer bounded away and their white tails
disappeared into the shadows.

"We're almost there," Maeve said, moving on without them. "The town's pastures are just beyond those
trees."

Dubric looked behind him, to the bramble-covered hill and the twisting, narrow path. The hill eased back to the south, connecting with the tree line as if together they embraced the grassy meadow. Even the mud beneath his feet smelled of spring and worms and life about to waken. He smiled and breathed deeply.

Expecting a larger metropolis, Dubric frowned as they caught sight of the village. Perhaps three times the size of Falliet, Barrorise was a ragged collection of homes and shops clustered around a well in the middle of a wider stretch of road. Dubric nodded a greeting to an old man leading a pair of goats, but the old man stood slack-jawed and silent as they passed. The little ghost waved.

The barge had docked; three thick-chested men unloaded barrels and crates while a short, round man counted the cargo and made notations on a scroll. A slender yellow pennon flew beneath the ship's company colors, shining like a bit of gold among tarnished coppers. Dubric pulled his notebook from his pocket and began his notes. "The boat is Casclian?"

"Yes, I think so," Maeve said. "I really don't know much about the shipments that come through, but I have sold fabric to Casclian and Deitrelian boats heading to the coast."

Dubric looked at the boat a moment more, then asked, "Has anyone questioned the captains about the missing boys?"

Otlee turned and stared at Dubric, his brown eyes piercing and keen. " 'Boys'? Sir, I thought we were seeking missing children."

Maeve watched Dubric, placing one hand on Otlee's shoulder.

Damn me to the seven hells. These two will know all

my secrets if I cannot keep my damned mouth shut. "A slip of the tongue."

Leaving the pair to catch up on their own, he strode to the village well and looked around him. The western side of the street had houses and shops, a grocer, a bootmaker, and a livestock paddock. North, far past the joining of the two rivers, a manor house sat on a high ridge overlooking the village. Two doors down and across the street to the east of the well stood the surgeon's shop. *B. Mulconry, Surgeon,* the sign proclaimed. Beneath it hung a crude rendering of scissors and bandages. Dubric pocketed his notebook and opened the door.

The walls were stained from leaking water and grimy fingers. Tracked-in dirt gritted the floor, as did bits of refuse and mouse droppings. The very air stank of mildew and rot and infection, rather than the medicinal tang he had long associated with physicians. He stepped aside to let Maeve and Otlee enter. The ghost grimaced and clung to Dubric, trembling.

A worn, exhausted-looking woman sat on a bench near the wall and cradled a sleeping toddler in her arms. Beside her sat a girl of perhaps nine with her arm wrapped and clenched against her belly while an elderly woman fretted over her. In the far corner sat a man with black and rotting fingers. All four stared at Dubric with suspicious eyes.

"He's a noble," the woman with the baby said.

"Feathers on a pony," the man muttered, leaning back in his chair and closing his eyes. He stretched out, crossing his ankles, and drew his hat low over his eyes. "At this rate I'll be dad-blamed lucky to get home b'fore bedtime. I should just let the frigging things fall off."

"Where would I find the surgeon?" Dubric asked.

The woman with the baby sniggered and pointed past him. "Pigshit Mul's right behind you."

Dubric turned and looked through a half-open door. A wide, balding man tended a man who lay facedown on a bench, his back scattered with bloody glass cups. "Just a moment," the bald man said without glancing their way. He pulled a glass cup from a steaming pot with a pair of tongs in one hand, and punctured the man's back with a slender-bladed knife in the other. Moving the knife away, he dropped the cup over the wound. Blood spurted upward, coating the cup, and the patient moaned, writhing on the table.

Dubric's ghost bolted through the wall.

"Only one more," the surgeon said, dipping his tongs into the pot again. "You paid for ten and ten you shall receive." He scrutinized the patient's back, then smiled. "Ah, here we go." Another puncture and spurt of blood, then the surgeon tossed his implements onto a cluttered table and faced Dubric.

"Surgeon Mulconry?"

"Yes, but Mul will be fine." He wiped his hands on his filthy apron, then reached for a grimy tin cup. "Sorry for the delay, milord. Please grant me a bit of your urine and I will find a cure for what ails you."

Dubric crossed his arms over his chest and glared at the man. Even Mul's hair was filthy with grease and flakes, and his skin had the pale, splotchy look of water-soaked bread.

Mul glanced at Otlee. "Oh. Your grandson needs his injuries tended?"

Dubric regarded the man with a long stare. Both castle physicians would likely want this man thrown in irons and flogged, with but one glance at his equipment and practices. "Is there a place we may speak? Privately?"

Mul smirked, leering between Dubric and Maeve. "Ah, yes, a private matter. Right this way." Filthy cup in hand, he walked down the hall.

Dubric turned to his companions. "Wait here." Making no effort to hide his grimace of distaste, he left Maeve and Otlee at the door and followed the surgeon.

The surgeon's office was little better than the treatment room, with jars of assorted ointments, bottles of sweet vitriol and other medicines, and bits of blood and filth scattered about. A desk hid beneath bloodstained papers and pans of noxious fluid, but Dubric saw no evidence of its surface. Two dead flies hung from a web in the window, spinning in a draft, but the spider was long gone. The plaster above the window had crumbled, leaving only rotting framework behind. The stench of death was intense and the air cloying in the small, dim room.

"What brings you here?" the surgeon asked, settling in behind his desk. He motioned Dubric to a nearby chair, which held a pile of blood-crusted bandages and a dead mouse. "An inadvertent pregnancy? Pain when you urinate? No iron in your rod?"

Dubric remained rooted where he stood. "I have come to examine the body you pulled from the river."

The surgeon stood. "Please! Take the damn thing! It's stinking up the place and scaring my customers." He hurried around the desk again and rifled through his pockets. "I don't know why you'd want it, but it's yours."

Dubric scowled. *The man did not even bother to ask my name. What sort of physician discards remains with such eager abandon?* "I merely want to examine it.

Nothing more. The remains should be returned to the family once I have finished."

"It's been here three days and no one has claimed it. Other than for morbid curiosity, no one even wants to see the filthy thing, yet they insist I keep it. Me! As if I'd have a use for a rotting corpse."

Disgusted, Dubric followed him to the far end of the hall. "You are the local surgeon. It is your duty to tend the dead."

"No, that would be the undertaker in Tormod. They should have taken it to him. Let him have the stink and the mess." He shuddered and unlocked a narrow door. "The disgusting thing is all yours, and good riddance, I say."

Dubric's hand snapped out, grasping Mul by the front of his filthy tunic. "A physician should have more care for the well-being of his people, alive or dead. A boy is dead. Someone grieves for him. That should matter to you."

"I tend my patients. I will do no more." Mul shrugged free and straightened his tunic. "I don't know who you are, but take the wretched thing and get out."

Dubric loomed over him and snarled, "I am Castellan Dubric Byerly, of Castle Faldorrah, and you are a disgrace to your profession."

Mul's chin quivered, but he straightened his back and said, "You're not at your blessed castle, Lord Castellan, you're in the Reach, and here I do as I please. Your arm does not reach this far and your name is barely a whisper. There's nothing you can do here." He winced and added, "Now, if you will excuse me, I have paying customers." He turned on his heel and hurried away.

Seething, Dubric made a note to have Pigshit Mul

removed from his post—by armed escort, if necessary—then he opened the door. The stench in the storeroom made him take a step back and his eyes watered. "Wretched excuse for a man of healing," he muttered, closing the door again. He walked back to Otlee and Maeve, his mind churning.

"Is it him? Is it Braoin?"

"No, milady. Far more than three days have passed since this person's demise. It may be best if you waited outside."

She nodded. "All right." Giving him one last glance, she left the surgeon's shop, closing the door behind her.

"And me, sir?"

"You are taking notes." Dubric turned to the hall again, Otlee following. He dug in his shoulder pack, then handed Otlee a small jar. "Put a smear of this under your nose. It will help with the stench."

"Yes, sir."

Dubric pulled his notebook from his pocket and handed it to Otlee. "I realize the paper is wet. Do the best you can." He smeared a finger scoop of goo under his nose and breathed a great deal easier. "If you must vomit, please, do it on the floor, not the body."

"I won't vomit, sir."

Dubric reached for the latch. "Then let us hope I will not, either." Taking a deep breath, he opened the door.

A grayish mound of meat and bone lay upon the table, one arm hanging over the edge and dripping sludge. A puddle had formed on the floor, leaving a dried pink streak to mark its path to a corner. The corpse was nude, and appeared to have no fingers, toes, or privates. Its belly gaped open, as did its throat and the cavern that had once been its mouth.

"Malanna's blood," Otlee gasped, following Dubric into the room. "Are you sure that's even human?"

"Reasonably so. Close the door. I will need help with the initial measurement."

"Yes, sir," Otlee replied. He stood just behind Dubric's left elbow and marked the page with his pencil. "Just give me a moment to note the number before starting in."

Dubric handed Otlee one end of the measuring string and walked to the body's head. Otlee held the other against the toeless stump of an oozing foot. "Five lengths, four fingers," Dubric said, pulling in the string as Otlee opened the notebook again.

"The victim appears to be male, red-haired, no eyes. The sockets are completely empty." With one finger, Dubric pulled the lower jaw open and peered inside. "All besides his wisdom teeth are present, but they're rotted. He never tended them. Put his age as fourteen to eighteen summers. His cheeks, lips, and nose have been partially removed. He has a contusion on the side of his head, softening his skull, but his scalp and ears are intact. I see a puncture near his temple opposite the contusion, perhaps from a stick or sharp rock while in the water. There are numerous abrasions and punctures on the face and torso, possibly from dragging along the riverbed."

Dubric pressed a finger into the victim's shoulder and water leached out, as if he were a sponge. "His flesh is waterlogged as well as rotted. Severe trauma to or severing of all extremities. He has half of his left index finger and a small part of the thumb but no other fingers on his left hand. All fingers on the right are missing." Dubric lifted the dangling hand and frowned at the dark lines across it. "Note that there are ligature marks on his right wrist. He was tied."

Otlee said nothing, but his pencil flew over the page.

Dubric stretched out a bit of his measuring string. "The hole in his belly is one length two by . . . nine fingers." Putting the string away, he pulled the flesh apart and peered into the cavern that had been the boy's belly. Grimacing, he reached in and extracted a dead bullhead. "There is a fish inside his abdomen."

Gritting his teeth, Dubric continued his examination but found little of note that was not fish-eaten or missing. "I estimate he was in the water a moon or so, considering the cool, wet spring. What a waste." He sighed. *And what I would not give for a towel to wipe my hands upon.*

"Yes, sir," Otlee said. The unbruised skin of his face had turned a pale shade of green. "Are we finished?"

"Not quite." Dubric took a deep breath and reached beneath the victim's shoulder, lifting and rolling him onto his side.

"The skin of his back is crusty, split open in places with burst and dried blisters from decay gasses. He floated facedown. Little bloating remains and the flesh beneath his skin is flaccid and decomposing. There are numerous shallow cuts across his neck and back." Dubric looked at Otlee and sighed. "Birds. Scratches and beak marks. Probably hawks, crows, or gulls."

Is there anything here to find? Balancing the corpse with one hand, he worked his way down from the head, noting injuries along the way. When he reached the buttocks, he paused, his heart hammering.

Otlee looked up as Dubric fell silent. "Sir?"

Dubric closed his eyes, then opened them again as he fought against the desire to wipe his hands. "Evidence of a sexual attack. His anus is torn, nearly shredded, and there is extreme bruising all about the area."

"Sir? I don't understand."

"He was raped, Otlee. Tied down and raped. Repeatedly."

Otlee took a step back, his mouth falling open. "And Missus Maeve's son?"

"I would assume so as well, yes." Dubric clenched his fists and started toward the door. *How am I going to tell her the fate of her son? Can I find him before it is too late?*

The girls nearly knocked Lars off his feet, squealing in their hurry to get to the merchandise.

"Hoy now, there's plenty for everyone," Atro the peddler said, unlatching the doors to his cart with plump sausage fingers. Display shelves opened along the sides, and he drew out a long rack of trinkets and utensils.

He stepped aside, grinning as Fyn and Kia shoved each other to get to a sparkly bit of jewelry, then waved as Lissea and Sarea came from the house.

"Have any spices today?" Jess asked, jostled aside by her sisters. "We're running short on nutmeg."

"Ah, that I do, lassie," the peddler said. He reached into the cart and pulled out a long, low case, opening it for Jess.

Beside her, Aly begged to see the puppets. Atro winked at her and opened the back door. Three battered puppets lay faceup in a box. He selected one and handed it to Aly. Giggling, she walked it around the cart.

Opposite from the squealing girls, Lars looked through an assortment of lenses and magnifiers, peering through them. He wondered if Otlee would like a good magnifier.

"Atro, back again so soon?" Lissea asked from behind Lars.

The peddler handed her a box of parcels and bags. "I know a good market when I see it. I recognize the girls, but have you acquired a grandson?"

"This is Lars," Lissea said. "He works with my son-in-law."

"Ah, from the castle, yes. That explains his discerning eye." Atro leaned his bulk past Lars, reaching for a magnifier with a gilded handle. "I received this lovely glass not a fortnight ago. It's from Blackmoor. Solid ivory with gold inlay."

Lars accepted the glass and peered through it, examining Aly and her puppet, much to her delight. Not quite as heavy as the examination glass he had back home, it magnified well, with minimal distortion. "How much?"

"I can't accept less than fifty crown for such a fine piece."

Shaking his head, Lars laid it back on the black cloth. "Otlee can buy his own magnifier for that much."

"Is that your brother?" Atro asked, opening another drawer of lenses.

Lars shook his head and knelt to examine the batch of telescopes and spyglasses. "No, he's another page, like me."

Kia walked over with a pair of ear baubles. "Otlee's

just a regular page, but Lars is Lord Hargrove's son, from Haenpar," she said. "He may act like a commoner, but he could probably afford to buy your entire cart." She gave Lars a chipper smile, then held out the ear baubles. "I only found red and blue in this style. Do you have them in green?"

Seething, Lars stood and closed the drawer. His father hadn't given him one penny in all the summers he'd paged in Faldorrah, and his salary, while reasonable and carefully budgeted each phase, did not offer him the luxury of buying an expensive magnifier, not to mention an entire peddler's cart of baubles. In fact, many times he'd fretted over replacing worn and broken necessities or buying appropriate books for his classes.

"Kia!" Sarea said. "Lars's finances and family matters are none of your business."

"But it's true. He's one of the richest and most powerful young men in Faldorrah, even if he never wants to admit it. Surely he can afford a mere fifty crown."

Scowling, Jess walked around the cart with a handful of spice tins. She looked at Lars with a sympathetic frown. "That's not the point," she said. "Mam's right. It's none of your business."

Lars walked past Jess and on to the house without looking back.

Braoin slipped again, swinging in the dark and cursing the weakness in his aching hands. The man had visited him early that morning, waking Braoin to agony and the crows of a rooster somewhere outside. He had no way to fight, no route of escape, and after what seemed like a lifetime of stabbing torture, the man had finished his business, then force-fed Braoin porridge and goat milk.

Alone again and lost in the dark, Braoin had cried until he had noticed a faint glow to his right. The ball of promise had grown and brightened until a thin shaft of light poured through the knothole. Braoin had watched with a desperate thread of hope, but it illuminated nothing more than plain-planked walls and shadows of tools.

Every movement had sent him swaying. He'd tried to flex his feet, his toes, but he felt nothing past his ankles. Were they even there? Had his captor cut them off and thrown them away? His neck hurt from supporting the weight of his head, his shoulders and arms ached, and his ass, oh Goddess . . .

This can't be happening, it just can't. Please, Goddess, no!

Braoin stared at the shaft of light. It crept from the wall toward the floor in a sluggish arc and he watched its descent while his mind wandered to thoughts of his betrothed. "Oh, Faythe," he said, his eyes stinging with tears again. Sir Haconry had commissioned a painting that would buy them a small home and give them a place to start a family. Braoin had wagered their future on the painting, his and Faythe's, and now it would never be completed. Their future would never come.

The light eased downward and Braoin took a sharp breath at what it revealed. Tiny red worms and fat red-black moths writhed on the floor, scouring clean a partially exposed skull. It lay on the infested dirt with its brow, its nose, and the tip of its chin rising above the insects.

Panicked, Braoin gripped his binds, inching upward and away from the horror on the floor despite the tearing pain of the cording around his wrists. Desperate and terrified, he climbed, ignoring the pain and the ghastly stench, closing his mind to the insects below. He imagined Faythe waiting on the beam above. If he could reach her, he could release his hands and break free.

He could go home to her again. To his life again.

Sweat stung his eyes, but he blinked it away and fought for another finger length, another higher grip.

Then his fingertips brushed wood.

Startled, he nearly fell but steadied himself and took a few deep breaths. His arms quaking, he pulled up, bending his elbows, then flung his right hand up over to grip the upper side of the beam.

He screamed as pain exploded in his fingers, and yanked his hand away. Something warm and firm landed against him and bounced away but he barely noticed. His grip slipping, he fell, screaming, his right hand—*my painting hand, oh Goddess*—burning in agony. He felt warm wetness on his face and he tasted blood.

He fell to the limits of his binds and lurched to a sudden, swinging stop, screaming again at the pain snapping through his wrists and shoulders. Whimpering, he looked to the silhouette of his arm against the shaft of light. His hand hung limp from a ruined wrist, with the index finger gone, the middle finger partially severed, and both oozing spurts of blood.

He turned his head away and wailed, swinging in the rancid dark.

Seething, Dubric grabbed Mul by the apron and yanked him to the hall. Otlee following, he shoved Mul into his office and slammed the door.

"You have but one chance to get me out of here and you will do it by answering my questions. The boy that you left to rot in that storage room was raped."

Stumbling against the wall, Mul turned to face Dubric. "It's none of my concern. I told you that."

"Someone raped and killed that boy and I need to know who."

Panic edged into Mul's voice. "It wasn't me."

He knows something. "Someone in the Reach has a taste for this. You live here, have heard the rumors. Who is it?"

His mouth clamped closed, Mul took a step back.

Dubric pulled his sword. "Damn you, tell me!"

Mul shook his head and turned away, his eyes squeezed shut.

Dubric leaned close and held his sword against the base of Mul's throat. "I could kill you," he whispered. "But you are merely a snake, not the killer. Who does this? Who rapes young men?"

"I can't!" Mul blubbered. "I have nothing, nothing but this business, nothing but boils and rashes and rotten teeth! I'm the fourth son, for Goddess' sake! He'll ruin me if I tell."

"Ah, so you do know." Dubric shifted the angle of his sword until it threatened to pierce Mul's quivering flesh. "Who?"

"I can't. He's family!"

"Who? He may ruin you, but I will leave your lifeblood on the floor, I will leave you to rot unclaimed and untended in a dark and filthy room, like you did that boy."

Mul blubbered, tears streaking down his face. "Martaen Haconry. My cousin."

CHAPTER

5

✝

Maeve was waiting outside the door, wringing her hands and pacing along the edge of the road, the little ghost crouching beside her. "What happened?" she asked the moment Dubric stepped through. "I heard shouting."

"I bullied my way through an interrogation," Dubric said, grasping her arm and leading her away. "What do you know about Sir Haconry?"

"He's a coldhearted bastard," she muttered, staring at her shoes. "Every spring and fall he takes his taxes, the best sheep, poultry, and grain, more than his rightful due. He leaves the people barely enough to survive, forcing them to buy back what should have been theirs to start with, at prices far higher than they should be."

Dubric shook his head and released her arm. "Besides taxes. Besides levies and laws and tolls and the suffering of the poor. What do you know of the man?"

"I heard he ran down a child in the road. He was on a great horse and the little girl was still in diddies. She didn't move quick enough so he charged his horse right over her."

Dubric had seen no female ghosts, nor ghosts of any children so young. "What else?"

"He beat his wife for producing a daughter, or so I

heard, and had her banished. He selects the mayors of our villages, picking men who will see his will done despite the needs of the people. There are rumors . . ."

He turned her to face him. "What rumors?"

"That he coerces boys to his bedroom and forces them to couple with him."

"Damn." Dubric ground his teeth. "Otlee!"

"I'm here, sir."

"I need two horses and I need them now."

"There's no stable here," Maeve said. "Only in Tormod. No horses, either."

No horses? Dubric turned to stare at her.

"I'm sorry, milord," she said, dropping her gaze, "but the largest animals you'll find here are goats or sheep."

He rubbed his eyes and tried to think, but a man yelled in the distance and he heard people running.

"What's happening?" Maeve gasped.

Dubric turned to see a dozen or so men running for the outskirts of town. He found himself following them down the road toward the riverbank, downstream from the dock.

"Dang, Girvan, I see it!"

"Not again!"

"What is it?" Dubric called out as he approached the group of men staring down at the river.

"Another body washed up," a barrel-chested craftsman said, glancing over his shoulder at Dubric. "Who are ye?"

"Castellan Dubric." He offered his hand and the craftsman accepted it with a firm but gentle grip.

"I'm Ungus Dwyer. The shoemaker. Glad to have ye here, sir."

" 'Bout damned time someone come," a man said

from the other side of the group. Agreement arose all around.

Dubric moved through the crowd and peered over the edge of the bank. A naked body floated facedown in the shallows, lodged in a tangle of brush and branches. Its back sported a good collection of streaks and slashes from talons and beaks, but far fewer than the corpse dripping in Mul's storeroom.

Dubric knelt upon the edge to examine the scene from above. He saw no footprints, only mud and sand and branches. "Is this where the first body was found?" The little ghost sat nearby, his feet hanging over the bank, and pointed at a passing bird.

Dwyer knelt beside Dubric and sighed as he looked at the body. "No, sir. 'Twas upriver, on the other side of town."

"This one sure stinks a hell of a lot less," a scrawny, wax-spattered man said, kneeling on Dubric's left. He offered his hand. "I'm Todd Morton, sir. Damn good to see ye."

Dubric met all eleven men in short order, including the village cleric, who struck Dubric as far too young to be spreading Malanna's lies. While the men stared down at the body, women clustered together on the far side of the road, clutching children to their skirts. Maeve stood among them, with Otlee.

"How we gonna get down there?" Morton asked, tugging on his beard.

"Yer a fool." Dwyer shifted, dropping his legs over the ledge. " 'Tis only ten lengths or so, with sand at the bottom."

"Otlee!" Dubric called, beginning his own descent.

"Yes, sir?"

"Take statements from every person here."

"Yes, sir." Otlee pulled a notebook from his pocket and asked for names.

Dubric inched forward then dropped, falling to a crouch as he landed. Dwyer dropped down beside him, then Morton, then the ghost.

"Stay behind me," Dubric said, "and do not touch anything unless I instruct you to. We must not compromise any evidence."

"Evidence of what?" Morton asked. "It's purty durn obvious a body washed up."

"Of murder, ye dingle," Dwyer muttered. "Let 'im work."

What I would not give for Lars and Dien's competence and aid, Dubric thought as he approached the body. His initial assessment of the scene remained unchanged; the area had not been trodden upon nor the body touched. It had arrived by current and fate alone. He felt off-kilter, examining a body without the ghost present, and still had no idea why all but one ghost had disappeared in the meadow. The tangle of brush shifted and his heart skipped a beat, sweat cooling his brow. He had to hurry before it washed downriver. He had no time to waste.

He waded into the river, gasping at the cold, and wondered how it happened that two bodies washed up along the same stretch of river within days of each other when so many had died over the years and been lost forever. "Someone fetch me a blanket, preferably two." The tangle shifted again, breaking loose from the bank, and started to float away. Dubric lunged forward, floundering in the chest-deep water until he grasped a cold, bloated ankle.

Still gasping, the muscles of his legs threatening to

give up and let him float away, he staggered to the bank, dragging the corpse behind him.

Dwyer and Morton waded in to their knees to help, but Dubric waved them off. "He stays in the water until I have a blanket to place him on. I do not want to lose the smallest bit of evidence to sand and mud. The water has washed enough away already."

Dubric looked at the body, his throat clenching. Dark-haired and slight of build, battered and sodomized, this corpse was much like the other. Dubric had no doubt the same person had killed both young men. He wondered if the latest discovery was Maeve's son, Braoin, but he pushed the thought aside. While not as rotted and waterlogged as its predecessor, the body showed early signs of decay. Blisters had formed along the red-green-tinged skin of his buttocks, back, and shoulders. A few had burst open, oozing putrid fluid onto his back. Although discolored, his fingernails remained attached to his bloated flesh.

Dwyer ran to him with an armload of borrowed blankets. Some were ragged, but a few were well cared for. Dubric hoped the loan would not bring too great a burden to their owners.

"Lay two of the worn blankets out, as smooth as you can," Dubric said. He turned the body sideways and crouched in the water, one arm beneath the chest, another the hips. Grunting, he stood and stumbled under the loose weight as he trudged to shore. As he laid the body on the closest blanket he saw Otlee lowering himself down from the edge.

"I've got everyone's name and statement, sir." Otlee's hair blazed red in the noonday sun, and the ghost limped beside him. "I told Mister Simorus to wait in case you wanted to talk to him. He found the body and hollered for help."

"Good job." Dubric knelt beside the corpse and continued his preliminary examination. "He has been dead a phase at most, judging by the blisters on his exposed skin. Again, obvious evidence of rape. Ligature marks on both wrists and ankles, numerous scratches and punctures on his skin."

Dubric lifted the body's right hand and examined it. "Index and middle finger are cut, clean to the bone. Some evidence of fish nibbling, but whatever cut him slashed the bone. It is a clean cut. A blade, perhaps. No noticeable skin or struggle remnants beneath the fingernails. They are discolored from rot but still attached."

Dubric rocked back on his heels, pressing his fingers into the victim's shoulder muscle. "Definite bloating, but limited water absorption. A day, perhaps two in the river, and he rotted for a time beforehand." Dubric pulled his measuring string from his pocket and gave one end to Otlee. "Height is five lengths, nine fingers. Black hair, cut short. Bruising on the back of his neck and between his shoulders. Possible strangulation. We will know for certain once we roll him over."

"Got it, sir."

Dubric walked around the body. "He wore shoes, tight ones. His toes naturally squash together, but there are no rub marks on his lower legs or calluses on his soles. Definitely shoes, not boots." He looked at Dwyer. "How many men in the Reach wear tight shoes?"

Dwyer blinked and reddened under Dubric's scrutiny. "Gosh, sir, I dunno. Most men round the Reach wear boots or plain slippers."

"Give me an estimate, that is all I ask."

"Couple of dozen, maybe. I repair two or three fitted pair a season."

Dubric heard Otlee note the information, his pencil dragging against paper. "And who wears fitted shoes? Surely not farmers."

"No, sir. Men of letters, the advocate up Tormod way, nobles, clergy, maybe a shopkeeper or two."

"The bottle maker wears them funny shoes," Morton chirped in. "I seen him polishin' them all the damned time."

Dwyer sighed. "Keane was right there on the road, ye fool, and he's done gone half bald. This ain't him."

Morton lowered his head. "Oh, yeah. My 'pologies."

Dubric resisted the urge to rub his eyes as he continued his first circuit of the body. "He wore a ring, on his left hand. The dent remains but the ring is gone." He walked around one more time and noticed nothing new. "Help me roll him over."

Dwyer knelt beside the shoulder, Dubric at the hip, and they rolled the victim onto his back. Dwyer gasped, scrambling away.

"You know this man?" Dubric asked. Despite the gaping eye sockets, he recognized the face as that of the unmoving ghost who had followed him to Maeve's.

The shoemaker nodded. "Yessir. It's the shoes, like ye said. I sold him his shoes, even repaired 'em not four moons back." Suddenly green, he cleared his throat and spat a wad of phlegm over his shoulder. "It's Calum the scribe. From Oreth. I'm sure of it."

At last, one ghost had a name. "What do you know about him?"

Dwyer shrugged and spat again. His words came shaky and slow, and Dubric feared he might vomit.

"Decent enough fella. Youngish, not more than twenty summers, I'd guess. Used fancy words. I only talked to him twice, ye understand."

"Where is Oreth?"

"Northwest of here quite a ways."

"Otlee?"

"One moment, sir."

Dubric watched Dwyer while Otlee pulled the map from his cloak pocket. "Yes, sir, it's northwest. About seven miles straight, maybe ten by road."

Dubric blinked, surprised. "A scribe journeyed ten miles for shoes?"

"Oh, no, sir. Every moon or so I travel to nearby villages. I'm the only shoemaker in the Reach, and folks, well, they need their boots resoled or repaired. Calum bought his shoes in Wittrup, I think. 'Twas nearly two summers back, but I'm fairly sure we met up in Wittrup that first time."

Dubric sighed. "And the second? Four moons ago?"

"Yessir, that was in Tormod, I'm sure of it. Just b'fore winter came. He brought his family with him, wife and two children. The little ones got new slippers."

Dubric's gut twisted as he looked at the corpse at his feet. *He is not a boy, but a man.* "Two children, you say?"

"Yessir. Twin girls, 'bout two summers old. Cutest little things ye ever did see, all laughter and spunk. It's a shame, them losing their daddy."

"That it is." His heart heavy, Dubric knelt beside the body. *Not only boys, but young men, with families. What predator attacks strong young men intending to rape and murder them? There has to be a clue here somewhere. Something to grant insight into the killer.*

He wiped his hands on his drenched trousers and

looked up at the two villagers. "Is there a place I can conduct a more thorough examination? Besides Mulconry's death house?"

Morton backed away, his face reddening, but Dwyer did not move. "We're scared enough as it is, milord. I dunno of anyone who'd bring a rotting corpse into their home, to their family. I'm sorry."

Dubric glanced at the sky, noting that the sun had recently passed its zenith. "Then this will have to do. When I have finished, the remains must be taken to the undertaker in Tormod, to be prepared for a decent burial, so please see that it is done. I will pay for whatever costs are involved, including transportation. Surely someone in this village has a cart or other conveyance."

Dwyer winced and swallowed. "That'd be me, milord, but night will fall before I could journey to Tormod and return again. I've got a mess of work waiting fer me as it is."

Dubric opened his purse and rooted through until he found a pair of coins. "Here. Five crown should pay for your trouble, and another five to pay preparation expenses. Feel free to keep any excess. Please tell the undertaker I will inform him—"

"I can't accept it, milord. I'm sorry." Dwyer stared at the coins in Dubric's palm as if they were made of dung instead of gold. "I . . . I've got me a family and I can't risk . . ."

Dubric closed his fingers over the coins, wishing his hands were clean enough to rub his eyes. "I understand. How much to rent your cart?"

"Milord, I can't allow—"

"I will not leave another young man to rot by a river. How much to rent your cart for one blasted evening?"

Dwyer stared at the body for long time then asked, "Can ye catch him, milord? Can ye put an end to this?"

Ghosts or no ghosts, the murders will stop. "Yes, I can."

Morton stared at the body as well, then both men raised their eyes to Dubric. Rage boiled behind Dwyer's otherwise calm face and his voice cracked. "Can ye avenge our children?"

"I swear I will see him hanged or set him dying upon my sword. You have my word."

Dwyer shook but he took a cleansing breath before taking Dubric's coins. "Then I'll deliver Calum to the undertaker for ye, even if it takes all night."

He nodded once to Dubric, then to Otlee, before turning away and climbing back to the road.

The axe securely in the chopping block and his hands sprouting blisters, Lars grabbed a bundle of kindling and carried it behind the barn. The land sprawled downhill before him, leading to the back fence. Beyond the fence, in a quiet little valley, stood another farmhouse and a pasture of sheep. Beyond that, another. He smiled. Water glistened beyond the farthest farm, a wide low patch of blue shimmering in the sun. He wondered if Sarea would want some fish for supper. His mind on catfish, he strode past the back of the barn and grimaced. Doing his best not to retch, he looked around but saw nothing but the closed doors of Devyn's shop.

"Goddess, it stinks back here," he muttered, striding forward again with the kindling in his arms. Wet and rotten, the scent of meat gone bad, it chased all thoughts of fishing from his mind. He added the kindling to the pile, stacking it neatly and trying not to breathe as he wondered what could smell so bad. A shadow fell across him and he was about to ask Dien about the stink, but hands grasped his neck and threw him backward.

He scrambled to his feet to see two workers moving toward him in a whiskey-scented haze. "Think you're hot piss, don't you, boy?" the taller one said, cracking his knuckles. "Walking 'round like you own the place, when you're just a hired hand."

The other giggled, brainless and mean. "Look at him, Rao! Ain't nothing to 'im. All pale and scrawny. He don't look like he's ever done a lick of work his whole miserable life."

"I don't want any trouble," Lars said, backing away.

Rao chuckled. "Puppies like you never do." He grinned, then lunged.

Lars tried to step aside but the other boy moved, too, blocking him. Lars grabbed Rao by the hair and pulled him in to knee his head, but the other boy, still giggling like a loon, shoved Lars against the barn wall, and Lars slipped, his knee barely grazing Rao's cheek. Lars grasped the laughing boy by the upper arm and flipped him forward, onto Rao, sending both of them to the muddy ground. The laughter stopped.

"I told you, I don't want any trouble."

"You found some," Rao growled, scrambling out from beneath the other, his hands curled into fists. His partner scurried away.

Lars blocked Rao's wild punch, stepped back to block again, then muttered, "Oh, hells," before punching Rao's face. Lars heard nasal cartilage snap as blood slopped from Rao's nose.

Astounded and blinking, Rao spat a mouthful of blood. "You broke my nose, you son of a swine!"

"Just because you fight like a fool," Lars said, then he felt himself flip backward and off his feet. Rao's cowardly friend had apparently returned.

He landed in cold, moist earth, the sudden slam knocking the breath from his lungs. Struggling to breathe, Lars tried to fend off the two men, but one held him down while the other punched and kicked. The ribs on his left side creaked from repeated blows and he tasted blood.

The beating paused and he fought to draw a breath, but hard, rough fingers encircled his throat, lifting his head before slamming it back to the mud again. Rao leaned over him, leering, and said, "Who's the fool now? Flann and me, we've seen you hanging 'round the house and sniffing after the girls. But you're just a worthless shit, ain't you? A sniveling baby."

Lars tried to shove Rao away, but Flann was pinning his hands above his head, and grinning at him with brainless menace.

Lars's head pounded and his lungs screamed for air, lurching within his chest, but even if they remembered how to work, he doubted he could draw a breath past the grip strangling his throat. *Goddess, I'm going to die.*

"He's just a scared little puppy," Flann said. "Too scared to even squeal. Look at him sweat. What a little diddle pup."

Rao lifted and slammed back Lars's head again. "Gonna piddle on the floor, puppy? Or have you learned your lesson?"

Lars struggled, his vision dimming. He felt one more slam of his head and a kick to his belly, then the hands were gone.

He rolled, drawing his knees to his chest, as the world faded to charcoal gray and he heard a door creak open. Someone yanked him upright and planted a couple of firm blows between his shoulder blades.

"Damn you, Stuart. Breathe, boy."

Another blow, harder than the first two, and the constriction in his upper chest disappeared. Cool air dragged like broken glass into his lungs and he coughed, struggling to find a rhythm to his breathing again.

Devyn released him and he fell forward, landing on his forearms. He stared at the ground between his hands and the blood dribbling on the black mud. He spat, fresh bright red leaching into black dirt. He forced in a breath, then another, coughed a few times, then his lungs remembered their job.

He rolled back until his backside rested on his heels, and looked up at Devyn. The old man shook, his hands clenching and unclenching, his face a deep and dangerous red. "Are you all right, boy? Did they peg you up the ass this time? Did they rip you?"

Lars shook his head and coughed, spitting again to clear his throat. "I'll be all right, sir. Thank you."

Devyn stared down the length of the barn wall toward the main yard. "I killed them once, and I'd do it again." He turned back to Lars. "But you're not dead, are you, Stuart?"

Lars staggered to his feet and stumbled to the old man. "No, sir, I'm not. You saved me."

Devyn's bleary eyes rolled as they looked at, then past, Lars. "I did?"

Lars nodded and Devyn took a shaky step toward Lars, then another, while grayish drool clotted the corners of his mouth. "But did I close the devil's eye?"

"Uh, sure."

Devyn grinned. Giggling, he turned and tottered to his workshop. He opened the door, releasing a cloud of rotting stink, then disappeared into the dark.

Dubric had found the first body's discovery location easily enough, perhaps fifty lengths north of where the Tormod River fed into the Casclian. Weeds and brambles were trampled and ruined, and a herd of swine would have made less of a mess of the scene. Climbing down the bank, Dubric doubted that after three days and one rainy night there would be much left, but the blatant disregard for proper evidence procedures sickened him. How could anyone discover the truth if clues were not gathered and protected?

Looming over the road, as if giving witness to the tragedy, a rambling manor house stood behind high stone walls, a finely crafted testament to the poverty and the toil of the Reach. Both bodies had been found within sight of it, a coincidence Dubric refused to ignore.

Furious, he stomped up the stairs to Haconry's manor and pounded on the door with his filthy fist. His hands smelled like wet corpse and his boots were flecked with thin blood, but he did not take one moment to tidy himself, or Otlee.

The boy stood in his accustomed position, one step behind and to Dubric's left, his hand resting on the hilt of his shortsword. They had left Maeve in the village, and, strangely, the little ghost remained with her. Dubric wondered why he saw only the one when so many were dead.

Dubric slapped the closed portal with his open palm

and left a blood and grime smeared print behind. "In the name of Lord Brushgar, I demand—"

The door opened, revealing a frail old woman. "My apologies, sir," she said, stepping back and lowering her wrinkled head. "We were not expecting visitors today. How may I serve you?"

Dubric brushed past the cowering woman, into a long, low hall of polished wood and brocaded carpets. Candles flickered from behind lamp lenses, magnifying the light and chasing all shadows away. "Where is he?"

The servant closed the door with barely a whisper of movement, her eyes never rising above Dubric's knees. "Where is who, milord?"

Dubric turned full circle, seeing little more than the long hallway. "Haconry."

The old woman seemed to shrink. "He is not accepting visitors this afternoon, milord. May I take your name and arrange—"

Dubric put one finger beneath her chin and raised her head until he could see her eyes. They were brown and yellowed, acutely aware, and vaguely familiar. "I am Dubric Byerly, Castellan of Faldorrah, and this is not a request. Fetch him. Immediately."

She blanched and stepped away. "I cannot, milord. My master has ordered—"

"You may leave us, Vidulyn. Lord Castellan Dubric is not known for his patience."

"As you wish," Vidulyn said, then hurried down the hall.

Dubric turned. Sir Martaen Haconry, Steward of the Reach, posed casually in the middle of the hall as if he had been there all along, his silk clothes shimmering in the candlelight and his eyes as cold and sparkling as a winter sky. Freshly shaven, he smiled broadly, showing a glimpse of yellowed teeth, and smoothed his carefully coiffed hair. "To what do I owe the exquisite pleasure of your visit, my Lord Castellan?"

"I received word of a murder, then arrived to find that there are several people missing. Why was I not notified sooner?"

Haconry's brow furrowed. "I did notify you." The silk whispered as he approached, bringing with him the scent of nutmeg. "I told Lord Brushgar when I attended luncheon at the castle last autumn, and I sent you several written notices that my beloved people's children were disappearing. No response arrived, and I could only assume my humble pleas had fallen on deaf ears." He raised an eyebrow as his eyes lit upon the shadow behind Dubric's elbow. "What have we here?"

Dubric ground his teeth. *He is lying. Even if one message went astray, or two, Lord Brushgar would surely have mentioned it to me.*

Haconry smiled at Otlee and leaned in. "You always did have a taste for commoners, did you not? A pity. Even in official garments his breeding is apparent. But he is a pretty lad, pedigree notwithstanding. Bright-eyed and eager, as your preference has always been, not that I can blame you." He touched Otlee's bruised cheek. "What's this?"

Haconry turned to Dubric and smiled, his voice dripping with sarcasm. "Tsk, tsk, my Lord Castellan! You surprise me. I surely thought you knew better than to succumb to the weakness of your rages. You must learn to be gentle with your . . . pets."

Dubric shifted his feet and his hand. "Remove your hand or your arm will no longer be of use to you, except as a doorstop."

Haconry waggled his index finger and stood straight

again. "Such brutality. It does not suit a man of your breeding, but you left that all behind, did you not? For a woman, no less. Truly a tragedy. She was a commoner, too, or so I hear."

"Why was I not summoned to avenge these dead children?"

Haconry stepped back, but his eyes remained cold and aloof. "Dead? My children are . . . dead? Are you certain?"

Dubric stomped toward him, holding back a snarl. "Yes, I am certain. I hear you have a penchant for boys."

Haconry tossed back his head and laughed toward the painted ceiling. "Of course I do! What's not to enjoy? Properly tended, they're soft and pliant and clean. Utterly delightful and eager to please." He winked at Dubric. "But you already know this, my Lord Castellan, do you not? Why else would you choose such a lovely specimen as your pet?"

"I have never touched my pages."

Haconry laughed. "My Lord Castellan, his face bears the mark of your lie. But no matter. You must stay and visit for a time, you and your delightful companion. We have much to discuss and tips to share." He winked again and chuckled. "Perhaps we could share something else instead."

"No," Dubric said, remaining near the door. "I have no time for this madness. What do you know about these dead boys?"

"My Lord Castellan, I assure you, I know nothing of dead boys, only living ones that come to me. What fault is it of mine that their parents cannot purchase garments to clothe them or buy food to fill their bellies? They appear at my door, begging to be taken in, begging to be cared for, to be loved, and that is precisely what I do. When I have aided them all I can, I send them home."

Smiling, he sighed wistfully at Otlee. "It's a mutually beneficial arrangement, I assure you. I don't dare suppose your pet is in need of food or clothing, or anything else? I'd be delighted to resume his training with a far gentler hand than you've shown."

Dubric pushed Otlee behind him. "He stays with me."

"A pity. I have not had such a lovely guest for a very long time." He started to reach for Otlee but glanced at Dubric and drew his hand back, his fingers curling toward his palm. "The Reach is not prone to breeding quality in its common populace, although the rare specimen does occur."

"Is that how you choose them? By their breeding quality? Then you kill the ones that do not meet your requirements?"

Haconry frowned. "My Lord Castellan, I am not so vile a beast to harm my pets. Even the homeliest specimen has its joys, and I would never harm them—unlike you. I am a gentle man, after all."

"So I hear." Dubric stood before Otlee, his hand resting on the hilt of his sword. "As a gentleman, would you allow me to search the premises?"

Haconry smiled, turning away. "I would be delighted to grant you a tour, but please remember that I have other duties to attend to and cannot spend an afternoon in idle gossip."

Motioning Dubric to follow, he walked down the hall to the first door and opened it. "My study. I recently added the chandelier. Isn't it lovely?"

Dubric peered into the sitting room before entering.

A low fire in the hearth burned cheerily, soft, plum-colored carpets covered the floor, and fine furnishings stood artfully arranged near low tables and a wall of books. A long, low cupboard beside one wall held a simple but exquisite collection of cut-glass bottles, most containing wines of varying hues.

One chair shifted, creaking softly. A plain-faced boy of perhaps eight summers peeked around the side, smiling shyly. "Did you need me?" he asked.

Haconry waved the child away. "Not now, Shoney. I am conducting business."

The child pouted and disappeared around the chair. Dubric heard the familiar sound of a page being turned.

"The harness maker's son, from Oreth," Haconry whispered in Dubric's ear. "A bright boy. He's shown progress in learning his letters. And other skills, of course."

"One of the dead lads came from Oreth." Dubric turned and stared at his host. "Would you know anything about that?"

"No, I do not believe so. Who might it be?"

"Calum, the scribe."

Haconry coughed a startled gasp, then patted Dubric's shoulder indulgently. "My Lord Castellan, you jest with me! Calum is not dead, nor is he a boy. He is a grown man, with a family. I had personal acquaintance with him many summers ago, but I assure you he is no longer of interest to me in that particular regard."

Dubric stepped back, shrugging off Haconry's touch, and snatched Otlee away. *He is more vile than old blood and rot! By the King, I need a bath.* "You knew him?"

"As a boy, yes. He proved very adept at letters and numbers. Who do you think taught him the skills to become a scribe? His mother?" Haconry shook his head and motioned Dubric and Otlee to the hall. "She was a serving wench in the tavern. A slovenly whore. I found him starving and filthy, little more than a street rat. I brought him into my home and offered him a future."

"And, after all that you gave him, it does not bother you that he is dead, found just downriver from your home?"

Once Dubric and Otlee had stepped through, Haconry closed the door. "Calum is not dead, my Lord Castellan. I spoke with him a mere two phases ago. The corpse pulled from the Tormod River had been floating for quite some time and bore no resemblance to Calum. Any fool could see that." He began to walk down the hall, his back to Dubric.

Out of habit, Dubric reached for his notebook, but stopped. "We found him today, downriver from the first body. He had been dead a few days, a phase at most, but endured significant torture before his demise."

Haconry turned, shocked. "Calum? Today? Are you certain?"

"I have received positive identification. You last saw him nearly two phases ago? In what capacity?"

Haconry's tone fell flat and emotionless. "We passed on the road." He shook his head, stepped away, and drew a deep breath. "I'm afraid your news has left me at a loss. May we resume the tour another time?"

Dubric nodded, bowing slightly. "I can see myself out." With Otlee following, he reached the main door and opened it to fresh air and a brilliant afternoon sky. He glanced back at Haconry, who still stood in the hall, shuddering.

Dubric closed the door and reached for his notebook as he descended the stairs.

CHAPTER

6

✝

Dubric stopped in the meadow west of Barrorise and stared at the ground. *One more step and the ghosts may return. Dare I brave them? What does it mean?*

"Sir?" Otlee asked, but Dubric barely noticed.

Just ahead of his boots there was a patch of trampled dead grass, along with indentations made earlier by his hands and knees. He had lost his ghosts there, had lost the weight and pain of their responsibility. When he walked to the same place would he see the pair or the horde? By the King, would he strike Otlee again?

"I am fine, lad," Dubric said, squaring his shoulders. He took a deep breath, then stepped into the abyss, his eyes closed.

Icy pressure, sudden and throbbing, slammed behind his eyes. He gasped a breath, then another, staggering forward. With or without the damned ghosts, he had to get Otlee to shelter before dark, he had to get the boy somewhere safe. He would not risk Otlee to the dark again.

"Dubric," Maeve said, "take my hand. We're here. We will help you through."

"No," he said, opening his eyes. "I will manage."

The horde milled about the meadow, reaching for him, pleading with their dead eyes and oozing hands. Maeve stood amongst them, with Otlee pressed behind her and her hand extended. She was gilded in the late-afternoon light, while the ghosts' spectral sludge shimmered dull swampy green.

He took a breath and counted the ghosts. Twenty-four of the wretched things stared at him. "Otlee," he said, reaching into his pocket without moving a step or looking away, "I want you to write what I tell you, but do not ask questions."

"Yes, sir," the boy said, taking Dubric's notebook from his hand the moment it left his pocket.

"Twenty-four ghosts, all male." Dubric squinted, ignoring Otlee's gasp as he looked for the youngest, smallest ghost—the crippled boy who had followed them all day. "The smallest is nine, perhaps ten summers. Crippled." He scanned the milling group for the eldest, settling on a skinny, bearded lad. "Eldest is early twenties, perhaps twenty-two. All are commoners, all have slender builds. There are three definite head wounds. Two are obviously strangled. All are bleeding. Somewhere."

He took a step toward them, his hands shaking and his eyes heavy and burning with cold. "Most are missing teeth and have bleeding mouths. Two are unclothed." He examined the ghosts, leaning close to them despite the pain it brought his eyes, and saw bruising on every limb. "They've been bound, hand and foot. What ties them together? Why these boys? What is the connection? What are they trying to show me?"

He stopped, staring, and shook his head. "A . . . string."

The ghost who had claimed his attention crouched

near the rear of the pack, his eyes glowing. Perhaps
Otlee's age, his hair had been clipped short and he
wore the faded and oft-patched garments of a field
worker on his scrawny, half-starved frame. His bare
toes dug into the dirt, and he held a vaporous stick in
his hands. Dubric ignored the other ghosts and focused on that one boy.

A black strand of thread or thin, fine cording hung
from his temple as if he had been strung like a bead
upon a necklace. Unlike the green ghost shimmer, the
thread held no shine but rather sucked every whisper
of light away.

Struggling to see past the ache in his eyes, Dubric
walked around the boy. No string on the other side, but
a hole, a swirling pinprick of black against the swampy
green, marked the boy's head like a brand. His hand
shaking in rhythm to the throb behind his eyes, Dubric
reached out to touch the hole, but the boy turned to
look at him, said something in his silent ghost voice,
then faded away.

Dubric sought the nearest spectre to examine its
head. A tiny but horridly black mark sucked color from
near the temple. The next ghost was the same, then the
next. Each ghost Dubric tried to touch faded away and
disappeared—unlike most ghosts he had endured, they
had no substance to them; they were merely thin vapor—until only three remained.

The pacing ghost, whose body rotted in Mul's storage room, sported the same mark partially hidden beneath his hair, as did the ghost of Calum the scribe.
But the little cripple, the brightest and most vivid ghost
of them all, had no such mark upon his head. He was
long dead, more solid, independent, and had dissimilar

wounds. Was he connected to the recent murders at all?

Sighing, Dubric rubbed his throbbing eyes and the little ghost faded away, leaving only Calum and the other behind.

"Otlee," Dubric said, grinding his teeth against the lingering ache in his head, "note that all but one have marks upon their heads and holes on their temples. One had a piece of string coming from the hole."

"Yes, sir." Otlee looked up and grinned. "You really do see them! This is great!"

"No, it is horrid, the things I see, the pain I endure."

Maeve approached him with worry etched onto her face. "Did you see Braoin?"

"No, I do not believe so," he replied, reaching for her hand and gently squeezing it. "But I want you to tell me about other weavers, spinners, and tailors in the Reach. People who would have access to thread or very fine cording. Can you do that?"

She nodded, pulling her hand away. "Yes. But we'd best hurry. It will be dark soon."

As he followed her, his mind reluctantly turned to the piles of yarn and cording in Maeve's own shop.

Lars walked into the house and carefully prodded his bruised cheek. Dien had just about scared Jak to death, yelling at him about his workers' attack. As soon as the chastised carpenter had left, Lars had received a merciless ribbing for letting himself get ambushed by, as Dien put it, "a couple of piss-brained fools." Dien had then sent Lars to talk to the neighbors and find out what they knew, what rumors they'd heard. While it wasn't prime investigative work, it was better than making hats. It was also more than he'd have been allowed if Dien knew the full truth of the attack, how close it had been. Lars pulled off his cloak and ignored the giggling blond bundle hiding behind a chair. Jess was cooking dinner and everything smelled spicy and meaty and good, making his stomach rumble with anticipation. Devyn sat at the table, muttering and teasing his wretched dog with a bit of string, while Fyn decorated hats nearby. As Lars watched, she burped and covered her mouth with an embarrassed giggle. Only Lissea looked out of place compared to the rest of the family. She seemed too quiet, too small, too invisible.

Lars heard a screech to his right. He jumped back, caught Aly in midair, and fell, rolling to the floor as he wailed in mock terror.

"I caught you," she proclaimed, sitting cross-legged on his chest. "I win."

He tickled her and she squealed, scrambling away. Laughing, he chased her across the sitting room, herding her from the kitchen, until she sprinted down the hall to the girls' bedroom and slammed the door.

Lars shook his head, smiling, and walked into the bath chamber. He lurched to a shuddering halt, then staggered backward. Kia stood in the bathing tub, drenched and soapy, her wet, dark hair plastered over, or rather around and beside, her breasts. She contemplated him with a knowing stare. Behind her, his reflection in Lissea's old oval mirror stared back at him, wide-eyed and pale, gaping beside the line of suds flowing down the round curve of her buttocks.

Kia smiled and sat, watching him without bothering to cover the slightest bit of skin, then leaned back in the water. She reached for the soap, letting it slip between her fingers and fall into the tub. "Are you going fetch my soap or are you just going to stand there?"

He saw his reflection lunge forward, grasp the handle, and slam the door closed. In shock, he stumbled back to the sitting room and out to the porch, where he waited until Sarea called him for supper.

Lights from Falliet shone not far ahead when the last shimmer of sunlight left the sky. Dubric trudged behind Maeve and Otlee, rubbing his brow as he tried to think. Of all the sheep he had seen since arriving in the Reach, at least half were black. Was the string hanging from the ghost's head actually black in color? Or did the blackness symbolize something else? Had the string, or rather whatever had punched it through their heads in the first place, killed them? What kind of murder weapon would that be? What the blue blazes did it all mean?

Muttering to himself, he followed Maeve into her home and urged Otlee to bathe. All three were filthy with mud, but Otlee looked spent and exhausted. Once the boy had gone, Dubric looked to Maeve and offered an apologetic frown. "I wish I had brought you better news today, milady."

She removed her cloak and hung it near the door. "You kept my hope alive. I can't ask for more." Sighing, she glanced at the pile of stuffed sacks beside the door. She lifted two, carrying them across the store.

"What is in the bags?" Dubric grabbed three, one in each arm and a third pressed between. They felt as though they were full of balls, loose and shifting.

"Yarn," she said. "Someone needs cloth woven." She

dropped her pair beside the smaller loom, then returned to the store for the last two bags.

Dubric placed his three beside her pair and admired the handiwork she had already begun. "It is beautiful," he said, touching the fabric. Smooth and even, it demanded to be admired.

She lugged in the final bags. "That's the commons. Simple twill, usually, although one family prefers herringbone tweed. Only so much I can do on a four-harness."

"What is the yellow thread? A place marker?" he asked, thinking about the string coming from the ghost's head. Located about one third of the full span from the left, a single strand of brilliant yellow ran from the fabric into the loom, disappearing in the back.

"My mark. All of my fabric has one yellow warp. Most people never see it."

He examined the fabric on the loom and, true enough, he could see not the slightest bit of yellow amongst the smooth, soft gray. It was well hidden, obscured by the wool.

"It seems a shame not to see it."

"I know it's there, and sometimes, if the fabric's folded, a glimpse will show through."

Behind her, the larger loom waited for his attention. One yellow thread stood amongst purples and blues, and the fabric took his breath away. It seemed to have a dimension all its own, brocaded and sleek, even with the speckle of yellow dancing from the depths. "What is this?"

"Survival," she said. "This fabric I ship. Sometimes to Casclia, but usually to Jhalin. Once I sent a bolt to Waterford. I like to think King Romlin wears my cloth."

"It is a work of art."

She blushed and once again she looked young, almost like a girl. "Thank you. Each bolt I make for shipment is a different color, depending on what dyes I have available, but I always let my signature peek through."

"As you should. An artist should lay claim to her work."

She drew away. "I'll see to supper. You might want to wash up after Otlee's finished." She glanced back, her smile shining, then left Dubric to stand sentinel with her looms.

Twilight had given way to darkness when Braoin heard the creak of the door. He gathered his strength and squinted to see a bit of the sky.

The door slammed, dashing his hopes, and the hated stink of his tormentor filled his nostrils. For the briefest of moments he wondered if the man would take his ass or his mouth this time, or select something worse.

"Look at you!" the man said. "Hanging there, limp and pitiful. After all I've done! Food, shelter! You filthy carp! I saw your cut fingers! Ungrateful, backstabbing swine!"

Braoin yelped at the strike across his ribs, then howled at the next, hearing the crack of bone through the pain of his screams.

"Shut your yap, you worthless piece of filth!" Another blow, and another, across Braoin's belly, his chest, his privates, his face. Bugs and bone crunched beneath the man's feet, each step bringing another slash of fiery pain.

The beating eased, then stopped, the dark filling with laughter. "You came to me so haughty! An artist!

Now look at you, no better than a piece of maggoty meat!"

Braoin said nothing, praying silently that the taunts would end and the rape pass quickly, but he froze at the unexpected cold of sharpened steel against his cheek.

"Ah, I have your attention at last," the creature of the dark said, tracing the blade down Braoin's throat. "Something new tonight for us. Something you've earned."

The tip pricked Braoin's chest, he felt a tight pinch, then he screamed at the slash on his chest. Something warm and wet and firm fell into his mouth and the man's hated fingers wrenched his jaw closed. He nearly choked as the thing caught on his tongue.

"Eat it. Eat your filthy nipple, or your balls come next."

Whimpering, feeling hot blood on his chest and tasting it in his mouth, Braoin chewed and swallowed.

"That's my good lad," the man said, patting Braoin's cheek before the blade moved again. "What shall we try next, eh? Your ear? Your liver?"

"No, please. Please don't." The blade traced downward from Braoin's belly to his groin, and he scrunched his eyes, turning his head to the side. "You're a lecher, and a coward."

The dark laughed and the blade slid lower, past Braoin's privates. "A coward, eh? I'll leave the choice to you, then, brave little boy. Me or the blade."

"Neither, you bastard," Braoin spat out, despite the agony.

"Wrong choice," the man replied.

Braoin screamed.

CHAPTER

7

✝

"Y ou're a pig," Jess whispered, glaring at Kia.

"He's fey, Jess. Accept it."

Jess plunged her hands into the dishwater. "Is not." She scrubbed a plate, then handed it to Kia.

"What does 'fey' mean?" Aly asked as she put away a recently dried cup.

"It means your sisters are going to stop it this instant," Sarea snapped.

Jess ground her teeth and plunged her hands into the scalding water again. Feeling sick, Fyn had retreated to bed without eating any supper, leaving Jess to help Kia wash dishes. And after what Kia had done, being stuck side by side . . . Goddess! Kia was lucky to be breathing, let alone able to speak.

"I'm just trying to help," Kia whispered in her ear. "I always suspected he didn't like girls. Now we have proof."

"So help," Jess snarled, "by leaving him alone."

"Like I'd waste my time on a boy who's fey."

"Why did you throw yourself at him, then? And why like *that*?"

"That's it," Sarea said. She stomped over to them, glaring, and her voice dropped to a dangerous whisper. "Kialyn, I can barely stand to look at you after what you

did. I raised you better than that. Since you can't be
trusted to keep your clothes on or act appropriately,
you're going to be confined to the house for the next
moon."

"Mam!"

"Don't 'Mam' me. You started this, and you're washing every dirty dish, pot, pan, utensil, and bit of laundry
until we leave. And if you ever pull another stunt like
that again, I'll have you scouring privy pots with the
lowest maids in the castle."

Kia glared at Jess but said nothing.

"And you," Sarea whispered, turning her angry gaze
to Jess, "for calling your sister names and getting upset
over something that is none of your business, you are
scrubbing every floor in this house and changing all the
bed linens tomorrow."

Jess almost laughed. Fyn usually made the beds and
swept the floors, but as sick as she was, it didn't seem
fair, so Jess had offered to do those jobs anyway, while
Kia had fawned over the carpenters all afternoon.

"What about me, Mam?" Aly asked, her eyes huge.

"You, little missy, are going to dust."

"Yes, Mam." Aly pouted, sniffling. Dusting made her
sneeze.

"Both of you leave Kia to her dishes. She needs to
think about what she did."

Jess handed her sister the washrag, and stepped
away, wondering what to do to pass the time before
bed. Grandpapa had gone to his workshop with the
completed hats, Grandmama had gone for a walk, and
Dad was muttering to himself, holding Cailin as he
pored over Lars's notes from the neighbors.

She contemplated reading or taking a bath, then
promptly rejected that idea—damn Kia—and even

considered going to bed. Then her eyes settled on the front door. "I think I'm going to get some fresh air," she said.

Lars started when the door creaked open, reaching for the lamp he'd set beside him. Jess paused, then, chewing her lip, continued to the porch. "Mind if I come out here for a bit? Kia took over doing the dishes."

"Sure," he said, his voice catching. "There's plenty of room."

"Thanks." Rubbing her arms, she stood near the rail and looked out to the stars. Silence surrounded them, laced with evening chill and the scent of growing things. She smiled and breathed in the night air, turning her head at an owl's call.

After a long while she left the rail and sat on the step beside Lars; he eased over to make room for her. Unlike other nobles she knew, he was quiet and reassuring, not demanding or vain, and she had never known him to flaunt his title or name. She glanced at him as she settled in, then turned her head away. Although his quiet presence was a comfort, something about Lars made her nervous, too.

He rubbed liniment into his hands as he stared out into the barnyard, the sharp, medicinal tang contrasting with the sweet, cool night air. He capped the bottle and leaned forward, his elbows on his knees. When he spoke, she jumped, startled. "Can I ask you a question?"

"Sure."

"What's it like, having Dien for a father?"

She shrugged and smiled. "He's a pretty good dad, but I don't know anything different. It's hard to compare."

He sighed, staring into the night. "Yeah, I suppose so."

"Can I ask you a question?" Hopeful, she glanced at him.

A shadow of a smile, then his normal stoicism. "Of course."

"Why do you do it? Work so hard, I mean. Here. At the castle. You cleaned the stalls, chopped all the wood, *then* went out to question the neighbors. Don't you like to, well, do anything fun or for yourself? What are you working so hard for?"

He leaned back and regarded her. "You really want to know?"

She nodded, afraid to say anything else.

Lars toyed with the liniment bottle and his voice lowered. "I don't want your dad and Dubric to send me away."

"They wouldn't do that."

He shrugged. "Yeah, well, I'm not taking any chances."

"Even if it tears your hands to tatters?"

He set aside the bottle. "I've had blisters before. They're not so bad."

She looked out to the yard, to moonlight on the pasture and the backs of sheep nibbling early spring grass. "But what else? You can't be a page forever. You're Lord Hargrove's son. Your name alone can get you whatever in the world you want. Surely there's something, a goal, a prize, you're striving for."

He turned to look at her, a smile appearing again for an elusive moment. "Actually, there is."

Jess watched him, letting his words find their own way.

He shook his head, looking into the night again. "You'll think it's dumb."

"No, I won't. I promise."

She felt silence stretch between them, thinning like an overspun thread, and she feared that she'd said the wrong thing. That she had trodden too close. When he spoke, his words surprised her.

"I want the one thing I never had. A home."

"You don't have a home?"

He laughed. "No. I have a bureau, a bed, some clothes, and a sword, all assigned to me. I have a name that's never claimed me as its own." He sighed. "And I have a job. That's it. At least for now. But someday, definitely someday, it'll be different. I know that now."

"You didn't know before?"

He shook his head. "Not until I came here. I've never really had a family, but for the first time in my life I almost feel like I do."

"I don't understand. I know you've had disagreements with your father, but what about your mother? And I thought you had a sister."

He stared into the night for a long time before he spoke. "I went back for a visit last moon, after the murders, because my father asked me to. After six summers away, I was so excited to be going home. But I was barely there, not even a full bell, and my mother . . . she has problems and, well, she didn't recognize me. She got upset, hysterical, and my father screamed at me, sent me right back to Faldorrah. Again." He sighed, and lowered his head. "I just got there and he sent me away, told me never to come back, that he never wanted to see me again.

"My sister is ten summers older than me, and I haven't seen or heard from her since I came to Faldorrah. My family doesn't want anything to do with me. But here, on your grandparents' farm, it's different. It's like I matter, at least a little. I'm still on the outside looking in, but for the first time in my life I can feel the fire in the hearth. Does that make any sense?"

"Yes, it does."

"You girls are wonderful, and your mam, your grandparents." He looked at her again and shrugged. "Even Kia, although some of the things she does worry me, but Aly, Goddess, she's the best."

Jess felt her brow furrow. "She is?"

"Yeah. I'm like a big brother to her, someone to wrestle and get horsy rides from, someone to read stories and tickle her. She has no qualms about me, no hesitation, nothing. She has no idea who my father is, and doesn't care. I'm just me."

Jess smiled. "She has known you for her whole life."

"I love all you girls, I do, but Aly . . . she's special, like she really is my kid sister and I'm her big protector." Lars leaned against the post and looked out to the night. "Your mam is fabulous, too. Did you know she let me change Cailin's diaper today? I'd never done that."

"Ugh. I've changed too many."

"Oh, it was stinky, sure, but still great. Working on the family farm and having a houseful of sisters, one a baby and another wanting to play with me all the time, is incredible. It makes me remember how much I want a home and family of my own."

"Ah." Jess stared into the night. *His sister.* She heard him shift around, but she didn't turn to look. She couldn't bear to look at him.

"Did I say something wrong?" he asked.

"No, of course not." She drew a shaky breath and did her best to ignore the stinging in her eyes.

She stood and muttered some nonsense about having to go inside. When she reached the door, she paused.

He asked, "Are you sure you're all right?"

Clenching the door latch, she lowered her head and pushed out the words before she lost her nerve. "I'm glad you're part of our family."

Lars started to follow, but uncertainty tugged at him, nibbling in his belly. Not only were women utterly confusing, but all the females inside were related. Would they turn on him because one was upset? Would he lose his precarious position of honorary brother? Would he make matters worse when he had no idea what started the problem in the first place?

While he sat on the steps, confused and uncertain, he heard the door open behind him and turned to see Dien's familiar bulk come through.

"I think we need to have a little talk, pup," he said without looking at Lars. He thundered down the steps and started toward the barn.

Lars followed, the nibbling in his belly feeling more like claws and sharp teeth.

Dien stopped and turned back to look at the house. "This should be far enough," he said. He put his arm over Lars's shoulder and turned him toward the barn. "I have a pretty good idea what you told Jess. The walls aren't very thick and, well, Sarea heard bits and pieces of your conversation. You're fine, lad, and we're glad you want to be part of our family. No harm done. But with Jess, you see, there's a whole different aspect involved. One you might not know about."

The big man paused and Lars felt his hesitation like a tremor in a bowstring. "But she's my daughter and I love her and I want to see her happy. That's my job, as her dad."

"I know," Lars said. "And I understand that if there's a choice to be made, I lose. I'd expect nothing else."

"Oh, it's not that, pup, not that at all. There is no choice to be made tonight, and Goddess willing, there never will be."

"I didn't mean to upset her."

Dien laughed, patting his shoulder. "I know, and she knows, too. You probably have no idea what happened. I feel your pain, pup, I do. Women can get blubbery over the strangest things. Sarea does it to me all the time. It's part of the magic of who they are. You'll learn about their quirks before you know it, but they'll still surprise you, still rip your heart out without warning or cause. Just the way it is."

Lars had no idea what he was talking about, but said, "Yes, sir," anyway.

"Tomorrow I think I'll send you to town to talk to the constable about Bray. We could use some soap and salt and other supplies, too, and it won't hurt a thing to get the stink blown off you. Decide if you want to go alone or take any of the girls with you. I'll leave that up to you."

What's this leading to? "All right."

Dien released Lars's shoulder and turned toward the house. He took a single step. "One more thing," he said, returning his attention to Lars. "I need to ask you a question and I don't want any safe, bull-piss answer. I want the bald, naked truth this time, however hard you think it may be for me to take. Man to man."

The teeth and claws in Lars's belly turned to full-grown ravenous rats, gnawing their way to his spine. *This is why he dragged me out here, so far from the house, so far from everyone else. He's going to punish me for walking in on Kia.* His fists clenched, then relaxed. "The truth. Man to man. Yes, sir."

Dien took a step toward him, looking into his eyes. He sighed as if fighting his own internal gnawing beast. "What are your intentions concerning my daughter? Concerning Jess?"

Jess? Lars startled, forgetting instantly about Kia. He expected his voice to shake, but it didn't. His words rang true but quiet in the night. "I think about her, sir, I admit. But not improperly."

"Go on."

He had played this conversation with Dien through his mind a hundred times. Never had he considered it would be confrontational, at night, in a barnyard. Always over an ale on a sunny afternoon, or perhaps in the office, a friendly man-to-man discussion. If it ever happened at all. He had always taken note to remind himself of that one last fact, that it might never happen at all. That he might never have the nerve.

Yet here it was, Dien demanding the bald, naked truth about how he felt about Jess. No polishing, no softening. *Tell it like it is, and let the dust settle where it may.*

Lars took a breath and leapt from the cliff, his voice coming out in a rush. "I'll be of courting age in less than a phase and Jess a couple phases after, if I remember right. I'd hoped to court her once she's of age. If she'd let me and if you'd allow it. But I promise I have no dishonorable intention. I will not mistreat her nor expect her to bow to me. I will not . . ." he paused, his hands clenching, "molest her. You have my absolute word on that. Beyond that I don't know, sir. I haven't spoken about it to her, or anyone. It's just been a hope."

His hands opened again and he stared Dien in the eye. "If I've spoken out of turn or offended you or your home, I apologize. You're my friend and in many ways a father to me, but . . ." He swallowed around his embarassment, laying the truth out in the night, "But I do think fondly of Jesscea and hope to court her. If that's permissible."

Dien stared at him for a long time. "Permission granted. Now get your ass inside before I change my mind."

Grinning, Lars trotted for the house. He wanted to whoop. Sarea paced just inside the door, the only person in the room, possibly the only person not in bed, and she jumped when he burst inside.

"Well?" she asked, her hand over her heart.

Lars almost laughed. *I'm here. I'm home.*

"He finally asked," Dien said.

Sarea gasped and hugged Lars, holding him close and dear. He hugged her back, the first time since leaving home that he had embraced any woman at all, and she kissed his cheek. "Welcome to the family, my son."

Dien laughed and pulled her loose. "Dammit, woman, let the lad go. I about scared him to death out there and you're gonna crush him. There's a lot of time and 'what ifs' ahead. No reason to get your hopes up."

Sarea backed away, wiping her eyes. "You're right." She beamed, sniffling, and pulled a kerchief from her pocket.

"What did I tell you, pup? There's no telling what'll set them bawling." He grasped his wife's hand and led her away. "We'll talk more later. Get some sleep. You've got a busy day ahead and plenty to think about, just stay in the house." He gave Lars one last nod then left, taking Sarea to their room.

His mind spinning, Lars readied for bed and settled in on the settee. After a long while, he slept.

Lars woke from a dream of a dark man stealing children in the rain to an aching bladder and raindrops blowing against the windowpanes. He rolled over and pressed his face into the pillow, but it was no use. He had to piss. Soon.

Muttering, he pushed away the blanket and sat. Barefoot and wearing only an old, stained shirt and sleeping trousers, he padded down the hall to the sound of snores coming from Dien and Sarea's room. The door stood ajar and he hesitated before peeking in. They lay spooned together, facing the door, Dien's thick arm draped over Sarea's waist and his hand holding her breast.

Embarrassed and reluctant, he cleared his throat and said, "Hey. I need to take a leak."

Dien yawned and rolled to his back. Sarea did the same, turning her face against Dien's armpit, before continuing onto her side and draping her leg across him. "So go," Dien yawned. They snuggled in and he resumed snoring.

Lars shook his head and stepped back, not quite closing the door again. "Okay," he said. "I guess that counts." His heart skipping, he reached for the back door and pulled it open.

Cool rain on a warm wind full of the scents of spring. Worms, mostly. Damp earth and bugs. Fish. The same smells as in his dream.

He watched the rain while his bladder reminded him what had brought him to this juncture in the first place. *I could just go right here. No one would know.*

"I'd know," he said aloud, sighing.

He took a deep breath and bolted from the doorway, slipping in the mud as he ran down the hill to the outhouse. *No dark man,* he assured himself. *Nothing but a rainy night. It was just a dream.*

Dripping but not drenched, he reached the outhouse and slipped inside to do his business. It took a few short moments—chiding himself all the while for being a coward—then he opened the outhouse door to begin his trek back to the house.

His initial fear set aside, he started up the hill, walking quickly due to the rain. He was perhaps twenty lengths from the house when a cold, wet hand came from behind and covered his mouth. He tried to bend forward and flip his attacker over his back, but his feet slipped in the mud and he found himself held up by the man behind him.

"Quiet now, Stuart. Rabbits and wasps, ye've gotta be careful," Devyn said, his rancid metal breath burning on Lars's cheek. "He likes the rain."

Lars let his breath out and Devyn pulled his hand away. "Goddess, you scared me."

"Damn straight I did. Good to be scared. 'Tain't safe, not on a night like this." Devyn, too, wore damp sleeping trousers. He stepped in front of Lars and squinted into the dark, somewhere to the west of the house. "Tell me, Stuart. Is it true, what I hear?"

Lars sighed. *I'm just getting wetter and wetter.* "What do you hear, sir?"

Devyn's shoulders slumped as he turned back to look at Lars. "That you're not Stuart a'tall."

Lars shook his head. "No, sir. I'm afraid I'm not."

"I feared it," Devyn said and, for a moment, Lars thought he might start to cry. "You're alive." The old man took a breath, then another, and stood a bit straighter. "Alive er not, come with me. I'll show you, Stuart, then you'll know."

Lars looked at the warm and dry house. "Sir, I really should get back to bed."

Devyn stomped up to him, his chin quivering. "I pegged them up the ass, and no one wants to know!" He balled his hands into fists. "No one wants to listen. No one wants to see!" He grabbed the front of Lars's shirt and said, "I died in that gaol. And the dead know, boy. We *know*. The dark ain't keepin' all his secrets."

He shoved Lars back and turned away, staggering in his loose gait up the hill.

Dumbfounded, Lars stood in the rain and watched him until Devyn turned and said, "I ain't got all night, boy."

Lars brushed rainwater from his eyes and hurried to catch up. "What do you know about the missing children?" he asked, falling in beside the old man.

Devyn stopped, his hands jerking. He muttered, bobbing his head, while tremors wracked his body. He licked his lips and glanced at Lars, reaching out, then used one shaking hand to pull back the other. "Stuart. I . . . Rabbits and wasps! Can't you see? Ain't I told you not to ask fool questions?" He blinked and bared his remaining teeth, the twitches subsiding. He took a smooth breath and his voice softened, sounding almost . . . normal. "Please, boy. Don't. This is hard enou—" Another shudder. "I died, but it was the wood colt what did it! But Stuart left! The red worms know!"

Goddess, what happened to him? Lars nodded slowly. "All right. No questions."

Devyn jerked, saying nothing, then continued up the hill as the rain lessened to a gentle drizzle.

They walked to the barn, Devyn sniffing the air, and Lars wished he'd taken the time to put on his boots. He was going to need a bath before he could even think about returning to bed.

"I never pegged my boy up the ass. Not my daughter. Not my granddaughters." Devyn looked at Lars. "And not you, not ever."

"No, sir," Lars said, wondering if he was allowed to talk at all.

Devyn twitched and grinned, showing all of his rotted teeth. "You're a good boy, Stuart. Come now, before they see we've gone." Lars followed, grimacing at the wet and rotted stench.

Devyn tittered and opened his shop door, beckoning Lars to follow him.

Nodding, Lars took a deep breath and entered. Devyn closed the door behind him.

Lars stood still in the dark and rancid room, feeling a worm crawl beneath his toes. Devyn shuffled away, muttering, and Lars saw a spark of light, then another, before the lamp lit.

Astounded, Lars blinked and took a single step backward.

Toys were everywhere. Hung on the walls, piled on the floor, stacked on tables. Puzzles, carts, and balls. Lead army men, fabric dolls, and wooden farm animals. Toys Lars had never seen Aly with, yet strung about as if a child routinely played there. Every bit of open space held toys. Everything except the workbench and the vat in the corner. Full of gray and putrid hides, it seemed to be the source of the stink.

"For my boy," Devyn said, gesturing around the room. A spasm shook his hands. "Nine summers. Crippled. The wood colt bastards pegged my boy, trying to feed him to the devil." Tears rolled down his cheeks and he took a breath, then another. "But he didn't die. I found them, saw what they did. I saved Stuart b'fore they kilt him."

Lars clamped his mouth shut, reminding himself not to ask questions.

Tremors increasing, Devyn tottered to a workbench and knocked a pile of felt strips from the lower shelf. "My boy was alive. The dark couldn't have him!" He pulled an old and battered box from the farthest reaches of the shelf and fell onto his backside as he stared at it.

Lars knelt before the old man and held out his hands.

"Hid it, I did, before I died." The box rattled in Devyn's shuddering grasp. "It's forbidden," he said, his rheumy gaze holding Lars's. "Stuart, be careful, rabbits and wasps. Don't let them see."

"I won't," Lars said, grasping the box before Devyn dropped it. The box was about as long as his forearm and as tall as his hand from the tip of his fingers to the base of his palm. Cobwebs and dust marred its rough wood surface, and the buckles were old and corroded. He saw no latch or lock. Carefully loosening the buckles, he pulled the leather strapping free and opened it.

Old glass vials filled with silver fluid, small brushes and paddles, an old and rusted knife. It looked like junk to Lars and he started to ask what it all meant, but he clamped his mouth closed as he looked Devyn in the eye.

Devyn swallowed and banged his head on the shelves behind him. "Like I told Braoin, don't you be lookin' beneath a girl's skirt now, Stuart. The devil might see you there."

"Beneath," Lars mumbled. "All right." He closed the lid and turned the box over, but he saw nothing of note on the bottom. Devyn continued to beat his head against the shelves:

This would be so much easier if I could ask questions. Glancing at Devyn, he opened the box again and emptied the vials and things on the ground. Tattered burlap lined the bottom. Lars picked at one edge to get purchase, then peeled it back.

He saw blackened hand- and fingerprints along all four edges, and a hole, just big enough for one finger. Devyn stopped banging his head and watched with glittering eyes.

Lars took a breath and pushed his finger through the hole. Something slick and soft lay beneath. Straining slightly to pry it open but not break it, he wriggled the false bottom free.

Devyn squealed and cowered away.

Black and red cloth woven in a reversible diamond pattern lay shimmering inside. Folded neatly and pressed flat beneath the wooden layer, the edges were worn and ragged and the fabric was speckled with dark stains. It looked fragile, old . . . and somehow dangerous.

Devyn rocked, wrapping his arms around his knees. "Stuart's death shroud. But he didn't die, did you?"

Lars pulled the cloth from the box and unfolded it. It was a full arm's length wide and about twice as long as he was tall. Smears and spots lay in crusty black patterns he recognized. "There's blood on here. Stab wounds, it looks like."

Devyn nodded, braving a glance.

"I found cloth like this," Lars said as he folded it

again. It felt slippery and warm. Repulsive. "The night I came. Near where they found the first body."

Devyn wailed. "The wood colt's back, not dead, not like they think. He took my Stuart to feed the devil."

Anxious to stop touching it, Lars returned the cloth to the box. "You know who he is. You know who stabbed your son."

Devyn lurched to his feet. "They pegged him up the ass, all three! Cut my boy. I saw, I chased them away." He staggered back, knocking half-finished hats from their molds. "They wanted to feed him to the devil."

"I understand that," Lars said softly as he replaced the false bottom on the box. "But that was a long time ago."

"No, no, no! Then! Now!" He leapt toward Lars and leaned close, his breath coming in shallow bursts. "Finish what you start, Stuart. Never give up. Not until the job is done. Not until the devil is fed."

Snarling, the knocked the box from Lars's hands and pushed him back. "They can see. You. Me. Red and black, black and red. It's not done. Not until the devil's fed."

Lars looked up at Devyn looming over him. "I don't understand! I have to ask questions!"

Devyn scrambled back to grab the box. He threw it at Lars and it hit him in the chest. "I didn't die for naught. I pegged them up the ass! I did. Now. Then. Does it matter?"

Lars held the box loosely, reluctant to touch it. "This cloth. Tell me what it does, why it's important. Just the cloth, if you can. Tell me why they stabbed your son on it."

Devyn panted, twitching like a man on a noose, and he fell, sprawling on the floor. "My boy. It saw my boy.

Showed my boy. Damn you, why can't you see?"
Devyn's back arched and he flailed.

Lars stood, approaching slowly. *Saw, showed, see.*
"Sight. This has something to do with sight, with seeing."

Devyn nodded, his gnarled fingers scraping against
the packed-dirt floor. "See the red worm, Stuart? Never
touch it. Never. Never the black moth. Never the
blood. Never the dead shall see but they'll feed the
devil."

Lars dropped the box and kicked it away. "It's silk,
black-and-red silk, like the scrap I found."

"The devil's eye," Devyn wailed, clawing at the dirt.

"And it can see. Somehow, it can see."

"Yes," Devyn cried, arching again.

Lars paced while he tried to think. "All right. You
found three men molesting your son and killed two.
One got away. Stuart bled on that cloth, cloth that you
believe can see. Somehow. I've heard crazier things. At
least it's a place to start." Hearing movement, he
stopped to look at Devyn.

Devyn crawled to his workbench, his head hanging
and his shoulders shaking with the strain. "Stuart start,
start Stuart."

"Fine," Lars said. "Tell me about Stuart. You can begin with why you keep calling me by his name."

Devyn climbed up his bench, tittering and tossing
tools and bits of felt aside. He pulled a board from beneath a scraper and turned, throwing it at Lars.

It spun through the air to the ground, bouncing
once before skittering past Lars's legs to land in the far
corner of the shop. He retrieved it and squinted to the
image painted there. A boy's face, barely visible in the
dim light.

"You're showing me Stuart's portrait," he said, carefully not phrasing it as a question. Devyn said nothing, he just turned to watch as Lars walked toward the lamp.

Lars paused, looking back and forth between the portrait and Devyn. "This is impossible."

Devyn staggered toward him. "Do you see, Stuart? My boy?"

Dread and confusion clawed through Lars's viscera. "It's a painting. Of me. When I was little." *The straight blond hair, gray eyes. By Malanna, even the mole beside my ear is the same. The cleft between my eyebrows.*

Devyn took a breath and nodded, his eyes glittering in the lamplight. "My boy. My Stuart."

"I'm not your 'boy,' " Lars said, shoving the painting back at the old man. "No matter how much you want me to be, I'm not. My parents are Lord and Lady Hargrove of Haenpar and I'll be fifteen summers old in a couple of days. I don't know how old Stuart would be, but I know he's not fifteen."

Devyn laid a shaky finger aside his nose and sniffed. "Same."

Lars thrust the painting forward again, but Devyn didn't take it. "I do not smell like Stuart."

Devyn tapped his nose again and nodded. "Same. Rabbits and wasps, boy, I haven't lost all sense." He took a deep, sniffing breath through his nose and nodded. "Same." He staggered to Lars, pushing aside the painting and lifting Lars's hair with his fingers. "Same." Touched Lars's forehead, eyes, lips, ears, the mole. "Same." Grasped Lars's hand and splayed apart the fingers. "Same." Fell to his knees at Lars's feet and tapped his second toe. It was longer than the big toe and curled slightly toward it. "Same." Devyn staggered upright again and held his palm against Lars's chest. "Same. My boy. My Stuart."

"No!" Lars said, stepping back out of range. "I am not your son!"

Behind him, the door opened and he turned, the painting still clenched in his hand. Dien stood there with his cloak hanging limp and sodden from his shoulders. He looked at Lars and sagged with relief. "He's not Stuart, Dev. We've told you. I'm sorry, but Stuart's dead. I buried him, remember? Almost twenty summers ago."

Devyn wailed, falling to his knees beside Lars.

Dien sighed and entered the shop. "C'mon, pup. Let's get you cleaned up and back to bed." He yawned and rubbed his face.

"No," Lars said, kneeling beside the old man. "He's trying to tell me what happened. I think it's important."

"He's lost his sense, pup, if he ever had it at all. He's been like this ever since I met him. He's mad, just mad, and he killed two men. Let it go."

Lars patted Devyn on the back. "He says they raped and stabbed his son. If that's true, they deserved to die."

Dien sighed and ran his fingers over the top of his head, ruffling his short-shorn hair. "Whether they deserved it or not, he did it, pup."

Lars looked up at Dien. "Stuart was his son."

"Yes, and two young men raped and killed him, a long time ago. That's all true."

"Three!" Devyn screamed, heaving upright and knocking Lars aside. "The wood colt!"

"They were brothers, Dev, I told you. And their only other brother was little. He wasn't involved. They didn't have a half brother, illegitimate or otherwise. I checked."

Devyn snarled then spat, his spittle foamy and thick. "Three. Three for the devil, damn me. Three!"

Lars stood. "See? I think he's trying to tell us, but can't."

"It's just the quicksilver gone to his brain, pup." Dien reached for Devyn and pulled him to his feet. "You, too, Dev. Back to bed."

"Pah," Devyn said. Muttering, he snatched fallen hats from the floor and put them back on their racks.

Dien gave Lars a look that allowed no argument. "Let's go, pup."

Lars nodded. He set Stuart's portrait on Devyn's workbench then followed Dien from the shop.

They walked in silence until they had nearly passed the barn, then Dien spoke. "You disobeyed me. I told you to stay in the house."

Lars stopped walking and curled his toes in the mud. "I asked to take a leak, you said to go. So I went. How is that disobeying?"

Dien turned and stomped back to Lars. "Now you're getting a lip?"

"No, I'm not." Lars sighed. "I'm telling the truth. I was almost back to the house when Devyn grabbed me and asked me to follow him. He seemed like he had something to say, so I did."

Dien loomed close and dangerous. "He grabbed you? Did he hurt you?"

"No, he didn't hurt me. He wanted to talk to me, wanted someone, anyone, to listen to him." Shaking his head, Lars started for the house again.

"He doesn't have anything worthwhile to say."

Lars stopped again and turned, staring at Dien.

"Don't. Don't start that, not with me." He swallowed, feeling tears sting his eyes. "You and Dubric both know that my mother's not in her right mind, that her illness is part of the reason I'm here instead of at Haenpar. I get her letters and they're rambling and incoherent. You've seen them. She thinks I'm two summers old, and sends me dolls and crib toys, for Goddess' sake. But I still read every letter, dammit. Every last one. Because she's my mother and because she has something to say to me. Even if it is nonsense. What does it hurt?"

Dien shook his head and frowned, shifting uneasily.

"She's the only member of my family that acknowledges that I'm alive. So what if she's a few apples shy of a bushel? She's my mother and she loves me. Or at least the memory of me."

Lars took a deep breath and pointed to the barn. "Who does he have? Who gives him so much as a thank-you? Yes, it's creepy that he thinks I'm his dead son, but there are worse things. The girls act like he's diseased, Sarea barely looks at him, and Lissea . . . I know that she's stuck with him all day, every day, but . . ." He shook his head and started to walk away.

"But what, pup?"

Lars stopped and stared into the rain before turning back to Dien. "Something in her eyes. I don't know. Something. I think she hates him. Not just married-forever-to-a-crazy-old-man hate. Something else. Like he messed up something so bad, she can never forgive him. Something she's paying for, and paying with blood."

Dien frowned. "She's angry, I agree with that. I've never seen her as snippy as she's been these last couple days." He sagged. "I don't know what's gotten into her."

Lars swallowed and took a step toward Dien. "What

happened to Stuart? Why is it so important to Devyn now?"

Sighing, Dien walked to him and put a heavy arm over Lars's shoulders. "Not in the rain, pup. All right?"

Lars nodded and, together, they walked to the house.

Sarea looked up when the door opened. "So he didn't run off," she said, smiling.

"You were right, love. Dev left the house, too. I found them together in the shop."

Sarea sighed and rubbed her arms. "I hate that place." Shaking her head, she turned away and walked to the stove. "I'll brew you some tea, Lars. You're drenched."

"Thanks," he said.

He walked down the hall to the bath chamber and heard Dien say, "He wants to know about Stuart."

Curious, Lars left the door open a crack as he peeled off wet clothes.

"Then we should tell him," Sarea said. "It was a long time ago. What can it hurt now?"

"When I got there, Lars was screaming that he wasn't Dev's son."

"Poor Dad. He did the same thing with Bray for a while."

"But now Braoin's gone."

"So this *is* all connected," Lars said, wrapping a towel around his waist. He blushed, lowering his head as he ducked toward the settee and rummaged through his pack. "Sorry, Sarea. I forgot to grab dry clothes."

"Pfft. It's just skin." She pulled three cups from the

cupboard and shook her head at him. "I see you're following Dien's example."

Lars stood straight, an armful of clothes clutched against his belly. "What example is that?"

She laughed and pushed a few hats aside to make room for the cups on the table. "He thinks that women like scars. I see that you're already getting quite a collection."

Lars blushed again and hurried back to the bath chamber with his clothes.

"How can a boy of fifteen have scars from three stab wounds, a gash across his belly, and some mangled curly mess by his knee?"

Dien said, "Because he keeps the peace, sometimes by force. Be glad you haven't seen his hip."

"What in the seven hells happened to his hip?"

Lars padded down the hall again, pulling a shirt over his head. "Gored by a very angry steer. Dislocated my thigh bone in the process and I couldn't walk right for almost two moons. The scar's a beaut, though. Almost as big as my palm."

Sarea stared across the table at her husband's smirk. "That was just last summer! You told me he fell off his horse."

"He did. After we got back to the castle."

Lars sat and reached for a biscuit. "It's all healed, no harm done." He took a bite, then looked Sarea in the eye. "What can you tell me about your brother?"

She took a breath and closed her eyes, her voice softening. "I was about your age and Stuart was nine when it happened. He was born crippled, and he was slow in the mind. He didn't talk, not like most people. He grunted, mostly, but Dad let him deliver hats sometimes, or press the fur into felt. I don't remember anything different about that morning, not after all this time. Just that Stuart went to town to deliver a hat, and he never came home.

"Sometimes he'd get distracted. Linger too long at the sweet shop, maybe play with the barn kittens up the road. Folks knew who he was and that he couldn't help it. Everyone watched out for him and we never worried, not until it got late. It was getting on to dusk and had started to rain, I do remember that, so Dad went out to find him."

Sighing, she stood and went to check the kettle. "Dad came home a long time later, carrying Stuart. He was bloody. Screaming. Mam came running, asking what happened, but . . . but Dad didn't look at her, he only looked at me. He told me to take the mule and ride for the castle. Ride all night if I had to. But bring back someone to catch the three bastards. Not Sir Jabbert, but someone else. Someone from the lord's castle."

She took a breath and lifted the steaming kettle. "Stuart was alive when I left. I didn't see how badly he was hurt, but he was screaming and thrashing around." She poured their tea and sat.

"Jabbert?" Lars asked. "I thought Sir Haconry was steward."

"Jabbert had only daughters. After he died, his grandson, Haconry, claimed the title." She sipped her tea. "Anyway, I rode, all night, to the castle. It was pouring rain. Sloppy. When I got there, I told whoever would listen what had happened and soon I was brought to Dubric."

She reached for her husband's hand. "It was the day before the castle faire was to start and Dubric couldn't come back with me, so he sent Dien instead."

Lars grinned. "So that's how you met."

"Yeah, pup, you should have seen her. A scrawny little sopping-wet mouse. Even after riding all night, she wasn't afraid of anything and insisted she had to go right back."

"I've never been scrawny," Sarea said, smiling. She shook her head and looked at Lars. "We rode back, through the rain. I was about spent by then, but we got here not long after sunset. My brother was dead, my father was screaming, insane with grief, and my mother barely spoke at all."

Dien said, "It was my first case after being promoted to squire, and I was determined to not make any mistakes. I recorded every detail and clue. I counted twenty-three stab wounds—and Stuart was a little fella, not much to him. Plus the other . . . damage. It's a wonder he lasted long enough to get home alive." Dien pushed aside his teacup and glowered. "The boy was a mess. No two ways about it. What little of sense I could get from Dev told me that he'd found the boy in the cemetery, being raped and stabbed. I'd guess that's what snapped his mind. No man needs to see that happen to his child. There wasn't much in clues to find—a night and day of rain had made sure of that—but I did get a name out of Dev in one of his more coherent moments. Bilton Haconry."

Lars blinked. "Haconry? Like Sir Haconry?"

"His eldest brother," Sarea said.

Dien nodded. "I rode up to the manor first thing the next morning, and what do I see? Two bastards running for the hills."

"The other was his brother, Didge," Sarea said.

"It took me the better part of two bells, and cost me

twenty-some stitches, but I caught them and dragged their asses back here."

He sipped his tea. "By the time I tossed them in the barn, they'd confessed. They admitted attacking Stuart, even admitted running when they'd heard someone was coming from the castle to get them." He sighed and stared into the cup. "I came up to the house to wash my hands and say good-bye to Sarea. I guess I lingered too long."

Dien looked up, to Lars. "I heard screams, and ran to the barn to find Devyn standing over them. He'd cut their pants off and had shoved tool handles up their asses. He looked at me, thanked me, then cut their throats."

Dien sighed and squeezed Sarea's hand. "I had to take him back to the castle. I had no choice. They were bound and helpless. Right or wrong, no matter his grief, it was murder."

"But who was the third?" Lars asked.

"There wasn't a third," Sarea said. "Martaen Haconry was ten summers old. He was the last brother, and he wasn't involved. There wasn't anyone else."

"What if they were lying?" Lars asked. "Even good witnesses lie. What if they were protecting the third man?"

"We thought so at first, too, but there wasn't anyone. I asked their friends, their families, people in the villages and farms. I couldn't find *anything* that led to a third person."

"Anything but Dev," Lars said.

"I came back every day I possibly could to help with the farm and look for other clues. But there were none. It was just the two of them, torturing a helpless crippled boy for sport. He wasn't the first boy they'd molested. They admitted everything."

"Council sentenced Dad to seven summers in gaol. He wasn't the same after that," Sarea said. "After a few moons of Dien coming up to court me, I moved to the castle and we got married. When Dad was released, he came back home and returned to making hats. And he was obsessed with Stuart and the third man."

She freshened Lars's tea. "But there wasn't a third man and Stuart is dead, no matter what Dad might say. He won't accept the truth. He thought Braoin was Stuart, and now he thinks you are. He thinks any boy who comes through that door is Stuart."

"But I saw a painting. It looks just like me."

Sarea put her hand on Lars's shoulder and met his worried gaze. "You do look a lot like Stuart, Lars. I thought so when you were just a boy. It's just coincidence—I think it's your coloring that does it—but I don't blame Dad for being confused."

"He's just mad, pup. Like we told you. Mad with grief, mad from felting with mercury, mad from seven summers in gaol for murder. Hells, I don't know. But I caught the pair responsible and Devyn killed them. That's all there is to it."

CHAPTER
8

†

Dubric rose before dawn to stretch his stiff muscles and back. He had insisted that Maeve keep the comfort of her bed, but the crippled ghost had claimed the settee and had refused to move. His options limited, Dubric found that the sitting room chair did not provide much in the way of ease or true rest. Nor did the floor. Nor the rug. Nor any other location he could discover.

I am getting too old, he thought, stumbling to the bath chamber. As he relieved the pressure of his bladder—one of the few aches he could attend to—his eyes drifted over the collection of objects in the room. A woman's hairbrush and a young man's comb. Shaving mug and razor. Soft, woven towels. A simple glass mirror in a rubbed pine frame reflecting his old, burn-scarred face and the painting behind him. A plain wooden bathing tub with a cake of goat-milk soap perched on the edge.

He finished his business and replaced the cover on the pot, then turned to the painting. The previous morning he had barely noticed it, attributing the view to dream and whimsy, but today he stood before it for a long time as his opinion shifted.

Springtime flowers framed the space, cascades of

mulberry and lilac dampened by a sparkle of water from below. The artist had stood upon the precipice above Maeve's waterfall, looking out to the river and the pastures beyond, catching a springtime morning in amazing detail. Dubric leaned closer, smiling. A finch hid amongst the flowers, its mate nearby, and a dragonfly buzzed about its business while sunlight shimmered on its fragile wings. He could imagine how the blossoms smelled, could almost hear the river and feel the waterfall's mist upon his face.

There was a tap on the door, and Dubric stepped away from the painting. "It is unlocked."

Maeve peeked around the portal. "I thought you'd fallen in."

"I was admiring your painting."

She took a shaky breath. "Braoin finished it last autumn. 'Life and Death on the River.' " She smiled sadly. "He always fretted over his titles."

"I see no death," Dubric said. "But it is an amazing piece."

"Oh, it's there. You haven't looked deep enough." She wiped at her nose with the back of her fingers and turned away.

"I will find your son," he said, following her to the kitchen. "In fact, this morning I intend to speak to his betrothed, then journey to Oreth and meet with Calum the scribe's family. Hope still remains. Do not give up."

"I can't go with you today," she said as she filled the teapot. "My work. I've fallen so far behind."

"Otlee and I can manage alone, milady. You must tend to your business. We will find your son, I promise."

She nodded and tossed strips of wood into her stove. "Of that I have no doubt. I only pray you find him before it's too late."

* * *

"I suppose ye want to hear about Braoin and me," Faythe said.

"Yes. All that you can recall."

Dubric sat in a home in the pitiful village of Myrtle, watching a plain-faced girl with blazing hair try to compose herself. Worrying a snag on a fingernail, Faythe stared at the table with her glorious curls obscuring her eyes. "We met at the spring planting festival in Tormod, just last spring. He and his mama, they had a table selling fabric and pictures. Did ye know he did beautiful paintings?"

"Yes, yes, I did."

She smiled, looking truly beautiful for a moment. "He painted a portrait of me. Would ye like to see?"

"Of course."

She left the table and disappeared behind a curtain, reappearing with a canvas in her hands. "He framed it and everything, said Jak let him have the wood fer free." She gave Dubric the painting. "I didn't believe him—Jak never lets the fellas have anything fer free—but I let him think I did."

It was her portrait, no doubt about it, painted by someone who saw loveliness in every freckle. In the picture, she leaned against a stone wall with ivy cascading beside her, the barest wind lifting her curls. Her eyes, shimmering and blue, reflected the sky, and a secret smile teased the corners of her mouth. "You are a beautiful girl," Dubric said, returning the painting.

She smiled sadly. "That's what Braoin always said."

"You mentioned someone named Jak. Who is he?"

"A carpenter, does all sorts of odd jobs round the Reach. Braoin's been working fer him, gosh, fer moons.

Mostly fer plastering, or fer painting, but sometimes fer carpentry work, too. He was too gentle with the hammer, I think, him being an artist and all, but it was good money, when it came."

"And you were betrothed?"

Her chin raised and he saw a hint of the smile from the painting. "Yes, sir. He even asked my pa, after he asked me."

"Was there someone else seeking your affection? An old suitor? Anyone who may have been jealous of Braoin?"

She frowned and shook her head. "Not no more, milord. Gilroy and I were a long time ago. A long time. Besides, he's gone."

"Gone where?"

"Why, to the dark, milord. Nearly two summers now. Everyone knows that."

Dubric's breath caught in his throat. "Two young men you knew have been lost to the dark?"

"Ye make it sound like I had something to do with it." Standing, she set water to simmer over the fire. "We were through six moons or more afore Gilroy disappeared. He took up with Tabby, the sneak. I might not be the prettiest girl in the Reach, but I ain't sharing. He wanted her so bad, he could just have her, I said."

"So this Gilroy was unfaithful?"

"Yessiree. I weren't never so relieved in all my life as the day I told him we were done." She shuddered and, behind her, the ghost knocked over a tin plate.

Dubric rubbed his aching eyes while Faythe knelt to pick the plate from the floor. "When did you last see Braoin?"

"Five days ago. We had plans the day he disappeared, but he came the day before instead."

Dubric blinked and Otlee looked up. Maeve had said Braoin had disappeared after leaving to see Faythe. "Why did he visit you a day early?"

"I don't know, milord, just that he needed to talk to his aunt and uncle. Something about an eye, I think. Never made no sense to me."

"His aunt Lissea and uncle Devyn Paerth?"

The ghost turned, grinning.

"Yeah, milord. Them."

Dubric looked away from the ghost and back to Faythe. "Who were Braoin's friends?"

"He knew some city boys I never met. Around here, though, his closest friend was probably Eagon. They talked all the time, been friends since they were little."

"Do you know his full name?"

"No, sir, not many folks round here use their after names. But Eagon's folks live on a sheep farm out in the briars west of town," she said, nodding her head toward the open window. "Bray and Eagon worked together, plastering and painting." She smiled wistfully. "Golly, they loved to talk about numbers."

"Numbers?" Dubric asked. "What do you know about the numbers?"

"Not much." She laughed a little, blushing. "I can't cypher so good, but Bray said that Eagon did patterns and things with his plastering. It never made no sense to me, add this, do that twice . . ." She shrugged, glancing nervously away. "Bray had a pattern book he loaned Eagon, and they talked about numbers and textures all the time. It wasn't none of my business, so I just let them talk. You know how men are about their jobs."

"Was there anyone Braoin's mother did not know of? Anyone he met on the sly?"

She scoffed, leaning forward. "Braoin? Hells, no. He loved his mama damn near as much as he loved me. He worked and he painted and we courted. Anyone who tells ye different is lying."

"What about this Jak? The carpenter? How did Braoin meet him?"

She stood and checked the kettle. "Everyone knows Jak. He works all over the Reach." She picked a dented, rusty canister from the shelf above the fireplace and reached inside, dropping a handful of tea into the water. "Last summer Eagon said Jak was asking around fer a plasterer and Braoin said he'd give it a go. He did real good at it, I guess. Got a bonus to his pay and three more plastering jobs after that. Even did Sir Haconry's place, down near Barrorise."

Dubric glanced at Otlee but the boy was scribbling away, noting every word. "Braoin worked for Sir Haconry?"

She said patiently, "Braoin worked, sometimes, fer Jak. Not creepy ol' Sir Haconry." She returned to the table and sat again, toying with the painting. "He did say something, though, after he'd finished plastering Sir Haconry's wall. Said he might want a painting. Said it would be real money. Enough to get us married. Maybe even enough to get us a house and a bit of land of our own."

She looked Dubric in the eye and said, "I told him not to do it. That all the money in the world wasn't worth bowing to that sneaky bastard. I told him that our own place didn't matter, that there was enough room fer us here, or at his mama's. She agreed, I know she did. She never liked old Sir Haconry none, either."

"Did Braoin accept the job?"

"I honestly don't know, milord. I do know he was thinking about some painting. That's what he did. Think about paintings before he started them. He never showed them to no one, nor talked about them, not till they was done. I don't know what he'd decided about Sir Haconry's offer, not fer sure, but I saw paint on his hands sometimes the past couple of phases. He was definitely painting something."

After a dank trek through tangled forest, Dubric and Otlee rode to the village of Wittrup, by far the largest settlement they had seen thus far. Snuggled on a mossy, rock-strewn peninsula, boats waited against nearby banks, some loading cargo for the float to the coasts or deeper inland, others unloading to carts heading north to Tormod or south to Castle Faldorrah.

Barkers called out offers for fish and wares and trinkets, the local peddler hawked from his cart, and a pair of whores leaned against a stone wall and smoked. The air stank of fish, sewage, and cheap ale. All the while filthy children ran about, some dressed in the ragged, short-legged pants of boat workers, others in loose peasant tunics. All were pitifully thin and none wore shoes.

Dubric sighed and rubbed his eyes. Three of his faint and vaporous ghosts had returned to their favorite haunts. They lazed near the piers, somehow oblivious to one another and to him. One, the lad upon whose temple he had seen the string, crouched on the muddy bank, his stick poised over the water. The second tried in vain to grab drinks and dice from a group of sailors, while the third stood across the road from the whores and attempted to market his own set of wares.

"I don't think I've smelled much worse than this, sir," Otlee said, his nose wrinkling. "Even that corpse was better than dead fish and . . . Ugh! What is that smell?"

"Rancid Blackmoorian ale, if memory serves." Dubric grimaced. Nearly fifty summers before, when war and death had brought him to the Reach, Wittrup had been little more than a quaint fishing village. After the beleaguered passage of time, he recognized the blacksmith shop but little else. Poor and crowded, the people were as wretched as the slimy rocks they trod upon.

The peddler waved to them, beckoning them close with his heavy hands. "Milord! Welcome to the Reach! May I interest you in a jewel for your lady or a slingshot for your boy?"

"No, thank you," Dubric said, looking past him to the boats lashed to the docks. *How many ships pass through each day? Each phase? If the boys were taken on boats, how could I track them?*

The peddler laughed, oblivious to Dubric's worries. "You're making me wish I sold boats, milord."

Dubric shifted in the saddle and turned his attention to the peddler. "I do not wish to purchase a boat."

"Then I am greatly relieved," the peddler said. "Is there anything I *can* interest you in? Anything at all?"

"Information," Otlee said.

"Atro is a fountain of knowledge," the peddler said, bowing. "What sort of information? Properties for purchase? Beautiful views? Mayors and businessmen?"

"Missing boys," Dubric said.

"Yes, the children," Atro said sadly. "You must be

Lord Byerly. I heard that you've come to find them. I am at your service, sir."

Dubric handed Otlee his notebook. "What rumors have you heard? What truths?"

Atro drew a thick and heavy breath then moved close, his voice lowering. "You are correct, milord, 'tis all boys we've lost, on rainy nights it seems. I saw one taken, pulled into the dark by a spectre. The lad was there one moment and gone the next."

"Where?"

"From the road near Reyburn, last spring. Saw him running toward me in a storm, a boy of maybe eleven, twelve summers. Saw him in a flash of lightning, then he was just gone. I looked for him, looked all over, but there was nothing."

Dubric asked, "What do the people say?"

"That it's a night spirit, milord, come to take our sons, to eat them up. Why else would a night spirit take them?"

Dubric thought of the two molested bodies and suppressed a shudder. "Who acts suspiciously? Who do the people suspect?"

"Everyone's afraid, milord, and they keep their children dear. But most hate Sir Haconry. Filthy man, the things he does to those poor boys."

Dubric looked Atro in the eye. "Does anyone else prefer relations with boys?"

Atro considered the question. "No, milord, not that I know for certain, but there are rumors . . ."

Dubric's hands twitched with anticipation. "What rumors?"

Atro glanced aside then leaned closer. "I'd heard tales that Devyn Paerth, hat maker up Tormod way, took some lads up the rear a few summers ago. Even went to gaol because of it."

Dubric sucked in a harsh breath. *But Devyn did not molest those boys.*

Something crashed at the peddler's cart and Atro stepped back to look. Two scrawny dock brats pulled a box from the cart, dropping it to the ground. As the box tipped, puppets fell out, the strings tangling together in the rocks and mud as they sprawled loose and contorted, like dead soldiers on a battlefield.

"Hoy, now," Atro said, bustling away. "Get your filthy nips off the puppets."

Atro shooed the children away as a whore approached, looking for some trinket or another. Leaving the peddler to conduct his business, Dubric continued across Wittrup.

Children held out their palms, running alongside the horses, and both Dubric and Otlee tossed coins. By the time they reached the ferry, nearly a score of children had swarmed them, some older than Otlee.

"No more than a half crown apiece," Dubric told Otlee, dismounting. "I do not want to support a whole village of children." He tossed Otlee his purse and approached the ferryman. The river churned and roiled, flushed with runoff from the Harvath and other sources farther north.

The ferryman spat brown fluid into the turbid mess. "Two horses 'cross the Casclian, eh? Don't see many horses round here. Skittish things, o'er water, 'specially this early in the season. Might see a mule er two mayhap, but most folks take oxen across. It's safer."

He spat again and leaned forward. "Fine boy ye got there. Must be trustworthy, too, ye givin' him yer purse like ye did. I'll trade ye straight up. A trip 'cross for ye and yer horses. I can keep the boy. I need a trustworthy lad. What say?"

Dubric sighed and rubbed his aching eyes. "I say I pay you a crown apiece to ferry my horses, not one penny for the boy or me, and you keep your head attached to your shoulders."

The ferryman stared at Dubric, his eyes resting a good long time on Dubric's sword, then he spat again. "Seems fair."

"Otlee!" Dubric hollered and the boy ran up, smiling and leading his horse.

"Half crown apiece exactly, sir."

"Fine job. Pay the man two crown and tie your horse."

"Yes, sir." Otlee bobbed a quick bow and paid the ferryman. As they crossed, he gripped the wooden rail and grinned like any child on an adventure. Dubric wished he could share in the amusement, but instead he leaned against his horse and shielded his eyes from the sun. The crippled ghost gripped the ferry's rail, grinning at the river, but the other ghosts floated behind, forever dogging his heels.

"Can I go?" Aly asked, looking up at Lars with pleading eyes. "Puh-lease?"

"That's up to your mam," Lars said. He read over the list and nodded. Nothing too complicated, or too heavy.

Sarea fished through her purse for a variety of coins. "Let me see your hands."

He sighed and curled them away from her. "They're fine. I put liniment on them again this morning."

She frowned and grabbed one, turning it over so she

could see his palm. Tsking, she let his hand drop. "You can't fib to me, Lars Hargrove. You're still blistered and cut. I told Dien that turning you into a farmhand was a mistake. You work in an office, for goodness' sake, maybe use your sword. You don't have calluses for farmwork."

"Oooh, soft hands are so manly," Kia sniggered from the sink.

Sarea shot her a glare, then returned to the purse. "There's a glove maker in town, and I want you to get yourself a good pair of work gloves. Don't let him tell you the leather's imported. It's sheepskin from the Reach. He cures it in his shed."

"Sarea, really, I'm fine."

She dropped a pile of coins on the table in front of him. "Don't argue with me. I'm a mother. You can't win." She snatched the list away and added another item. "See if you can get some chamomile or peppermint for Fyn's stomach. She vomited again this morning." She started to hand the list back to Lars then changed her mind. "Oh, and pickles, we need pickles. Don't want the girls to catch colds this spring."

He smiled and shook his head, waiting for her.

Jess carried in the morning milk. "What's the money for?"

"I'm sending Lars to town to pick up a few things."

"Don't forget, I want some cream pastries!" Kia chirruped.

Jess put the milk pail on the floor near the cellar door. "We need salt. And some raisins would be nice."

"Already on there," Sarea said, skimming the list one more time before handing it to Lars. "Walnuts, too. There you go. I think that's everything."

"Can I go?" Aly asked again, looking between Lars and Sarea. "I like pastries and raisins."

Sarea nodded, and Lars turned to Aly. "Sure thing." Glancing up, he added, "You want to come, too, Jess?"

Surprised, she turned to grin at them. "Can I?"

Sarea asked, "Your chores all done?"

"They are till supper."

Kia groaned and flung suds at her sister. "This is completely unfair. Why can't I go?"

"Because you're being punished," Sarea said. "Go on, Jess, fetch your cloak and Aly's. Have fun, but be back before dark." As Jess ran off, Sarea patted Lars on the cheek. "You have fun, too. There's a little extra money there in case you kids decide to get a tonic or a snack. No reason to rush, just get my girls home in time for supper."

"Yes, ma'am." He pocketed the coins and folded the list, tucking it away.

Jess appeared with a basket tucked over her arm and Aly's cloak in hand. Once Aly was bundled, Lars escorted them from the house and down the lane, Aly skipping on ahead, giggling, while Jess walked along beside him.

After a mile or more of friendly silence, Jess leaned close. "Just to let you know, the pastry shop also sells soft candies. Aly really likes the caramels."

He grinned, watching Aly skip. He glimpsed the tallest village roofs peeking through the trees ahead; one had the gentle curve of Malanna's temple. "I'll be sure to surprise her, then. Have to keep my girl happy."

He saw a momentary pang of sadness pass over Jess's eyes, then it was gone, like smoke on a breeze.

He was about to ask her what was wrong when she

called to Aly, "We're going to stop and look at the rabbit!"

Aly squealed and started running.

Lars watched her go, worry tingling down his spine. She was far away, but Jess didn't seem concerned. "The rabbit?"

Jess nodded and broke into a jog. "I think you'll like it."

Giggling with delight, Aly rounded a bush and disappeared to the left, into a line of trees. "Aly, wait!" Lars called after her as he ran beside Jess. "Get back where I can see you." The village was farther down the lane, perhaps another mile or so. *What can Aly do in the trees?*

She appeared again, her hands on her hips and her hair blowing in the warm breeze. "I thought I was supposed to wait at the rabbit."

Jess laughed. "It's okay, really. The rabbit's within sight of the road. She'll be fine."

They had nearly reached Aly when Lars motioned her ahead, and she giggled and zipped off to the left again. Jess turned to follow, but Lars paused to look at the sign hanging above the path.

On the sign, made of weatherworn wood, whitewashed letters said *Cemetery*. No pomp, no humble homage to death; just a simple sign. His mouth went dry and he coughed before moving again.

He hurried after them, their names hovering in his throat, but he halted after a few steps. Aly climbed onto the head of a massive stone rabbit, then slid down its back, laughing all the while. Jess leaned against it, her hand on its nose, regarding him with mirthful eyes. "Lars Hargrove, I'd like to introduce you to your grandfather's rabbit." She bowed with a flourish and grinned at him.

"My what?" Astounded, he approached the sculpture, taking in every shape and shadow while Aly climbed up it again.

Jess dropped her hand from the creature's nose and took a step toward Lars. "King Byreleah Grennere was your grandfather, wasn't he?"

"My great-grandfather. He died in the War of Shadows." A huge carved insect lay crushed between the rabbit's front paws. Made of black stone flecked with veins of red, it was shaped like a moth, but had a stinger and head like a hornet.

An inscription was carved on the insect's exposed belly:

In Memory of the King
The Hare
Byreleah Grennere
Felled Sixth Moon, 2214
Rescuing the Reach from the Devil

Lars knelt and touched his great-grandfather's name, his eyes stinging. "I didn't know this was here."

"There's more," Jess said. She pointed behind the rabbit to a paved path that led past rows of modest grave markers. "My grandmama told us all about it." As Lars started down the path, Jess grasped Aly's hand. "Before the armies came, the Reach was ruled by a man named Foiche and he bred special wasps. He could command them to sting people, I guess. I'm not sure what else."

The path led down a gently sloping hill, through a ring of birch and fir to end at a windowless white stone structure with a beautifully aged copper roof. Lars approached the building, Jess trailing behind him. A plaque hung beside the door.

"Grandmama says there were lots of armies: the Hare, the Cudgel, the Hawk, the Sheep. All the royal houses came to free the Reach. But it was the Hare that defeated Foiche. He was found with the Hare's white-and-red flag shoved through his chest. But the Hare was dead, too, stung by Foiche's wasps."

"That's not quite accurate," Lars said. "Dubric said that the royal houses fought shadow mages, and my great-grandfather died in northern Faldorrah by being incinerated. He was an archer, like my father. If he killed Foiche, it was with arrows, not a flag, and I've never heard anything about wasps."

She shrugged. "I just know what my grandmama says. That's not a very good poem, by the way."

Squinting at the plaque, he leaned close. The copper's patina blurred the fine engraving, making it difficult to read.

The wite hare come
Wit the arm'y it led
Blak wasps swurm'd
Hare drop'd th'm de'd

Red an blak
Blak and red
A lone wasp stang
The rabb't bled

Hare crush'd the wasp
Wasp bit the hare
The thred's a death
R'main ev'r ware

"It is pretty bad. But I guess this is where your granddad got his rabbits and wasps. He's old enough to remember the war." Lars shook his head and stepped back to look at the building again. "What's inside?"

"A body," Aly whispered with grave emphasis.

Jess laughed and released Aly's hand. "It's supposedly your great-grandfather's crypt."

"Let's take a look." He reached for the latch but found it locked.

"Grandmama said it was vandalized, so it's kept locked."

"Who would have the key?"

"I have no idea."

Lars peered into the lock and frowned. "Would we get in trouble if we went in anyway?"

He felt Jess come close behind, and Aly crouched beside his knee, peering up at him. "I don't see how," Jess said. "It is your family, after all, and if we don't damage anything . . ."

He grinned and slid his pack from his shoulder. "Seems reasonable. Want to learn how to pick a lock, Aly?"

"Sure!"

He rummaged into the pack's side pocket and pulled out two slender strips of metal. "Peek inside. See the pieces in there? The curved rod thing and the hook?"

Aly squinted into the hole, climbing onto him for a better view. Her heels dug into his thighs as if they were dulled daggers. "Yeah. And there's a spring!"

"Yes, ma'am. Okay, slip this tool in there and lift the hook. Be sure to hold it steady. The spring will make it slippery."

He smiled at Jess while Aly tinkered with the lock. "Your dad's gonna skin me."

"No," she said, kneeling beside him. "He taught all us girls how to spring a lock when were were nine or ten summers old. Just in case. I have to see what I'm doing, but Fyn can do it in the dark."

"Got it!" Aly said. "Now what?"

Lars placed the other strip in her free hand. "Keeping the hook out of the way, push that rod thing to the side. Toward the middle of the door."

Click! The door popped open a hair, the hinges creaking.

"I did it!" Aly jumped to the ground, excited and squealing, while Lars returned the picks to his pack.

Jess laughed, spinning her sister through the air. "You sure did. We'll tell Dad all about it when we get back."

Lars opened the door, checking both sides of the latch. The outer remained locked but the inner worked stiffly. If the door happened to close, they would not get locked in.

Jess walked past him. "It's beautiful."

Lars looked inside. The walls, made of the same white stone as the outside, had been carved to depict battle scenes. Armored men on horses and common men on foot, all under the banner of a hare, fought a gruesome legion of slathering beasts and skeletal men under the banner of a wasp. On the wall to the left of the door, a bearded man with a bow led the charge against a massive, naked man with the wasp army behind him. Strands flowed from the huge man's arms and mouth, like thin tentacles, reaching for the hare's army. The far wall showed men writhing in the tentacles, body parts cut off and falling away, while others fought and died against the dreadful beasts. Only the archer stood fast, unafraid and pressing forward with the rabbit pennon fluttering all around.

The third wall showed the archer taking aim, his horse rearing while being gripped by a tentacle. The opposing man held out his hands and sent insects swarming forth, most surrounding the archer but some attacking men and horses.

Lars turned again, to the final wall. One side of the door showed the wasp's leader dead, arrows in his chest and a rabbit sitting astride him while dead insects fell from the sky. The other side depicted a funerary march with the hare's pennons hanging limp. People knelt, crying and tossing flowers.

He stepped back, away from the door, and bumped into something cold. Breathless, he read the inscription around the top of the walls, beautifully carved in the white stone and accented by rows of moons with diamonds etched inside them.

Grace Be To He Who Broke The Black Thread Of Death And Crushed Clothos's Red Worm Of Blood. Here Lyeth The Hare, The Hope, The Salvation Of The Reach.

"It is beautiful," Lars said, but his mind was on red worms. Dev had mentioned them, too. He turned to look at Jess and Aly. They stood near the middle of the crypt, beside a stone coffin with a red-and-white fabric folded and draped across it. The stone lid was carved to depict an armored man clasping a bow in his hands; the cloth lay across his belly. Lars recognized the tips of the hare's ears on the top layer of worn and ragged folds. Although long familiar with his family's mark, he had never seen an actual battle pennon before. He touched the fabric, lifting a corner to feel the weave. "May he rest in peace."

Drawing Malanna's holy mark upon his chest, Lars walked around the casket. Rabbits danced along the sides of the white stone box, some crushing insects beneath their feet while others nibbled flowers or bore arrows upon their backs.

Aly skipped and jumped, mimicking the rabbits, and Jess backed against the far wall, covering a smile with her hand. "Settle down, Aly," she said, struggling not to laugh. "This is supposed to be a somber place."

Lars was about to say that dancing and skipping was a fine way to be, but Aly stumbled and fell against the pennon on the stone coffin, knocking it to the floor.

"Aly!" Jess said, but Lars was already there, lifting Aly to her feet again.

"You all right?" he asked.

She nodded, her eyes huge. "I'm sorry, Lars. I didn't mean to hurt your grandpapa."

"I don't think he'll mind," he replied with a smile.

Jess helped him refold the pennon, but as they started to put it back where it belonged, she paused. "What's that? On his stomach?"

Lars leaned over the coffin and frowned. Someone had gouged a ragged divot in the polished stone and smeared it with dirt. A dead moth lay in the hole, its wings crusty and crumbled, its once plump body merely a husk. It had been snarled in shiny black string, wound round and round, like a thread cocoon.

Jess grimaced and plucked the pitiful bug from the hole. "Why would anyone ruin such a beautiful monument?" Disgusted, she tossed it out the door, where it skittered away in the breeze.

"Some people just do things like that," he said, laying the pennon across the casket. "I don't understand why, either."

That done, he paused and looked around the crypt one more time. "Thank you for showing me this, Jess. You can't imagine how much it means to me."

She stood in the open doorway, her hair teased by the wind, and for a moment he could see the woman she would become. "You're welcome. We'd better get going, though. Still have a lot to do today."

"Pastries and raisins!" Aly said, skipping from the crypt.

Smiling to himself, Lars followed them outside and closed the door, making sure it was locked and secure once again.

CHAPTER

9

✝

By the time they reached Oreth, Dubric, Otlee, and their horses were filthy with mud. The wide, oft-traveled road connected the northern reaches of Faldorrah with Casclia's southern marshes. Innumerable carts, wagons, and porters braved the mud and chill to get their wares to market.

A couple of miles south of town, a cider merchant's wagon had broken an axle, spilling kegs and blocking the road. One of the rolling kegs had slammed into a passing poultry cart, knocking cages loose and freeing several geese. Tempers had flared, blows were exchanged, cider was spilt, and the geese—surely the more intelligent participants in the accident—fled, with the little ghost happily chasing them. After trying to quell the argument to no avail, and capturing one errant goose, Dubric admitted defeat and left the two men to resolve the issue on their own.

All the while his wretched ghosts had looked on. Even when geese ran through them and passersby rolled a keg across their feet, the ghosts remained, flickering and translucent.

By the King, he had been in the Reach two days and already despised them. If he had been a pious man he might have prayed that the merchants would not kill each other and add to his burdens. But he was convinced that the addition of two fools would make no difference compared to the weight of the twenty-four souls already tugging on the back of his eyes. He could not see them—like the three in Wittrup, most had likely returned to their favorite haunts—but their weight was a constant reminder of his responsibility to the dead.

The air smelled like rain and wind tugged at Dubric's cloak. He did not want to face another cold, wet ride, nor subject the boy to one. He hoped Oreth had an inn.

He rubbed his aching eyes as they rode into town. As the first Reach settlement not constructed on a riverbank, Oreth possessed a unique quality: It was clean.

The homes were prim and well maintained, the roads smooth and free of debris. Even the children appeared to be clean and well mannered in comparison to their brethren from Wittrup. None approached with their palms outstretched, and several chased an inflated bladder-ball across a nearby pasture, happily playing without care, undue noise, or need of supervision.

"Oh, no," Otlee said, returning Dubric's attention to matters at hand.

"What is it?" He looked where Otlee pointed and muttered a low curse. Sir Haconry tossed an armload of books into a carriage not fifty lengths away. *Curse him.*

"Halt there!" Dubric called, heeling his horse to a canter.

Haconry smiled and drew on a pair of gloves. "Ah, my Lord Castellan. What a pleasant surprise."

Haconry's carriage stood outside a tidy brick dwelling with a whitewashed fence. A cleverly scripted sign proclaiming *Calum Floret—All Manner of Scripts, Records, and Words* hung from a lamppost beside the gate. Dubric pointed to the sign as he eased his horse to a stop. "I should arrest you," he snapped, dismounting. "You are interfering in an official investigation."

Haconry regarded him with a cool stare. "Nay, my Lord Castellan, I am retrieving my property." He flicked his fingers toward the house as if shooing a fly. "Investigate at will."

"Your property? What sort of property would you retrieve from a murdered man's home?"

Haconry smiled. "Personal property. Good day, my Lord Castellan." He started to enter his carriage, but Dubric's hand on the door halted him.

"I could toss you in gaol for a few days, a few phases. Perhaps then you would not be so quick to challenge me."

Haconry brushed Dubric's hand away. "Your gaol is a full day's journey to the south. Mine, however, is much closer and surely more painfully appointed. I remind you, for the last time, that while your castle may belong to you, the Reach belongs to me. Take care what you threaten, as well as who you menace with your insubstantial postures, or I may have no choice but to call your bluff and leave you to rot in the dark with the other vermin."

His eyes were as cold and depthless as stone. "While you were rotting in my gaol, my Lord Castellan, I would claim responsibility for your pet. Given your heavy-handed proclivities in that regard, you would likely judge that aspect of incarceration to be particularly grating, while I would find it ever so pleasurable. Perhaps you should bear that near the forefront of your mind while you continue your 'investigation.' Good day."

His hands clenching and unclenching, Dubric stood

silently as Haconry slammed the door and the carriage whisked away, taking potential evidence with it.

"Did he just threaten you, sir?"

"No. He threatened you. He will regret that particular transgression."

They tied the horses to the fence and approached the house. Dubric knocked, rain beginning to patter all around them.

A crying, puffy-faced young woman snatched the door open. She looked them over, top to bottom, and frowned. "At least you have the decency to knock," she said, then blew her nose. "State your business, then leave me to mine."

He bowed. "Dubric Byerly, milady. Castellan of Faldorrah. I have come to investigate your husband's disappearance."

"He's not my husband," she said, turning to glance over her shoulder. "Wait here."

The door closed.

Otlee looked up, confused, but Dubric had no answers for him.

The door opened again, a different woman this time, younger, pregnant, and very haggard. "Please, milord," she said, backing away. "I apologize for my sister's rudeness. Please come in."

"You are Madam Floret?"

"I was," she said, her chin lifting. "I've been expecting you. I only wish it were under better circumstances. Please, follow me."

She led him past the first woman, who clutched two wide-eyed little girls, then down a well-lit hall. "Calum's office is this way. We can talk there."

She reached a set of double doors, took a breath, then threw them wide.

* * *

Lars followed the girls from the spice merchant's shop, pausing outside the door to mark their purchases off the list.

"Can we get another caramel?" Aly asked, dancing around.

Their first stop had been the pastry shop, and Aly had already eaten six candies and a fruit puff. He feared she would turn into a bowl of sugar. "We'll see." Lars glanced at Jess. "Last thing on the list is a crock of pickles."

"What kind? Does it say?" She looked over his arm and frowned. "Three places sell pickles. What kind do you like?"

"Dill and garlic!" Aly chimed in. "Then can we get more caramel?"

Jess laughed and started down the road. "You know garlic gives Kia gas."

Aly tossed her head and danced along beside her sister. "Okay. Sweet pickles, then. Long as I get caramel."

Lars followed, shaking his head. To him, a pickle was a pickle. "What kind of pickles do you like, Jess?"

She sighed, twirling, and flashed a mischievous grin. "I like the chunky ones with slices of onion and mustard seed. Mam does, too, but Dad likes dill. Kia and Fyn like sweet little pickles."

"Then let's get the onion ones. The kind you like."

Aly walked along a board, balancing. "We usually get dill."

Lars stopped to add a single word to their list. "Look! I made a mistake." He showed it to Jess. "Don't know how I missed it before."

"Caramel?" Aly asked, her mouth dropping open and her eyes pleading.

Jess laughed. "Well, what do you know?" She showed the list to Aly and pointed to the remaining item. "Onion pickles."

"Aw, fiddle." Aly rolled her eyes and sighed with dramatic flair.

Lars smiled and tucked the list back in his pocket. "Lead the way, ladies."

Jess knelt beside Aly and pointed. "See that store with the blue barrel out front? We'll meet you there."

Aly skipped ahead, and Jess fell in beside Lars. "Thanks for the pickles, but it's really not necessary."

"I know," he said, braving a glance.

She smiled and walked along, swinging the basket.

By the time they reached Aly and the blue barrel, the wind had picked up, but Lars barely noticed. He was too occupied trying not to look at Jess.

They paused at the door to Halgren's dry goods store, and Lars fidgeted, glancing across the street to the sheriff's office. "I'm going to check in. Okay? See what they know about Braoin."

"Go," Jess said, smiling. "I know you have work to do."

Glancing back often, Lars walked to the sheriff's office. Finding the door unlocked, he let himself in and grimaced at the smell.

Two men were conducting business across a desk. The unwashed, portly man in a stained physician's coat turned, obviously startled at the interruption. He dropped the leather pouch he was pocketing and narrowed his eyes at Lars.

The pockmarked man behind the desk stood calmly, closing a drawer. He had a dark glower, and he shifted his sword belt on his narrow hips. "We don't allow kids in here. Go home to your mama."

Lars knelt to retrieve the fallen pouch and felt coins shift inside. He tossed it to the smelly physician. "I'm not a 'kid,' I'm a page from Castle Faldorrah, and I'm here to ask about search efforts for Braoin Duncannon."

"Told you, Sherrod," the physician said, quickly tucking the pouch away, "the Byr's here."

Lars rocked back on his heels. "You've already met Dubric—that simplifies things. What can you tell me about Braoin?"

Sherrod moved from behind the desk, his dark gaze skittering over Lars like ants assessing a potential meal. "I can tell you it's none of your concern, kid. Boys disappear in the Reach. It happens. End of story."

Behind him, the physician nodded, licking his lips.

"Um-hmm," Lars said. The sheriff had shifted his sword belt again, fiddling with it. *He never uses it, might not know how. It's alien, awkward, uncomfortable.* "But, you see, I'm not asking about 'boys,' I'm asking about Braoin Duncannon. He's . . . family."

"Family, my ass. You ain't his mama," the sheriff said, stretching to come nose to nose with Lars, "and he ain't got no snot-faced brothers."

Lars stared calmly at the sheriff. "Just answer my question. What do you know about Braoin's disappearance?"

The door creaked open behind Lars, and Sherrod's gaze shifted. He took a step back and said, "I told you, kid. Boys disappear. Braoin's one of them. Sorry I can't be more help."

"Is there a problem?" Lars heard a man say, and the voice sounded vaguely familiar. As the sheriff retreated another step, Lars glanced back and nodded in greeting.

"No trouble," the physician said, brushing past, and the outer door slammed behind him.

"Ah. That's good, because I brought it with me." A big man with a big smile and hardworking hands, Jak the carpenter strode forward, dragging a young man with him. "Hockers said Flann here pilfered a bottle. You know about that, Constable?"

Sherrod stepped away from Lars and returned to his desk. "I might. You here to pay for it? Two and a half crown."

"No, he is," Jak said, pushing forward the giggling hellion Lars had fought the day before. Flann wore the same clothes, complete with mud and Lars's boot-prints, and he stank like moldy sheets. He gave Lars an obscene gesture and Jak smacked him on the back of the head. "Quit fooling around, and pay the man."

"I ain't got no scratch," Flann whined. "I done told you, you ain't paid me yet."

Jak glanced at Lars and rolled his eyes, as if to say *Can you believe what I have to endure?* Then he reached for his own purse. "I want a receipt this time," he said. "From both of you."

Flann slipped from Jak's grip and started for the door. "Sure thing. I'm heading back to work, boss," he said, slamming his shoulder against Lars. Their eyes met and Flann grinned. "Next time you'll piss your pants, little puppy," he whispered.

He blew Lars a kiss and left the sheriff's office.

Intending to return to Jess and Aly, Lars followed him through the door and strode across the street, watching Flann saunter away under a darkening sky. Lars had nearly reached the dry goods store when someone touched his arm.

Jak stood behind him, slightly out of breath. "Lad!

Divine fate brings us together again. You come to town to see about that job?"

"Actually, sir, I'm just here to pick up a few things for the Paerths. I already have a job."

Jak looked past Lars, to Jess comparing pickle jars in the window. He winked. "I see that. One with added benefits, no less."

Lars said nothing.

"Laddie, I could use a solid man like you. Someone to watch over my work crew and keep them to task while I dredge up business. They're likely picking their noses and sleeping on the barn roof this very moment."

"Then I'm very relieved that the Paerths are paying you for the job, not by the day."

Jak burst out laughing and draped a heavy arm over Lars's shoulder. "You're a funny one, lad. That you are. Tell you what, I have a small project pending, in Myrtle. A fence repair, perfect for one industrious lad like yourself. What say I have you do the repair and give you a full crown for your trouble? Shouldn't take you more than a day or two. Good money that, certainly better than any farm boy round these parts." He leaned close and whispered, "Could get your girl there a ribbon for her hair."

"I can't. Sorry. I have a job."

Jak drew his arm away and regarded Lars, nodding. "You're a hard man. Two crown, whether it takes you one day or two. That's damn fine money, lad. Don't be a fool."

"No. I'm honestly not interested." He started to walk into the store, but Jak touched his shoulder.

"Now you've got me intrigued. It's more than that girl, isn't it? What's your story? How can a lad your age turn down two full crown?"

"I'm a page. I don't need a second job."

Jack paused, confusion on his face, then he shrugged. "Can't blame a man for trying. Ol' Jak won't bother you no more."

He offered his hand and Lars grasped it, finding the grip firm and friendly. Jak left, waving a good-bye as he climbed onto his mule cart, then drove away.

Lars straightened his back and entered the store, wondering if Jess had found the pickles she liked.

Madam Floret shuddered as she strode into the office. "Calum would have been livid, had he been here to see. He maintained records for that beast for summers and not once did the wretch touch his things. Despicable man."

"Sir Haconry, I presume?" Dubric picked up a ledger that lay upon the floor. Much of the office remained painfully neat, organized, and structured, but one shelf stood empty, and several more had been ransacked. Books and papers lay strewn on the floor, desk, and chairs, while others remained crisply in position.

"Vile bully is more accurate." She shuddered again and forced a smile. "Please excuse my bluntness, milord. I wish that man hadn't entered my home. And I wish my Calum weren't dead."

Despite himself, Dubric glanced at Calum's ghost. "Haconry informed you of his death?"

She took a step back and looked at him. "No, milord. He barged unannounced and uninvited into my home and demanded that I deliver his books."

Dubric held her crisp gaze and reached into his pocket for his notebook. "You knew your husband was dead?"

She stared at him, indecision weighing in her eyes, then she stepped past him and closed the doors. "He disappeared nearly three phases ago, milord. When nightfall came and he was not home, I knew he was dead." She licked her dry, cracked lips and stared at him. "I had feared for moons that it would come to this, to Calum's death, but he insisted he was safe. Even with our marriage, the children, he was wrong."

Dubric glanced around the ransacked room. "You mentioned that you had been expecting me. Would you care to explain?"

"You haven't come because of the letters?"

"What letters?"

She wavered, her steadfast demeanor gone like smoke, and she gripped the door latch behind her. "Calum sent dozens of letters, begging you to help us. You didn't come because of his letters?"

"I am aware of no letters, milady. I received word by rider."

She swallowed. "From the south? Myrtle? Reyburn?"

"Nay, milady. Falliet."

She staggered to a chair and fell into it, her face ashen. "Please, milord, tell me the rider was Braoin Duncannon, on his mother's jenny."

"You know Braoin?"

She looked up at him, her lip curling in. "Yes, he's godparent to our daughters. Was he the rider, milord?"

Were Braoin and Calum connected to the other victims as well? "No, milady, he was not. He is one of the missing boys."

She closed her eyes and her hands clenched together. "How can Bray be missing? He knew where all the eyes were, all the places to avoid. But Calum did, too."

"The eyes? What places?"

She stood weakly. "It's all on the map." She turned, her back to Dubric, and fiddled with her bodice. She turned back with her chemise mussed and a piece of parchment in her hands, folded so many times it had begun to tear on the creases.

"Braoin made it. One for each of them. Take it!" she said, shaking it at Dubric. "I can't bear to look at it again."

He accepted the parchment and unfolded it, revealing a hand-drawn yet incredibly detailed map of the Reach. Red and black ink diamonds were scattered along the roads and rivers, some beside notations of boys' names and dates. One part of the map demanded his attention; the markings there threatened to send him to his knees.

The ghost peered at the map, poking with grubby ghost fingers and rustling the parchment, but Dubric barely noticed. Four diamonds, two red and two black, were circled twice at the location of Devyn Paerth's farm. The same farm Braoin had visited before he disappeared. The same farm where Devyn had murdered two young men many summers ago. The same farm to which Dubric had sent Lars.

His stomach twisting, Dubric handed the map to Otlee. "What do the diamonds mean?" he asked, afraid to hear the answer.

"Not diamonds," she said. "Calum said they were eyes."

"All right, eyes, then. Do you know what they mean?"

"Bray used to say they were the devil watching, but it never made any sense. Except to them. They'd meet about once a moon and search an area of the Reach, looking for eyes. Bray would mark all three maps while they discussed the missing boys."

"Three maps?"

She took a breath and tried to hold his gaze. "Yes, milord. Calum, Braoin, and Paol."

Dubric added to his notes. "Paol?"

"The priest's apprentice, in Tormod. They've been friends since they were children."

Dubric grimaced, but continued his notes. He had ceased worshipping decades before but Lars attended services regularly. Did that put him at greater risk?

"Milord, you look distressed. Is Paol missing as well?"

"I have never heard of him before this moment, so I have no idea," he snapped with far more venom than he had intended. He wondered if the pacing ghost was Paol. *I must get to Devyn's farm!*

She stepped back from his anger, and moved toward the door. "I'll retrieve Calum's notes for you, if you think they might help."

"Milady, my condolences for your loss, but, please, one thing before you go."

She turned, her hand shaking on the door latch. "Yes?"

"Did your husband suspect Sir Haconry?"

She nodded, turning away. "Yes. He never found proof, but because of his concerns, he kept a duplicate set of Haconry's books. I'll fetch those as well." She opened the door, then paused, hanging her head. "If there's anything else you see that may aid you, please take it. I have no need for these things any longer."

CHAPTER

10

✝

Dubric left Madam Floret's home to find that the pattering drizzle had become a full torrential downpour. The sky had turned a noxious shade of green, and wind whistled from all directions at once, spurred on by flashes of lightning.

"We have to get to Lars, be certain he is safe," Dubric said, lashing a sack of books to his saddle.

"I agree, sir. He's where Braoin disappeared." Otlee shoved bundles of papers into his saddlebags, then climbed onto his gelding. "Can we make it in this storm?"

Calum and the other ghost wavered and faded in the wind, more wisp than substance, while the child ghost remained solidly formed but terrified. Dread roiled in the pit of Dubric's stomach and he shuddered, staring at the ghost's hauntingly familiar face. Never before had the little boy's resemblance to Lars seemed like such an ominous portent. "We must."

Braoin's injuries had sapped him, and the taste of infection filled his tattered mouth, tainting his entire head. Every breath he took stank of death and rot and tasted raw and bloody and full of pus. Frigid water had dripped on his face for a long time, longer than he could count, longer than he could remember, each drip punctuated by the pinging of hail on the roof. When the door opened, he barely had the strength to open his eyes. He opened them anyway, hoping to see a glimpse of the sky.

He did—a bright flash of lightning against the blue-green terror of a spring storm. The man stood in the open doorway, blocking his view, blocking his hope.

Braoin let his head fall and closed his eyes, berating himself for his exhaustion when he should resist whatever horror his captor brought. His admonishment barely began before he forgot it, drifting away with weakness and fatigue.

He screamed suddenly, swinging through the air while sharp, bright pain exploded from his ribs.

"Look at you, you girly chaff! Grinning away like a fool while I'm talking to you!"

Braoin gasped for a breath, each a burning torture. "Be pegged. You can kill me but you'll never take my soul."

Another blow to the same ribs, and Braoin cried out again.

"Are you so sure?" the man said, leaning close and covering Braoin's face with his breath. "I think I can. In fact, I think tonight would be the best night to do just that."

Lightning flashed, a crackle of flame and a roar, illuminating the edges of the man in blue and purple glory.

"Go drown yourself."

When the beating came, Braoin drifted away, thinking of painting the sky rolling over the fields. The painting needed a house, perhaps three silhouetted trees, and a barn. He smiled. Yes, a barn. Something to catch and reflect light from the sky.

"You have to be awake!"

Braoin screamed as fire shot through his bicep.

"Damn you! It won't work if you're not awake."

Braoin felt a tug at his arm, a rod of cold fire slipping through, and saw a long streak of metal wink in a flash of lightning. He knew what he'd seen. He'd seen them his entire life. *A needle, Goddess, he skewered me with a weaving needle.*

He heard a scrape and the man sat down, laying Braoin's head in his lap. The thought of what was to come made Braoin retch. He thought instead of Faythe, her eyes sparkling and blue, and she kissed him, her fingers ripping at his cheeks, tearing into the corners of his jaw—

"Wake up!"

Braoin flinched as pain shot from his jaw and ears, but he struggled to see Faythe and not the shadow looming above him.

The needle hovered above his eyes and he focused on its forearm-long shaft, his breath catching. There was a smear of black along the metal. *Is that my blood?*

"I'm only gonna tell you this once, you wretched whoreson. You remain awake or she'll skin me for failing."

Braoin wanted to laugh but his mouth hurt too much. "I hope she kills you and feeds you to the hogs!"

"Bastard! Son of a whore! Misbegotten whelp!" Each exclamation brought another flash of pain, along with a flash of lightning, and a stab with the needle.

"Look at me!"

Braoin shook his head and scrunched his eyes closed. He tried to think of Faythe or painting or the feel of spring grass beneath his toes, but instead he thought of his mother.

Another stab, through the flesh along the slope of his shoulder, and his eyes snapped open.

"That's better," his captor said, holding Braoin's head tight in the vise of one hand while pulling back the needle with the other. "Now, don't move."

Braoin barely struggled when he felt the prick dance along his temple. As it slid home, puncturing through to the other side, every whisper of his vision and thoughts turned black and red.

Otlee jumped when Dubric screamed.

"Sir!" Otlee called, yanking his gelding to a rearing halt at the Tormod bridge and reigning about. Lightning crackled across the sky and the air seemed to heave. Dubric slumped in the saddle, holding his head and wailing, while a thin, white line of vapor streaked from his left temple.

Dubric cried out again, the vapor growing crisp then fading along with the scream. A breath, then another screech of pain and a brightening streak of white. Again and again, ebb and flow, bright and faded, while Durbic held his head and wailed.

Goddess, what's happening?

Otlee reached for Dubric's reins. "What can I do?"

"Kill me," Dubric rasped. "I have never received a ghost like this. Aaach! For King's sake, boy! Kill me!"

"Sir! I can't do that!"

The white streak faded away and Dubric sagged in the saddle, panting. "I see him, it is Braoin, I am sure of it, but something keeps pull—"

He reached for Otlee and shrieked, the vapor from

his temple illuminating the side of his face. Then only the storm marred the silence as Dubric fell from the saddle and shuddered in the mud.

Lars followed Jess and Aly from the store and nestled the jar of pickles in the crook of his arm. "Goddess, it's gotten cold."

Jess fastened Aly's cloak, protecting her from the drizzle. "We'd better hurry. I think we're going to get drenched."

They had barely left town when the wind picked up and it started to pour. Lightning crackled through the black and roiling sky to the northwest and the air smelled sharp and dangerous.

Lars handed Jess the jar and lifted Aly, holding her against his chest as he picked up the pace.

Jess wiped her hair from her eyes where it had clung, curling and dark. "We're not going to make it. We should turn back."

"We'll make it. I gave my word I'd get you girls home."

Aly blinked raindrops from her eyes. "I'm cold."

Lars leaned into the wind and wrapped her tighter in his arms. "I know, but we have to keep going. We're almost halfway there." He tucked his cloak around her but the wind and rain yanked it away.

Lightning burst across the sky with a deafening roar, brightening the landscape to brilliant purple-white. Lars halted, his breath catching in his throat. He pressed Aly's face close against his neck and squinted while Jess trudged past.

There. Something glowing and red at the crest of the hill.

"Jess, wait," he said, reaching for her.

Another burst of lightning, and he saw a silhouette against the bright sky. A man, dark and muscular, staring at them with eyes the color of blood and fire.

"What's wrong?" she asked, barely audible over the storm.

He stared at the glowing eyes and shuddered. "We have to find shelter. Now."

She turned, slowly, following his gaze, then screamed and backed into him. Lightning flashed again, a burst of thunder and light, and the man, naked and black and burning hellfire red, was closer, nearly halfway down the hill. He appeared to be grinning, fading in and out at the whim of wind and rain.

"The crypt," Lars said, dragging her forward again. "Run!"

Jess ran off the road, Lars right behind her with Aly screaming in his arms. Jess dropped the jar of pickles and it burst, but both kept running.

Closer the darkness came, sauntering down the hill as he faded to nothing and became definite once again, somehow skipping leaps of distance in the process. Jess turned down the path and scrambled toward the rabbit with Lars on her heels. As they pounded down the lane leading to the crypt, he glanced over his shoulder. The dark man, naked and aroused, strolled into the cemetery as if he had all the time in the world. As he turned toward Lars he flickered and disappeared, then appeared again, several steps closer.

Lars sprinted, shifting Aly in his arms and shrugging his pack off his shoulder. "Hold her!" he cried to Jess as he tossed Aly and yanked the pack loose. He reached in the side pouch and closed his fingers over the picks, dropping the pack at his feet.

Aly wailed while Jess screamed, "It's at the rabbit! Goddess, what is it?"

Lars slammed the picks in the lock and flicked the first upward, catching the hook. "Almost, almost." His hands twitched and the hook slipped. "Bastard!" he snapped, trying again.

"Lars . . ." Jess said, backing against him. "You'd better hurry."

Up, snap, and the latch clicked free. Lars yanked the door open and shoved the girls through.

He heard laughter intermingled with Jess's screams, but he didn't turn to look. Something cold touched his neck, painful and sharp and stinking of sweet spice, but as soon as it touched him it faded away again. He stumbled, grabbing his pack as he threw himself through the doorway.

He fell and rolled to his back to see death reaching for him. Its teeth were long and viciously yellowed, corpse's teeth hanging from raw and bleeding bone, and Lars saw threads of breath leave its hideous maw to curl around the half-bone fingers, twirling into strands. Lars swung his pack, knocking the arm aside. It dissipated in a breath of smoke and wisps of darkness but the thing laughed again, strengthening and ebbing in the storm while lightning flashed all around.

Lars lunged for the door. It slammed and latched, snapping off a vaporous hand and pitching them into the dark.

"Come back out and play, little boy," the fiend chittered, its voice fading to a threaded whisper before booming again. "Open it or I'll rip out your bowels and lop off your head!"

Surrounded by blackness so complete it hurt his

eyes, Lars backed into the coffin. "Jess, Aly, you all right?"

"What is that thing?" Jess cried from the dark. Hail pattered on the roof, surrounding them with metallic pings.

"I don't know," Lars said. He shuddered and touched the back of his neck. "I think it scratched me."

"Oh, Goddess." He heard her move, heard her trip, then he felt her warm hands on his arm. "Where?"

"Back of my neck."

A rapid tap at the door and a voice cold and dark and dead. "Come out and play, little boy. I want to peg you till you scream, then eat you up."

Her fingers felt along his neck from his shoulders to his hairline and paused, trembling. "It's wet, warm. A small cut, I think."

Boom! The door shook and the air trembled. "Open this cocksucking whore of a door, you mongrel bastard!"

Aly screamed. "I want Mam! I wanna go home!"

Jess shuddered, her fingers shaking like a leaf in a wind, a terrified staccato against his upper spine. "I can't see it. What if it gets infected? What if it . . . if it makes you sick?"

The door thundered again, as did the storm outside.

Lars brushed her aside and pulled his boot dagger. "Here. Take this so you can defend yourself if I go mad." He held out the dagger and she slowly took it from his hand.

Rap. Rap. Rap. "Let me in. I just want a nibble. Just one. The little girl will be enough. We can share her, peg her till she's spent. Don't you want to hear her scream?"

A metallic ting as his dagger touched the stone wall. "You're not going to go mad. Don't say that."

"I might. Goddess, Jess, I don't know what that thing is or what it might have done to me."

"It obviously can't get in," she muttered.

The door rattled again as the thing outside rabidly yanked on the latch, but it held.

"I want to go home," Aly whimpered.

Jess moved away. "We can't, honey. Not yet."

"When, Jess? I don't wanna be in the dark with a body."

"It's just Lars's grandaddy. Nothing to be scared of. Come here. Let's see if we can get you dry, okay?"

"Open this damned door!"

"Open it yourself," Lars muttered. He started pacing, trailing a hand along the wall to keep him on track. All the while, the thing pounded the door and demanded to be let in, demanded to be fed.

The storm raged on.

PART 2

MEASURE

CHAPTER

11

✝

Dubric was barely conscious, and Otlee struggled to get him on his feet against the force of the storm. The white streak coming from Dubric's temple looked like thread or very thin yarn, its strands twirling together and disappearing into the storm. Dubric had stopped screaming, but each brightening of the strand wracked him with tremors.

"Let me die," he said, spitting water and blood.

"I can't do that, sir." Slipping in the mud, Otlee helped Dubric to his horse. "You have to ride, sir. You have to help me."

Dubric arched back, caught in another brightening strand, but he reached for the saddle as it faded away. "Ride, yes. To Lars." He fumbled one foot into the stirrup, then started to hoist himself up. "No one will harm him. No one would dare."

"Yes, sir. To Lars." Otlee pushed up on Dubric's backside and released a relieved sigh when the old man fell onto the saddle and moaned.

"Stay there, sir." *Rope, I need rope,* Otlee thought, running to his horse while thumbnail-size hail pinged all around.

Lightning struck nearby, and Otlee's horse reared, but did not run. The reins hung in the air, held taut but tied to nothing, and Otlee swallowed. *Goddess, what's happening?*

Afraid to breathe and terrified to move, he stared at the reins. Rain and wind blew against them, and he squinted at a shadow of a shape deflecting drips and hail. A figure, small and hunched, not there at all, yet somehow real, crouched in the mud.

Is that a . . . ghost?

"I'm not going to hurt you," Otlee said, swallowing his fear. "And you're not going to hurt me, either. Right?"

The shape stood, limping a step toward Otlee, then another. The horse followed. "Thanks," Otlee said as he yanked a coil of rope from his saddle.

Hearing no reply over the madness of the storm, Otlee ran to Dubric. Unconscious and bleeding from his nose, Dubric hung limply across his charger's back. Otlee tied him to the saddle and hoped that he wouldn't slide off.

He had nearly finished—only two knots left—when something cold and frantic scrambled up and over him. "What the—" Otlee looked up to see the ghost pointing.

Otlee turned, slowly, his heart stopping. A man, naked and black with glowing red eyes, sauntered toward him from the pasture north of the road. His form solidified and faded, matching the rhythm of Dubric's white glow and brightening as lightning streaked across the sky.

"Two in one night," the thing said, its voice rumbling and low like distant thunder. "And such lovely boys they are, stinking of pious Byr. So tasty, so fine." It licked its rotting lips and laughed, threads spewing from behind yellow teeth to spin and twirl like tentacles. They reached for Otlee, black writhing horrors with gleaming red-worm tips, each with tiny eyes and claws. The tentacles thickened and twirled, coming to eat him up.

Something cold dripped against the back of Otlee's neck. The ghost fumbled around his collar, then grasped and pulled, yanking him backward and up. Otlee screamed, frantic, but Dubric's horse bolted forward, taking him with it while the dark creature chased after, howling with rage.

The toy twitched and bucked, its muscles thrashing in vain. He drew the thread through, humming and looping the strand around his arm while it glowed a brisk and comforting red.

Worms crawled up his leg, hungry for fresh meat. "Not now," he said, brushing them off as the glow in the fresh thread faded. "Perhaps I'll give you a taste later. After I'm all through."

Each pause stopped the toy's twitching, but he hurried again, pulling another arm's length of thread through its head and brightening the glow once more. Mama would be furious—she preferred the thread to be all one color, not fade in and out—but surely she wouldn't want her red babies to be unduly injured, either. He had crushed far too many preparing the toy for dyeing. To kill more was unthinkable.

He pulled and pulled until his arms ached, then he pulled some more, watching the toy's face all the while and paying close attention to its twitches. Try though he might, the glow brightened and faded with each pull, damn thing.

"Ah, there we go," he said as he neared the last bit of

the first skein. "What do you see, girly boy? Do you see the devil's eyes? I'd love to see his eyes. I hear they're red and black, like the worm and moth, like raw and dyed silk. Are they? Can you see?"

"Gah!" The toy drooled, its eyes sunken and its mouth gaping.

He smiled, draping the first skein across the toy's chest, where it flickered and thrummed its luscious color. "I appreciate the offer of your mouth, but I can't tonight. Mama's set me to work."

He tied a new skein to the end of the old and pulled again, setting the toy's muscles to twitching and the thread to its fade and glow. Concerned over the dyeing strength on the second skein, he watched the toy's eyes as they shrunk and shriveled away. If he pulled too much through, if the toy left him nothing from which to make dye, the thread would tear and crumble. Even worse, Mama would lose precious length.

"Far better to snip when you're through and waste a bit of raw silk," he said, smiling at the toy's pallid face, "than to leech perfectly good thread. None of the red is to be wasted, not on worthless girly boys like you, but I've plenty of black and the worms to make more."

The toy's eyes disappeared, sucking into its skull with a slight pop. He stopped pulling and stared at the toy's face with trembling apprehension. *Did I pull too far? Not quite far enough?*

"Damn you," he muttered, reaching for the scissors. Only a couple of lengths of undyed silk left. "Why couldn't you have finished the skein?"

After easing his frustration by punching the toy's forehead with his scissors, he cut the thread and gathered the skeins, leaving the toy to swing as whim took it. A few days would pass before stench and rot overpowered any use the toy might have, but it certainly could no longer fight or get away.

He trudged from the shed and closed the door. Toys weren't as much fun after dyeing, damn things. Why couldn't Mama let him play a little longer?

Grumbling under his breath, he walked through the storm, protecting the thread under his coat. As he entered the house he smiled, looking at the skeins in his arms. Silk always looked prettier dyed red and this batch was brilliant and brisk, even with the streaks of faded black. Mama would be happy.

He wondered what color his golden boy would dye. Surely vermillion or crimson. A deep, warm red. Like blood.

Lars stopped pacing and listened. The thing had ceased pounding on the door, leaving only the storm and their breathing.

"Is it gone?" Jess asked.

Aly whimpered, tweaking his heart. "Can we go home now?"

His fingers tracked along the door. "No. Not until morning, after first light."

"I wanna go home."

Lars struggled to not curse. "We have food and shelter, and we're safe right here. He might have stepped away to give us a false sense of safety, to lure us out. I'm not taking chances with you girls. We're safe right here, and here we'll stay."

Jess said, "We have Kia's pastries, walnuts and raisins, some soda, salt and spices. Oh, and a square of milled soap. I wouldn't call that food, if it were up to me."

"Dammit, Jess, I'm doing the best I can."

She sighed, harshly, and he wondered if it showed her exasperation for him or herself. "How can we tell when morning comes? It's pitch black in here."

He resumed pacing. "I don't know."

She sighed again. Louder.

Had there been an odds-taker handy, he would have bet a whole moon's wages that she had just rolled her eyes and thrown her arms in the air. *Does she expect me to know everything?*

Aly's voice sounded very small, almost mouselike. "Don't fight. I'm scared."

"We're all scared, honey," Jess said without a hint of sighing or sarcasm.

Lars stopped pacing and worked his way to the rear of the crypt, across from the girls. He tripped—*I give her my dagger and she just drops it in the middle of the floor*—and he picked it up, only to take one step and run headlong into the wall.

He rubbed his sore forehead and sat, leaning into the corner and closing his eyes.

"You all right?"

"What do you care?" he snapped. He laid his dagger where he could find it easily and he willed his anger to go away.

"I care." Her voice sounded as quiet as a whisper. "I'm just scared."

"I'm scared, too," he said, softer this time.

Movement in the dark, then Aly crawled onto his lap, damp and shivering, and hugged him. "Don't be scared, Lars."

He held her close, tucking her into the crook of his arm and stroking her wet hair while wrapping his cloak over her. Movement again, then Jess kicked him, stumbling over his legs.

"Sorry for kicking you, and for what I said." She sat beside him, every bit as wet and cold as Aly, and passed him some kind of blanket. "We might as well try to get warm. If you can forgive me."

"Where did you get this?"

She covered the three of them. "Your grandfather said we could borrow it."

He felt Aly nod. "He did. I heard him."

The war pennant. Lars smiled and made sure Aly was covered. Jess leaned in, not quite touching him, and he groaned and lifted his arm. "Let's get you warm, too," he said. "And you're forgiven."

She hesitated then snuggled in, cold and shivering against his side. Aly fell asleep almost immediately, and Jess relaxed against him not long after. Her head drooped, rolling toward him, and her forehead warmed the side of his neck.

Lars smiled. He had protected his girls as best he could. Now if only he could get them home.

The door latch jiggled. He held his breath and pulled the girls closer while his heart beat steady and slow. "If I were alone you'd feel my blade," he whispered. "You can't have them. I gave my word to keep them safe and see them home again."

The latch rattled once more, then fell still. After the storm blew past and rain had ceased pattering on the roof, Lars drifted to a fitful sleep, dreaming of fiery eyes and corpse teeth.

The kids hadn't come home.

Dien struggled to remain in the saddle and keep his horse on the road as he called for them, but the damned gelding pulled at the bit and shied at every burst of lightning, as skittish as a mouse in a room full of cats.

But they continued on, Dien snarling at the storm and refusing to succumb to the sting of hail on his head and back.

He held a lantern in one hand, glass protecting the flame from wind and rain, and desperately searched the edges of the road for the slightest sign that the kids had sought shelter. He rode to the next farm, scaring the daylights out of the young couple and their two little boys when he banged on their door, but they had not seen his children. Nor had the next farm, nor the next.

He rode to the cemetery and turned in, guiding his horse through grave markers and sculpture. No sign of them. Down the lane to King Grennere's crypt. Locked.

He grit his teeth and returned to the road. The gelding wanted no part of it, but Dien kicked him ahead anyway. "We're finding the kids, you wretched beast. Get a move on."

He pulled the horse to a halt fifty, perhaps sixty lengths from the cemetery gate when he saw something on the road. Lantern in hand, he dismounted, dragging his horse forward.

"Oh, Goddess, no! I beg of you, please, in all your mercy! Not my girls! Not my son!" he cried, falling to his knees.

A jar of pickles lay shattered on the ground, the fragments spread out around Aly's drenched and muddy shoe.

CHAPTER

12

†

"Let go of me!" Otlee cried, clenching the reins for dear life while Dubric's horse barreled through the night. He straddled the charger's neck but the ghost was sitting on Dubric and clinging to Otlee, half strangling him.

The creature had chased them through Tormod, up streets and down alleys, the tentacles and strings snapping at the edges of Otlee's vision, but Otlee had driven the horse to the river and the spectre hadn't followed.

At least he thought it hadn't followed.

He rode back to the road, and north, galloping as fast as he dared through the hailstorm. Dien's in-laws' farm lay somewhere ahead. It might not be safe, but if Dien was there, or Sarea and the girls, he could get help.

Lars was there, too, surely. They'd received no word nor heard any rumors that he'd gone missing. Maybe Calum had left something at the farm, marking the map as a reminder. Maybe Braoin had gone to get it and had disappeared after.

Maybe the red-eyed man had simply snatched Braoin from his life and the map meant nothing at all.

A flash of light and thunder boomed overhead, making Otlee cry out. He looked around him, expecting to

see red eyes and yellow teeth, but he saw only farms
and the familiar shape of a big man, far ahead, on a
horse.

"Dien!" he called, urging the horse faster, but his
voice was lost to wind and thunder. Another flash and
Dien was gone.

"No, no, *no!*" Otlee cried, alone in the storm once
again.

He reached the place in the road where he'd seen
Dien and he reined up, Dubric's horse snorting and the
ghost nearly choking him. Otlee stared at the mud and
waited for another flash of lightning.

There! Hoofprints.

Otlee kicked the horse and charged to the west,
down a narrow lane winding through a stretch of trees.
The landscape opened before him, revealing a sloping
valley and farms nestled along the lane with fields and
barns and grazing sheep.

A horse stood untied before the third house, a big
horse with familiar tack: Dien's gelding.

"Almost there, sir," Otlee called back, turning toward the farmhouse. Windows blazed with lamplight
and the front door stood open, spilling illumination
onto the porch. Otlee rode to the steps, jumped from
the saddle, and ran through the door.

He saw a worn and cluttered sitting room that
opened to a kitchen, with Dien, his wife, and an old
man arguing near the cupboards. Dien was dripping
wet and furious. Sarea was crying and clutching a
muddy shoe.

Dien said, his voice low and dangerous, "What do
you know about the kids?"

"I rammed 'em up the ass! I already told you! You
saw! You were there!" Devyn cackled and yanked a dish

from the cupboard, dashing it on the floor. "Broken children, broken lives. Why can't you see? It's all the wood colt's fault."

"Stop calling Lars a wood colt! He's not a bastard, and he would never hurt Jess and Aly," Sarea said, frantic.

"Stop it!" an old woman cried. She rushed from a hallway and hurried to the old man.

"How did you know he was adopted?" Dien asked, so soft Otlee barely heard. "I've never told a soul. Not even the boy."

Sarea looked between the two men, her mouth working but no noise coming out.

"I know what I know!" Devyn said, his face turning red. "And the wood colt's doing this! I saw him, damn you! I saw him follow his murdering father! Rabbits and wasps! Why can't you see?"

"Lars's father is Castellan Hargrove of Haenpar," Sarea choked out. "He's not here, and Lars hasn't hurt anyone."

Devyn laughed. "Goat piss. Tell her the truth. Tell her how you've sent your daughters into the storm with a nameless whoreson. And he's killed before, ain't he? You've chosen a killing bastard for your own daughter. Tell her."

Dien said, "It appears you already have. How did you know, damn you. How?"

Sarea gasped and shook her head. "No! It's a lie!"

But Otlee saw on Dien's face that it was true.

Devyn tapped his nose. "He reeks of filth, like before, like Stuart. Wood colt bastard stink in my house and my barn." He grinned. "They all do, you hear? All of 'em. They're dying for it, pegged up the ass, like before. Then they're fed to the filthy worms."

"Where are the kids, Devyn?"

Another dish burst on the floor. "I told you! I told you! I pegged them up the ass! Like Stuart! For Stuart! Damn you! You were there! You know! Now he's gone!"

The old woman rushed around them and stood in front of Devyn. "Stop it. Ye're upsettin' him."

"Upsetting him?" Dien snarled and lifted her, setting her aside. "Woman, you haven't seen upset."

Otlee felt cold rush past him and the wind freshened, blowing papers from the table. Scowling and holding down her skirt, the old woman turned toward the open door and took a single step, then she fell silent and stared at him.

"Dubric's hurt," Otlee said, his voice cracking as Dien spun around. "And I saw a black monster on the road."

"You've ruined it," Mama whispered. "Look at this, the black streaks. Look at what you've done."

He stared at his mother while rivers of rainwater poured off him and puddled at his feet like piss. The house smelled like her. Like soap and dried honeysuckle and old blood. "It was the worms. I didn't want to hurt your worms."

Her lips pursed to a thin line. "Don't you lie to me. I set you to a task and you failed. Just like always. A simple task, and what do you do? You make excuses. Just like when you wasted the old cloth. Just like when I had to send you away."

"But it's almost two skeins. And see how bright it is?"

"I can't use the dark streaks, not for the eyes, you know that. I've told you and told you. I only hope there's enough this time. I want to see him again. Don't you?"

He hesitated, unsure how to answer. He'd never met the Devil of the Reach, had never been blessed with his presence. Mama mistook his hesitation for denial and she stood, clenching the freshly dyed skeins. "You don't want to see him, do you? You don't care about what I want. What we need. You just want to play with your boys. Is that all you think about? Is that why you keep putting older boys on the list even though young ones make brighter dye?"

He shifted on his feet and stared at the puddle. "I bring you your thread, just like you ask."

"Yes, but what about the rest of it? Why do you have to . . . do those despicable things?"

He sniffled, wiping his nose on his sleeve. "I dye your thread. The more they suffer, the more they *hurt*, the brighter your thread is."

"So cut them," she said. "Beat them. Break their bones, their spirits."

"I do," he said, fidgeting. "Just like you want."

She shook her head and shuffled away. "Like *I* want, my backside. You disgust me, lusting after them like you do." She stopped and raised her head, then turned to stare at him. "You're not lying with your brother, are you? Not after all the trouble I went through to beget him in the first place."

Trouble you went through? You poisoned me, forced me to couple with you. He winced at the old memory. "He's my son, too, Mama, and no, I haven't."

"At least you did that right the first time," she muttered, turning away again. "I only had to lie with you because you'd failed with that crippled boy! You always fail."

His hands clenched as he let his breath out slowly. After the mistake with the Paerth brat all those summers ago, the boy's sister had left for the castle, for the Byr. Mama was furious when she heard that the vessel had been broken and the cloth ruined. Then, knowing that the Byr might return, she had decided to create a new vessel. She had poisoned him, stolen his seed, and before he had regained his senses she had packed him away on a river barge heading to the coast. He had stayed gone fifteen long summers.

He smiled. Oh, the young men he had enjoyed, the young men he had killed. He had taken a few, then moved on to take a few more. It had been a grand life, but Foiche and family had drawn him home again. After all, Mama needed her thread.

Mama hung the skeins on pegs. "If you'd do what I asked instead of playing with your prick all the time, the cloth would be done by now. You don't think of that, do you? You don't think of anything but your prick and poking those boys with it. That's all you think about, that's all you do. Nasty things."

"But they're my toys," he whispered.

"They're my dyers!" she snapped, slapping his face. "And you keep a civil tongue in your head, boy, before I snatch it away."

"Yes, Mama," he said. "They're your dyers and I'd best remember that."

"You'd best," she said, turning away. "And don't you come here again stinking of whiskey and blaming my worms. That's why your thread's bad. The whiskey and the nasty things you do. Why I let you dye at all is beyond me."

"Yes, Mama," he said, not really listening. The new fabric was nearly finished and it shone in the lamplight, red diamond eyes flickering, watching. Thread he had dyed. *All those boys,* he thought, licking his lips.

She started to wind the thread onto her shuttle. "You still pissing the bed, Tropos?"

He felt embarrassment on his cheeks. "No, Mama. I use the clip, like you taught me."

"You'd better," she said, shuddering. "It's disgraceful. Nasty. Pegging boys and pissing the bed. And to think I pushed you from my loins. Even worse, I let you back in."

"Yes, Mama." He remembered her loins. Even after eighteen summers, he remembered. Boys were better. Much better. Especially when they screamed.

She sighed and snipped the thread from the full shuttle, then sat at her loom. "We're getting close, I think. One more young dyer ought to do it."

"Why not two older ones?" he asked, hopeful.

"One young one," she said. "The older ones don't dye as well. With the Byr here we won't have time for two." She slid the shuttle across, settling the thread in the threshold, and looked back to him. "Don't disappoint me, Tropos. Not this time. It's too dangerous."

"Yes, Mama," he said, then he watched her make devil's eyes.

CHAPTER

13

†

The storm had passed, but Duric had not wakened. Dien had come and gone several times, searching for Lars and the girls without luck, and Sarea had long ago stumbled to bed.

Alone in a quiet house, with only a single lamp and Dubric's muttering and thrashing to keep him awake, Otlee sat reviewing Calum's papers and books. Braoin was dead, Lars and the girls were missing, and the elusive, definitive clue had to be within reach. It just had to.

He yawned, adding to his ever-expanding notes. Braoin, Calum, and Paol had spent more than the past two summers searching the Reach for connections between the missing boys. Calum had listed a timeline for the disappearances in his journal, along with the missing boys' names, home villages, and ages.

Dubric's initial guess had been accurate. Twenty-two missing, at Calum's last count, the youngest ten summers, the eldest twenty-three. Adding Calum, and Braoin, that brought the total to twenty-four, the same number Dubric had counted.

Otlee frowned. But Braoin had not been dead then, so Dubric was off by one. Did that matter? Did it mean anything? Was it an inconsequential error? A meaningless mistake?

He looked up at the crunch of heavy footsteps on the porch. Dien trudged in, brushing rain off his cloak, and after tossing it aside he fell into a chair. "I've looked up and down that frigging road, but there's nothing. Not one frigging clue. The rain took it all." He rubbed his short-shorn hair. "How's Dubric?"

Otlee shook his head. "No change."

"Dammit!" Dien sighed heavily and leaned his head back on the chair. "How are you? You sure that thing you saw didn't hurt you?"

"Yeah, I think so." Otlee felt tears sting his eyes, but he ignored them. Without Dubric and Lars making decisions or offering alternative theories, their team seemed diminished and shattered. *That thing gutted us,* he thought. *I just take notes and Dien makes sure Dubric's decisions are enforced. Dubric and Lars do most of the investigative work. What in the seven hells are we going to do?*

"I'm going to try to take a nap, go out again in a couple of bells," Dien said, standing. "Try to get some rest."

"Yeah," Otlee said, returning to his research.

He'd heard Dien snoring for quite a long time, and his own eyes had grown dry and tired, when he suddenly sat straight and stared at the copy of Haconry's ledger.

"That's it," he said aloud. "The devil's eye!"

20-LN Devil's Eye Silk (red/black diamond pattern) 672CR

"Haconry paid six hundred and seventy-two crown for twenty lengths of Devil's Eye silk! I did it! I figured it out!"

No longer sleepy, he added the information to his own notes, then looked for Calum's map.

He couldn't find it in Dubric's bags or his own, nor was it in Dubric's cloak pockets or in his tunic.

"Oh ding, oh choke it," Otlee said, rabidly searching through their gear a second time. No luck.

"It has to be here, it has to!" He dumped the saddlebags and rooted through the contents. "All those diamond eyes, but where were they? How can we find out what they mean without the map?" Otlee's hands shook and he crouched on his knees, tearing at his hair. "I have to find it!"

He stood and looked out the window to clear skies and an approaching dawn, then turned to look at Dubric. "What should I do, sir? What in the seven hells should I do? I can't let Lars die!" Frantic, he scratched a note and snatched up his cloak.

Dubric slept on, oblivious, while Otlee ran out the door.

Startled, Dubric sprung from the settee as a dead, bleeding face leered at him and stuck out its tongue. The crippled ghost fell onto a clutter of books and notes and returned his tongue to his corpse mouth. Dubric did not see or feel any other ghosts.

That ghost will be the death of me. Dubric fell back to the settee and tried to catch his breath. *Where am I?* he thought, looking around. *Did Otlee find shelter or did someone find us?*

He heard footsteps and stood, sagging with relief as he saw Fynbelle enter the kitchen.

"Oh! You're awake," she said, wiping at her red nose. "I'll wake Dad."

"Thank you," he said, relaxing and rubbing his aching head. Lars's gear waited in the corner; Otlee's pack stood beside it, while books, notes, and other gear lay strewn about.

Dien lumbered down the hall, pulling on his shirt as he walked. "Sorry I overslept, sir, but we'd best get going. Is Otlee readying the horses?"

Confusion gnawed at Dubric's belly. "Where are we going?"

Dien sat and yanked on his boots. "Didn't Otlee tell you? The kids are missing, have been since last night, and he saw some dark, naked creature in the storm."

"I have not seen Otlee. What naked creature? Who is missing?"

Dien stared at Dubric with fear creeping over his face. "Lars, Jess, and Aly are gone, and what in the seven hells do you mean you haven't seen Otlee? He was here when I lay down for a nap. He told me about a dark, naked man with red eyes and strings coming from his mouth. Said he was part of the storm. It sounded like nonsense, but it scared the boy to death."

The familiarity of the description turned Dubric's bowels to water. The Devil of the Reach had shunned clothing when wielding his dark magic, and as little more than an animated corpse, he had indeed been darkly colored with red, dead eyes. *Foiche? By the King, I killed that murdering bastard decades ago.* Dubric stood, ignoring the arthritic creak of his knees, and reached for his boots. *He is dead. I buried him myself. We killed the moths, the worms. Destroyed everything.* "Lars is gone? Where? How? And Otlee, too? Where did he see the spectre? Did he say anything about moths or worms? Black and red cloth?"

"Oh peg," Dien growled, scrambling for the door. "No, sir, nothing like that. Maybe he went to the privy or the barn or—"

"Otlee wasn't here when I got up, Dad," Fynbelle said. "That was a bell or more ago. I haven't seen him at all."

"Shit!" Dien ran through the door, calling Otlee's name.

Otlee walked along the riverbank, trying to keep to the grass and limit the mud on his boots. No sign of the map, but if it had fallen in the river it could float all the way to the sea.

He found churned mud, where Dubric's horse had scrambled down the bank the night before. Humming, he followed the trail back to the road and into Tormod, passing a greeting nod with a carpenter and a cart of workers.

In town, he tried to remember where he'd ridden the night before, but he saw few familiar features other than benches before a stage and a sign advertising events for the festival. Everything else had been lost to the night and the storm. Praying he'd find the map before it was too late, he began a systematic search of roads and alleys.

"He's not in the barn, sir, nor Dev's shop, or the coops."

Dubric ran up the hill, frantic, as a cartload of workers rumbled into the yard. "Or the privy, the sty . . . Where would he go? Why would he leave?"

Devyn grinned at him. "Boys don't leave. You know, you see what's left!" He pointed at Dubric and spat. "Ruined boys and ruined lives. Taken and kilt and left to follow you. And for what, eh? Just so the devil can see?"

"I'm sorry, sir," Dien said, lumbering up to them. "He talks nonsense most days."

He knows I see ghosts? "Maybe it is not nonsense," Dubric said, slowly approaching Devyn.

The ghost ran in his awkward gait through the coop and up to Devyn. Devyn grinned and knelt, whooping, "Stuart!" He fell to his back and laughed, wrestling with the boy.

That is Stuart? Still? After all these summers? And Devyn can see him? Dubric pursed his lips and knelt near Devyn. *We have not caught Stuart's killer, Foiche is loose, and Otlee is gone!*

Dien trudged over and dragged Devyn from the ground. "Quit pitching your damn fits."

His face contorted in fear, Stuart bolted, disappearing into the house while Devyn mewled and wailed, cowering.

"Let him go," Dubric said.

As Dien released him, Devyn fell screaming to the ground. He reached for Dubric. "They took Stuart once. Can't he stay? Why can't he stay?"

Dubric knelt beside him. "Do you know where the children are?"

Dev shook his head. "The wood colt got 'em! The devil sees!"

"It's just raving nonsense, sir."

Dubric grabbed Devyn by the shirt and shook him. "Where? Where does he take them?"

"Up the ass! He took Stuart and pegged him up the ass!"

"Damn you, I know he molests them! Where are my pages?"

"The wood colt knows! Not me, not I, not the eyes I have."

"Rats' whiskers," Dubric snapped, shoving him away. "I do not have the time nor the temperament to indulge in this." He turned and stomped to the horses. "Where did Otlee see that black corpse?"

"Near the Tormod bridge. It chased him most of the way here," Dien said. "But, sir, when Devyn said the wood colt molested Stuart, you said you knew? Knew what? How?"

Dubric paused to look his squire in the eye. "The man stalking the Reach kidnaps boys, molests them, then kills them. Otlee and I examined the bodies of two young men, both tortured and violently raped."

"No," Dien said, sagging. "Not our boys, not my girls."

"He does not harm girls," Dubric said, climbing onto his horse. "That gives me great hope that your daughters are safe."

Dien mounted and reined his big gelding about. "But our boys?"

"We will find them. We have to. There is no alternative." Dubric kicked his charger in the belly and galloped to the road.

Otlee yawned as he left the peddler's cart. A bag of candy in his pocket and a bottle of tonic in his hand, he turned left and passed Haconry's housekeeper hurrying to the store with a basket over her arm. He wished her good morning and she replied in kind, though she seemed distracted. Intent on his quest, he sipped his tonic and searched along the street, behind barrels, in ditches, and between buildings.

He queried the butcher, the advocate, the undertaker, and the sheriff, asking them and others if they'd seen a big piece of parchment lying in the mud. None had, but he refused to give up. He had lost it; therefore, it was his responsibility to find it.

The weight of two dozen ghosts fell hard behind Dubric's eyes like sharp and deadly ice as they approached the cemetery gate. He held on to the saddle while his head threatened to burst open, and he wondered again what made his ghosts arrive and depart so unexpectedly. They appeared suddenly in the road, transparent and thinning in the breeze. A new ghost stood among them, with paint flecks on his hands and blood streaming from his anus and chest. He resembled Maeve, with dark hair and eyes and a similar shape to his mouth. Dubric closed his eyes as he rode through Braoin and waved off Dien's concern.

"There's a constable in Tormod," Dien said, "but he wasn't much help last night."

"Perhaps my presence will expedite matters," Dubric said. He rubbed his aching eyes furiously, trying to ease the pressure of the ghosts tugging upon them. Some departed but many remained, the empty, aching weight of the dead pulling on his soul.

Lars stared at a thin blue line, a mere thread of color in the otherwise endless black. Jess lay on the floor beside him, her lower back and hip warm against his leg, but the rest of her lost to the dark. Aly, however, had sprawled over him, her knee digging into his bladder and her arms wrapped around his neck. She snored, little congested rumbles, and drooled on his chest.

Was it morning yet? Could he dare hope the dark monster was gone?

He dozed. He had no idea if the latch had rattled ten minutes or ten bells before. He saw only endless black and a single promise of blue. Like the dark, it seemed steadfast and unchanging, neither brightening nor darkening.

He decided that it must be moonlight on the door; surely sunlight would be golden, not blue. He leaned his head back and closed his eyes, moving Aly enough to get her knee off his aching bladder.

He yawned, shifting in his corner, then his eyes flew open.

Aly was gone.

His heart hammering, he reached through the dark for her, but found nothing but his dagger beside his leg and the pennant they had used as a blanket. No Jess, no Aly. Only the blue light remained.

"No!" he cried, lurching to his feet. "Jess! Aly!"

"We're right here," Jess said from somewhere beyond his reach. "Aly had to pee. We didn't want to wake you."

Lars fell against the wall and tried to settle his heart. "Thank the Goddess."

Movement, a stumble, then Jess touched his arm and chest. "We decided to eat Kia's pastries, too. Want one?"

He almost laughed, reaching for her, his hands stumbling over her arms. His girls were fine. "Sure."

"Wish they were caramel," Aly said.

He found Aly's face, the top of her head, her back,

and he knelt to lift her. "Wake me next time, all right? You scared the daylights out of me."

Jess pressed a crumpled pastry into his free hand. "Speaking of daylight, when can we go home?"

"How long do you think we've been in here?"

"Forever," Aly said.

Jess laughed, and Lars felt her bump against his arm. "I honestly don't know. All night? A couple of bells?"

"Forever," Aly insisted.

Lars took a bite of his pastry. "Did you hear anything outside?"

"Not since that thing left, no. And that seemed like a long time ago."

But is it long enough? Lars finished the pastry and set Aly on her feet. "I'll open the door and check, but I want you girls to stay back here, where it's safe."

"All right," Jess said. "But be careful."

He searched with his feet until he found his dagger. Settling it in his hand, he followed the wall to the door and grasped the latch. "Ready?"

"We're ready," Jess said.

He took a breath and opened the door a crack, then pulled it wide, his breath falling out in a rush.

Aly squealed, and he turned back to make sure that the girls were all right. Morning sunlight flooded his eyes, temporarily blinding him, but after a moment he could make out Jess clutching Aly to her while covering her own eyes with her hand. Both were filthy, mud-spattered, and rumpled, but he doubted he had ever seen anything as wondrous in his life.

"Let's go home," he said, walking to them while golden light streamed through the open door.

*   *   *

Dubric followed Dien into the constable's office.

"You again," the constable said to Dien, leaning back in his chair. "I've already told you. This has happened before; there's nothing I can do. I can't afford to waste time and men on a needless search, especially on worship day." He glanced up at Dubric's entrance and added, "I'm sorry for your loss."

Dien loomed over the constable's desk, shuddering, Alyson's muddy shoe clenched in his fist. "You have to assign me men. Someone. Anyone. We have to find my children."

The constable looked at Dien as if he had heard the story a thousand times before. "Mister Saworth, please."

"I told you, sir," Dien said, turning to Dubric. "This piss-for-brains won't do a frigging thing to help me."

"The dark took them," the sheriff said, standing. "There's nothing I can do."

Dubric's breath caught and he tasted bitter bile. *No. Not my boys. Not yet.* Three ghosts stared at him, battered and bleeding, and he refused to accept that Lars or Otlee might soon join them.

He brushed past Dien and glared at the constable. "What is your name?" he snapped, pulling his notebook from his pocket.

The constable's eyes narrowed as his chin raised. "Glis Sherrod, Constable of Tormod. Who the seven hells are you?"

Dubric stared the man in the eye. "Dubric Byerly, Castellan of Faldorrah. I do recommend, Constable, that you offer this man whatever aid is at your disposal."

Sherrod barked a laugh then sat again, leaning back in his chair. "I will not waste nor risk men to the dark, sir. What it takes it does not return. His children are gone. I feel for his loss, but I can't—"

"You don't feel a single frigging thing," Dien snapped. "I spent most of the damned night looking for them, and you refused to help me. Well, it's daylight now, you worthless coward, and they're still missing, so you'd better get off your scrawny backside and find some able-bodied men to help me, or I'll feed your wretched carcass to the crows."

"Don't threaten me."

"Fine," Dubric said. "Then I shall. Aid this man or I will arrest you on charges of treason."

"Treason? Pah." Sherrod leaned forward again. "I'd heard you'd come to the Reach at last. Lord Castellan Dubric finally deems a few missing peasants worth his time and is wandering the Reach asking questions. I'll answer your questions, old man. It's actually very simple. The dark comes and takes a child, and they don't come back. Mystery solved. Now get out of my sight."

"Have you bothered to look for evidence of kidnapping? Of murder? Of anything at all?"

"My lord, after nearly three summers of this, I know what's left to find. Nothing, that's what. No bodies, no weapons, no footprints or clothes. Nothing." Sighing, he leaned back in his chair. "You're wasting your time here. The dark doesn't give back what it takes. Ever. And it's a waste of time and energy to try to change it. There is nothing treasonous about accepting the truth."

Dubric snapped his notebook closed. "How do you retain your position with such an attitude? Do you not care about your people? Those innocents you have sworn to protect?"

Sherrod jumped to his feet and banged a fist on his desk. "I can't protect them from the dark. I am only one man, and there's nothing I can do once they're gone."

"It is not the dark, you fool," Dubric said, turning away. "A man takes them. A mortal, fallible man. He tortures them, then he kills them. I will find him or die trying. He will not take my pages from me, or Dien's daughters from him."

Dien following, Dubric stomped outside and fumed.

Dien blew his nose, his rage and grief thundering all around him. "What do we do, sir? How can we find the kids?"

Dubric reached for his horse. "I am positive that the children are all alive. That gives me great hope. You found the shoe on the road, so we know that Lars and the girls left Tormod. Perhaps they found a place to hide from the storm, after all."

"How can you be sure of that?" Dien grasped his own horse and climbed into the saddle. "How can you know they're all right?"

Dubric regarded him with an even gaze. "I know they live. Beyond that I have no certainties. Take hope in that, please, and show me where you found the shoe. It is the only clue we have."

Tears glistening on his cheeks, Dien nodded and climbed on his horse. He kicked the gelding in the belly and galloped from the village.

They reached the broken pickle jar and Dien dismounted, letting his reins fall to the mud. "I found it here, sir. Last night."

"During the storm? Before Otlee arrived?"

"Yes, sir."

Dubric examined the scene, circling it while his gaze landed where it would. Muddled footprints washed away by the storm, puddles of water and ruined pickles, all set sparkling by shards of glass. He stood and looked about, gauging the distance to town. "How much farther to the farm?"

"Mile or so," Dien said, pointing down the road. "We're roughly halfway."

Dubric frowned at the curve of the temple roof peeking from behind trees. "Faced with a sudden storm, would Lars turn back, this close to home?"

"No, sir," Dien said. "If the distances were similar, he'd head for home, especially with the girls. He wouldn't turn back."

"Let us walk it, then, shall we?" Dubric led his horse around the broken glass. "We can be certain that they arrived here. Let us assume that they continued after the jar had broken. That Lars would press for home instead of retreating to town."

Dien sighed and ran his hand over his head, but nodded. "I've been up and down this road a dozen times thinking the same thing, but all right. We can walk it again."

They worked their way down the hill, checking both sides of the road and looking through the brush, brambles, and dead weeds while the ghosts followed. Dubric paused near the cemetery entrance to remember an old friend. "I never thought I'd see that stone hare again," he mumbled, closing his eyes. "By the King, it seems a lifetime ago."

He walked on, his eyes scanning the ground, and said, "I see footprints! Boots and a girl's shoes, coming from the cemetery."

"What?" Dien cried, running to him. "Where?"

They looked at the trail and Dien fell to his knees, laughing. "He found shelter, the closest he could. Damn that boy."

Lars is all right. Praise the King. Dubric smiled in relief and patted his squire's back. "Of course he did. I would have expected nothing less."

Dien leapt to his feet and followed the trail, weeping. After a few steps he climbed onto his gelding.

Dubric mounted his own horse and followed Dien down the road. Near the bottom of the hill, Dubric clenched the reins and gasped.

"Sir? What's wrong? It's the second time you've stopped here."

Dubric took a cleansing breath and blinked, shaking his head to loosen the unexpected airy sensation. "Nothing. Never mind about me." Braoin, Calum, and the unnamed pacing lad had gone, leaving only Stuart to flicker in the road. He grinned at Dubric, then ran ahead in his awkward, crippled gait.

Lars opened the porch door to see Otlee's pack lying open beside the settee and Dubric's drenched saddlebags. Their disheveled appearance and strewn contents worried him.

Sarea staggered over to them and pulled all three into her arms. "Thank the Goddess! Oh, Jess! Aly! Everyone's out looking for you kids." She kissed her daughters, then looked Lars straight in the eye. "And bless you, boy. Goddess bless you." She soundly kissed his forehead and hugged him tight.

"There was a storm," he said, blushing, "and a man . . . a thing . . . on the road."

"He was real scary," Aly said, hugging her mother's skirts.

Sarea held them all, marveling at their presence, while Kia and Fyn tugged on them. "Where were you?" Sarea asked.

"The crypt," Jess said. "Lars knew just what to do."

"It wasn't like that," he said, crushed beneath hugs. "There just wasn't anywhere else to go."

Sarea wiped her eyes. "The crypt's locked."

"Uh-uh," Aly said, grinning. "Lars showed me how to unlock it. I did it all by myself."

Jess shook her head and smiled. "During the day, silly. Last night, in the rain, Lars unlocked it. Even with that man right behind us." She shuddered, shaking her head.

"But you kids are all right?" Sarea asked, looking them over and hugging them again.

"We're fine, Mam. But I broke the jar of pickles."

"And I lost my shoe. And Lars got scratched."

Sarea looked to Lars last and held his face in her hands. "Pickles and shoes I can replace, scratches will heal. But you brought my girls home safe. Thank you, Lars. Thank you. Dien and Dubric will be so relieved when they get back."

He shrugged, forgetting all about Dubric's and Otlee's bags. "All in a day's work, ma'am." He stepped back, embarrassed, and nearly stumbled over Fyn. "And I'm behind on mine. I'd best get to feeding the horses before Dien has my hide."

Shaking his head, he glanced at them with a whisper of a smile on his face. Content, he opened the door and headed to work.

He walked to the barn, smiling despite himself. It felt good to be home.

The ewe had birthed a pair of coal-colored lambs; he fed her before continuing to the horse stalls. Dien's gelding was gone so he mucked that stall first, filling the feed bin with grain and replacing the bedding with clean straw. That done, he saw to his mare, leading her out and tying her to a post. She favored her right front.

"Ho, girl," he said, kneeling beside her. "Whatcha got there?" He lifted her right forehoof, then reached into his pocket for his file. "Just a stone. We'll get it out of there." Dubric insisted that his pages carry their files at all times. Slim and flat, with a small hook sharpened in the tip, it was a useful tool. Lars slipped it beneath the mare's shoe to wriggle the wedged-in bit of white into his palm.

A tooth, slightly bloody, with a bit of flesh still attached. *By the Goddess, is it human?*

"I told them! I told them!" Devyn screeched. "I didn't peg you up the ass! No!"

Startled, Lars stood, shoving the tooth in his pocket, and stared at the old man from over his mare's back. "What did you just say?"

"Ha-ha! Not you, not my granddaughters!" The old coot danced a little jig, tossing his half-finished hat in the air, then tottered toward Lars, swaying from post to post. The mare stepped away from him, prancing nervously. Oblivious, Devyn tapped Lars on the chest, his breath a cloud of noxious fumes. "Ha! You saw him, didn't you?"

"Saw who?"

"The bastard, the Devil of the Reach!" Devyn leaned close and asked, "My granddaughters? Did they see him, too?"

Lars nodded, slowly. "Yes, sir, they did. But they're fine. I brought them home just fine."

"Ha!" Devyn patted Lars on the chest again and grinned, his breath whistling between the gaps in his rotting teeth. "And Stuart? Did you find Stuart? He's gone again."

Lars took a hesitant breath and shook his head. "No, sir, I didn't. I'm sorry."

"Damn that bastard!" Devyn grabbed Lars's shirt and shook him. "Why not? Why the bloody hells not?"

"Let him go, Dev," Dien said from the door.

Devyn's eyed rolled, rheumy and blue, toward the big man stomping toward them. "See. I told you."

"I told you to let him go."

Devyn backed away, muttering, then fled to his workshop.

Lars watched him leave, turning back only to be crushed in Dien's embrace.

"Thought I'd lost my girls, pup," he said, shaking. "And I thought I'd lost you."

"I gave my word," Lars said, choking out the words and struggling to draw another breath. "It never touched them."

"So I hear." Dien released him and took a step back. "Damn, you're a sight for sore eyes."

Lars nodded. His eyes stung and he didn't trust his voice.

"Jesscea said you were scratched by the man chasing you. May I see the wound?"

Lars looked up, astounded, to see Dubric standing behind Dien. Lars wiped his eyes with the back of his hand. "Damn, Dien, it wasn't so big of a catastrophe you had to fetch Dubric."

Dubric looked him over head to toe, raising an eyebrow at his filthy, damp clothes. "Otlee is missing, and he, too, saw the black man before he disappeared. The scratch? May I see it, please?"

Otlee's gone? Lars turned his back to Dubric and pulled down his collar. "The thing that chased us was a large, dark man, naked and pitch black, with glowing red eyes. He had strings coming from his mouth and winding round his hands, and he was made of smoke. I know that sounds unbelievable, but that's what it looked like. I'm not sure if a string touched me, or if he did, or if he had a weapon of some sort. Whatever it was, it stung. Do you think he took Otlee?"

Dubric touched the wound, pushing Lars's head down to get a better look. "Did you see any insects? Black moths, perhaps?"

"No, not then, not in the storm. What happened to Otlee?"

Dubric's fingers paused, pinched, then pulled away. "There you are."

"Ow!" Lars winced and turned back to them, rubbing his neck. Dubric held a tiny red grain between his fingers. "What's that?"

Dubric squinted at the bit of red then crushed it, smearing it into blood-colored goo on his fingertips before wiping them on a post. "A noxious little worm. You mentioned you saw an insect?"

"Yes, in the crypt, yesterday afternoon. It wasn't black, though. Just a plain white moth tangled in some thread. Are you going to tell me what happened to Otlee?"

Dubric opened his notebook and licked his pencil. "Byreleah Grennere's crypt? You entered it yesterday?"

"Yes, sir. Twice. Once just to see it, then later to get away from that strange man and the storm. Why? Did something I did hurt Otlee?"

"No, of course not," Dubric said, starting his notes. "Tell me about the moth first, then the man who chased you."

Lars rubbed the back of his neck, then began his tale.

"Found it!" Otlee grinned and rolled the map tight as he walked past the alehouse. He'd searched alleys and gardens, rooted behind refuse bins, even looked in drainage pipes, but he found the map precisely where it had fallen, beneath Dubric's bedroll near the Tormod River bridge.

Relieved, he slung the sodden bedroll over his shoulder and stuffed the map in a case as he walked. He jumped, his eyes growing wide as someone yanked him back and placed a stinking cloth over his face.

He kicked and tried to squeal. He dropped the map and his bag of candies as he struggled, but no one seemed to see him and he could not escape. His vision faded to red, then black, then he knew no more.

CHAPTER

14

†

Dubric followed as Lars and Dien argued their way across the barnyard. "Where are we going?" Lars asked.

"You're not going anywhere. That's an order," Dien said.

"Yes, I am! He's my friend, too."

Dien stopped, his head lowered, then turned to stare Lars in the eye. "And you, whether you like it or not, are my son. You could have died last night. That thing put a pegging bug in the back of your neck. What the hells does that mean? What if it was supposed to eat you from the inside or corrupt your mind or make you sick? What if it had touched the girls? What if you'd died?"

"He is right," Dubric said, catching up to them.

Lars stood his ground. "No, he's not. I have a duty. Responsibilities. You two can't just—"

"You are not going!" Dien growled, then turned and resumed his furious trek to the house.

Lars started after him, but Dubric grasped his arm. "Let him go, lad. Please."

"Dammit, Dubric, it's my fault! If that thing had taken me, maybe Otlee would be okay. I *have* to go."

Dubric grabbed Lars by the shoulders. "It is not your fault, and you must not get involved in this."

Lars shrugged off Dubric's grip. "Faldorrah first. You made me swear to protect these people, and I'll be damned if I'll turn my back on Otlee. He's part of my duty, too."

"Lars, listen to me. Please. The Wasp was a sick and demented mage who slaughtered countless innocents. I killed him once. If he has returned I will kill him again. But you will be a distraction. I may try to protect you when I must remain steadfast and unflinching. I cannot allow that weakness. The risk is too great."

"Then I absolve you of it. Let that giggling bastard try to touch me again. I'll leave his guts steaming in the pegging mud."

Dubric's voice fell soft. "He cannot be killed that way. You are young, rash, and justifiably angry. He can take that, pull it from you, use it against you. He killed thousands of my men in the war, Lars, thousands, by setting them upon one another. Only calm determination and unblinking focus can stop him. You have to stare a mage down to kill it. You have to be cold and unfeeling and oblivious to your own pain and loss. Any emotion—anger, fear, even love—will get you killed."

"I don't care," Lars said. "Otlee is my friend. I won't desert him."

"Yes, you will, because I am commanding you to."

"No. I can't, Dubric. I won't."

Dubric gripped Lars's shoulders again. "Yes, you will. Foiche could not reach you in the crypt, for it is a holy place, protected from his power and corruption. A sanctuary. Do you remember when you told me that Jess threw the moth away?"

Lars said, "Yes. It was just a dead moth."

"No, it was part of a holy spell. We put the moth

there to keep the Reach safe after we killed the body Foiche inhabited."

"What? You hate the Goddess. You'd never use a holy spell."

"I did not always despise her. I used her magic many times during the war. It was a simple but powerful spell. Foiche's spirit, like the moth, was caught and unable to escape, but Jesscea released him when she threw the moth to the wind. He is no longer contained, and he has touched you, marked you. He needs a host, a boy or young man to house his spirit, and someone in the Reach is helping him.

"Boys your age are being tortured, molested, and killed. Twenty-four ghosts, Lars! All marked and prepared, *weakened* for Foiche. I will not allow that to happen to you. I dare not. Time and focus are of the essence, no matter how many ghosts I bear, for the Wasp is free once again."

"What about Otlee?"

Dubric took a shaky breath. Only Lars knew the extent of his curse, but some truths were harder to face. "Otlee lives, for I do not see his ghost. I *will* find him. He will not die. But you are not ready to face a shadow mage, especially not one like Foiche."

"Why in hells not?" Lars asked. "I took the damned vow. I do my job. I'm going to help." Lars shook off Dubric's grip and started to stomp away, but Dubric's words stopped him.

"No, you are not. That is a direct order. You are going to stay here, on this farm, because I command you to."

"Dubric, please."

"No. You are too young, too headstrong, too unpredictable, and you are not ready to face a mage. Stay here. Stay safe. Do not leave the house between sunset and dawn without escort. Do not disobey me. Please. More than Faldorrah depends upon it."

Dien thundered to them, a scrap of paper in his hands. "Otlee left a note," he said, thrusting it at Dubric. "He went looking for some lost map."

Dubric read:

> Sir,
> I lost Calum's map but I will find it. It's our
>   only clue.
> I'll be careful.
> Otlee

Relieved, Dubric folded the note and tucked it in his notebook. *Why did he not see he is far more valuable than a map?* "He left of his own accord, praise the King, and is likely fine. But we must find him."

Lars said, "Then let me help, Dubric. Please."

Dien hugged Lars. "Help by protecting our family, pup. You keep them safe, you hear? There's no man I trust more than you."

Lars nodded, his eyes moist. "No one will touch them."

Dubric reached for his horse. "Foiche will not dare to approach you during the day; he will be too weak. But do not leave the house after dark if you are alone. Not for any reason."

Lars took a deep breath. "I want to go."

"I know," Dien said, turning his horse. "But you'll stay. We'll be back before you know it."

Dubric met Lars's pained gaze and held it. "We will find him," he said. "You have my word."

*   *   *

Dubric and Dien rode into Tormod to find a bustling town in the midst of its morning routine. They rode through every road and alley, searching for Otlee without luck. While several folks said they had seen him, none knew where he had gone. Dubric and Dien found no evidence of his intended destination, only preparations for the coming festival and people hurrying through their days.

While passing near the alehouse, Dubric pulled his charger short and leapt from the saddle.

"The frigging map," Dien said, his voice cracking.

Dubric picked up the case and looked up to his squire. Muddy parchment extended beyond the green-painted wood. "Yes, and Otlee was here," he said, his voice cracking as he picked a candy from the mud. "He was right here."

Dien dismounted and searched the area. "So many tracks, sir. People, carts, pack animals. Where do we start?"

Dubric looked up and saw the curve of the temple roof above the humble shops and homes of the village, the rounded shape mimicking a woman with child and symbolizing Malanna's gift of life. "Braoin had a friend named Paol," Dubric said, reaching for his horse again, "And Paol lives in the bitch's womb. We start with the pegging Goddess. She knows, somehow. She always does."

Dien looked to the temple and winced. "Will you manage, sir?"

"For Otlee, I will stare the bitch in the eye, even if it kills me."

Once past the final cluster of shops, Dubric said, "Why am I not surprised?"

A black carriage waited beside the temple steps;

Dien noticed Dubric's stare. "Sir Haconry's coach. I see that bastard's livery every time we come up here. Do you think he's involved?"

"Yes," Dubric said, guiding his horse to the carriage. "And he has touched Otlee in my presence."

"Where's that bastard you work for?" Dien called out.

Haconry's driver, a slight, slender man with graying hair, jiggled the reins nervously as Dubric and Dien dismounted. "He's not here, milord, but inside."

"Prayers in Malanna's church are at night," Dubric said, striding to the carriage. "It is difficult to pray to the cursed moon during the day."

The driver nodded. "I know that, milord, but it's business, not prayer, the master seeks."

"Our boy's missing and we're searching this frigging coach," Dien said, his hand falling to his heavy sword. "You can either stand aside and let us, or you can die right here."

The driver climbed down from the seat and hurried out of the way. Dubric yanked open the carriage door.

The carriage was decorated with opulent velvets and satins, all in shimmery black, with red piping and minute details. It stank of nutmeg and clove and tobacco. A small boy, perhaps eight summers old, lay sleeping on one seat. He woke with a start as Dubric entered the carriage.

"Who're you?" the boy asked, cowering away.

"Castellan Dubric," he said. "I need you out of that carriage."

The boy looked past Dubric to Dien and shook his head, his eyes growing wide.

"C'mon, lad," Dien said, holding out his hands. "Let's get you out of there."

"Can't," he said. "S'posed to stay right here."

Dubric lifted the boy. "We will not hurt you."

He handed the squirming child to Dien, then returned his attention to the carriage interior. He ripped down the fore bench's back to reveal a compartment full of decanters of liquor. The seat lifted away to expose a deep, wide box with blankets and a brazier. Cursing, he threw both cushions out the door and into the mud then dumped the contents of the boxes as well. Both boxes were solid wood and lined with silk. He found no secret compartments.

The rear bench's back pulled away easily, but the shallow box contained merely a sword and a spyglass. Dubric tossed both aside. The seat base refused to budge. He searched for a latch, a release lever, but found nothing.

He found nothing between the drawn curtains and beveled glass windows. No apparent doors in the carpeted floor or tufted fabric ceiling. And no discernable access beneath the rear seat.

He climbed down, grinding broken decanters and fine blankets into the mud, then strode to the rear of the carriage. The boot was locked from the outside and large enough to hold a boy, especially one as small as Otlee. "Break it," he said to Dien. "I want this open now."

"Then perhaps you should take the time to request access, my Lord Castellan," Haconry said. He strode down the temple steps, his silk clothes gleaming in the morning sunlight. "Tsk, tsk. I never would have believed that a man of your standing would embrace such rude and uncivilized methods. From genteel breeding to uncouth vandalism. How utterly tragic. I weep at the thought."

Dubric turned, his hands clenching. "What have you done with him?"

Haconry blinked. "Once again you have me at a loss, my Lord Castellan." He glanced at Dien before returning his smirk to Dubric. "Did you tire of the lovely golden boy? Even I would not have believed that you would prefer this bear over such a delight. Or were you too heavy-handed in his care? Perhaps he perished under your gentle hand?"

Dubric stared into Haconry's eyes and slowly pulled his sword. "Where is he? Tell me or I will leave your entrails in the mud."

Haconry laughed. "Ah, my Lord Castellan, you jest with me. If your boy is indeed missing and I had knowledge of his whereabouts, slaughtering me would serve no purpose. In fact, it would be a great hindrance. A man of your experience must realize that dead men do not divulge their secrets." He winked and added, "Alive, I do not divulge mine either, at least not to grown men."

He smiled, assessing Dubric from toes to brow and said, "It surprises me that you have misplaced the lad. He obviously adored you and your affections."

Oblivious to Dubric's fuming, Haconry turned his attention to the boy cowering behind Dien. "That precious child is entrusted to me. Return him."

"Do it," Dubric said through gritted teeth. "He has the law behind him in this instance, whether we like it or not."

While Dien seethed, Haconry motioned to his driver, who replaced the cushions. Haconry drew the boy to him and asked, "I can expect full reimbursement for the damages, can I not?"

"Open the boot."

"Alas, I cannot, for the key was misplaced some time ago, during a hunting expedition, I believe." He grinned and helped the boy into the carriage. "Several things were lost that night. Aah, such delightful memories."

He reached for the door frame, but Dubric grasped his shoulder and yanked him back to the ground. "Do not taunt me, nor tempt me further. There is little I would enjoy more than gutting you like the swine you are. Open the boot before I open your bowels. This dance is finished."

Haconry smiled, staring into Dubric's eyes. "The dance has barely begun, my Lord Castellan. You have no evidence against me, nothing but your ill regard for my dalliances, which, I assure you, are none of your concern. The Reach belongs to me, and I have never misplaced a boy in my care. Unlike you, I tend my pets gently and protect them from harm."

"Open the pegging boot," Dubric snarled slowly, his sword at Haconry's throat.

One eyebrow rose. "I have no key, as I told you. Your brute may break it, if you desire, but you will find nothing more than old gear."

"Do it," Dubric said.

Dien moved past them and pulled his sword. A few hard slams with the hilt in his fist and the lock broke. He pulled the boot open and looked to Dubric. "He told the truth, sir," Dien said, pulling a moth-eaten tent from the compartment. "A tent, cooking utensils, old blankets."

Haconry's gaze remained steady and cold. "Shall I send the list of damages to you or to your employer? You have left me without suitable transportation; I will be compensated for the inconvenience as well."

"Seek payment however you wish," Dubric said. Seething, he returned his sword to its scabbard then climbed the temple stairs, his ghosts' responsibility throbbing behind his eyes as if they beat upon his skull with their dead and rotted fists.

The temple loomed above them, passing judgment as always, but Dubric squared his shoulders and took a cleansing breath. "Let us get this torture behind us."

He hesitated before grasping the latch, expecting a jolt of some sort, but he felt nothing but the cold metal. By the King, he despised the Goddess, hated the stink of her temples, the blind fealty of her believers, but most of all he hated the fear tainting his mouth.

"I will not bow before you, no matter what plagues you set upon me." He gritted his teeth and pulled the latch, yanking the door open. His ghosts and their weight disappeared in a blink of white light.

Sunlight shone through windows around the base of the ceiling dome, the slanting rays illuminating white granite columns and rows of pews. The floor was tiled with white and gray granite, the fixtures were of polished nickel, and the air smelled faintly of evergreen. Far ahead stood an altar covered with an embroidered cloth; an unlit white candle stood upon it, waiting for the evening's services.

The metallic taste of fear in his mouth turned to the bile of disgust. After nearly fifty summers, so little had changed. Malanna's messengers demanded opulence borne upon the backs of the unwitting and easily misled. It sickened him.

Dien on his heels, Dubric strode up the main aisle, not caring that his boots tracked mud on the floor. Childishly, he wished that he had ridden his horse through the main doors and let it drop manure where whim took it.

They approached the altar, where Dien briefly knelt to draw the Goddess' symbol over his chest. Dubric turned his head away before he saw the meaningless and nauseating ritual. Having to breathe her stink was bad enough. "Get up, before I lose my patience."

"Yes, sir." They climbed the steps past the altar and up to the clergy's dais.

"Damn lazy fools," Dubric muttered, looking around. Three doors stood open; two leading to halls, the third to a cluttered office. "Anyone with sense would know we were here. I do not have time to dawdle while priests and friars scratch their backsides."

He took a deep breath and called out, "Is anyone here?"

A bird burst from a beam far above him, its wings beating against the streaming sunlight, but he saw no one, nor heard the movement of any people. Grumbling, he strode toward the closest door and leaned into the hall. "Damn you, is anyone here? I do not have all day."

"Sir?" Dien asked, wincing. "Are you sure cursing in the temple is a good idea?"

"They are lucky I do not burn it to the ground," Dubric muttered, striding across the dais to the other hall.

"Yes, sir."

"Hello, there!" Dubric hollered.

There was movement from behind, and Dubric turned to see an elderly friar hustling down the first hall. "Pardon me, milord," he gasped, out of breath. "I was indisposed. How may I serve you?"

Indisposed, my backside. Haconry likely sought to

purchase a boy from a temple-sponsored orphanage.
Dubric took a deep breath and let it slowly free. "I have come to speak with a young man named Paol. I was told I could find him here."

The old man scurried over, squinting through finger-smeared spectacles. "Yes, Paol is here. May I ask who seeks him?"

"Dubric Byerly, Castellan of Faldorrah."

He expected surprised obedience or perhaps humble respect, but instead the friar burst into a toothy grin and grasped his hand. "Milord Dubric! By the Goddess, sir, it's been a lifetime since I've seen you. I never thought you'd grace my door. Praise be!"

Dubric blinked, astounded. "Have we met before?"

The friar bowed slightly, then struck the pose of a foot soldier at attention. "Treacy Mannix, milord. I served under you during the war."

Dubric took a step back, his jaw falling open. "Mannix? By the King, you were barely a lad last time I saw you."

He laughed, nodding. "Aye, sir, that I was. Fourteen summers old and proud to bear your colors." He smiled at Dien. "Decide to show your son a bit of his history, sir?"

"Not precisely."

Mannix laughed, winking. "You wouldn't believe it, young man, but Lord Dubric was one of the fiercest knights I ever did see. Oh, the tales I could tell. Once, under cover of darkness, he rescued six soldiers taken prisoner by the enemy. They were scheduled to be executed, but Lord Dubric wouldn't hear of it. All alone he crossed a swamp and freed them, guiding them back through the swamp even though one had a broken leg. The enemy thought spirits had taken them."

"It was a broken arm," Dubric muttered. "And there were four men, not six."

Mannix didn't seem to hear. "And then there was the time we laid siege to a keep in Casclia. Darned driest dirt you ever did see, just sand and rock. And hot! Son, you haven't ever sweated as much as we did in Casclia. But your father there, after a phase or more of siege, decided enough was enough. He had us create a diversion, so most of our men were whooping and hollering at the gate while he and a couple of bowmen crept like spiders over the back wall. A few quick arrows, a slashed throat, and we were basking in the cool bathing pools by suppertime."

Dien chuckled, glancing at Dubric. "And to think all you've ever told me of the war were tales of your sore feet and arduous treks through the snow. This is much more interesting."

"War is not interesting," Dubric muttered. "It is merely long moons of walking, broken by a few bells of death and terror."

He looked at Mannix and frowned. "We jimmied a tower door, Mannix. We captured one guard and bribed another to open the gates. For King's sake, the siege had lasted nearly a fortnight. The people were half starved and ready to surrender by then."

"He's being humble," Mannix said, and leaned close. "The best one, though, the one I tell my grandchildren, is when we'd been fighting in the caves of Morant. Dankest, darkest places you can imagine. Full of nasty beasties that would rather eat you than give you the time of day. Deep in its bowels we faced an army led by Laoch the Black. They had us outnumbered three to one—"

"Two to one. At least get the facts accurate."

"Two to one, yes, sir, but what was worse . . ." his voice lowered to a whisper, "they had magic. Dark, evil magic."

Dubric remained silent but crossed his arms over his chest.

"We laughed at the odds and fought them anyway. Man to creature, sword to claw. We had right on our side and from the start the battle was ours, but Laoch's mage had other plans.

"He set the stones to trembling, trying to get the cave to collapse upon us, but Lord Dubric here, he walked right up to that mage, and let him have it. There he was, sparks flying everywhere, the very ground shaking and trembling in fear, but Lord Dubric laughed at that filthy mage and stared him in the eye. Killed him quick as a wink without care for his own safety.

"No man I ever met before or since would stand toe-to-toe with a dark mage. But your father did, yessir. More than once, if truth be told."

Dubric sighed and tried to will his frustration away. "He's not my son, but my associate, and it was my duty."

Mannix bowed stiffly. "Perhaps, milord, but every other general on the battlefields sent others to face the mages. You faced them yourself. Not once in the summers I served under your banner did you send a common man into harm's way while you remained safe. Not once."

Dubric sighed and rubbed his tired eyes. He had not intended to visit old memories. At least the ghosts had left him at peace.

Mannix bowed again. "And not once did you leave a

man behind. Common or noble born, we were all the same under the banner of the Cudgel."

Dien said, "You never told me why your banner was a cudgel and not a leaf."

Dubric clenched his fingers. "My men called me 'the Cudgel' because I would tolerate no chicanery. I was . . . blunt."

Dien smiled innocently. "You, sir? Blunt?"

Mannix chuckled. "Aye, milord, that you were. But you were fair. Always. A man of unquestionable character and faith."

Dien looked back and forth between them. "How many mages did you kill?"

"Seventeen."

"Pah!" Mannix said, shaking his head. "You're not counting the ones that died fighting your banner. More than half the mages in the northern territories fell to us. Surely they numbered closer to fifty. You led an army far better than most men swung a sword and should count the victories accordingly, milord."

Astounded, Dien stared at Dubric. "You killed seventeen mages? Yourself? You never told me that."

Dubric pulled his notebook from his pocket. "I did not come here to reminisce. May I speak to Paol, please?"

Mannix winked. "What'd I tell you? Straight to the point, just like I remember, and never taking a bit of credit for himself."

Smiling, he bowed to Dubric. "Right this way, milord, but Goddess, it is grand to see you again."

Dubric felt his cheek twitch into a reluctant smile. "Thank you. It is good to see you again as well."

Mannix led them down the first hallway. "I'd heard you'd become Castellan for Lord Brushgar all those summers ago, but I never understood why. The pair of you barely saw eye to eye on anything, and I always assumed you'd rule a province or even be crowned King."

Dubric tried not to glance at the religious tapestries on the walls. He knew what they depicted. Visions, and lies, of hope. "Assumptions change."

"I'd wager you got those scars battling a dark mage after the war ended. I'd heard that a few holed up here and there and were rooted out like vermin, many with dangerous traps to protect them."

"You would lose that wager. A common fire scarred my skin."

Mannix paused, looking at Dubric over his shoulder. "You, milord? No mage in the northern territories could touch you, yet a common fire forever marked your skin? How can that be?"

Dubric took a slow breath. "Because my skin burned."

Mannix took a step back, then turned away. "I do hope that my grandson isn't in any trouble, milord. He's a good boy."

Dubric rubbed his eyes and tried not to grumble. "I merely need to speak with him concerning the disappearances. He is a potential witness, not a suspect."

Mannix sighed, nodding. "I am forever thankful that I wake each morning to find him here. So many have vanished."

He knocked, then opened a door, spilling music into the hall. "Milord Dubric is here to speak with you. Tell him the truth, whatever it may be."

Dubric heard an affirmative grunt mixed amongst the melody as Mannix stepped away, leaving the door open.

A young man lounged inside, his clerical robes open

to reveal the tunic and hose beneath, and he lay upon an unkempt bed with his bare feet tapping on the wall. He held a worn and battered dulcimer against his belly, plucking the strings in a repetitive melody, practicing the same bit over and over. "Just a moment, all right?" he said without looking toward the door. "I've almost got these bars memorized."

Dubric said, "I was not aware you were a musician."

Paol nodded, his foot tapping along with the tones, then he set the instrument aside. "Hoping to be. Have to pass the entrance recital to be accepted at university, though." He rolled and sat, his feet on the floor once again. "So," he said, bounding off the bed and tying his robe. "What can I do for you?"

Dubric glanced at Dien, who closed the door. "As your grandfather mentioned, I am Dubric Byerly, Castellan of Faldorrah, and I understand you were an acquaintance of Calum Floret and Braoin Duncannon."

Paol stopped tugging on the laces, his dark eyes locked on Dubric's. "What did they do now? Did my grandfather send for you?"

"You tell me."

Paol sighed and fell upon the bed again, reaching for the dulcimer. "I don't know what muck they've told you, but it was all their idea, all right? I didn't want to do it. I swear."

"Which idea was that?"

He leaned back and groaned. "The church's birthing records. I know, I know, they're supposed to be private, but Bray and Calum can be very persuasive, you have to understand that."

Dubric sighed and rubbed his eyes. "May I sit?"

"Of course." Paol pulled a pile of laundry off the only chair and dropped it on the floor.

Dubric opened his notebook. "There are a few facts you may need to be aware of."

Paol winced. "That stealing from my grandfather's temple is a crime? I'm aware of that. I did it, but I swear to you it was their idea."

"Actually, the fact you might want to be aware of is that both Calum and Braoin are dead."

Paol looked back and forth between Dubric and Dien, his mouth working and his skin turning ashen. "Dead? Both of them? How? Why?"

"I had hoped you could tell us."

Paol raked his fingers through his hair and shuddered. "What do you want to know?"

"Everything. Start at the beginning."

CHAPTER

15

†

Paol stared at the floor, his hands on his head, and rocked. "I hadn't seen them for a few phases, sure, but we weren't scheduled to meet again until the planting festival. Oh, Goddess, they can't be dead."

"Please, you must tell me what you know. Let us start with Calum, all right?"

"No, you're wrong," Paol said, rolling back to lean against the wall. He drew his knees to his chest. "It starts with Braoin. He's the one that noticed the connections between the disappearances."

Dubric nearly snapped his pencil in two. "Connections?"

"Everyone seems to think that children are missing, but that's not right. It's just boys disappearing without a trace. The missing girls, some of them, have come home." He raised his eyes to Dubric. "With all the rivers around here, some get snatched by sailors. They have their fun and the girls, some of them anyway, come home. The boys never do."

"Go on."

"We—I mean Bray, Calum, and I—we thought that the rumors were wrong, so we asked around. Of the girls that disappeared, six these past two summers, all were lost along the rivers, in a town, and most during the day. Only one boy was, and his parents said he'd been talking for a long time about joining a boat crew."

He banged his head against the wall. "The rest of the boys disappeared after sunset. No one knew where they'd gone, or how they were taken, and none ever came back." He took a breath and stared at Dubric. "And now you tell me that Bray and Calum fell prey to this thing? Impossible. They knew the patterns, the places. They weren't that stupid."

"Braoin disappeared several days ago, and I pulled Calum's corpse from the river the day before yesterday. Tell me what you know of patterns and places and how the killer chooses his victims."

"Calum wasn't the body in Barrorise. I heard a body had been found, and I went down to help drag it to town. That was Bray's friend Eagon. At least, I think it was. He was too decayed to know for sure."

Dubric sighed. *One more ghost with a name.* "Calum was found later, farther downriver. Do you know anything about Eagon? How he disappeared?"

"He disappeared like many of the others. Walking home."

"What do you know about him?"

"His folks live on a sheep farm somewhere near Myrtle, I think. I never met them. His lover, Loman, though, used to live in Wittrup, and Eagon often visited his mother to give her most of his pay. She's crippled, and after Loman disappeared she had no way to make money." He shrugged. "Eagon had a good heart and did everything he could for her. One night, he left Donia's place but never made it home."

"Loman? When did he go missing?"

"Mid-autumn, I think. Bray kept track of all the

missing for more than two summers. I can't remember for sure."

Dubric added to his notes. "And this Eagon, and Loman, they were lovers?"

"Yeah. Wittrup isn't the best place to raise a son."

"What do you mean?"

Paol winced. "There are only two ways for a boy to make money in Wittrup. Selling his back, or selling his ass. Letting sailors have a few minutes of skin pays better, and Loman needed money for his mother's medicine." He frowned and stared at the ceiling. "Eagon was born fey, but life made Loman that way. They got on well and never hurt anyone. Why should I care?"

"All right. Loman met sailors to make money to take care of his mother, and after he disappeared Eagon took over. Did Eagon sell his wares, too?"

"No. He had a regular job. Working for Jak the carpenter."

Dien shifted his feet and grumbled.

"As did Braoin, I hear," Dubric said, glancing back at his squire.

"Some, but not really. Bray never liked Jak, said he didn't use him enough. Even when Eagon volunteered to work with Bray, show him the ropes, Bray barely made a scepter after expenses."

"Why did Braoin not find other work?"

"Not much work to be had, here in the Reach, especially if you have no skills. There's no extra money for wages, anywhere. Everyone's poor. Most take what work they can get."

Dubric noted the information. "How did Braoin and Eagon meet?"

"Eagon's mam and stepdad raised sheep. Bray's mam weaves their fabric. They'd been friends since they were kids. Bray even taught Eagon to read. In fact, when Eagon turned up missing, it had him sweating, and not just because they were friends."

"Why was that?"

"Because Eagon borrowed a book from Bray, and his mother'd paid a king's ransom for it. He needed to get it back, but Eagon was just gone, and the book, too. Missus Maeve was furious."

"What kind of book?"

"I'm not sure, but I think it was about yarn. Something like that anyway. Might have been about weaving. Eagon was addicted to patterns, repetitions, connecting mathematical sets. There's a lot of mathematics to weaving, I guess. Eagon and Bray talked about it a lot."

Faythe had mentioned Eagon liked number patterns. "You mentioned before that the abductions were connected?"

"Yeah." Paol stood and pulled open a bureau drawer. "We all were trying to be extra careful when it was a dangerous night." He pulled out a scuffed and wrinkled scrap of paper and handed it to Dubric. "Those are the number of phases between disappearances, as best we could tell."

Dubric unfolded the paper and read a list of numbers.

$$1\ 2\ 3\ 4\ |\ 1\ 2\ 1\ 2\ 3\ 2\ 3\ 4\ 3\ 4\ 3\ 4\ 3\ 2\ 3\ 2\ 1\ 2\ 1\ 4$$
$$3\ 2\ 1\ |\ 2\ 3\ 4$$

Paol pointed to the tenth digit. "We didn't keep track until here. Bray mentioned the pattern after the fifth disappearance we'd tracked, and when we started asking about earlier ones, they fit, too. Bray gave us this list of numbers and it never missed a disappearance, not once, all these moons. He called the list 'the Devil's Eye.' Strange fellow, our Bray."

"He never explained why he called it that?"

"It's some mathematical thing, something about a diamond pattern that Eagon figured out. I never understood all of it. I mean, it's a list, right? Phases, not gems. And what does any of it have to do with eyes? Bray had his oddities."

Dubric noted the name Devil's Eye, and it tugged at his memory but did not match any recollection he could name, other than the Devil of the Reach himself. "Have you ever heard of Foiche?"

"Yes," Paol said, his brow furrowing. "Grandfather said he died in the war."

Frowning, Dubric stared at the list. "Never mind. The numbers in this Devil's Eye, they represent phases?"

Paol sat on the edge of his bed. "Yeah. Well, sort of. They're actually mid-phase. No one disappears on a phase, but in between. The fourth or fifth night, on quarter moons. We all knew not to be outside after dark on those nights. I can't imagine that Calum or Bray would make that sort of mistake."

Opposition to the Holy Days. The Nights of Shadow, Dubric thought as he added to the notes. "Where on the list are we now?"

Paol leaned forward and pointed to the paper, to the final 4 of the middle section and the 1 before it. "Here." He pointed, counting backwards, to the 1, the 2, and the 1. "Bray, Calum, Eagon." Paol drew his hand back. "Damn them. They knew! How could they have done this?"

Dubric thought of Lars. "Because young men think they are immortal."

"I've never thought that," Paol said, leaning back again.

"You mentioned locations. Is there a pattern to those as well? Does the pattern have anything to do with a map?"

"Those who have disappeared have done so after leaving a village. No one has disappeared in town, nor traveling from farm to neighboring farm. Calum kept most of the records, but boys have disappeared all over the Reach, even as far away as Harvath. We each had a map. They showed where we've found red-and-black cloth and if we've destroyed it. It's usually up in a tree or tied somewhere high. It's not always easy to get to."

"Who makes the cloth? Who puts it in the trees?"

"I don't know. Calum thought it was the same guy who's stealing boys. Bray thought it might be someone else. We never found anyone with the cloth or making it. Whoever it was, they were good at climbing trees."

"Do you know how many boys disappeared from each village?"

"No, not specifically. Most of the villages have lost at least one, and some area farms have reported missing sons. Tormod has lost the most. Six, I think. Calum kept track, not me."

Astonished, Dubric said, "Six young men in two summers? No wonder the Reach is so impoverished."

Paol stared at the ceiling, his chest shaking as his breath fell. "Yeah. And here I am. I'm marked, aren't I? The last of the three bastards."

"The what?"

He smiled sadly, his hands clenching against blankets wadded beneath his hips. "We called ourselves the three bastards. The best educated ne'er-do-wells in the Reach. We all had dreams. Bray and I were going to go to university, then bring our knowledge back. Calum intended to unseat Haconry. Together we were going to make the Reach into a place to be proud of, instead of the cesspool it's become."

"What about Haconry? What is his part in this?"

"I don't know, but it surely has to do with money. That's all he cares about. That and power."

"He was here earlier. Do you know why?"

"Yeah. He comes once a moon or so. He wants the church gone, but grandfather refuses to leave. He says someone needs to speak out against Haconry's sins."

Dubric paused, watching Paol carefully. "What of young boys?"

Paol regarded him with an uneasy stare. "You know about that?"

"How can the people let him get away with such atrocities?"

"Because they're weak."

"So it is true? People give him their children?"

"Yes. Some. Not as many as he might like, but there's always a fool or two who can't plan ahead. Haconry is a coward, an opportunistic wretch. He sees a weakness and he exploits it."

"How so?"

"Imagine a poor farm, nothing special, barely worth notice. The mother is a drunk and the father gambles away what money he gets. They farm enough food for themselves and their family, sometimes have a little extra, but come spring and fall, when taxes are due, they have no money to pay. It's all been spent on liquor and dice. Faced with debtors' prison, the loss of their farm, or the payment of a son, which do you think they'd choose?"

"I would choose prison before my son," Dien muttered.

Paol nodded. "As would most parents. Or they'd pack up and leave. But the Reach is full of fools. Haconry has created his own crop of children, and he farms them, picking the fruit as whim strikes." Paol sighed and stood. "At least, that's how I see it."

"Is it true that Calum was loaned to Haconry?"

"Yeah. He hated him for it. And he hated his mother, too."

"What about Braoin? What about you?"

"No, neither of us. Bray's mother is one tight-fisted woman. Good-hearted, but she doesn't flinch, if that makes sense. Haconry could never catch her at a loss. I don't know if he ever tried. If my mother hadn't died, I very well could have been one of his boys. But she did, and my granddad raised me. Haconry isn't stupid enough to openly challenge the church, or my grandfather." He shrugged. "Like I said, he's a coward at heart."

"Has Haconry tried to catch the kidnapper?"

"He sent a proclamation once, offering a reward, but that's all." Paol frowned and ran his hands through his hair, raking it into spikes. "I'm sorry I can't be of more help."

"Never you mind about that," Dubric said, standing. "You have been more help than you realize. If you think of anything else, please notify me as soon as possible. My page is staying with the Paerths, on their farm north of Tormod. He will be able to take your information, should the need arise."

Paol nodded. "Old crazy Dev. Yeah. Do you know if Bray ever talked to him about his missing son? From summers and summers ago? Bray seemed to think it was important."

"Stuart's killers were caught, a long time ago," Dien said.

Paol looked up at him, his brow furrowing. "Bray thought that one escaped, but now he's back. He thought Devyn might know why, not that the old guy ever makes much sense. Seeing your crippled son cut up and raped . . . I can't imagine staying sane after that, the poor bastard."

His thoughts churning over Stuart's elusive killer, Dubric packed away his notebook and thanked Paol for his insights. "In the meantime, remain here, in or near the temple, and do not walk about after dark, even on supposedly safe nights."

"I'm not leaving this room once the sun sets. I promise you that." Paol fell back on the bed and picked up his dulcimer. Frowning, he played a sad and lonesome tune.

"Lars! Wait!" Aly called from somewhere behind.

Worried, trying to not look at Otlee's things piled by the settee, Lars paused in the open door and turned to see Aly running toward him with a broken toy cart in her hands.

"Can you fix it?" she asked, fidgeting. "I found it broken."

"Sure thing. Let's see what you've got here." He knelt and accepted the toy, flipping it over to look at the underside. "You've snapped the axle, but I can make you a new one. There's plenty of scrap wood in the barn; I'm sure something will fit." He glanced up, looking at Sarea. "If it's all right with your mam."

Sarea stood, pushing away from the table, which was covered with hats and trims. "Of course it's all right." She rummaged through a box. "Have you seen my scissors?"

"Last I saw, they were with the ribbons," Lars said.

"That's what I thought." Sarea rooted through scraps, muttering about Dev moving things, as Fyn helped her search.

"Did you forget my cart?" Aly asked, her hands on her hips. She grinned at him and skipped through the door. He followed.

Once inside the barn, he lifted her and set her upon the workbench while he rummaged through drawers of old and rusted tools.

Aly said, "Can I ask a question? No one else'll answer me."

"Sure. Ask away." Lars found a small mallet and set it on the bench before resuming his search.

She sighed, banging her feet against the bench. "What's fey?"

He chuckled, shaking his head. "Why would you want to know about that?"

Bang, bang. A long pause.

He stood and looked at her, concerned. "Did something happen?"

"No. Yes. Sorta." Shrug. *Bang bang.*

"You going to tell me?"

She frowned, her lower lip curling in. "I better not."

He looked her in the eye. "If something happened, something bad, you have to tell. I'll help any way I can, I promise, and you won't get in trouble."

Hopeful, she looked up at him. "Promise?"

"I promise."

Bang bang, and her attention shifted back to the

broken toy. "Well, the other day, Kia said you were fey, like it was something bad, but I dunno what—"

Lars thought he might fall over in shock. "Kia said what?"

Aly looked up at him, suddenly timid. "That you were fey. But no one'll tell me what it means! You're not bad, are you? Even though you and Dad had a fight?"

"Your dad and I just disagreed about work stuff. It wasn't a real fight."

He took a breath, then another, before looking at Aly. "But you asked a question. I'll try to answer. First of all, fey means that a boy likes a boy. Kissing and stuff like that."

"Eww!"

He let his breath out and held her worried gaze. "And second, I'm not. I promise."

"Oh, good," she said, grinning.

"And third, I don't know whether it's bad or not. Some people think it is, some don't. I haven't decided. Don't you worry about me, all right? I'm not fey. I like girls. Kia mentions it again, you just tell her she's wrong. And your dad and I are still friends, I promise."

" 'Kay." *Bang bang.*

He found a set of grippers and reached for Aly's toy. "Any other big, dark secrets you need to let out?"

The banging stopped. "Well, um . . ."

He shook his head and tried to pry the axle from one wheel. "Let me guess. Kia says I'm afraid of soap or that I'm the reason Fyn's been sick. No, wait. I know! It's my fault it rained last night." The first piece slid free and he set the wheel aside.

Aly laughed. "No, silly." She giggled and her voice lowered to a whisper while her feet resumed banging.

"One of my sisters likes you, but I'm not s'posed to talk about it."

"Oh?" he said, hoping he didn't sound as concerned as he felt. He thought of Kia beckoning him into the bath chamber and his throat closed, cutting off his air. He stifled a shudder and reached for the other wheel, then he thought of Jess, laughing as they walked through town, and he smiled.

"Yeah."

Kia, no way, but Jess, that would be . . . great. But it's not Jess. Can't be. Can it? "I like all of your sisters, and I like you. You know that, don't you?"

"Well, yeaaah." From the tone of her voice, he was certain she was rolling her eyes, even though his attention remained on the wheel. "But I mean she *likes* you."

He didn't know whether to feel worried or terrified or utterly elated. *Let it be Jess. Let it be Jess.* "And you're not supposed to tell?"

Bang bang. "Nope. She'd kill me if I did."

He sighed, his hopes falling. *Dammit, it's Kia. Jess wouldn't threaten Aly. Would she? It's Kia. Has to be. She's calling me fey after I rejected her in the bath, hoping that I'll prove her wrong. What a mess.* Worried that the bath was only the beginning, he said nothing, even as Aly's banging foot stopped.

"I just did, though, didn't I?"

He nodded and winked at her, pushing aside his worry. If Kia tried something again he would just tell her, straight out, that he was absolutely not interested. "That's okay. It'll be our little secret. I promise." The axle pulled free and he reached for a split hunk of wood.

"So you're not mad?"

"Of course not." He pulled his page's file from his pocket, then wriggled the sharpened hook into a crack. He worked a long strip off and tossed the big hunk back into the scrap bin.

"And you won't tell that I told?"

He smiled at her and pinched his mouth. "My lips are sealed."

Bang bang. "You have any secrets?"

He laughed, whittling the strip down. "Of course. Everyone does." He tried it in the wheel—too big—and scraped off more.

Bang bang. "Like what?"

"Like if I told, they wouldn't be secrets." The axle nearly fit, so he set the first wheel upon the bench and gently pounded the axle in.

"But Laaaars!"

He threaded the axle through the bottom of the toy cart and scratched a mark where he wanted to cut it before pulling it out again. "But nothing."

"Please? Just one? I told you two!"

Chuckling, he cut off the excess axle. "I didn't know we were making a trade. I thought I was fixing your cart."

Bang bang, and a heavy sigh.

He whittled the end, trying the fit then whittling more. He hated to disappoint her. "All right. You win. One secret."

" 'Kay." She turned and sat cross-legged on the bench, her head on her hands, and eagerly watched him.

He threaded the axle through then pounded it into the final wheel. "I like being part of your family." Smiling, he spun the wheels and handed her the toy.

The toy set aside, she tilted her head. "What's the secret?"

He lifted her from the bench and set her on her feet. "That was the secret, silly."

"Oh." Unimpressed, she accepted the cart then graced him with a smile and a polite hug. "Thanks for fixing my cart. I like having you in the family, too."

CHAPTER
16

†

Dubric and Dien hurried from the temple and climbed onto their horses. "Braoin may have been right. One of Stuart's killers may still be loose," Dubric said. "The coincidences are too numerous to deny." *And I have seen his ghost. We have not brought his spirit justice.*

"Yeah, I'm thinking the same damn thing," Dien said. "Dev never made much sense, just crazy talk about a wood colt doing it. I've never gotten a name, a description, anything but his madness, but Stuart died eighteen summers ago. If it is the same killer, he's not a young man. He's in his mid-thirties, at least. My age."

"Perhaps older," Dubric said, guiding his charger from the temple grounds. "How many men are between thirty and sixty summers of age in the Reach?"

"Hundreds, surely," Dien said, "but clues never lead to everyone. Certain names have a habit of reappearing."

"That they do. You flinched while I questioned Paol about Jak the carpenter," Dubric said. "Why?"

Dien looked to the north. "He and a crew of boys are repairing the barn roof. At least two of his former employees are dead."

"And Lars is there," Dubric muttered. *I lose precious*

time riding back and forth between the farm and the village. Do I ride to question Jak? Or do I further examine Calum and Eagon's remains? How best can I serve Otlee? "We must talk to Jak," he said at last.

"Yes, sir," Dien said. "I didn't see him on the way here, but we've been in the temple a good while. He might be back at the barn by now. Do you want me to ride ahead and fetch him?"

"No. We remain together."

They turned north and soon saw a lumber-laden cart rattling down the road ahead. "That's him, sir," Dien said, urging his gelding to a canter. Dubric followed.

A broad-shouldered, middle-aged worker cringed as they approached, and pulled his mule to a halt.

Dubric brought his horse alongside the cart. Flat-bedded, with slat-walled sides and an open back, it was neatly stacked with bundled lumber. Dubric saw no area that could possibly hide Otlee. "You are Jak?"

"Yes, milord," he said, nodding awkwardly.

"Have you perchance made the acquaintance of a young man named Braoin?"

Jak stared ahead before turning to face Dubric. "Braoin, milord? Is he lost? In some sort of trouble?"

"What do you know of him?"

"He worked for me, from time to time. Plastering, mostly. Painting. Haven't seen him around lately." Jak shrugged. "He seemed a nice enough lad. Had a real talent with the brush."

"When did you last see him?"

"Nearly a phase ago, milord. Braoin came to me asking for the rest of his wages because he was going after Eagon. I haven't seen him since."

Dubric's pencil paused, then continued writing. "Eagon, you say? What can you tell me of him?"

"Scrawny, red-haired lad. Nervous sort, couldn't sit still to save his life. He and Braoin did the painting jobs, Eagon the base work and Braoin the detail."

"And this Eagon left, you said?"

"Yes, sir."

"When?"

"A couple . . . three phases ago, I guess." Jak looked to the sky, then nodded. "He left in the middle of plastering Lord Haconry's library. That would have been nearly a moon ago, give or take a couple of days."

"What were the particulars of his departure?"

Jak laughed. "Like most boys who tire of working, he just didn't show up one morning, milord. Weren't no particulars."

"But it upset Braoin?"

"Yes, sir. He was in a foul humor after that. Moping around, not his usual self."

Dubric noted the information. "Were any others of your crew friends with either Braoin or Eagon?"

"I suppose so. They all worked together." He looked at Dubric, his eyes narrowing. "Is there some problem with my boys? You thinking they're up to something?"

Dubric continued to write, asking, "The four repairing Devyn Paerth's roof. What are their names?"

"Struthers, Nally, Flann, and Rao." Jak frowned and added, "Flann's damn near an idiot and Rao can get mean, but the other two are decent enough. All can swing a hammer. I can't ask for more than that. Want me to fetch them for you?"

"No, thank you. I will summon them as needed. How about a smallish, redheaded boy? A stranger to the Reach. Have you seen him this morning?"

Jak said, "Yes, sir, I have. On the road, 'bout dawn. He waved hello. He was coming to town when I took my crew to the Paerth's farm. I thought he was looking for something."

"But did you speak to him? Have you seen him since? In town, perhaps? Or with someone?"

"No, milord. I haven't. Not since passing him on the road."

Dubric added Jak's statement to his notes. "Is there anything else you would like to add?"

Jak swallowed and glanced at Dien. "Just a plea for the new boy, from the Paerth farm. He's a good lad, a hard worker. I know he's infatuated with the master's daughter, any fool can see that, and I know a man worries over his daughters. But he's a fine boy, a damn fine boy, even though he's turned down my offers of work. I just want you to know that I'll take him in if the master casts him out. It's not safe to be a lad in these parts without a good roof over your head."

Jak fidgeted with the reins. "There. I've said my piece. If you need anything else, I'm happy to oblige." He clucked to his mule and, glancing over his shoulder, drove north.

Dubric turned back to Dien. "How long have you known him?"

"Three days. He talked Sarea into fixing the barn roof the morning before we came. Seems competent at his work and pleasant to deal with, for the most part. He was gone most of yesterday, though. Said he had to look at a shed repair and a bad wall. I had no idea he's been talking to Lars."

Dubric watched Jak rattle down the road. "He works exclusively with young men, and that worries me."

"Last time I checked, sir, apprentices are usually boys and young men. We've got two of our own."

Dubric put away his notebook. "I may be jumping at

shadows. Any tradesman in the Reach could be involved, or someone far removed from such things. I
must keep that in mind." He turned his horse toward
the main street. "There are two bodies that may yet
yield clues. We must hurry if we have any hope of finding Otlee before nightfall."

Jess's mother was in the back room feeding the baby
and her grandmama had gone to take her afternoon
walk, leaving the girls to make hats. Jess braided strips
of felt into a band. Fyn sat beside her, searching for the
glue and looking queasy.

"Are you feeling any better at all?" Jess asked.
"You've been sick practically since we got here."

Fyn stood. "I'm all right. Just want to go home."

Even though it was late afternoon, Kia hadn't finished the midday dishes and she rolled her eyes, turning to face them while she wiped her soapy hands on a
rag. " 'Fess up, Fyn. You only want to see creepy ol'
Gilby. You're just playing sick so we'll all feel sorry for
you."

"Next time I throw up, I'll be sure and do it on your
lap so you can see how good I am at pretending."

"You wouldn't dare. Do you have any idea how much
this dress cost?"

"Too much," Fyn muttered, searching the cupboard.
"But you never worry about things like that, do you?"

Kia tossed her head and plunged her hands into the
dishwater. "I still think you're pining after Gilby, just
like Jess is sighing after Lars. I don't understand either
of you. One's a lazy good-for-nothing and the other's a
hopeless fey noble."

Aly stuck out her tongue at Kia. "Lars doesn't kiss boys."

Kia rinsed a plate, squinted at it, and put in back into the soapy water for the umpteenth time. "Yeah, sure."

"It's true," Aly insisted.

Jess reached for the scissors, but they were gone. Again. How could Granddad expect them to finish hats if he kept hiding tools? "Let it go, Kia," she snapped. "Leave Lars and Gilby alone."

"Why? One's not worth the spit he uses to polish his shoes and the other is a lost cause."

Fyn found the scissors and glue behind the settee cushion and came back to the table. "And you're just jealous and mean."

"Jealous? There's nothing to be jealous of."

Fyn burped again, then said, "It doesn't bother you that your younger sisters have boys that like them? You're the eldest, and no one likes you. All the castle boys know what a witch you are. That's why you've been flirting with the work crew. You've no hope left at home."

"Fyn," Jess whispered, glancing at her.

Kia turned, her eyes narrowing. "That's not true. Lots of boys like me. I've had dinner with Deorsa, Serian, Moergan . . ."

Fyn put a line of glue on her hat. "How many have had dinner with you twice? Have any kissed you? Ever? Have any asked you to Lord Brushgar's spring faire? Gilby asked me moons ago, and I'll bet my best dress that Lars is gonna ask Jess." Fyn winked at Jess's gaping astonishment and added, "Might even kiss her, too."

Kia took a step toward them, her lip curled in a

sneer. "I'm the eldest. You're less than a moon past thirteen, and Jess won't be fourteen for another couple of phases. You're both too young to be courted, or kissed."

Fyn shrugged, pressing feathers into the glue. "So? I've been asked and I'm going to go. How about you, Jess? Lars ask you yet?"

Jess shook her head, looking back and forth between her two sisters. "No, of course not. And he's not going to. Asking day's less than a phase away, and besides, he's not interested in me like that. I'm like his sister."

Fyn smiled. "You sure?"

"He's fey," Kia said. "And a high noble. His working around the farm doesn't prove a thing. Even if he liked girls, which he doesn't, high nobles don't ask commoner girls to the faire or anything else, no matter how much they try to act like they're commoners. We're lucky if the regular nobles notice us."

"What's the matter, Kia? Afraid you'll get stuck with a lowly stable boy or kitchen lackey for a sweetie?" Fyn made smooching noises then laughed.

Kia's voice dropped to a low growl. "You'd better be glad you're sick."

"And you'd better be ready to eat your words come faire time, when you're sitting at home alone while Jess and I are dancing."

"I . . . I don't think I'm going," Jess said. "No one is going to ask me." She shrugged and cut felt strips. "I'm not popular or anything. I'm too tall, too plain."

"And too peculiar," Kia added, smirking. "Out of all the girls in the castle, you're the only one considering university. You'd spend your life in a book, if it were up to you, and everyone knows it. No one's going to ask you to the faire, least of all Lars, and you're definitely not going to get asked to the dance. Heck, asking day's only a few days away and it takes at least a moon to have a party dress made, let alone all the other pomp and glitter."

Fyn set aside her glue and wiped her hands. "What do you want to bet?"

"Excuse me?"

"You heard me. I think you're wrong. I'll wager that Jess'll be asked to the faire long before you, and I'll even bet that Lars will be the one to ask her. Early enough to go to the dance and *everything*."

"No way. It's not going to happen."

Jess drew a shaky breath and said, "Can you two please not do this to me?"

Fyn grinned. "You're so sure, take me up on it. What's your wager, Kialyn? Money? Clothes? Favors?"

"No one is going to ask me to the faire or the dance," Jess said.

Fyn patted her on the back. "Yes, they will. Be positive. It's more than a moon away. You'll get asked, I'm sure of it, but Kia the snootypants won't."

Kia crossed her arms over her chest, wincing when she remembered her hands were wet and soapy. "I should tan your hide."

Fyn grinned. "You'll have to wait for that. I'm still sick. But you're scared to make the wager. You can gripe and gossip about everyone else, but you know deep down it's all lies and your own cowardice."

"I am not a coward."

Fyn grinned. "Prove it."

"Don't, Fyn," Jess said, staring at the tangle of felt strips. "Please. Don't put me in the middle of this."

"In the middle of what?" Lars asked as the door opened. Filthy and exhausted, he closed the front door and pulled off his muddy boots. "I've been all over the valley. No sign of Otlee."

The girls' conversation stopped, and all three returned to their assigned duties.

Jess glanced at her hat and picked five felt strips. As she heard footsteps enter the kitchen, she tried to keep her hands steady and her face emotionless.

"What's going on?" Lars asked. "Am I interrupting something?"

Jess stared at the felt. "Nope."

Kia said, "No."

"Of course not," Fyn said, touching Jess's arm.

But Aly said, "Fyn wanted Kia to make a bet, but Kia's chicken."

"Ah," Lars said, walking away. "It must be a dilly of a wager."

"It is!" Aly said. "It's about who's going to ask Jess to the spring faire."

Jess closed her eyes and cursed.

Silence, then Lars said, "Oh?"

Before Aly could answer, Jess said, "Aly, so help me, if you utter one more word, I'll beat you to within an inch of your life." She opened her eyes and stared at the felt, trying to ignore her embarrassment.

She felt Lars's gaze on her back, felt Kia's smirk like a ping between her ears, and felt Fyn grasp and squeeze her hand.

Fyn released her then turned. "We're making lamb stew for supper. Did you happen to notice if there were any early greens in the garden?"

"Actually, I didn't look. I can, if you want, and I didn't mean to interrupt. Your grandfather needs the oil can and he said it's in the house." He paused as Jess resumed braiding. "At least I think that's what he said.

Other than calling me Stuart, he's difficult to understand sometimes."

"Yeah, we know," Fyn sighed. "I think it's in the cellar. I'll show you."

Jess braided. She heard the cellar door creak open and footsteps descend, then braved a glance just in time to see his head disappear under the floor.

Kia made a face and flung some cold suds, spattering Jess's dress. "Real men don't take off muddy boots," she whispered. "They leave the mess for us to clean up. He's fey, Jess. Face it."

Smirking, Kia returned to her dishes, leaving Jess to work in relative quiet and peace.

Lars ducked a coil of stained rope and some ancient and dusty bundles of dried flowers as he descended the stairs. The air smelled damp and spicy, like squash and apples waiting to be baked. Shelves hung on mud-and-beam walls, each loaded with boxes and jars, and bins stood in a row along the near wall. He peeked into one—turnips—and smiled. He liked turnips, but one happy thought kept the smile on his face: Jess *had* threatened Aly. If she'd been telling Aly to keep the secret, instead of Kia, maybe things weren't hopeless after all.

Fyn muttered something he couldn't quite hear, and knelt to open a low box. Shaking her head, she glanced at him with a rueful smile. "I can't believe we forgot carrots for the stew."

He smiled back, peeking into other bins, to see apples and onions, salt pork and potatoes. Not much remained, but there was enough to last until the first berries and vegetables of spring.

Fyn tucked her hair behind her ears and rummaged through the straw, finally locating three carrots. Always the thinnest of the three elder girls, she seemed unusually pale and fragile. He felt a twinge of protectiveness as she pushed herself to her feet, and he hurried to help her.

She smiled as she declined his help. "I'm all right. Don't look so worried."

"We're all worried about you."

She laughed then, like the Fyn he had known for the past six summers instead of the ghost he had seen the past few days, and her cheeks brightened. "I'm fine. Really I am. There's absolutely nothing wrong. I promise."

She gave him a genuine smile, peaceful and happy, her eyes sparkling, and he took a quick step back as she deliberately covered her belly with one hand.

He stared at her belly and blinked his astonishment. "Oh, Fyn, no. You can't be."

She laughed and closed the door to the carrot box. "Why not? It's a perfectly normal way to be."

He swallowed, forcing himself to talk. "Gilby?"

"Who else would it be? We've been seeing each other for more than a summer, you know."

"Yes, but . . . You're so young."

She smiled and handed him the carrots. "I'm obviously old enough." Turning away from him, she walked toward the far wall and rummaged through the shelves of assorted containers and junk. "Don't tell anyone, all right? Gilby needs to get things straightened with his father first, and I don't want Dad and Mam to get all upset. Here, hold this."

She handed him a box of jar lids and tin cups. They

clattered as he shifted the box to one arm and tucked the carrots in a pocket. "No one knows?"

"Nope," she said. "Well, no one but Gilby and me. And you." She burped, covering her mouth with the back of her hand. "Gosh, I'm getting tired of that." She laughed, pushing aside another box.

"How far along are you?"

"Almost three moons. Ah, here we go."

He barely had time to wonder how she could be so matter-of-fact and unconcerned before she turned back to him with the oil can in her hand. "You won't say anything, will you?"

His stomach tied itself in greasy knots. He wanted to beat the piss out of Gilby. For Goddess' sake, Fyn was barely thirteen.

I'll kill him.

She touched his arm and he blinked. "Lars! Don't. Please."

"What he did was wrong. Forcing you to—"

She shook her head gently. "What makes you think he forced me? I love him and he loves me. I chose to do this. I wanted to." She regarded him with calm assurance, a happy smile teasing her lips, and he didn't know what to think.

She reached out and lifted his chin, closing his mouth. "I'm fine. Really. Everything is fine, I promise. Just, please, keep this to yourself until after we're back home. All right?"

"Your parents need to know."

"They will. We're going to tell them together, once Gilby gets things sorted with his father."

Lars shoved the box of lids and cups back onto the shelf. Gilby's father was Sir Newen Talmil, a castle noble. Also a lecher, a sneak, and an all-around ass. But, for Fyn's sake, Lars tried to be nice. "I don't know if he'll be able to. Sir Talmil isn't the most understanding man I've met."

She sighed, her hand falling to her belly again. "I know, but we'll manage, whatever happens."

He took a breath and straightened his back as he looked at her. "Fyn, you're like a sister to me. If you need anything, I mean anything, you let me know, all right?"

She beamed, nodding. "I will. I probably shouldn't have mentioned it, but I want to go home so badly and I had to tell someone before I burst. Thanks for listening."

He gently took the oil can and handed her the carrots. "You're welcome. I mean it, though. If you need anything, for you, for the baby, whatever, you let me know."

She hugged him quickly, burping as she pulled away. "I will, I promise, but today I just needed someone to talk to." She sighed, looking at the light streaming through the open door. "Guess we'd better get back to work."

She wiped her hands on her apron and stepped onto the stairs. "Don't forget to look for those greens. It would be nice to have something fresh in the stew."

"For the baby," he whispered.

She gave him a smile and a slight nod. "Oh! One more thing."

"Sure," he said. "Anything."

Fyn glanced up to the kitchen then leaned over the stair rail to whisper, "Ask Jess to the dance." She winked at him, then hurried up into the light.

*   *   *

Dubric found Piras the undertaker's shop tucked behind the tanner's, and he entered. A shortish, bushy-eyebrowed man looked up from cleaning his instruments. "How may I serve you, milord?"

"I am Castellan Dubric and this is my squire, Dien Saworth. We have come to further examine the bodies pulled from the river near Barrorise. Are they in your possession?"

"One is, milord. The other has already been retrieved."

Madam Floret must have come for her husband. "Then I shall examine the one that remains."

"Right this way, sir," Piras said, limping toward a hallway.

They followed, Dubric noting the medical implements, anesthetics, and examination table in the immaculate entry room. "I thought Mulconry was the local physician."

"I'm no physician, milord," Piras said, glancing over his shoulder. "Besides undertaking, I barber and pull teeth, stitch up a wound now and then. I don't know diddly about herbs or poultices or medicines, and I'm certainly no surgeon. At least, not yet." He reddened and turned away.

They reached a door and Dubric watched his host pull out a set of keys. "Not yet?"

"No, sir," Piras mumbled, his face growing a deeper crimson as he sorted through the keys. "I shouldn't have said anything." He selected a key and slid it into the lock. "This corpse is rather, um, drippy, milord."

Dubric pulled the vial of mint from his pocket. "I have already seen it. What should you not have said?" He wiped a smear of goo under his nose and held the jar out for Piras.

Piras sighed and nodded his thanks as he accepted the mint and myrtle. "I'm not of fine blood, milord, just a common man trying to provide a necessary service. Sir Mulconry never took care nor showed concern when he tended the dead, and he's just as likely to pull a good tooth as a rotten one. Someone needed to step forward and fill the need. I'll never be a full-fledged physician, but I do hope to offer a choice, at least for some folks."

He sighed and handed the jar to Dien. "Some of the high bloods in the Reach don't take kindly to a common man tending to the living. They say it's a nobleman's job. I apologize, milord, if I've offended you, but I've a family to support and barbering doesn't pay well, nor keep me busy." He smiled. "And my wife can't stand to see me idle."

"Mine's the same way," Dien muttered.

"No offense taken," Dubric said. "I would much rather work with a man of ethics than someone like Mulconry. Have you performed many postmortems?"

"I've done a couple, milord, more for my sake than for any official purpose. Only after folks have requested that I nail the coffins shut." He shrugged and seemed to shrink, drawing into himself. "I was curious, more than anything else. What's hooked up where? What's this part look like, or that one? The human body is an amazing thing, milord. Fascinating."

Dubric pocketed the mint again. "Yes, it is." He looked the undertaker over from his leather boots to the top of his thinning pate. "Can you read?"

Startled, Piras leaned back. "Me? Goodness, milord, not many commoners in the Reach can read."

"I did not ask about others, I asked about you."

Piras blushed again and fidgeted. "Aye, milord, some. I practice when I can."

Dubric turned his attention to Dien. "Please note to remind me to have physician Rolle send some introductory medical texts here. Anatomy, common ailments and injuries, basic medicines. Perhaps an anatomical illustration or two and a selection of essential equipment."

"Yes, sir."

Piras gaped, his eyes huge. "Milord, that's not necessary. I never asked—"

"I realize that," Dubric said, patting the man's shoulder. "I offered. The expense is immaterial when compared against a man with a quest for knowledge and a group of communities in desperate need of his service. Far better for you to provide basic medical care for the Reach than Pigshit Mul."

"So you have met him?" Piras asked.

"The man is vile. I would rather have my horse sew my stitches than allow him to look at a wound at all."

"But books are so expensive, milord. It would take me summers to repay you."

Dubric nodded toward the door. "Let us see to that examination, shall we? While the mint is still fresh? And repayment is not necessary. It would be my honor to aid you."

"Yes, milord, whatever you say." Piras took a breath and opened the door.

Steps led down, into the dark. Piras lit a lantern and led the descent into the cellar. "He was very warm when he arrived, milord, and I've done what I can to cool him, but the damage from exposure and maggots is quite extensive. I hope you can find what you're looking for."

Dubric nearly tripped down the stairs. "Maggots?"

Piras reached the bottom and turned to the left. "Yes, milord, but there have been no flies about for moons." They walked past a wrapped body to a closed door.

"Who's that?" Dien asked.

"Missus Glafisher, from Wittrup. She died in her sleep the night before last. Someone is supposed to retrieve her tomorrow or the day after."

"Why have they waited so long?" Dubric asked. "I thought most people were buried in a day or two."

Piras nodded, his hand pausing on the door. "They are, in the summertime, but it takes time to dig a grave in the Reach. The soil is rocky and hard, especially near Wittrup. There are a few places on the peninsula with arable dirt, but not many. I tend the bodies and keep them cool until their graves are ready. I'm likely the ice man's best customer. Ready, sirs?"

Glancing at Dubric and Dien, he opened the door.

Dubric nearly staggered back from the stench. Beside him, Dien grimaced, but Piras limped through. He opened the lantern and lit a wood taper in the flame. Once he had hung the lantern on the hook beside the door, he carried the glowing bit of wood to the adjoining wall and lit another lamp, then another.

A body lay upon blocks of ice and straw, covered with a sheet of stained cloth. Dubric approached slowly, noting the placement of the stains and the gray-pink fluid trailing toward the drain.

Despite its first appearance, the liquid was clotted not with blood and rotted flesh, but rather clumps of red worms, writhing together and being carried away by current until they clumped on a mesh-covered metal grate.

"Sir? Are they the same worms as the one you found in Lars's neck?"

Dubric rubbed his eyes. "That they are. Was he in this condition when he arrived?"

"No," Piras said, lighting the final lamp. He blew out the wood taper and returned it to the holder. "I thought he and the other were drowners—with all these rivers, I see one from time to time—but when I prepared a table for Missus Glafisher, they started to stink up the place. Before I left for her, I put them in here, on ice, until I decided what to do with them."

Dubric approached the body and his stomach lurched. "When was this?"

"Yesterday morning, milord. Perhaps ten bell." Piras rummaged in a drawer and pulled out something soft and pale. "I would have bled them both then and there, but neither had any blood."

Dubric turned to stare at him. "Excuse me?"

"No blood, milord. I tried to open a low vein to drain from, but nothing happened. No fluid at all, other than river water." He handed Dubric and Dien soft, flimsy gloves. "Their blood vessels had collapsed. It's as if something drained them dry. Even clotted blood leaves golden fluid."

"What is this?" Dubric asked, examining the loose, translucent material.

Piras pulled whitish gloves over his hands. "Sheep gut, milord. I have the glove maker make them for me. They stretch a goodly bit and I don't worry about touching rancid bodies when I wear them. If you put the seams over the tops of your fingers, they are more comfortable and you can still feel everything."

Dubric grimaced in apprehension as he pulled the snug and cloyingly dry gloves on, but he smiled as he flexed his fingers and ran his fingertips over the buttons of his jerkin. He retained full movement and much of the sensation of touch. Amazing. Even his rheumatism did not object to the slight pressure on his joints. Better yet, he would not get corpse mess on his hands. *I must remember to have the castle glove maker create these for me.*

Piras reached for the edge of the sheet and pulled it back.

Despite himself, Dubric gasped. He had accepted that the body would be covered with clothos worms, that they would have created considerable damage to an already decayed corpse, and that the remnant would form a new level of putrid disgust and muck.

He had not, however, considered that Calum would be the corpse in question.

His dark hair had peeled back from his skull and slumped behind his head in one oozing piece. His arms and legs lay desiccated and nearly boned, lost beneath a sea of writhing worms. His privates and belly were gone, as were his cheeks, nose, and most of his face. His internal organs lay exposed from his pelvis to his throat. Worms gnawed and crawled everywhere, creating a low burble that tugged at the edges of Dubric's hearing. They erupted from the flesh, bits of red the size of salt grains, slithering beneath their larger brethren.

"What do you see, sir?" Dien asked.

"This is not Eagon's body." Dubric circled the corpse, his attention landing where it desired. "Eagon had red hair and was much smaller. This is Calum, but he is in worse condition than Eagon was two days ago. The worms' presence seems to have accelerated the decay by a marked amount."

"I checked his temperature just this morning, milord, and saw worms only on his belly and one spot on his upper chest. Not this infestation."

Dubric touched Calum's thigh, and the wormy meat fell away to reveal white bone. "Who retrieved the other body?"

"I do not know, milord. I was out fetching Missus Glafisher yesterday afternoon. When I came back he was gone."

Dubric sighed and walked toward Calum's head. "Was it as infested as this?"

"No, milord. Merely water-rotted, as far as I could tell."

"And you have no idea who took it?"

"No, milord. I don't generally lock up the embalming rooms or cool storage. Folks tend to be afeared of corpses, not want to take them. I assumed the lad's family heard he was here and came to take him home. Families have come while I was out before and I never thought much of it. Folks round here are honest. I've never had anyone not pay their due."

Dubric pulled down Calum's jaw to look into his mouth, wincing as it snapped free. "His throat is full of the vile things."

The shed skins of the clothos worms lay crumpled around and upon the body in a pale, pinkish drift. Countless writhing red horrors coated the young man's heart and lungs. While Dubric watched, the heart split open and a fresh swarm of worms burst into Calum's chest.

Dubric looked at Piras. "Yet you locked the stairway door today. Why?"

"I didn't know who he was, and I dared not let worried families in." He looked down upon the body and frowned. "A dead son is tragic enough, but to have him rotting before your very eyes? I couldn't in good conscience just let his family see him like this, not without warning them first."

The worms chewed away the meat along the back of Calum's neck and his skull rolled to the side, gaping jawlessly. Dubric noticed that the flesh around a tiny hole at the temple remained unchewed.

The marks on the ghosts' heads! "Do you have a bone saw?"

"No, milord, but I do have a small handsaw. I'll fetch it."

When Piras had left, Dien frowned at the swarmy meat and asked, "What happened?"

Dubric frowned and gently lifted one of Calum's arms. It snapped free, the tendons and ligaments no longer holding the joint together, and the forearm separated from the wrist. "I do not know for certain, but I would guess that the frigid water stunted the worms' growth and development. Once the body warmed, the eggs began to hatch."

"Even though Piras put him on ice?"

"It was just too late." Dubric lay the arm bones beside the body and knelt to retrieve the hand. "When we finish here today we must burn the remains. We must be certain we have killed these vermin."

"One of the bastards is crawling up your leg."

Dubric snatched the red grub from his calf and dropped it to the floor. Nearly as thick as his index finger, the fat worm wriggled toward him, but he smashed it beneath his heel.

Dubric and Dien walked around the corpse, crushing every worm squirming on the floor. "Why is Calum laying here to rot and be eaten, but Eagon is gone?"

Dien grimaced at the mess. "His family came and took him home, or the killer stole him. There's no other reason I can see."

A pair of worms thrashed together beyond the edge of the straw, fighting over a bit of moldering meat in a warped mockery of a mating embrace. Dubric killed both. "Do you think his family found him?"

"Doubtful," Dien said, staring at the wounded body. "We'd have to ask them to be sure, but there's no frigging way I'd take something like this home."

Calum's left foot slumped to the side and rolled onto the straw, the upper ankle joint collapsed by squirming worms. Dubric lifted it and put it back where it belonged. "Why would the killer want him back? Why him and not Calum?"

"Maybe something on the body you didn't notice, maybe the killer changed his mind and decided he wanted to play some more, maybe there's another reason we haven't considered."

Dubric frowned, his gaze gliding over the corpse. "Perhaps he was not infested."

"Sir?"

"What if whoever took Eagon knew that Calum was infested, that this would happen to him, while Eagon was not?"

Dien nodded, pushing loose, buggy flesh toward the skeleton. "Something about the body might lead us to the bastard. Yeah, that makes as much sense as anything else."

"Like any thief, he took what was useful and left the refuse for others to discard." Dubric looked up as Piras limped through the door with a worn hacksaw in his hands.

Dubric accepted the saw. "This body and everything

possibly tainted by the worms must be destroyed. By fire if possible."

"As you wish, milord. I have a pyre oven."

Dubric took a breath and brushed a clot of worms from Calum's forehead. "That should work quite well, thank you." Saw blade balanced on Calum's brow, Dubric started to cut. He winced at the grating sound of steel against the smooth bones of Calum's skull. He did not cut clear through; instead, he turned the head and worked the saw blade around the edge in an effort to protect the brain and whatever else might be within.

The oozing mess that had once been Calum's head snapped free of the vertebrae, leaving only the spinal cord and dry, crusty veins to hold it in position. Grimacing, Dubric cut those as well to give him easier access to the back of the skull.

Both sides of Calum's skull were punctured on the sutures between the temporal and sphenoid bones. Dubric cut directly through one hole, but just above the other, and the top of the skull popped off with a crisp snap. Dubric stared at what lay within, his mouth going dry.

Beside him, Piras whistled through his teeth while Dien stood astounded and silent.

The inside shone gleaming and white, completely void of blood and worms. A black thread hung downward from the uncut temple to the base of the skull and, strung on it, like a bead on a string, was a pitifully dehydrated clump of gray sludge. The plum-size lump lay in the skull's bowl with brittle bits of vein hanging about it like dead roots on the edge of a riverbank.

"Milord, I have never in all of my days seen anything as pitiful as that wad of muck. How did his brain collapse like that?"

Dien pointed his pencil toward two dangling and desiccated pustules that sagged from the fore section of the shriveled brain. "Are those his eyes?"

Dubric suppressed a shudder. "I believe so, yes." Gingerly, he reached in and lifted the clump of dried tissue. It snapped free from the brittle bundle of nerves entering the base of the skull and he saw no worms anywhere within the brain pan. "It feels like dry clay, stiff and unyielding, and is very light." He turned it over, noting that the threads ran into the underside of the lump. He glanced at Piras. "Do you have a sack? A box? Something clean I can place this in?"

Piras nodded and limped away while Dubric examined the remnant of Calum's brain. The strand of thread on one side was a deep, shiny black, but the other was a rich, dull scarlet. Stiffer and somewhat thicker than the black string, it tended to curl as it hung between his fingers, and it felt strangely warm.

"Are they two separate strands, sir?" Dien asked.

"I do not know. We will have to cut it open to find out. I dare not pull either end free."

Piras held out a ceramic basin and Dubric placed the brain within it.

While Piras carried the basin to a nearby table, Dubric circled the body again, but saw nothing else besides worms and rotting meat. "Let us finish this before these worms grow wings," he said, lifting the stained sheet from the straw. "Scrape the grate. We must not let a single one escape."

Together the three carried Calum and every bit of straw to the pyre oven. They lit it afire, watching red and black smoke rise to the chimney before Piras slammed the door closed.

CHAPTER

17

†

Dusk had gathered close by the time Dubric and Dien reached the ferry port across from Wittrup. They had queried every business owner and home in Tormod but had found no sign of what had happened to Otlee. They spoke little that evening as they rode west. All lines of evidence led to dead ends, leaving only Calum's shriveled brain and Eagon's missing corpse as potential threads to follow.

Dubric dismounted to ring the ferry bell. He felt wracked with a level of fear and shame he had not experienced in decades. *Braoin died and Otlee is missing. How could I have failed both boys?*

He heard a cart approach, and both he and Dien loosened their swords in their saddle scabbards as it rattled closer. Dubric remounted, turning his horse around to face whoever traveled toward them, while the ghosts seemed intent on getting in his way.

Atro the peddler eased into view, yawning behind his rickety mule. "Peace be to you, Lord Dubric," he called, waving. "Thank you for calling the ferry."

"You are most welcome," Dubric said. "Are you always on the road this late?"

"Aye," Atro said as he climbed down from his cart. "Some nights much later, I'm afraid. Don't suppose I could interest you in a trinket or two? Perhaps some tobacco or a bauble for your lady?"

Dubric sighed and rubbed his eyes. His "lady" had died forty-six summers before. "Thank you, but no."

The peddler opened the back of his cart and pulled himself in. He appeared again with a rolled parcel in his hand and a book tucked under his arm. "How about you, Master Saworth? A lovely bauble for your beautiful wife or daughters?" He unrolled the fabric parcel to show a selection of bracelets.

"No," Dien grumbled. "Not today."

Atro's face fell and he rolled the strip of fabric again. "I've got just the thing for you, though, I'm sure of it." He tucked the roll of fabric under one arm and pulled the book from beneath the other. Presenting it to Dubric, he said, "All the things a village boy should know but might not. Knot tying and rabbit snares. How to bait a hook and set a tent. Curing leather. What berries are safe to eat. It's got beautiful drawings, real true-to-life pictures. The cover says it's *The City Boy's Guide to Country Living*."

"I see that," Dubric said, politely thumbing through despite the stinging in his eyes.

Atro beamed. "I thought that boy you have might like it."

"He is missing," Dubric said, closing the book. He tried to ignore the pain in his heart and clenching throat.

"Have you seen him today?" Dien asked.

"Yes, I have," Atro said, taking the book from Dubric. "He can't be missing, milord. Boys go missing at night, round here, and yours purchased a tonic and a bag of candy from me just this morning. In Tormod. He was fine, milord, just fine. Maybe he got lost, or found some children to play with."

"You saw him?" Dubric asked.

"Yes, sir, I certainly did, this morn in Tormod. But not since. I assumed he was with you. Like I told you before, boys only disappear at night, and I didn't consider—"

"He's gone!" Dien snapped. "Taken in broad daylight."

Atro blanched and returned the book to his cart. "Then I am sorry for your loss. Is there any way I can help?"

The last traces of pink and gold left the sky, chased away by a chilly wind, and Dubric drew his cloak tight around his shoulders.

"No more than you already have. I assure you, whoever the culprit is, I will find him and bring him to justice."

"Aye, and bless you, milord, for all that you do." Atro closed and latched the cart door before turning again to Dubric. "Have you had much luck in your search?"

"Some." Dubric squinted into the night and the light coming from across the river. His horse shifted, stomping its hoof.

Atro leaned against his cart. "Have you many possible culprits, milord?"

"Some," Dubric said again, covering a yawn with his hand. He intended to spend the night at Maeve's, then ride to Myrtle to visit Eagon's family. Part of him dreaded visiting her while bearing such bad news, but another part was anxious to see her again. The juxtaposition of the two worried him, tangling in his lower belly. Involved with his own thoughts and concerns, he was in no mood to exchange banter with the peddler, particularly over details of his investigation.

He merely wanted the day to be over with. He wanted to find Otlee. And he wanted to get some sleep.

Atro did not seem to notice Dubric's fatigue or concern. "Word around the Reach is that you've found a pair of bodies, milord, and that they'd been damaged in a most disgusting way. Why would someone do such a thing?"

"I am not at liberty to say," Dubric replied. He sighed and glanced at the ghosts, frowning at Braoin's mutilated body.

"Yes, milord, but to think 'tis someone living here, in the Reach. Folks are scared, and with good reason. Many are mistrusting their neighbors, thinking that they've gone and done these things. 'Tis deplorable to consider such madness."

The ferry pulled up to the dock and the ferryman hacked up a clog of phlegm, then spat into the river. "Oh, shut yer damn yap, Atro. M'lord Dubric is too busy for ye to be bendin' his ear and tryin' to lighten his purse. Git on home now and peddle yer wares t'morrow."

"Are you not taking the ferry?" Dubric asked, frowning.

Atro laughed. "Oh, no, milord. I'd hoped that Orlek would bring other travelers across the river so I might interest them in a bauble or two, but as he's scared them all away, he continues to be a disappointment."

Orlek the ferryman spat into the water again. "Watch yer manners, Atro. I ain't scareda nobody 'cept maybe that son of yers. He pitches a fit ever time I take him 'cross the Casclian. Cussin' an' carryin' on like a beast. 'Bout damn near flips my ferry."

Dubric blinked, staring at Atro. "You have a son?"

The peddler climbed onto his perch and gathered up his reins. "Aye, milord, that I do. I never knew my daddy and I know how hard that can be. I took in a orphan, summers ago, to give a poor kid a father. He's a fine lad.

Apprentice carpenter. He'll earn a decent wage some-day and not have to haggle for every penny of profit."

"Does he work for Jak?"

"Yessir, that he does."

"Foul-mouthed hooligan, that's what he is. Gets wild crossin' a friggin' river!"

Atro sighed and his mule tossed its head. "Flann nearly drowned as a boy, and he's afraid of water. Doesn't make him any less of a good lad."

Dubric wished enough light remained to see by. Beside him, he heard Dien open a notebook. "How long has your son worked for Jak?"

"Near to three summers going," Atro said. "He's a few moons shy of becoming a journeyman, and does a fine job carpentering. Makes a father proud, it does, to see his boy learning an honest trade."

"Did he know any of the missing boys?"

Atro chucked the reins and the mule backed away. "Yes, milord. Last time I talked to him he was most upset. He'd worked with a couple of the lads."

"How long ago did you last see your son?"

The mule stopped. "Day before yesterday. At ol' Devyn's farm. I saw him on the roof of the barn, right there, plain as day. Now, there's a place I can make a good sale. All them granddaughters, all wanting trinkets. I could've spent the morning there, could've cleaned out half of my display cart, if it weren't for Squire Saworth there. He's damn near as tight-pursed as you, milord, begging your pardon."

Dien grunted.

"Did you speak to your son?"

Atro sat straight up and tilted his head. "No, milord. 'Tis not right to interrupt a man while he's working."

"Speakin' of which," the ferryman chimed in, "are we gonna stand here an' jaw all night?"

"One more moment," Dubric said, watching Atro. "Your son . . ."

"He's a damn fine boy."

"Blubberin' idiot, ye mean."

"Let's see you get your fat backside up on a barn roof."

Dien growled, "Don't make me knock your heads together."

The argument stopped, and Dubric dismounted. "One last thing, please. On your travels throughout the Reach, have you seen any suspicious men? Anyone harassing boys? Has your son mentioned anyone who has bothered him?"

Atro tapped his bristly chin. "Now, milord, can't say that I have, least no one in particular. We've got merchants running their cargo by road and by river, folks heading into town to buy seed, scores of people going 'bout their regular business. I haven't been looking for suspicious folks, but I'll be sure to keep my eyes open."

"Thank you," Dubric replied, leading his horse onto the ferry.

"You're welcome, milord." The peddler waved his good-bye and clattered away.

Orlek watched him leave. "That's ol' Atro. Too worried 'bout makin' a crown an' playin' with his puppets to notice what's going on 'round him. Hells, milord, he coulda sold the wretch the knife an' he never woulda noticed. He ain't much brighter than his boy."

"Have you seen anyone suspicious?" Dien asked, tying his horse beside Dubric's.

The ferryman pushed off. "Aye, that I have. I see suspicious types damn near ever' day, workin' in Wittrup like I do. Place is full of 'em. Sailors an' merchants, whores an' gamblers, poor folks trying to weasel a pence from someone's pocket. But have I seen anyone botherin' youngsters? Other than folks just shooin' 'em away, I can't say that I have."

The current grabbed the ferry and it twisted to the side, but Orlek did not seem to notice. He just pushed it forward again, working it across the river. "Children, boys mostly, been disappearin' fer damn near three summers now. Wittrup's done lost its share, one of 'em my nephew. We watch 'em careful these days, ye hear? Don't no one touch one of ours without folks noticin'."

He paused and glanced over his shoulder to look at Dubric. "Remember just yesterday, when ye took my ferry 'cross? How ye sent yer boy to give the kiddies a coin er two?"

Dubric nodded. "Yes, I remember."

"All that day and into the night folks was askin' me 'bout ye and 'bout yer boy. Where'd ye go? What'd ye say? Who were ye?"

"What did you tell them?"

Orlek laughed, working the ferry closer to shore. "I told 'em that ye was Lord Dubric hisself an' that ye was gonna catch an' kill the dark beast, just like ye did back in the war. My daddy done told us kiddies all about ye, milord, back when I was just a lad. Some of the old folks, they still r'member how ye done did the work while the King took the credit. I then told ever'one that ye protected yer boy from me, that yer boy paid the kiddies, not ye, an' that ye love that boy as if he were yer own. I could tell."

"Those are all nice things to say. Thank you."

"No need to thank me, milord, no need a'tall. Ye just catch that beast an' kill it. 'Tis all we poor folks want." He paused, the ferry shuddering in the current, and took a deep breath. "Is it true, milord, what folks'r sayin'? 'Bout the boys they done found?"

"What are people saying?"

"That he had his way wit' them. Laid wit' them, like a man wit' a woman, only worse."

Dubric closed his eyes to the ghosts of three young men following him and their reflections flickering on the water. He thought of Otlee, only twelve summers old, and he wanted to vomit. "Yes, it is true."

Orlek nodded, sniffling and wiping his face on his arm. "Thought so. Damn shame, it is. Only reasons to take a boy are to work him or ruin him." He continued to push the ferry across the river. After a long while, when the ferry dock waited a mere push or two away, he said, "Can ye do somethin' fer us, milord? Fer the poor folks of Wittrup?"

"That depends upon what it is."

Orlek nodded and shoved the ferry home. "When ye catch the bastard, can ye make him suffer? Can ye make him pay?"

The ferry shuddered to a stop and Dubric untied his horse. "I will bring justice to your boys, I swear upon my life."

Orlek opened that gate. "Then ye are the saint my daddy spoke of, milord. Thank ye."

Dubric sighed, rummaging through his purse for two crown. "I am no saint, but I will fulfill my duty to your people. You have my word." He placed the two coins in the ferryman's cup. "You mentioned your nephew is one of the missing. What can you tell me about him?"

Orlek's eyes glittered in the moonlight. He straightened his back and met Dubric's gaze. "His name were

Loman, milord. My sister's boy, Goddess rest her soul. What would ye like to know?"

Dubric heard Dien open the notebook as the questioning began.

The wind had picked up by the time Dubric and Dien rode into Falliet, and black wisps of clouds danced among the stars. The village had settled in for the night, no one was about, and all of the homes were closed off from the wind and chill. Like the other dwellings in the village, Maeve's lights shone with a welcoming golden glow, and smoke rose from her chimney. Her jenny brayed a quiet greeting as Dubric rode to her shed, and he sadly scratched her long ears before lugging his gear to the house.

"I've known her for nearly twenty summers, sir. She's family. I don't know if I can tell her about Bray."

"Neither do I, but we must. Better us now than from gossip days later when he is pulled from the river."

"If anyone finds him at all," Dien grumbled. "Of all the lads missing, only two have been found. And Otlee, sir. What in the frigging hells are we going to do?"

"We will find him, even if it kills us." Dubric took a breath, squared his shoulders, then approached the door.

He had barely tapped his knuckles against the wood when he heard movement within, and Maeve appeared from behind the opening door.

"Dubric! Dien! What are you doing here? Have you found him? What's happened?" She smiled, hopeful, then she backed away, covering her mouth with her hands. "No!" she wailed, dropping to her knees. "Braoin!"

Dubric rushed through the doorway and tossed aside his burdens, the papers and books scattering across the floor. "Hush, hush now," he said, kneeling beside her.

She turned into his arms, clutching at his chest. "My boy, my baby!"

He held her while Dien closed the door. "His ghost came to me last night. I am sorry, so sorry, that I was not fast enough."

He stroked her hair, her back, and looked at Dien, who watched them with confusion. "Fetch her some tea. Please. And a blanket."

The big man nodded and hurried across the shop, disappearing into the house.

"What am I going to do, now that hope is gone?" She shook, tremors shuddering through her body.

"I do not know, but you will survive. I promise. We both will. Otlee is missing, too." He held her as best he could until Dien returned with a blanket. Together they helped her into the house and to a soft chair near the fire.

She stared into the flames for a long time without speaking, tears rolling down her cheeks as the tea cooled untouched beside her. The cat, Lachesis, leapt to her lap and she petted it without moving her gaze from the fire.

Dubric and Dien settled into the kitchen with their limited evidence while Maeve came to terms with her grief. Neither spoke.

"Where are my manners?" she said at last, pushing away Lachesis and the blanket. Her voice sounded hollow and far away, like a cry from within a forgotten well. She staggered to the kitchen, tugging on her hair with a shaking hand. "You must be hungry."

"We can manage," Dubric said. He set the last armload

of papers and notes upon the kitchen table. "Please, tend to yourself. Would you rather we retired to a different location this evening? We could stay in the shed or seek shelter with a neighbor."

"No." She leaned against the doorjamb and blew her nose. "I'd rather not be alone. I'm glad you're here." She lowered her head then turned and staggered away. "Help yourselves to whatever you can find. I think I need to lie down."

Once she had left, Dubric opened her cupboards, locating a tin of fruit and jars of dried vegetables. Dien ventured to the porch and cellar then returned with a pair of potatoes and a smoked fish. While Dubric set water to boil, Dien sorted through the mess of books, notes, and other evidence.

"So you're positive Braoin's dead?" Dien asked. "You told Paol he was, and you told Maeve you saw his ghost."

"Yes, yes, he is, and yes, I do."

Dien's eyes narrowed. "How?"

Dubric swallowed as the last remnants of his secret ripped away. "It is my curse, seeing the dead until I avenge them. I have been cursed since Oriana died. I wish I could escape it, but I cannot. I should have told you sooner."

Dien sagged with relief. "I knew there was something, all the headaches you get. How much a pain in the ass you are when we have a murder. That's how you know Otlee's alive. How so many other boys are dead."

"Too many dead," Dubric said. "But not Otlee, not yet. We have to find him. Somehow."

"We have so little to follow." Dien sighed. "He could be anywhere."

Dubric located a knife and began chopping the potatoes. "The missing are connected somehow. What are the age ranges and disappearance dates for the boys we have confirmed?"

"I'll get right to it, sir. The information's here, I just haven't sorted and cataloged it yet."

Dubric grunted his approval and continued to assemble the soup while Dien created order from the chaos they had brought to Maeve's kitchen.

Once the soup had begun to simmer, Dubric excused himself and went to check on Maeve. She lay upon her bed, crying softly, her back to the open door.

"It is I," he said, striding in. He pulled a blanket from the back of a chair and covered her with it. "I have set out a pot of soup, if you decide you are hungry. If you need anything, Dien and I are both nearby."

She rolled onto her back and looked at him. "Did he suffer? Do you know if my son . . ." She winced and wiped her eyes.

"I have no way to know," he said, remembering the pain that had slammed through his head as Braoin's ghost appeared. "But I do believe that the end came quickly for him."

She nodded and clutched a pillow to her chest, rolling away from him again. He wanted to climb in beside her, hold her close and let her cry, ease her pain as best he could, but he still loved his wife. To lie beside another woman, even to give innocent comfort, was reprehensible.

And he was old enough to be her father. Damn near old enough to be her grandfather. To think such thoughts, even with pure intent, could quickly lead to a dangerous path.

Sighing, he left her to her pain and went to the privy room. He closed the door and sat upon the edge of the tub, allowing himself to relish his own grief. Oriana, his bride of three short moons, had died unexpectedly so long ago. He felt her loss as if it were a physical thing, a needle still stuck deep within his heart. He had lost everything in that fire, everything except his own miserable life, and he hoped—nay, prayed—that the same pain would not haunt Maeve for the rest of her days.

He took a deep breath and turned his face toward the ceiling, much like he had as a young man when seeking answers from the Goddess. The memory of those days disgusted yet comforted him, and when the words came they flowed softly from his lips like water burbling in a summer creek.

"For more than forty summers I have asked nothing of you. I have borne your curse upon my heart like a beast bears burdens upon its back. At your command I have done my duty to the souls wronged, and I have reviled you in my heart. I have seen and suffered the deaths of many, far more than the single death a mortal man should endure. My sins are my own, I admit, and I have never denied what I have done—nay, I have laid claim to it every day of my wretched and contemptible life. You have despised me, and I have returned the same care. You owe me nothing and I owe you even less."

He paused as tears stung his eyes. "I deserve the plagues you have placed upon me, we both know that simple truth, but the woman crying in the next room has done nothing to warrant such pain, nor have the families whose sons I seek, nor Otlee, whose innocence is surely lost. Can you not aid them? Can you not ease their suffering? Can you not bring them hope? Smite me as you will, I will never beg your mercy or forgiveness, but do not torture these good souls as you have tortured me. I once believed in your magnificence, your grace and kindness. Do not take that illusion away from these people. They have so little else to live for. So little to believe in."

He stood and cleared his throat, coughing away an obstruction that had settled there. "Thy will be done, as it is and as it will always be."

Unsettled, he washed his hands and splashed water on his face. He dried himself and looked into the mirror, seeing an old, scarred man with haunted eyes, and he shook his head. Not all scars were visible, he knew that as well as he knew his own soul, and many would never heal.

He took a moment to wipe the washbasin clean—he did not wish to create additional work for his hostess—and neaten the washstand. Once finished, he took a deep breath and looked into the mirror as he smoothed his shirt and collar, then paused, his burn-scarred fingers trembling.

Braoin's painting hung on the wall behind him, a reflection of the waterfall he had seen but two days before. The same painting, yet very different.

In the mirror, the mist looked like deadly, sparkling shards of ice. The birds perched with sinister intent, the leaves were poised and ready to cut open skin, and the sky had filled with foreboding.

He turned and stared at the painting. A beautiful piece of artistry, exquisite in every detail, from the insect's wings to the dewy blooms. A masterful work.

Back to the mirror. The same painting, certainly, yet the opposite effect. Was it the lighting, the brushstrokes? Something else?

Maeve had said that the title, "Life and Death on the River," was correct, that there was death in the painting. *Is this what she had meant? That the death is in the reflection? The reverse of life?*

He pulled the painting from the wall and held it before the mirror. The river seemed darker and deadly; the pastures beyond were not green and growing but grayish and rotted. The workers in the fields seemed but charred sticks, and the mill far back, nearly obscured behind the fields, was not a mill at all but a ruined relic of dark stone.

And it had burned.

He turned the painting around again to look at the details. A lovely and cheerful spring morning, but . . . He squinted, leaning close, then nearly took a step back as his eyes lit upon the conceit. Two brush strokes for each bit of detail, one beside the other, some so tiny he could barely see them. A shadow and a highlight. A damp stone and a scorch mark. A feather and a fang.

He frowned and stood straight again, still holding the painting before him, and he happened to glance in the mirror.

Something was written on the back of the canvas.

Startled, he turned it around to look at the back and he muttered a low curse.

A row of numbers, a portion of the set he had already seen.

1 2 3 4 1 2 1 2 3 2 3 4 3 4 3 4

"Damn that boy," he said. Tucking the painting under his arm, he left the privy room and hurried to the kitchen.

CHAPTER

18

†

During supper, while in the midst of a rambling complaint about the dismal state of her life, Kia's foot rubbed Lars's. He kicked it away and drew his feet back. Kia sighed, toe-tickled his shin, and resumed her incessant griping. Lars tried to avoid Kia's feet and remain focused on his supper, but he jumped when Sarea slammed her palm on the table.

"Kialyn Rebeka, I think that's enough."

"Enough of what, Mother? It's not my fault Fyn's hogging all the greens," Kia huffed, crossing her arms over her chest. "And everything else," she muttered, eyeing Lars.

Fyn sat to Lars's right and she barely glanced at Kia as she ate. "I'm not hogging anything. I've got one spoonful, same as you."

Kia snapped, "I saw Lars bring them in. He handed them to *you*. Asked *you* if they were all right. Looked to me like he picked them just for *you*, and *you've* been sneaking them ever since."

Lars stared at Kia, his spoon poised halfway between the stew and his mouth. "She was cooking."

"Actually, I was," Jess said with a sigh. Sitting beside Kia and across the table from Lars and Fyn, she picked at her stew and seemed to shrink with each volley of the argument.

Dammit, she's right. Frowning, Lars glanced at Jess before returning his attention to Kia. "I didn't pick them for Fyn, I just saw a clump of new dandelions and thought they might taste good." He shrugged and plunged his spoon into the stew.

Kia leaned forward. "You sure were in the cellar together for a long time. How long does it take to get a couple of carrots and the oil can?"

Lars felt his cheeks get hot but said nothing.

Jess wiped her mouth and stood, pushing away from the table. "May I be excused?"

She didn't wait for an answer; she simply turned and walked to their bedroom. Lars helplessly watched her go.

"Nighty-night," Devyn tittered, a carrot slice falling from his mouth to land on the floor. He leaned over, picked it up, and set it on the table, balancing it on its edge. It fell over and he set it upright again. Grinning, he fished a hunk of potato from his stew and started marching the carrot and potato along the edge of the table. Beside him, Aly watched with delighted interest.

Sarea rubbed her forehead and groaned. "Would you kids *please* stop it?"

"Why do you have to have such a filthy mind?" Fyn asked. "Did it ever occur to you that maybe, just maybe, nothing happened?"

Devyn's potato approached Kia's arm and she brushed it away. "Something happened. I don't know what, but it was definitely something, and I'm going to find out."

"There's nothing to find." Fyn picked a dandelion leaf from her plate and popped it in her mouth. "Tasty!"

Kia leaned forward, her voice lowering. "Look at you, you tramp. Like a cat who just ate a plump pigeon. You snuck him down to the cellar on purpose. And not just to get him to pick you some greens. What did you have to promise him, Fyn? The same things you do to Gilby?"

Fyn gaped and dropped her fork. "What?"

Sarea slammed her palm on the table. "Kialyn!"

"I'm sitting right here, you know," Lars said. He took a breath and stared at Kia. "Nothing happened. Fyn got some carrots, I got an oil can, nothing more. Why in the world would you think that I'd do anything even remotely improper? She's like my little sister!"

"Sister? Like heck. Grandfather's right. You're chasing all our skirts like a mongrel dog. That's why Dad calls you 'pup,' isn't it? Because you're just a damned dog."

Sarea lurched to her feet. "I've heard all of this nonsense I can take. Kia, get your ass to the porch. Now. Until you learn to be civil. You can't talk to anyone that way, especially not Lars."

"Mother! Can't you see what's going on? That black ghost nonsense is just a lie he and Jess concocted so they could stay out all night together. Now he's done with her and is after Fyn."

Sarea pointed to the door. "Now, Kia."

"Fine." She wiped her mouth and stood, flouncing away from the table while everyone watched her go.

"There was too a ghost," Aly yelled after her. "It was scary. Real scary, like it wanted to eat us up. And Lars kept me out all night, too!"

Bewildered, Lars looked back to Sarea. "Have I done something to her that I don't know about?"

Sarea sighed and pushed away her plate. "Not that I know of."

"She's just a jealous bitch," Fyn muttered.

Sarea rubbed her forehead again. "For that comment, missy, you can go to your room."

Fyn shrugged, ate one more dandelion green, then left the table without further comment.

Almost immediately after Fyn closed the door, an argument erupted from the girls' bedroom. Lars stared at his food, his ears burning as he heard his name in the midst of the argument. "Maybe you should talk to Fyn," he said, glancing at Sarea.

"Is she still sick?" Aly asked.

Lars lifted his head and looked Sarea in the eye. "Please."

"Fishies!" Devyn grinned and reached for Kia's abandoned plate and bowl. He dug around with his finger and pulled out a carrot slice then made it dance with his potato hunk.

Lars looked into Sarea's eyes a moment more, silently imploring her, then he sighed and resumed eating.

Dubric set aside his tea and flipped to a fresh page in his notebook. He tried not to look at the window, tried not to think of Otlee being lost at night, but worry and shame refused to leave him at peace. Somewhere out there, a sick, demented man tortured his page, doing unspeakable things. And Otlee was such a small boy. How much could he endure?

"We'll find him, sir," Dien said, picking at Calum's shriveled brain with a slender awl. "Even if I have to break every head in the Reach."

"I hope we can save him as well," Dubric said.

"We will, sir. We have to."

Dubric frowned and stared at the brain. "Cut it. I want to see those threads."

Dien set aside the awl and readied a fine fillet knife. He cut the dried tissue carefully, his large hands handling the knife with gentle precision. Humming softly, he split the forebrain from the rear and exposed the thread's path in the base of the brain.

"It passes through the optic nerves," Dubric said, leaning over the pan. "I think. I have not delved into brain anatomy for decades, not since university, but those strands do come from the eyes, and I think that mass is part of the internal workings of the nose."

Dien poked the lumps along the bottom of the brain. "The bottom of his brain curled up like a shriveling leaf. Whatever it was, it pulled damn hard."

"Could the string have affected the senses?"

Dien set aside the knife. "Sight at least."

"Maybe perception," Dubric said. The thread faded from red to black and he lifted it carefully, letting the red part curl around his fingers. It tingled, thrumming as if it were alive. "Feel this."

"But why, sir?" Dien asked, accepting the thread. He frowned as it clung to his fingers. "What perceptions?"

Dubric reached for the map Otlee had gone to retrieve and unrolled it on the table. "Calum's wife said he called these diamond marks 'eyes.' Perhaps there is a connection to sight. Perhaps he shows the boys something when he kills them?"

"Or when he tortures them." Dien placed the thread in the pan. "Devyn always mutters about the Devil's Eye and how it sees but doesn't see. It sounds like nonsense."

Dubric looked at the channel the thread left through Calum's optic nerves. "I do not think it is nonsense at

all. If there truly was a third man responsible for Stuart, perhaps your father-in-law is not as crazy as he
seems. Lars mentioned that Devyn ranted about sight
and seeing."

"All right, sir, the bastard wants them to *see*. But
what? What's he showing them?"

"What if he is not showing them?" Dubric asked,
staring at the brain. "What if he is taking images from
them? The brain is shriveled, after all, leeched away."

"He's taking their sight?"

Dubric thought of Braoin's painting, life and death,
two views, two sides. "Perhaps, or the things they *have
seen*. The thread does pass through other parts of the
brain. There is no way to tell what memories are stored
there, what perceptions."

Dien leaned close and examined the lump. "But,
why, sir?"

Dubric glanced at the three ghosts. Otlee still lived,
praise the King. "That is what we must discover."

Dien had gone to bathe while Dubric tidied the
kitchen. Dishes washed and excess food stored away,
Dubric poured himself a fresh cup of tea and wandered
to the sitting room. Several of Braoin's paintings
leaned against the settee, their brilliance calling to
him. *Such a loss*, he thought. He looked away from the
paintings to three of Calum's books sitting upon a
small table, along with an assortment of papers he had
judged to merit further perusal. Many of Calum's
books remained at the Paerth farm. He hoped that he
had not left a vital clue behind. Sighing, he sat and
reached for the first book of the stack.

He began to read Calum's journal, immediately

struck by the scribe's boring and pedantic reflections. Each page listed the date and a description of the weather, then slid into an itemized list and rumination of the day's events. Incredibly organized as well as utterly dry, the mundane and irrelevant details brought a yawn to Dubric's throat. In all his summers taking notes, he had never listed what color of mud had stained his stockings nor how long it had taken to scrub them clean.

He noticed when Maeve rose and set to work on her weaving, and he did his best to ignore his ghosts. But in his entire sixty-eight summers he had never read anything less interesting than Calum's observations of milk being stirred into a bowl of porridge.

Thankful for the distraction, Dubric looked up as Maeve walked into the sitting room with a scrap of paper in her hand. "I found this on the floor of my shop. It's not mine."

He glanced at the paper, the peculiar list of numbers Paol had given him, the same list that matched the painting leaning against the settee. Paol's list must have fallen to the floor of her shop when they came inside. "It is merely evidence we took from a witness. Your son painted it as well. Not only was he a brilliant painter, he was cautious and clever." He retrieved the canvas and showed her the numbers painted on the back.

She paced, tugging at her hair while the air around her seemed to vibrate like a strummed thread. "Why would Braoin paint a warp pattern? That makes no sense. Nothing makes any sense."

He nearly dropped the canvas as he stared at her. "A what?"

She turned to him and shook the paper while tears coursed down her cheeks. "These numbers. They're a warp pattern for a reversible diamond weave. Why? Why would he care about this? Why would anyone care about this?"

A diamond weave! Could it connect to the diamonds on the map? Dubric set the painting aside and reached for his notebook. "Braoin gave these numbers to his friends. They connected the disappearances, but no one knew what they were nor how he found them, only that they corresponded with dates. You are certain they are a weaving pattern?" He flipped through to Paol's notes. *The Devil's Eye.* Devyn had mentioned it by name. The thread through Calum's brain . . . Diamond "eyes" on the map. Sight. *What are we following?*

She resumed pacing. "Of course I am. I've done scores of reversibles. Hundreds, maybe thousands. Warping follows fairly standard patterns." She stared into Dubric's eyes. "You think these numbers mean something, that Braoin left them for a reason?"

"I certainly do," he said, adding to his notes. "He left the painting here, where you could find it, where you would recognize the significance of the digits. That in itself may be a clue as well. What sort of fabric would this make?"

She sat and dropped the list in her lap. She stared at it, and he noticed a twitch beside her left eye. "You have to understand, it might not be a reversible, it all depends on what order and combination the heddles are raised. It could be a jacquard, could be an even weave, but if I were to string this, it would be for diamond reversible."

She looked up to Dubric while tears ran to the corners of her mouth. "I sell a lot of fabric. That's how I earn my living. Braoin knew . . ."

She paused, shaking her head as her eyes grew wide.

"He knew that I'd recognize the pattern! Why didn't he just tell me? Why did he have to go looking for it in the first place?"

"Because he was a curious, principled boy," Dubric said gently. "He tried to help. Tried to stop it."

She lowered her head. "Then it's all my fault, isn't it? I taught him to think and ask questions, to reason things out for himself. I insisted he care about his life, about others, about helping people. Because of my stupid principles he went looking for this damned pattern, and feared it enough to leave it behind as a message for me. And Otlee, not wanting to lose a different clue, disappeared."

Her chin quivered, and the last shred of strength fell. "I killed him. I killed my son and that sweet little boy." She ripped the paper into tiny shreds. "My work, my Goddess-damned work and hopes for my son got him killed. If I'd been content to be poor, if I had kept my place, kept Braoin ignorant and raised him to expect no more from life, he wouldn't be dead. And Otlee might not be lost."

Dubric knelt before her and touched her hand, stilling its shudders. "Look at me, Maeve. Please."

"You're not supposed to be here," she cried, slamming her free fist against the arm of her chair. "I'm supposed to grieve alone. My whole life I've been alone, except for Braoin. Now, when he's gone, I'm not alone anymore? Why?"

"I am not going anywhere," he said, grasping her fingers. "I promise. And I will find whoever did this to your family."

"How could a mother kill her son?"

"You did not kill your son. You were a good mother. A fine mother. And you loved him."

"That doesn't matter now, does it? He's still dead. Like all the others, he's dead." She drew her hand from beneath Dubric's and curled away, crying.

Dubric hung his head, his mind spinning. The list of numbers had a name. Taking a deep breath, he looked at her again. "Does 'the Devil's Eye' mean anything to you?"

Abruptly she turned her head and stared at him. "Where did you hear that?"

He saw a shimmer of fear and uncertainty in her eyes, hiding behind her grief. "As part of my investigation."

She swallowed, shaking her head. "It's a fabric, a reversible weave, that's forbidden. No one makes it, not anymore."

By the King, he wanted to add to his notes, but the notebook lay upon the floor and he dared not pull his gaze from hers. "Why not?"

"Foiche the Devil wore only clothes made from a certain cloth. A red-and-black cloth that was woven to look like eyes. He also made flags from the cloth and hung them from trees and posts and buildings. People said anywhere the cloth was, he could see. He could watch his people, spy on their lives. After he was killed, all the weavers swore never to make that cloth again."

A shiver danced up Dubric's spine at the mention of Foiche's name. "Could these numbers make that cloth?"

"Maybe. I suppose so. The pattern for his cloth is supposedly written in one place. I've never seen it, but my weaving master told me that he had, that it was marked on stone."

"Where?"

She shook her head and cowered away from him. "It's forbidden. A dark place."

He reached for her, grasping her shoulders. "Where, Maeve? Please, I need to know."

She nodded and swallowed, holding his gaze. "It's north of Wittrup. Do you know where the road to Oreth crosses over a narrow creek?"

He had crossed that creek twice. "Yes."

"Follow the creek north. They say that a tower's near where the creek begins, but it's black and burnt and ruined."

Dubric pulled back, releasing her. *The burnt place in Braoin's painting.* "I have been there before. Foiche's watchtower."

Her hands shaking, she pulled a hankie from her pocket and blew her nose. "Now that I think about it, some of the old folks used to call it the Devil's Eye, because he watched everyone from there, and he could see everything. But that was a long time ago, when I was just a child. 'Stay away from that creek because it leads to the Devil's Eye.' 'Don't step in the water or he'll see you and take you away.' Things like that. Stories to scare children."

"They were not merely stories. Foiche the Devil brutalized the people of the Reach. In that tower, I saw horrors beyond the imaginings of a sane man. People tortured and butchered for sport, children mutilated. It was a relief to burn it and salt the ground within its shadow. But I never knew it was called the Devil's Eye."

He stood and turned away.

"Where are you going?" she asked.

He sighed, stopping in the doorway and looking back at her. "To make more tea and get Dien. If we intend to visit that blackened horror again with the hope of rescuing Otlee, we have much planning to do. I dare not enter without preparing in every way I possibly can."

He strode to the kitchen and tried to ignore the
tremble in his hand as he filled the teakettle.

The last of the dishes washed, Lars put away the
plates while Jess wrestled the stew pot into a cupboard.
Fyn dried and sorted eating utensils into their drawer.
Kia had pitched a fit, refusing to work and leaving
them with the mess.

"Thank you for helping," Fyn said, offering him a
smile. "But you didn't need to. It's our responsibility."

Lars shrugged and stacked the bowls. "I dirtied
them, too. I'm glad to help." Jess knelt beside his right
knee and he glanced at her back before taking a deep
breath and dragging his attention away.

Fyn winked at him and tossed the drying rag onto
the pile of forks and spoons. "I'll let you finish up, then.
G'night, Lars, g'night, Jess."

"Night," he called after her. He dried the last bowl
and added it to the stack before putting them all in the
cupboard.

Jess muttered a soft curse and started pulling pans
from the cupboard. "I swear, Kia has the organizational
ability of a turnip. How does she expect anyone to fit
anything in here?"

"She doesn't," he said, kneeling beside her. "I think
that was the point." He reached in and pulled out a
greasy skillet and a baking pan with dried and crusty
bits in the corners. "These need to be washed again."

Sighing, Jess stood. "So do these." A pile of pans and
utensils lay at her feet. "So much for getting any sleep
tonight."

"I'll get fresh water and put it on to heat," he said,

reaching for the bucket hanging on the wall. "Be right back."

"Dad and Dubric said you weren't allowed outside after dark by yourself."

Lars stopped and lowered his head, sighing. "I am perfectly capable of going to the well to get one bucket of water. It's five steps from the back door."

"I know," she said, her voice soft and tentative, "but I can go with you. If you want. So you won't get into trouble."

He didn't know whether to feel embarrassed or elated, but he couldn't help but smile as she followed him down the hall and out the back door.

The night spread wide and dark above them, each star a pinprick of sparkle against the sky.

While he primed the pump, she walked past him and looked up to the stars. "Nights like this make me feel so small," she said. "The sky seems so big at night, don't you think?"

"I used to, until I learned more about it. Now it's like a giant storybook."

"What do you mean?"

He filled the bucket and set it on the ground. "We'd have to step away from the door for me to show you."

She looked at him, her eyes sparkling in reflected lamplight. After the briefest of hesitations she nodded. "All right."

He fell in beside her and they walked around the side of the house, past Devyn and Lissea's bedroom window. Utter blackness overtook them, the sliver of moon lost and hidden behind the house, and Lars looked at the sky as he led her around a tree to a clear patch of ground. "Here's a good spot."

He sat, leaning back on his elbows, and she sat

beside him, both looking to the stars. He pointed straight up. "Do you see that reddish star there, the one that's twinkling?"

"Just to the left of that greenish one? Yes."

He grinned. "Okay, imagine that red star is a dragon's nose, its nostril. Look to the right, to that green one, and think of it as the dragon's eye. See the curved line of white stars beyond that?"

He turned to look at her, smiling as her mouth fell open. "They twist onto themselves, almost like a snake."

"Yes. And past the dragon's twist, to the right, do you see a straight line of stars? Five of them?" He saw her nod, saw her smile. "And moving upward, almost a circle?"

"More like an egg," she corrected, glancing at him.

He grinned. "That's Harim, the hunter. The line of stars is his sword . . ."

She looked back to the stars and laughed, pointing. "And the curly thing is Blathshel, the dragon. Just like in the ancients' myths."

"Exactly. Supposedly their great deeds sent the ancient heroes to the heavens, but Dubric says that the ancients made up stories to match the stars."

"How many stories are there? In the stars?"

He looked to the sky again, searching for an easy-to-see constellation. "Lots. Like over there, to the west. See that clump of really bright stars?" When she nodded, he led her across the great spider to the farmer who saved a village from her hunger. Then he drew her attention to the north, to the war cat and the running horses. To the west again and the king of birds.

The wind picked up and clouds moved across the sky, obscuring the stars and bringing damp chill with them. Lars shivered, looking along the brush line for glowing red eyes, but he saw none. He realized he was holding his breath. "Guess we'd better get back to work." He helped Jess to her feet and brushed off his trousers. They walked to the well, but he paused before grasping the bucket. He didn't want to go inside, didn't want to go back to being just her brother again.

"Jess?"

She had opened the door, but she stopped to look at him, the wind teasing her hair and the light from inside turning her skin warm and golden. "Yes?"

He stared into her eyes. "I didn't touch Fyn. I've never wanted to touch Fyn. Nothing like that happened in the cellar. I promise."

She nodded, chewing her lower lip. "All right."

"And . . ." He took a deep breath, then another, fidgeting. *What do I say? What do I do?*

She closed the door, watching him. "And?"

"And, um . . . Um. This was fun."

"Yes, it was," she said, looking as nervous as he felt.

He moved a step closer and started to reach for her hand, but stopped as she smiled shyly and lowered her eyes.

A million thoughts tangled in his head, begging to be said, to be acted upon. But he was five days short of courting age, she two phases, and he had given his word that he would wait until she was old enough. Until they were both old enough.

Lars pulled his hand back and took a deep breath as the first cold raindrops landed on his brow. He had given his word. Hopes and wants were immaterial when faced with the measure of a man's word. He knew that as well as he knew his own name.

He forced a smile and lifted the bucket, sloshing

cold water on his leg. "We'd better finish those dishes. It's getting late."

"Sure," she said, opening the door for him.

As he walked past her he looked into the pale green depths of her eyes and nearly stumbled. Embarrassed, he carried the bucket to the stove and set the water to heat, wondering all the while if he could remain merely her brother for two more phases, or if he would ever become anything else in her eyes.

By the time he crawled to his pillow on the settee, his thoughts had snarled into worries. He fell asleep to the sound of rain, dreaming of the apparition that had chased them the night before. This time it caught them at the door. It snapped Aly's neck and tossed her aside, then reached for Jess. It snatched out her lovely green eyes, and, grinning, it ripped out her throat with its teeth.

"You killed them. It's all your fault," the black thing laughed as Jess fell dead at its feet.

Then it held Otlee before him, naked and bleeding and blinded. "Want to watch?" it asked, grinning, and thrust Otlee toward its engorged penis, just as it had threatened to do to Aly.

Lars jolted awake. *I kept the girls safe. I brought them home. And you don't have Otlee. You can't! It's just a bad dream. A horrid, bad dream.*

Shaking, he stared at the ceiling for a long time, until sleep overtook him. When he opened his eyes again, Aly grinned down at him with another wheel broken off her cart. He smelled griddle cakes and sausage, heard Kia and Fyn arguing and the baby's hungry cries. Another day of family had begun, thank the Goddess.

CHAPTER

19

✝

Dubric woke well before dawn and brewed a pot of tea. He and Dien had spent half the night planning their search of Foiche's tower. Dien had not yet risen, but Dubric could not sleep. Too many memories and fears twirled in his mind.

The water heating, he sharpened his sword while Lachesis meowed at his feet and begged to be petted. Hot tea finally in hand, Dubric sat at the kitchen table, reviewing his notes and wishing the damned cat would get off his lap, or at least stop shedding on it.

Why did I not bother to retrieve my notations from the war? He sighed, flipping a page. *When I left the castle, why did I not consider that somehow Foiche's power remained? So many similarities, so many dead, in the same place as before.* He rubbed his eyes and closed the notebook. *By the King, why did I not see?*

Maeve entered the kitchen, looking as if she'd slept not at all. "I thought I heard someone up and about. Good morning."

"Good morning," he replied, standing to tidy the mess on the table. "I apologize for the clutter. I shall remove it immediately."

"Oh, never mind about that. What harm are a few

papers and things?" She freshened his cup of tea, then poured one for herself. "Have you always seen ghosts?"

"No." The tea warmed his throat, and he nodded his thanks.

She sat across from him and offered a sweet biscuit. "What happened? You seem too good a man to carry such a burden."

He looked into his teacup, into the soothing brown liquid. So long ago, a lifetime, and yet the pain of Oriana's passing had never healed. "My wife, she . . . she was a servant of Malanna. There was a fire. I tried to save her, but I failed. She died."

Maeve reached out and touched the back of his scarred hand. "Oh, Dubric! I'm so sorry!"

"It is all right," he replied, forcing a smile. "It was a long time ago." He took another sip of tea. "The Goddess cursed me for my failure, so now I must seek justice for those who were not meant to die."

"What a burden it must be."

He shrugged and set his teacup on the table with a slight clatter. "We all bear the burdens of our past."

"You must have loved her very much."

"Yes. I still do." Sighing, he ate a biscuit.

"How long have you been alone?"

"Forty-six summers."

Her eyes opened with astonishment.

"It does not matter, not anymore. What is past remains there, no matter how we may wish it would change."

She shook her head and smiled sadly. "I assumed you'd been recently widowed."

He laughed. "Goodness, no. I was twenty-two summers old when Oriana died. She was nineteen. We had only been married three moons."

"So no children?"

How long has it been? he wondered. *How long since I simply talked with someone about life and regret and whatever else came to mind? How long since I talked with a woman? How long since I allowed anyone to come near me?* He sighed and picked up his cup again. "We wanted a family and did a good job trying. She missed her courses our second moon together, and again the third. The Goddess took both of them. My wife and my child."

She touched his hand again. "I'm sorry."

"Thank you, but there is no need. It was not of your doing and nothing can be done to change it." He sipped his tea and asked, "How long have you been widowed?"

"I've never married."

He considered her, raising one eyebrow. "I never would have guessed. It must have been difficult raising a child alone. Did his father at least aid you?"

Maeve laughed harshly. "This will sound horrid, I know, but I have no idea who his father was."

"Oh," Dubric said, returning his attention to his tea. "It is none of my business."

"No, it's all right. 'Twas a long time ago. Painful though it may be, it can no longer hurt me." She leaned back in her chair, cradling her teacup in both hands. "When I was still a girl, I worked dyeing thread in a shop, as did a friend of mine, and we walked to and from work together. One night a man accosted us on the road. She escaped; I didn't. I couldn't get away, and he took what he wanted."

"Oh, Maeve," he said.

"My father felt shamed and disgraced, and my betrothed deserted me, disgusted by my lack of virtue."

She paused and looked at the ceiling. "That was bad, but when I discovered Braoin was growing inside me, my fa . . . my father disowned me. He thought I'd done it to embarrass him. I was alone, all except for Lissea and her family. I barely knew her, but she took me in.

"I couldn't bear to have the midwife kill him, and once I saw him I couldn't give him away. 'Twas not his fault, what had happened. So I raised him to be a good man, a far cry from the bastard that begot him and the two that turned their backs to me when I most needed their help."

She smiled then and looked into Dubric's eyes. "And he was a good man, a damn good man. He loved Faythe, he worked hard, he treated people with respect and kindness. From him I learned that even the worst curse can bring a blessing."

Dubric stood and walked to her side. "I will find who killed him, I swear to you I will. I will find the man responsible and I will see him hanged."

She reached for his hand and squeezed it. "I know you will."

They looked at each other for a long moment, until Maeve blushed and drew her hand away. "I'd best see to breakfast. I know you wanted to be on the road first thing." Giving a quick smile, she stood and hurried to the pantry.

Dubric watched her disappear down the hall, and the pounding of his heart begged that he follow her. He took a single step then paused, shaking his head. "Mind your manners, you old goat," he mumbled. He reached for his tea, and wondered what he was going to do.

* * *

Lars sat on the settee, staring at Otlee's gear while the family made hats. *There has to be something I can do.*

He grasped Otlee's pack and opened it. The girls had put everything back, but it was disorganized and messy, nothing like the way that Otlee kept it. Items were thrown in without regard for use or convenience or Otlee's preference.

He's coming home. He has to.

Lars dumped the contents on the floor between his feet and methodically returned each item to its rightful place. Dry socks and clean trousers. A ragged, second-hand book—*Understanding Optics and Light.* Two feathers. A mathematics book and a half-written literature paper dissecting an obscure poem. A broken pencil and a brand-new one. A vial of aromatic mint. Keys. Boot wax. A library token. A tin of headache powder.

Lars examined each thing before he put it away and tried not to cry. He set aside the survey map, along with some official-looking papers and books, hoping he could glean something from them. He packed slowly, taking his time, until only one thing remained.

He picked up Otlee's journal and rubbed his fingers over the mud stains, loosening and brushing away the dirt, then he opened the battered cover. "You always took excellent notes," he said softly, smiling at the opening paragraphs, a retelling of Otlee's first day as Dubric's page.

"Help me find you," he whispered, and began to read.

When Dubric and Dien reached Wittrup, the sky glowed a glorious pink to the east, and the first shimmers of sunlight glinted on the river. Gulls glided over the water, seeking fish, and dock workers toiled under packs, parcels, and boxes of goods.

Even with the stink of rotting fish and festering sewage, Dubric breathed deep. It was going to be a lovely day, brilliant and clear. A good day to hunt mages.

They rode to the ferry, Dien tossing coins to the children along the way, and Dubric tried to keep his stomach from twisting into knots. He had always been of the opinion that some secrets were best left dead and buried. He had brought no shovel to dig up his past, nor any particular equipment or armor. He had only his memories, his sword, and his determination to find one bright, inquisitive boy.

He said little more than the barest of polite pleasantries as they ferried across the Casclian River, and he rode in silence to the creek, wishing that he could enjoy the feel of morning sunshine on the back of his neck.

The previous night's rain had turned the creek into a coursing, muddy ditch, crossed with puddled wagon tracks and hoofprints. They rode across, the horses flicking splatters of mud and water onto their flanks and their riders' shins. Once past the creek, Dubric kept his charger along the northern edge of the road and looked for any travel-broken openings in the weeds and brambles.

Perhaps fifty yards beyond the creek, he reined in and dismounted, pulling his sword. "A wagon or cart," he said, crouching before the battered weeds as he examined the trail. "It is pulled by a single horse or mule." He took a step forward, into the brush, dragging his hand along the tips of the dead leaves and sticks and ruffling them in the morning breeze. "It is not traveled often. Grasses remain along the tracks and there is little exposed dirt."

Squinting, he stared into the brush, at the cart-broken path leading north. He sighed and turned back to Dien. "There is no telling what we might find or face."

"Yes, sir," Dien said. He drew his sword.

Dubric mounted his charger and reined about to lead the way through the tangle, his hopes soon faltering. No one had traveled the route for days; the occasional hoofprint lay obscured by rain and left little more than a circular dent in the grass. He saw no human footprints, no discarded bits of refuse, nothing but broken weeds and the ghost of a trail from a passing cart.

The trail led through a stand of trees, along the faint remains of a long-forgotten stretch of road. Birds tittered as they rode through, and a squirrel scurried from their path. Uncheered by the natural peace in the scrap of woods, Dubric clenched his teeth and kept riding, with Dien right behind.

A grassy hill rose before them, then faded, only to reveal another. Despite the open grassland, Dubric could see no evidence that sheep had ever grazed there; the land was wild and untended, marred only by the faint cart tracks and the ruins far ahead. Soon, Dubric saw the first remnants of the old tower, a black and charred post thrusting up from the fields. Three hills later he could see much of its decayed and crumbling form, the ancient metal beams and bricks crumbled into a haphazard pile on the ground. Skeletal remains of houses were clustered around the main ruin, their wooden beams and mudded walls blackened and decayed. Decades of seasons had washed away much of the charring and ash, but the tortured remains of Foiche's compound still looked burnt and dead.

As had Byreleah Grennere, before the tower had begun to fall.

"That's it, sir?" Dien asked, bringing his horse alongside. "It's just a jumble of ruins."

Dubric swallowed away the acrid taste in his mouth. "That is what remains of Foiche's tortures. I had hoped I would never see them again."

Weeds had grown between fallen beams and rusted machinery, sprouting amidst the charred and battered bricks and steel. Four scorched, concrete posts still stood, rising from the ground like black, accusing fingers pointing to the sky. Three were as tall as five men standing on one another's shoulders, but the fourth towered above them, its shadow stretching far across the field. Broken crossbeams remained attached to its crusty, crumbling surface, sprawling out like the legs of an upended ant. Several more beams lay like lashes upon the ruined machinery cowering in supplication below.

Old books in the libraries of Waterford showed that, before the mages, people had embraced technology and science. They had created great machines of steel and steam; some traveled faster than a man on horseback, others milled lumber or wove vast amounts of cloth. Smaller ancient mechanisms burned images on coated tin, or measured time. But, for all of their knowledge, the ancients fell before the rise of dark magic, just as the mages later fell to the armies of light.

Dubric dismounted and led his horse around the crumbling testaments to a forgotten time. "Watch for pits and sinkholes."

Dien looked around him. "Pits and sinkholes? That's a bit of an understatement."

Dubric sighed and rubbed his eyes. They walked along the edge of a nearly circular pit as large as Maeve's home, a vicious hole cleaved in the earth by a massive burst of fire and shards of metal. Time had softened the perimeter with erosion and weeds, and had filled part of the depth with sparkling water, but the scar itself remained.

Fifteen men from his army had been instantly incinerated in the explosion. One moment they were living, breathing beings, the next they were nothing more than ash and flame. They had not had time to scream, pray, or even blink. Dubric could not remember their names, and it shamed him.

Grinding his teeth, he walked along the edge and searched for the cart tracks again. "This is but one of many. Some are rather small, the landing points of steel balls the size of a man's skull. Others are much larger." He stopped walking and pointed past the ruined tower. "If my memory is accurate, a single blast hole beyond the northern wall was large enough to hold three hundred men and all of their gear. Seventy-two disappeared in the explosion. My best lieutenant was one of them. I cannot remember how many were injured." Shaking his head, he resumed walking. "It has likely become a pond by now, and fish have fed on what pieces we could not recover."

Dien shoved aside a hunk of cement. "How many men faced this madness?"

The widest path wound between heaps of piled bricks, and Dubric trudged along, looking for crushed grass. "Seven thousand, on our side. Only two thousand walked away once the battle had ended. Eight hundred more were carried. Nearly fifteen hundred were never found or identified. We had faced worse battles, but not many." Dubric located the cart tracks and followed them between crumbling masonry and rusted steel. The path led past the great tower's foundation, skirting along its western edge.

Dien looked around him then shook his head. "I know you don't like to talk about the war, but how'd you do it? How did you get to him? He had magic, the high ground . . ."

"Determination and a great deal of luck," Dubric said. "Scores gave their lives so that a handful of men could scale the eastern wall and enter the second floor of the main building. Once inside, they set fire to whatever they could find. Fire consumed the base building and spread to the tower."

Dien picked up a filthy shard of glass as long as his forearm and tossed it into the weeds. "Brave bastards."

"Yes. They knew they would die." They paused near the tallest post, a square shaft of concrete and steel wider than Dubric could spread his arms. A long stretch of the original wall remained attached to it, and smaller posts and twisted, rusty rods poked out from the masonry. A series of metal numbers in the style of the ancient people had been bolted to the bricks. They were corroded from exposure to the elements. The same set of numbers Braoin had painted, but with the last two digits missing.

A corked bottle lay in the mud and broken masonry just off the path. Dien picked it up and cursed as he opened and sniffed it. "Sweet vitriol, sir," he said, handing the bottle to Dubric. "A lot easier to handle a boy if he's not able to fight back."

Dubric pulled an evidence bag from his pack. An

aromatic, medicinal fluid, sweet vitriol—or ether, as the castle physicians sometimes called it—had long been used to deaden pain or put surgery patients to sleep. Most physicians, but few others, had access to similar anesthetic concoctions.

The evidence packed away, Dubric added to his notes. "How accessible would you gauge sweet vitriol to be?"

Dien rubbed the top of his head. "Here? I don't know, sir. I'm damn near positive Dev has a bottle in his shop as a solvent, and I know I've seen it several places about the Reach."

"Each locale can regulate its own intoxicants and medications, damn them," Dubric said, moving forward again.

"And it wouldn't take much of that shit to take Otlee down."

The tracks led behind the wall; he led his horse around the corner. Another line of broken masonry stretched before him, but a wide, wheel-marked path lay between it and the wall, with only occasional bricks scattered upon the bare ground. On the mossy north-facing of the wall, locked forever in deep shade, few grasses and weeds grew along the pathway. Dubric doubted if much snow accumulated there either, or torrential rain. The pile of bricks to one side and the wall to the other offered continual shelter. A pair of finches had built their nest in the bricks, and they fluttered about, scolding as Dubric and Dien walked past.

The wheel tracks on the path, while softened by wind and rain, remained reasonably fresh, as did the unshod hoofprints of the horse. Other than the angry finches and occasional dried remains of spindly weeds, he saw no life or sunlight, only the deep blue sky far above.

Behind him, Dien grumbled, "I found another bottle sir, but it's broken. There's also a rotting bit of cloth—a handkerchief, maybe—and a whiskey bottle." Dien paused, sounding ashamed. "Lars and I found a whiskey bottle near the river, but I never thought much of it."

"Gather them. Whiskey is common here. I have seen several bottles lying beside the roads, and I would not have considered it a viable clue, either." Dubric followed the muddy path, but paused to stare at the gray and mossy wall.

Shackles hung from the bricks at eye level, spaced nearly an arm's width apart. The moss on the wall between them had been scoured away in patches that roughly resembled the shape of a person. Smeared, dried blood decorated the bare patch he associated with the head, and other dark flecks stained the bricks at hip level.

"Aw, piss," Dien said.

"What is it?" Dubric asked, turning, but he soon found himself cursing as well.

A pair of skulls, stripped of flesh and missing their jaws, stared at him, moving slightly in the breeze. They hung suspended on shiny black twine from either side of a hole in the wall of loose bricks. Between and below them, leg and arm bones hung over the opening, along with cut strips of red-and-black-patterned cloth and ragged feathers. Reddish clay smeared the ground from inside the opening out toward the path, giving the hole the appearance of an open toothy maw with its tongue hanging out.

"We seem to have found it, sir."

"That we have." Dubric crouched before the opening and peered inside. The tunnel stretched into utter darkness. "Light the lantern."

While Dien readied the light, Dubric snatched a strip of fabric from the maw. The black-and-red diamond pattern reversed on each side—one side black with red diamonds, the other red with black—and although the cloth was wind-ravaged and faded, it retained strength and flexibility. Frowning, he folded the fabric and put it in his pocket, then squinted into the dark.

Not again. Not here.

"Sir? Is there something wrong? You look ill."

Dubric rolled back until his backside rested on his heels. "After the tower fell, we chased Foiche and his guards through a tunnel much like this. Hundreds of soldiers, myself included, crawled after him. We were not far behind when the tunnel filled with smoke and flame and collapsed. I was lucky. The man ahead of me had his shield strapped to his hip. Its shelter created a pocket of air to breathe, and I was close enough to an exposed opening to be unearthed and found. Everyone near me was crushed or suffocated."

Dubric sighed and wiped sweat from his brow. "There is nothing as black and horrifying as being buried alive, being trapped and unable to move, barely able to breathe. I have not well endured enclosed spaces since then, nor caves. Truth be told, I have not even entered a cave since the war ended, though I used to enjoy exploring them."

"I can go by myself," Dien offered.

"Nonsense." Dubric smoothed his tunic and took a deep breath. "I have managed before and will do so again." Grasping the lantern, he crept past the hanging bones and into the darkness.

He had barely left the light from the opening when he paused. Not only did he see prints from hands and knees, but something had been dragged through the tunnel, several times in both directions. Gouges and scrapes marred the packed clay, starting and stopping with angled, directional scars of disrupted earth. The air and the clay beneath his hands had the stink of a cesspool, gassy and vile, but he saw no evidence of excrement or rotting meat.

Dubric noted the condition of the tunnel floor, then continued on as it curved to the right.

The ceiling opened above him, and he stood before stepping down into a pit. Rusted metal beams angled far above, creating a jagged, peaked ceiling, while black strands hung down all around them with insects and small birds tied at the ends as if they were hovering in mid-flight. The bricks and metal of the walls were painted black, while the floor was reddish clay. A pole with a lantern hook stood not far ahead to his right. Partially obscured by the dangling insects and just beyond the reach of his light, he saw shadows in the darkness but could not discern what they were. A clear path wound through the curtain of dead bugs and tiny birds, and Dubric followed it. Lantern held before him, he strode toward the shadows and paused, holding out his hand to stop Dien.

A blackened altar of rough wood stood below a throne of red brick. An ancient and rotted corpse wrapped in red-and-black diamond cloth sat upon the throne, with a curtain of black strings flowing from its slippered feet and cascading down a set of brick stairs. Grinning a toothy leer, it stared down at the altar. The corpse clenched a shiny black whip in one hand; a large wasp rested on his other bony palm. Something beside the corpse shifted in a draft and Dubric turned, his lantern held high.

Large, dead birds hung from twine in the shadows, seven on either side of the corpse like acolytes attending their priest. Ripped black cloth draped over their extended wings, hanging in tatters to the ground. Their eye sockets were dark and their mouths hung open, some with red string tied around their shiny beaks. A few had clothos worms roiling on their decaying flesh, and black strands spun between their claws.

"Goddess-damned son of a whore," Dien gasped, yanking down some of the suspended insects that had snarled onto his clothes. "What kind of temple is this?"

"Foiche's," Dubric said. He walked to the altar slowly, trying not to lose his breakfast. The altar stood chest high and nearly square, with iron loops about two-thirds down on the near side. A board as long as his spread arms lay across the far side, facing the corpse and strapped down with black twine. Near each end of the board, grooves were worn into the edges. Tiny, glistening bits of black twine sprouted from the grooves, and cut strands of twine hung from the irons. The acolyte birds watched, swaying in the shadows, and a chill danced up Dubric's spine.

"So this is where the bastard tied them down?" Dien asked. He looked at Dubric with horror.

"It would appear so," Dubric said. "There is no blood to speak of. No evidence of cutting. They are brought here, but must be killed someplace else. Otlee is not dead, nor is he here. Where could he be?"

A pile of discarded clothing lay to the right of the altar, beneath the widely opened robe of a large raven.

Dubric knelt beside it. Pants, shirts, boots, undergarments, and coats in a variety of sizes and qualities lay amongst purses and books, spectacles and jewelry, fishing gear and tools. None were Otlee's.

Dubric handed Dien the light and lifted a pair of mud-stained trousers. "Coins remain in the pockets and pouches." Dubric shrugged his knapsack from his back and pulled a bag from inside. He sorted through the clothes, folding them as he stacked them aside. He paused as he reached the bottom of the pile. "What have we here?"

He held up a gold ring with a sparkling green stone. Surely worth several hundred crown, it lay untended and forgotten in the clay as if it had no worth whatsoever.

He placed the ring and loose coins in the side pouch of his pack and stood again, brushing off his aching knees. "List and pack the clothing and other items. I shall examine the altar."

Dien nodded and set to work, laying his sword beside his knee while he retrieved his notebook.

Ignoring the shifting shadows, Dubric walked around the altar and plucked a few short strands of thread from the length of board. "They were tied down, they struggled," he said, rubbing the strands between his fingers. The corpse grinned down at him and he shuddered.

"He wants Foiche to watch, but why? What is he trying to prove? Why not kill them here? Why bring them here at all?"

He looked at the nearest birds. Loath to touch them, he pulled another sack from his pack and nearly yelped when Dien came to his side.

"While I gather these, would you please get samples

of the various twines and label where you retrieved them from?"

Dien set down the sack of clothing, then lumbered around the altar to the corpse. "I'll bust that bastard into pulp when I get my hands on him. So help me, he'll frigging wish he'd never—"

Dubric had put but three birds into his sack when he heard Dien stop. "What is it?" he asked, turning.

Dien reached between the corpse's feet, past the curtain of string. "There's something in there."

His task forgotten, Dubric walked over.

Dien pulled out a brown parcel and turned, handing it to Dubric. "It's a canvas sack."

"So I see." Dubric accepted the bag and opened it while Dien reached between the feet again. Three carefully folded letters lay inside, all addressed to him. He opened one and read a woman's heartfelt plea for his aid in finding her son. Another letter, from a farmer asking Dubric to come and locate a missing neighbor boy.

"Two more sacks, and a parchment parcel. It's sealed."

Tucking the first batch under his arm, Dubric accepted the sealed package and frowned as he turned it in the light. The seal, a flecked gray wad of wax bearing Haconry's mark, snapped beneath his fingers.

More letters, all addressed to Castellan Dubric, Castle Faldorrah. Three were written in Calum's dull and familiar hand.

"Damn," he muttered, glaring up at Foiche's grinning corpse. Dubric crammed the letters in his pack and thrust the bundle at Dien. "Take the evidence to the entrance to this room and give a shout if anyone approaches."

"Yes, sir."

Dubric reached for Foiche's leg. As he dragged the corpse from its throne he said, "I killed you once, you bastard spawn from the seven hells. I'll be damned if I ever set eyes upon you again."

Foiche clattered to the floor, the joints breaking apart, and Dubric climbed to the throne to knock down the last bits of fabric and bone. That finished, he yanked the remaining birds into the moldering pile, dropped the step box onto it, then shoved the altar against the bones. He lifted the lantern from the floor and took a deep breath.

He spat on the ground then smeared his saliva under the toe of his boot. "May you burn for eternity, and may your vile plots come to naught." After dashing the lantern on the pile of bones and wood, he turned and walked to Dien, flickering shadows leading the way.

They crawled through the tunnel to fresh air, and both turned to watch smoke rise to the sky.

Late morning hung fat and lazy over the farm when Jess left the house. Tired of assembling hats and trying not to dwell on what had happened to Otlee, she had turned her thoughts to baking. A carpenter on the roof waved a greeting and she waved back, then she walked to the henhouse and went inside.

The henhouse was dark and steamy, thick with the scent of chickens roosting in the heat of the day. A few scratched the dirt and weeds outside, but most sat upon their nests and fussed softly at her as she searched for eggs.

Of the first three hens, two had eggs. Six hens later, she found a third. Three more barren nests. Beginning to worry, she reached under another hen. "C'mon, girls. I know it's early, but I need six eggs for nut bread." Success! Patting the hen, she placed the fourth egg in her basket and moved down the line.

She found two more eggs with a hen to spare, counted them again just to be sure, then left the hen-house with a smile on her face and a recipe running through her head.

On the ramp, she turned to latch the door, then gasped as someone grabbed her. The basket of eggs went flying, rolling in the mud, and cold, rough hands slammed her against the wall.

One of the carpenters leered at her, licking his teeth, while another held her tight against the hen-house. "Dangit, Rao. Looks like we done caught us the quiet one."

Rao, the one gripping her right arm, said, "I was hopin' for her sister. She's been givin' us the look, not this here bit o' nothin'."

The first one reached for a handful of her hair, sniffing it. "A bird in the hand, my papa always says. She does smell purty. An' she's got nice titties, too."

Her eyes darted between them, noting the other two moving closer and blocking her in. With one, maybe she'd have a chance, but four? "Let me go!" she demanded.

Rao, his shoulders and upper arms bare to show his wind-tanned muscles, grinned and tweaked her breast, leaving a grimy smear on her dress. "Your granddad just went to the outhouse, girlie, and he's too crazy to care. We already whipped that pigshit farm boy's ass once. He ain't gonna save you neither. And your daddy's gone. You're all ours now."

She spat in his eye and struggled to get away, but

they held her against the wall, laughing and cutting off her shrieks with filthy hands across her mouth while they took turns groping her.

Anxious to get back to Otlee's journal, Lars lugged a box of felt hats to Devyn's shop and paused, listening. *Was that a squeal? One of the girls?* He dropped the box and strained to hear. Silence echoed all around him, nothing but wind and birdsong. Something was wrong, but what? It was too quiet, this early in the day, because . . .

His mouth fell dry. No hammering. Then he heard it, an indignant shriek cut off. Snarling, he vaulted over the sty fence and hit the ground running. Pigs squealed as they scattered out of his way. He cleared the far fence and ran toward the outbuildings.

"No, please . . ." drifting on the wind. *Jess!*

He paused only long enough to pull his dagger from his boot, then he sprinted, rounding the henhouse.

All four workers clumped together, laughing and tossing their quarry between them, taking turns kissing and groping her. Jess's dress was torn, and the farthest pulled her hair to tilt her head back, kissing her in a vicious mockery of desire.

Snarling, Lars bashed the nearest's skull with the hilt of his dagger and yanked the boy away, throwing him to the ground. The next gasped and tried to throw a punch, but Lars dipped low and turned, opening the fellow's thigh. He dropped, screaming, and showered Lars with a burst of blood.

Two left—the pair who had tried to strangle him a couple of days before. They shoved Jess away and came at him together. Both pulled hammers from their belts, and the bigger sneered, "Guess we didn't whup you good enough last time, did we, little puppy?"

Lars lunged. Snap, twist, and one hammer fell to the mud, its wielder's wrist broken. An elbow to the face sent him sprawling. Lars ducked the other's swing, sweeping with his left leg as he bobbed. The fourth down but uninjured, Lars rolled forward and pinned him to the ground with his blade through the boy's shoulder.

He regained his footing and gasped a deep breath, running to Jess while the carpenters writhed and wailed behind him. She cowered by the henhouse door, hiding behind her knees with her arms up and covering her face.

He knelt before her, afraid to touch her but needing to know. "Jess. Jess! Are you all right?"

She squealed, flailing at him, but he reached between her pummeling hands and grasped her by the armpits. He let her hit him, let her scream and kick. One gentle shake. "Jesscea!"

Her eyes were wild, her head rolled, and she shuddered in rapid waves, but he drew her upright. "Jess," he said again, softer as he tried to search her crazed and alien eyes, "did they hurt you? Did they—"

Reason snapped back into place; he saw its flash in the soft sea green of her eyes. A wail burbled in her throat and she leapt forward, into his arms.

Unsure of how to hold her, terrified of doing more harm, he hugged her gently and asked again if she was hurt.

"Four of them!" she cried against his cheek and neck. "What could I do against four?"

"Nothing," he whispered, stroking her hair. "It's all right now. Shh, it's all right."

He glanced back at the injured carpenters. They wouldn't be mobile anytime soon. "Can you walk?"

Jess nodded, her head thumping against his throat. Her shudders slowed to small tremors, and she pulled her hand from his back and stared at it. "Goddess, you're bleeding."

"Not me. Just them. C'mon, let's get you inside. To your mam." Jess trembling in his arms, he helped her to the house.

Sarea burst through the door, nearly knocking them over. "Oh, Goddess, what happened?"

"The carpenters—" Lars started, but Sarea pulled Jess away and his voice dried in his throat.

"Inside, both of you." Sarea helped Jess in, and Lars followed. "Goddess, Lars. How bad are you hurt? Where did they cut you? You've got blood everywhere."

"I'm not." His knees felt weak but he took a breath and kept moving. "Did they hurt Jess? Did they—"

Lissea was there, peeling off his shirt. "Hold still," she said. "Ye've got a deep gash on yer back."

"I do?" Startled, he stood dumbly in the middle of the sitting room while Jess and Sarea disappeared down the hall.

"Kia! Fetch me a bowl of water and a clean towel."

"Yes, Grandmama," she said, running.

"Is Jess all right?" he asked. "Where's Jess?"

"She's fine," Lissea said. "Hold still."

Fire erupted on Lars's back, between his shoulder and his spine, and he winced. Something hard and heavy hit the floor. It sounded like metal.

Kia appeared, shoving a bowl of steaming water at her grandmother. She grimaced and paled. "I'll fetch some thread."

"Yow!" he yelped, twisting away.

"Hold still, boy," Liss snapped. "Ye've got dirt and rust crammed in there and I gotta get it out."

"What? How? They never touched me."

She slammed something into his palm. "They touched ye, all right, and yer lucky to be standin' here. Now hold still."

Dumbstruck, he stared at the broken nail hook in his hand. Snapped loose from the hammer, one end was sharp and metallic, the other rusted and filthy, coated in blood. While Lissea cleaned the wound, he clenched the hunk of ruined metal and let his pain flow into it, all the while staring at the hallway entrance. He wondered if Jess was hurt, and if he should have killed the bastards instead of merely dropping them.

He endured the stitches without making a sound, then yanked on his shirt as he hurried to the hall. "Jess? Sarea?" he called. He heard crying ahead, saw Fyn burst from the bath chamber and run to her room. She came back with a blanket, and he followed her, pausing at the bath chamber door.

"Is she . . ." he asked, afraid to look.

"She's fine," Sarea said. "Come on in."

He peered around the door and his breath fell out in a rush. Jess sat upon the edge of the empty tub with her torn and muddy skirt hiked up to her knees. She tugged the blanket around her shoulders while her mother bandaged her leg. "Thanks," she said, smiling at him. "And I'm sorry if I hit you."

He shrugged. "It's okay. You all right?"

She nodded, wiping her eyes with the back of her hand and leaving a streak of mud behind. "Thanks to you. Banged my knee, scared the breath out of me. But I'm fine. I think."

"Good." He smiled, nodded, then turned to go.

"Lars, wait." Brushing past her mother, she came to him and wrapped her arms around his neck. "Thank you." He felt the warm dampness of her lips against his cheek in an astounding jolt, and a tightening of her embrace.

He hugged her back, holding her tight while his heart hammered. "You're welcome," he whispered in her ear.

CHAPTER

20

✝

Dubric and Dien rode to Myrtle, then to the home-steads beyond, searching for Eagon's family. They found a farm hiding behind a tangle of hawthorn and stick bushes, a decrepit house on a rocky strip of land. A few sheep grazed behind a stone fence, and a thin line of smoke rose from the chimney. The place looked dusty and tired. Neglected.

Dien put away his notes. "This seems to be it."

Dubric looked at the three ghosts but none paid the least bit of notice. Calum and Braoin screamed, while Eagon paced back and forth, oblivious and flickering. "Let us hope they have useful information."

They rode through the yard past two large dogs slavering and snarling on chains. An unshaven, rum-pled man in a filthy tunic threw the door open and stomped out on bare feet. "What ye want? Taxes ain't due fer damn near a moon!"

"We are not here to collect taxes," Dubric said, shift-ing in the saddle. "We are here to discuss your son."

"Rotten little good-fer-nothin' bastards." The man turned toward the open door and hollered, "Stoc! Hawley! Get yer asses out here!"

Two prepubescent boys, both scrawny, barefoot, and

filthy, came outside, cowering. "We didn't do nothin', Pa!" the taller of the pair said.

The man slapped him across the face, knocking him to the dirt. "His lordship says you did, filthy shit. What'd ye do? Steal a pumpkin? Draw dirty pictures on his walls? Piss in his garden?"

"No, Pa!" the boy cried, covering his head with his arms.

"What the peg do you think you're doing?" Dien asked.

The man pulled the boy from the dirt by the scruff of the neck and shook him. "I've tried my damnedest, milord, I swear I have. But he's contrary, like his mother."

"Contrary, my pimpled ass," Dien said, sliding from the saddle. "The kid's terrified."

"Let the child go," Dubric said, holding up his hands in an effort to calm both men. "I am Castellan Dubric, from Lord Brushgar's castle, and I am here to talk about Eagon, not either of these boys."

The man dropped his son and kicked him in the backside as the boy scrambled for the door. "Eagon's gone, damn near a whole moon now. I ain't seem him and he ain't comin' back." He looked Dubric in the eye and added, "And good riddance, I say. I didn't want his kind around the little'uns."

Dubric felt Dien bristle beside him. "His *kind*?" Dien asked.

The man's gaze shifted to Dien, and he spat. "He was queer. A fey boy. Laid with other fey boys, maybe animals. Damn thing to have in a good man's home, filth like that."

Dubric took a slow breath and struggled to remain calm. "May we talk inside?"

"Suit yerself," the man said, shrugging. "Just don't expect the slut I married to feed ye. She barely feeds us." He turned away and strode through the door.

Dubric and Dien looked at each other then followed.

Lars pulled his sword and scabbard from his gear and took a moment to strap it on. Flexing his shoulder and trying to loosen his arm, he left the house and walked down the porch steps to the yard. Screams of pain filled the air, along with low, guttural wails, and he grunted in approval. A few cuts and bruises were too good for them.

Breathing deeply, intending to remain calm and in control of his faculties, Lars walked around the chicken coop and paused. The four wretched savages remained physically in one piece, but all were bleeding and battered, cowering away from him.

Oblivious to his own pain, he dragged a scrawny freckled lad from the mud. A punch to the face sent fresh blood down Freckles's shirt and he crumbled, whimpering like a terrified baby. "Which one of you started this bright idea, eh?" Lars asked, tossing Freckles aside. "Who decided it would be good sport to assault my girl?"

He reached for Flann and yanked him upright, pulling the dagger from his shoulder. "Was it you, dung heap?"

Flann called Lars a filthy name and spat in his face.

Lars considered stabbing Flann again, but decided to elbow him in the nose instead.

"Ho, there!" a man called from behind, and Lars turned, dropping Flann.

Jak skidded to a halt, his hands held up before him as he stared at the bloody blade. "I've got no quarrel with you, lad. Put that pigsticker away before you hurt yourself and let me see to my boys. Whatever they've done, you've overstepped your place."

Lars growled low in his throat. "Stay back. I'm warning you."

"He's crazy!" one of the boys wailed. "Look what he did to Nally's leg!"

"The farm boy started this!"

"Get us out of here!"

Lars kicked the nearest one. "Shut your damn yaps."

Jak took a single step closer, craning to see past Lars. "Damn, laddie. Why?"

Lars wiped the dagger on the tail of his shirt. "They assaulted Jess, tried to have their way with her. I did my duty, to her and to Faldorrah."

Jak took another step and blanched at what he saw. "Your duty?"

Lars put the dagger away. "I'm not a farm boy. I'm a castle page, and I should have killed them for what they did."

Jak stopped and raked his fingers through his hair. "You're really a damned page? I thought you were joshing me, trying to get me to leave you be." He winced and looked past Lars again, frowning. "Guess that explains it, then. Your girl, Jess? She all right?"

"We didn't do nothin'! He just attacked us for no reason! Ow! Shit!"

"Shut your fool yaps!" Jak hollered over the din. "How bad they hurt her, laddie? She need a surgeon?"

"She's bruised and scared to death. They mauled her, but if they'd raped her, they'd already be dead. I'd have seen to it." Lars took a deep breath, flexing his bloodstained hand beside the hilt of his sword. "Remove them from the property immediately or I'm turning the lot of them into carcasses."

He glared at Jak. "I don't care if the roof is half done. You're dismissed. And don't ever come back."

Jak nodded and looked to the four. "All right, lad."

Lars stood aside while Jak carried and dragged his work crew to the cart.

"Stuart?" Devyn asked, shuffling into view. He held a shovel in his hands and drool had collected at the corners of his mouth. "You do it? You peg them up the ass?"

"I'll kill them if they come back," Lars said, his voice low and even. "Or if they touch her again."

"They hurt my granddaughter," Dev whispered, twirling the shovel to point the handle at the retreating crew. "But you're a good boy, Stuart. You don't need to rot in gaol for me."

Dev started toward them, but Lars grasped his arm. "She's okay, Dev. I got here in time."

"So they didn't . . . they didn't . . . ?"

Lars shook his head and held Dev's gaze. "No, they didn't rape her. She's all right and I've sent them away. They won't come back, and Jess will be okay."

Devyn's hands shook and he stared after the bleeding boys. "But the third! He'll get away again! We have to find him!"

"We'll find him," Lars said softly. "I promise. For Otlee, and for Stuart. I won't let him escape again."

Dev nodded hesitantly. "You'll find the wood colt and kill him, won't you, Stuart? For hurting my granddaughter, for pegging my boy."

Lars put his arm over Dev's shoulders and hugged the old man. "Yes. And for taking away your life and sanity. I'll see him dead and you'll have your justice. You have my word, sir."

Calling Stuart's name, Devyn fell to his knees and wept while Lars watched Jak drive away.

An old crone named Baerta and a timid woman named Glinni stood in a pitifully tidy kitchen and watched Dubric. The man, Horace, thumped his fist on a cracked and battered table, making it shift on its unlevel legs. "Fetch the lordships some tea!"

Glinni jumped, but Baerta stared at Horace and bared her few teeth. Dubric could not see the boys. A ragged blanket hung in a doorway, blocking the view farther into the house. The floors were smooth-swept, hard-packed dirt, the walls cracked plaster with straw shoved in the holes; Dubric heard wind whistling through. The place stank like a swamp, rotten and moldy with an undercurrent of mouse, even though it was painfully neat.

"Tea is not necessary," Dubric said. "I merely have a few questions."

"So ask 'em," Horace said, falling onto a chair held together by twine.

"First, I am sorry to inform you that Eagon was pulled from the river five days ago."

Glinni turned, startled, and almost dropped a mug. "Only five days?" she asked. "He went missin' nearly a moon ago."

"He was a good boy," Baerta said. Tears glistened in her eyes and her chin quivered.

Eagon's mother shook, her hands jerking like dying fish. "Parents should never hafta bury their babies."

Her voice cracked and warbled as it tore from her throat.

"No, madam, they should not." Dubric took a slow breath. "Please tell me about him and about his friends, especially Braoin Duncannon and a boy named Loman."

Horace's eyes narrowed. "The Duncannon boy weren't nothin', but Loman? Pah. Good riddance, I say."

Baerta gave him a withering glare then looked away, but Glinni merely clenched her hands until her knuckles turned white.

Dubric asked, "You met Loman?"

Glinni nodded, but her husband answered. "Met him? Hells, I dunno how many times I threw him out the door." He grumbled and stared at the table. "Eagon'd bring the good-fer-nothin' bastard back, though, no matter how many times I kicked his ass. He'd sneak the rotten whore in and hide him."

Baerta glanced at Horace then snatched her gaze away and stared beyond Dubric's right shoulder.

Dubric wrote a few notes while he carefully worded his next question. "Why did you not approve of Eagon's friendship with Loman?"

Horace leaned forward. " 'Cause of the foul things they did. Damn filth, all of it."

"He was a good boy," Baerta said, still staring over Dubric's shoulder. "And he tried hard to please ye. Nothin' he ever did was good enough. You never 'preciated him."

Horace leaned back again and crossed his arms over his chest. "He coulda pegged a girl instead of that whorin' fey boy."

"Stop it!" Glinni cried, tugging at her hair. "He's dead! It don't matter no more!"

"It may, madam," Dubric said, watching the three. He hoped the two little boys were not listening. "Your son was molested before he died, as was the other young man we have found. If your Eagon had acquaintance with others who preferred the company of young men, I need to know. Other lives are at stake."

"He weren't 'molested,'" Horace said, smirking. "His girly-boy friends pegged each other to death."

"Yer a beast," Baerta muttered.

"Don't ye start, Mother!" Glinni wailed, covering her face with her hands.

Baerta took a deep breath and stared at Dubric. "Eagon was always different, even when he was little, but he was a good soul. He helped other people, was p'lite, a hard worker. He felt all by hisself all the time and no one understood him. Not 'til he met Loman." She smiled. "They was happy with each other, more'n I can say fer my girl an' the worthless bug over there."

"Watch yer lip, ye old hag."

She turned to glare at Horace, raising her chin. "Ye may scare me daughter, but ye don't scare me. Yer a filthy weasel, a rotten slug, and I ne'er shoulda let ye marry her."

"I took ye into my home, and that bastard brat clingin' to her skirts. And ye got the gall to call me a beast?"

Glinni slammed her fists on the wall and Dubric saw tufts of her hair between her clenched fingers. "Stop it! Stop it!"

The pair turned away from each other, staring in opposite directions.

"Bastard."

"Witch."

Dubric sighed and rubbed his eyes. "Perhaps I am not making myself clear. A young man is dead—more than one, if truth be told—and I need to locate the man responsible. I do not care about your family squabbles. I do not care if Eagon preferred romantic relations with other young men, married women, or milk goats, nor do I care what your opinion is of such things. I merely want to gather what factual information I can and proceed with my investigation. We have established the fact that he preferred other men. Fine. What other men? Do any of you have names?"

Horace grimaced. "I only knew 'bout that skin peddler. He was bad enough."

Dubric looked at Eagon's mother. "Madam? Did he see any others?"

She stared at her hands for a long time before she nodded.

Dubric added the information to his notebook. "Do you know who they were?"

A long, shaking pause, then she nodded again. "It's my fault, ye know. All mine."

"We know that, Glin," Horace said, rolling his eyes.

"Nonsense!" her mother said, rubbing her daughter's back. "Ye did what ye had to. Eagon never blamed ye for what happened."

"Yes, he did," Glinni whispered, teardrops falling on her hands and arms. She stared at the base of Dubric's throat. "When he was 'bout six summers old, I had a run of bad luck, so bad I sold myself to sailors and travelers, but it weren't enough. I gave him to Sir Haconry and he paid my debts. I've never forgiven myself." Wailing, she buried her face against her arms. "Ye have to understand. I was desperate. We woulda starved."

Dubric tried to keep his face emotionless, but the

thought of Haconry made his skin crawl. "Eagon blamed you?"

She shook her head, shrugging off her mother's touch. "I don't think so. He told me that he'd had a good time, that Haconry was fun and nice and they'd played games."

Lifting her head from her arms, she stared at Dubric. "He wanted to go back. Haconry laid wit' him, took my son to his bed, and my boy wanted to go back!"

Horace smirked. "He was a filthy queer, even as a little one."

"He was my grandson and a good boy," Baerta interjected.

Dubric ignored the arguing pair, keeping his attention on Glinni. "Were there any others? Besides Haconry and Loman?"

She picked at her fingernails. "No. And he never had no friends, not really. Except Loman and Braoin." She sniffled and looked up. "He just had his puzzles. Bray'd help him with them sometimes, like that one they made on the wall."

The wall? "What sort of puzzles? Number puzzles?"

Horace slammed his palm on the table and Glinni jumped. "I thought I told you to stop babbling about that number nonsense of his!"

She shook her head rabidly and cowered away.

Dubric took a calming breath and said, "Sir, I will say this only once. If you interrupt me again while she, or anyone else, is giving an account of past happenings or other evidence, I will arrest you, throw your carcass in the local gaol, and drag you to the gallows myself. Close your mouth or I will close it for you."

Horace's jaw dropped open and he stared at Dubric, but Dubric turned his attention to Baerta.

"The same rules apply to you, madam. I am here to get information, not witness squabbles. If neither of you can offer constructive details or information potentially helpful to the investigation, keep your thoughts to yourselves."

He took in a deep breath and blew it out through his nose, willing his anger to dissipate along with it. "You were saying, madam? Something about puzzles?"

She glanced at her husband and shook her head, paling, when he stared back at her. "I . . . I was wrong."

Blast! Dubric glared at Horace. "Do you or do you not have any definite information about Eagon's friends and habits?"

"He was a freak. Made me sick to look at him. I pointed him to girls, but he kept chasin' that skin peddler."

Dubric turned to Baerta. "And you, madam? Do you have anything to offer other than the fact that he was a 'good boy'?"

"Salt of the earth, he was. Always willin' to offer a hand."

Dubric nodded. "Then I must request, nay, demand, that the pair of you wait outside. From this moment on, the remainder of Glinni's testimony is a private matter, ensured and protected under the laws and lordship of Faldorrah." He paused to stare at both. "This is not negotiable and I will arrest you if you do not comply. Immediately."

Both blustered, but Dien opened the door and they stomped away, leaving Dubric and Eagon's mother alone, while Dien guarded the door.

"He *was* a good boy," Glinni said. She wiped her nose and raised her eyes to Dubric's. "A bit rowdy, but he never brought me no grief or caused no trouble."

Dubric sat across from her. "I am certain he was. I hear he did plaster work for Jak the carpenter."

She smiled. "Yes. Was good at it, too."

"How long had he worked for Jak?"

"Nearly three summers. Eagon was one of the first lads he hired when he come to the Reach."

"And Jak paid him well?"

Glinni raised her chin and he saw a mother's pride in her eyes. "Yessir, he did, when there was work to be had. Sometimes he'd get paid a crown or more for a single day's work."

"A goodly sum."

"Yes, milord, it was. He gave it to us, Horace and me, to help."

"Does your husband have regular employment?"

She shook her head and stared at her hands. "No, milord, he don't. Our farm keeps him busy."

Dubric glanced around the dilapidated home with its broken walls and shattered furniture. "Does the farm bring in income?"

She ran her hands through her hair. "No, milord. It barely feeds us. Without Eagon, I don't know how we'll pay taxes come spring."

"Eagon has been missing a moon. Has your husband had no luck finding work? How will you manage?"

"We always do, milord. Even with Eagon gone. But, to be truthful, he weren't around much after Loman disappeared. He got real quiet, barely talked to anyone, and he started givin' us half his earnings instead of all of it."

"Do you know why?"

"Loman's mama. She was ill and crippled. Without that money she woulda died."

"What is her name? Where could I find her?"

"Donia, I think. Donia Glafisher. I've never met her, but she lives in Wittrup, I think. In one of the monger flats."

Dien cleared his throat. "Sir?"

Dubric gave Glinni an apologetic frown and turned toward Dien.

"The woman in Piras's cellar was named Glafisher," Dien said, his tone grim.

Dubric nodded. Another body, but no ghost. Had she starved after Eagon died and could no longer provide for her? He rubbed his aching eyes and turned back to Glinni. "Tell me about Loman. What did you think of him?"

"Decent enough boy, I guess. Considerin'." Her fingers twitched in abrupt spasms. "He, he sold hisself on the docks."

"Did he try to get Eagon involved?"

"No. Never." She raised her eyes again. "I heard him several times tellin' Eagon to never go near the docks. I think it shamed him."

"What did they talk about?"

"Gettin' away, mostly. Goin' someplace where no one knew 'em. Gettin' their own farm." Her fingertips tapped the table in an erratic rhythm. "Loman was like my son-in-law. Ain't that strange?"

She swallowed, shaking her head, "I'd of helped 'em get away if I could. Horace hated 'em both, I know he did, and he only tolerated Eagon 'cause of the money. Loman was a decent boy, quiet, not prone to trustin' folks, but he was polite and I know he loved his mama. They didn't want to leave 'cause of his mama."

"What other boys were like Eagon and Loman?"

She shook her head, leaning back against the chair, and wiped her nose. "I dunno for sure. There was another boy workin' the docks they used to talk 'bout sometimes. I think his name was Jasper. He left a couple of summers ago, looking for richer pastures. He never come 'round here."

"Did Eagon have enemies? Anyone who might want to hurt him?"

"No. 'Course not. He was a good boy."

"How well did he know Braoin Duncannon?"

"You think Bray had somethin' to do with this?"

"Were they close?"

She stared at Dubric for a long time before answering. "They played together sometimes as kiddies, but Bray started comin' 'round again 'bout a summer or two ago. He started workin' for Jak, too, and we'd see him ever' now and then workin' on Eagon's puzzles."

"Did you trust Braoin?"

"Sometimes. I wanted to, I did, and he seemed like a decent boy, but he was . . . forgetful, I guess. He'd stare off and his mind'd wander away. It was spooky, but he'd smile right after and write somethin' on a bit of paper. Strange boy. Very polite, but an odd one just the same."

"Did you ever see what he wrote?"

"Yessir, but I can't read a lick. Not even my name."

Dubric pulled a slip of paper from his pocket and showed it to her. "Can you read numbers?"

"No, milord. I can count, yessir, but not read 'em. But Eagon had a real talent with numbers. Said they fit together like puzzles. He used to write 'em down all the time. Want to see?"

"Of course," Dubric said.

Glinni led them to a tiny, closet-size room off the kitchen. She stood aside while Dubric looked through Eagon's few things. A plank, painted with a landscape,

hung beside the door; Dubric easily recognized
Braoin's precise style on the varnished wood. Scattered
among Eagon's grimy clothes and worn furnishings
were scraps of paper and parchment with lines and circles drawn in repeating patterns, much like the mo-
saics and pavers on temple floors. Similar patterns
were drawn in sprawling clusters on the patched plaster walls and ceiling and scratched into loose moldings.
"These are the puzzles your son made?" he asked,
glancing back at Glinni.

"Yessir. He'd sometimes work on them for days at a
time, trying to get them to fit together." She smiled.
"Never made no sense to me, but it made him happy.
He told me he used them for plasterin', for makin'
pretty textures on the walls."

"And the number puzzle he and Braoin worked on?"
Dubric asked, hoping he did not sound as eager as he
felt.

She chewed her lip then nodded. "I'll show you," she
said, her voice barely above a whisper.

She stretched past Dubric and pulled the painted
board from the wall. "They worked on it most of a
whole day," she said, holding the plank so that it faced
her. "Surprised me when he covered it up."

The back of the painting had the same series of
numbers Dubric had already seen. His heart fell. He
had hoped to glean new insights into the pattern, find
another clue, something to lead him to Otlee. He
started to thank her, but, beside him, Dien said, "Sir,
look at the wall."

Dubric did, and nearly gasped.

He stared at repeating mage marks, diamonds fitting
together point to point and textured into the plastered
wall. Mages used straight lines for their marks, never

the Goddess' curves. Dubric swallowed as he looked at the tiny, perpendicular lines that made up the design. Each diamond had a smaller diamond within it, making them look like eyes.

Dien said, "It's like the cloth."

"Yes," Dubric said, leaning close. There were three sets of diamond-eye patterns, each slightly different, but two were scratched out, leaving only the third unmarred. All three had numbers written in tiny scratches across the top row of marks and along the sides, but only the third set matched Braoin's number pattern. It had a worm drawn beside it and circled in red pencil.

"Braoin had Eagon figure out how the cloth was made," Dubric whispered, scribbling in his notebook. "That's how they tracked the disappearances." Dubric pointed to the worm drawing. "Did Eagon ever mention seeing a red worm or a black moth?"

Glinni's eyes widened as a crash sounded from the back of the house, and she clutched the painting.

The two filthy boys came through the blanket-covered doorway and ran to their mother. Both had red marks on their cheeks and their black toes curled against the dirt floor.

"Mama!" one said, while the other wiped his runny nose with the back of his arm. "Pa's comin' through the window. He fetched the axe." Footsteps and crashes thundered behind them, and the boys cowered, whimpering.

Glinni paled as a crash rocked the house, then another. "You have to go. Please."

Dubric glanced at the boys. "The moth and worm, madam. It may be important."

She shook her head and dragged her boys away from him.

Horace stomped through the doorway, an axe clenched in his hands. "Yer done talkin' to my wife. Git out," he said, swinging against a nearby wall and leaving a ragged hole much like the ones stuffed with straw. He pulled the axe free, then slammed it onto the table, cracking it further.

Dubric swallowed, his attention on the blade. The blunt end led the swings, not the sharp. Horace was intent on destruction, not murder.

Dien loomed large and dangerous beside Dubric. "She can answer this last question."

Horace stared at them, snarling as he broke a chair under the heavy blade. "Ye've no 'thority in the Reach or my home."

"Your hovel," Dien snapped.

"Git out." Horace swung the axe against the kitchen wall beside Dien. The axe punched through to the other side, knocking plaster onto Dien and over Eagon's rumpled bed. Horace yanked the axe free and prepared for another swing. "I'm glad the fey cur's dead, ye hear? Now git before I crush your skull."

Plaster dusting his shoulder, Dien started to pull his sword, but Dubric's hand on his arm stopped him. "Not in front of the children."

Snarling, Dien shrugged off Dubric's touch and took a single step toward Horace. "We'll be back," he said slowly, his voice lowering to a whisper. "If I hear you know one frigging thing about our missing boy, I'll bust both your legs, then open your belly. I'll feed your guts to the hogs while you scream, and no little wood splitter is going save you."

Horace blinked, his smirk faltering, as Dien loomed over him and snatched away the axe.

"They'll eat your sorry ass alive, and fight over your guts," Dien whispered, tossing the axe aside as Horace swallowed. "Busted up and eaten alive by hogs. You tell that to whoever has our boy. Pray it isn't you, dung heap, because there's nothing I'd rather see than two sows fighting over your shitty liver."

"You have made your point," Dubric said. He nodded good-bye to the woman in the corner, then turned and walked away.

Once outside, he said to Dien, "Search the outbuildings."

"Yes, sir," Dien said, and he stomped to the nearest shed.

Dubric untied the horses and watched the house. Horace did not come out to refute them. Dien spent mere moments in the shed before he appeared again and stomped to a leaning barn.

One of the boys braved the porch. "Pa says there ain't no boys here, no boys but us."

"Is that the truth?" Dubric asked, watching the child.

The boy did not flinch or glance away. "Yessir."

"Have you seen a red worm or a black moth?"

He shook his head. "Nawsir."

"Do you have a cellar?"

"Nawsir. Them's fer rich folks."

Dien left the barn and strode to Dubric. "He's got a still in the barn, sir. Corn mash whiskey. And a marked deer. No sign of Otlee or any trouble."

Dubric relaxed his stance. "Poaching and bootlegging do not concern me."

"Me either, sir. Otlee isn't here."

Dubric nodded to the boy and wished him well, then climbed on his horse. Dien beside him, they galloped from the farm and into the evening.

Rao limped along the road between Tormod and Wittrup while Flann lagged behind, stumbling like the piss-brained fool he was. "Page, my ass," Rao said. "He's just some snot-nosed kid. And then Jak, the bastard sumbitch, tells us we ain't got a job no more." He tried not to move his weak hand. The busted wrist hurt like a buzzard, and the bruises from the punches and kicks didn't feel much better. Knowing that by morning he'd be stiff, barely able to move, he trudged on despite the pain.

"Yeah," Flann said, stumbling behind.

"Bastard whoreson messed me up." Rao stopped, looking back the way they had come, but he saw nothing more than shadows of trees in the deepening twilight. "We shoulda killed the swine when we had the chance, instead of leavin' him pissin' in the mud."

"Yeah," Flann said.

Grumbling, Rao returned to trudging down the road. "And the friggin' girl. Piss, it shoulda been her sister. She wouldn't a screamed, no sir. She'd been beggin' for it."

"Begging, yeah. Begging to touch her titties."

Rao spat a bloody, snotty mouthful of muck from his mouth. "You got titties on the mind, my friend."

Flann laughed. "Yeah."

Rao grumbled and kept walking while Flann sang "The Song of Titties," a malformed, bawdy mess of dirty words and lust.

The song finished, Flann left the road and started toward the trees, unfastening his pants as he went.

"Where do you think you're going?" Rao asked. "You're not gonna climb some fool tree again, are you?"

"I touched me some titties today," he called back, grinning. Rao could just see him in the gathering dark.

"Do that shit later. We need to get home."

"Don't wanna do it later. I wanna do it now." Wriggling and laughing like a damn fool, Flann grabbed his pecker, jerking it and pointing it at his friend. "Wanna come along?"

"Piss, no. My slapping hand's ruined." Rubbing his wrist and cursing the farm pup as well as his randy friend, Rao grumbled and paced along the edge of the road while Flann giggled and wriggled away.

Darkness enveloped the road. Flann's eager grunts came faster, then faded in the quickening wind. Rao kept moving, pacing over the same strip of road. He heard gravel crunch, and goose bumps prickled his arms.

"What in the seven hells?" he muttered, listening. Something was moving down the road toward them. *Is that a cart?*

"Someone's coming," he called to the dark, but Flann didn't answer. *Piss, be just my luck that the idiot passes out after slapping his stick.*

The cart came closer with a clop of hooves and a creak of old wood. "Who's there?" Rao called out.

"Me," Jak's voice said, pulling closer. "Glad I found you."

Rao's breath came out in a rush. "Yeah, good, 'cause I'm not." For a moment there he'd thought that death came toward him, but it was only Jak, and Jak never even beat his wretched mule. Disgusted with his own cowardice, Rao turned and walked toward home again. Flann could just sleep it off on his own.

"Wait." Jak jumped from the cart and walked toward him. "Let me take you home. It's not safe to be on the road alone."

"Then get your scaredy-shit ass back home," Rao said, walking away.

"Where's Flann?" From the dark, the mule's tack jingled.

"How should I know?" Rao walked on, muttering.

Jak did not respond; silence filled the dark.

Pisser, Rao thought. *Probably scared, out in the dark all alone. I hated working for you anyway, you bastard.*

Lost in his thoughts, he yelped in surprise at the sudden constriction at his throat, yanking him back toward the mule cart.

Dubric and Dien reached Maeve's not long after the sun's last golden light left the sky. Lantern light fell upon them, and Dubric turned to see the wind tugging on Maeve's skirt and shawl.

"I was getting worried," she said. "You haven't found Otlee?"

Dubric winced. Two nights gone. "Not yet."

Maeve sagged. "Supper's ready whenever you are."

"How are we going to find him, sir?" Dien asked.

"I am not certain, but we will find a way." Dubric watched Maeve walk back into the house. "We must find Otlee, and she must bury her son."

"We're running out of time, sir."

"Then let us hope luck is with us." They discarded their muddy boots on the back porch and walked into the kitchen, lugging the bags of clothing and belongings they had found near Foiche's tower.

Maeve pulled a deep pan from the oven. "I hope you like spiced pork." She set the pan on the stove and pulled strips of meat from the red sauce.

"It smells wonderful. Thank you." Dubric walked behind her, and found himself looking at the curve of her waist as she moved. He shook his head and continued on to the washroom.

Hands and face clean, he and Dien sat at the table with Maeve amidst strained silence. He had taken but one strip of sauced pork from the dish when an all-too-familiar pain fell behind his eyes.

Desperate to breathe, Rao struggled to pull the cord from his neck, but he was held fast, pulled off balance, and dragged away. His assailant shoved him facedown over the back of the cart; the rough planks scratched his belly. He heard the cart creak as he bent into it, then the cord loosened for the briefest of moments while his assailant changed his grip.

Instinct demanded that he breathe, and air tore through his throat before being cut off again. He felt his pants rip down, his goods swinging free while he was shoved against the back of the cart. Something hot and hard poked his buttocks twice, then rammed in, lifting his feet from the ground.

He tried to scream, but he had no air, no strength. His flickering red vision dimmed, twirling away, and he faded, falling into it. The constriction loosened at his throat again, just enough to let a whisper of air through. Enough to remain conscious, almost enough to remain aware, but not enough to waken his muscles from their terrified clench.

Ripping pain spread inside him, throbbing and tearing with each thrust, pain he could not escape or fight. The dark slammed his face against the floorboards of the cart, grinding him against the wood as the twine at his throat tightened again.

The dark finished, then pulled free, granting Rao a full lungful of air before slamming him over onto his back as if he were no more than a moldering sack of grain. He landed on something hard and lumpy that was snarled in the choking twine.

"You're mine," the dark said, its teeth glimmering faintly. It leaned in and tore at his genitals with its teeth, biting and hissing, while Rao tried to scream.

Rao tried to back away, but the weighted twine around his neck was stuck beneath him. The lumpy thing lodged against the cart floor as he struggled. It caught under him, tightening the twine, and he gagged and fought against it, his own weight and terror choking his life away.

The dark grinned. It moved, a shadow in the night grasping Rao's thighs and holding him still while hot blood warmed his belly and groin.

Rao tried to scream, but he had no air. The thing shoved his legs up and ground him against the cart again.

Dubric panted through the pain, pressing his palms flat upon the table. Braoin's death had brought him agony, a sharp, bright stab through his skull, but the newest ghost, a half-naked lad with a variety of fresh bruises and a mark across his throat, arrived with minimal fuss. Pain, yes, but not torture. And no string marked the ghost's head.

A common murder, Dubric thought. *It is not the same at all.* He pushed his plate away and leaned forward, resting his throbbing head on the table while he caught his breath and the ghost completed its arrival.

"Dubric?" Maeve asked, rushing to him. "What happened?"

"A murder," he said, sitting straight again. Maeve backed away with her hands over her mouth.

"Otlee?" Dien asked, turning ashen.

Dubric shook his head, panting through the pain. "No. Otlee lives. This ghost is a young man, beaten, with his pants gone and genitals mangled. I expect it is a lover's quarrel, or that he was caught with another man's woman."

Maeve fell into a chair across from him. "A man's dead. How can you be so matter-of-fact about it?"

"Because it is my job," he said. "Most murders are uncomplicated. Rage. Lust. Greed. I have seen many people murdered over happenstance. Being in the wrong place at the wrong time, or insulting the wrong person in the wrong way. A woman murdered her husband because he failed one time too often to put his dinner plate in the washbasin. A man murdered his son, thinking he was a burglar. And, more than once, one man has murdered another for having relations with his wife."

He paused while Maeve stared at him with a horrified expression. "It is what I do. I find whoever lost control of their rages for that one terrible moment, and I bring them before Council to face whatever justice they deserve. And, occasionally, I track a rabid beast who has no control over his rages and lusts. Those, generally speaking, I kill, as all rabid beasts must be killed."

"Pegging right, sir."

"You will kill the man who murdered my son?"

He nodded. "Yes, milady, I will. Animals like that tend to refuse capture. I would prefer to have them judged and hanged, but I have not known that to happen before."

"But not the man who killed tonight?"

"The man, or woman, who *murdered* tonight. If a man takes a life saving his family, or himself, or if someone dies due to accident or war or disease, I see no ghost. If I see a ghost, the victim was murdered, and the ghost will remain until justice has been served, preferably by Council. Merely capturing the murderers is not enough; they must be judged, and the judgment delivered."

She stood, tears rolling down her cheeks. "But a young man is dead! Someone's son! Doesn't his death matter to you?"

"Of course it does," he said, softly. "But if I let my feelings cloud my actions, if I lose impartiality, I do no one any good. Every death tears at me, yet I must find those responsible, and I must make them pay. For if I do not, perhaps no one will. I deliver justice to the dead, and that, milady, does far more to aid their loved ones than if I were to succumb to sorrow."

She stared at him, blinking through her tears.

Dien said, "Would you rather have us wring our hands, or stay focused and catch the degenerate?"

"I would have you rip the bastard that killed my Braoin to shreds and feed the remnants to the hogs."

"Then that is precisely what we will do." Dubric reached for his tea. "Or an equivalent."

Maeve sat and looked at them. Nodding, she ate.

* * *

Worry gnawed at Lars's belly.

Jess had barely uttered a word since she'd been attacked. After they'd finished supper, while Sarea and Kia tidied up, Fyn had taken him aside to tell him that Jess had bruises everywhere. Her back, her belly. Her breasts. That she'd been lucky; if he hadn't come when he did, no telling what might have happened.

Not knowing what else to do, he had thanked Fyn for keeping him informed, then staggered to the porch. He stared into the night and watched rain clouds roll in.

His eyes ached. He had been unable to read Otlee's journal while worrying over Jess, and he felt powerless, unable to help either of them. The stitches on his back itched, the blisters on his hands burned, and he was tired deep down to his bones.

The door creaked open behind him, but he didn't turn to look. Jess had come out and talked to him other evenings, but tonight she had gone to bed, crying. It wouldn't be her, and no one else mattered.

"I'd like to talk to you," Sarea said, sitting beside him, "if that's okay."

"Sure," he said, shrugging. "Talk away."

Sarea took a heavy breath and fidgeted with her hands for a long time. "I don't know where to start."

"You could always start by yelling at me. That's what Dubric does. It seems to work."

She paused, turning to stare at him. "Why in the Goddess' grace would I want to yell at you?"

"Because I wasn't quick enough. Because I didn't

kill them when I had the chance. Because of me, Jess was hurt."

"None of those things are true," she said, hesitating before she draped her arm over his shoulder. "I came out here to tell you to stop blaming yourself."

"Yeah, sure," he said.

"All right. Lars Hargrove, you pull your fool head out of your ass and listen to me. If it wasn't for you, Jess would be seriously hurt instead of just scared and bruised. She could have been raped, Lars. Raped. Or even killed. But because you were there, because you kept your head instead of simply killing anything that moved, she will be fine, and those rotten boys will have to live with what they did.

"I didn't hear a thing until they were screaming in pain, and neither did my parents. You heard *Jess*, whatever sound they let her make, and you went, immediately, to her aid. Yes, she's scared, yes, she has bruises, but she's alive and she wasn't raped. That's a lot. No one expects you to be perfect, no one but you. You did the best you could, far more than anyone else could have, and we're very proud of you, and thankful. Let the rest go."

He stared into the night. "I can't. It's not good enough."

"It's good enough for me. And it's good enough for Jess."

"No, it's not. She wouldn't even look at me at supper."

Sarea squeezed his shoulders. "She's worried that you won't like her anymore."

Startled, he turned his head to look at her. "What? Why?"

"Because she wasn't strong enough to fend them

off." Sarea paused. "She's afraid she's not good enough for *you*. You've saved her life twice now."

"That doesn't matter."

"Maybe not to you. I know you've spent your life learning how to fight efficiently, how to think on your feet and handle situations like those without stopping to consider the implications. You just do it; it's part of you now, trained so deeply that you're barely aware. I know that. But to Jess, it feels like she's weak and needs rescuing. My daughters don't like thinking they're weak little girls."

"They're not," he said. "Especially not Jess. Four men attacked her as a pack. No one could have escaped that unscathed. She was unarmed, for Goddess' sake, and taken by surprise. I *was* armed, and I knew what I was running into, yet they still hurt me."

"I know, and she knows, too. Just give her a little time to accept it. She does adore you, after all."

"What?"

Sarea smiled, laughing softly. "She's had a crush on you since she was in diddies. I thought you knew."

Astounded and beaming like an idiot, he didn't know what to say.

Sarea said, "It'll be our little secret."

He nodded, feeling his cheeks heat up. Before he could stop himself, he blurted out, "I think I love her."

Sarea smiled and ruffled his hair. "I know. We gave you permission to court her, remember?" She leaned close, grinning, and nudged him. "Are you planning on asking her to the castle faire? It's only a few phases away."

He shrugged.

She patted him on the shoulder and stood. "I've heard several boys are talking about asking her. Maybe you should think about that instead of dwelling on things you can't change." Sarea walked toward the door and paused, turning back to look at him. "You have a unique opportunity here. Don't dawdle too long. Once we get back to the castle, it's gone forever."

He nodded, smiling at her. "Thanks, Sarea."

"You're welcome." Sarea entered the house, closing the door behind her.

I am running out of time. Dubric sat at the kitchen table, poring over his notes and the materials they had found at the Devil's Eye and listening to the rain. Dien grumbled across the table with Calum's ledger open before him. Maeve had returned to weaving, and Dubric was relieved she had left. He did not want her to see the dead birds or the folded clothing.

The four ghosts—Braoin, Calum, Eagon, and the nameless new arrival—languished around the kitchen as their preferences demanded. Dubric ignored them, wishing that they would go to other haunts as the other ghosts had. Not once in all the summers he had been plagued with the wretched spirits had they ever done a single thing to aid in an investigation. They wailed, they oozed, they annoyed, but little else. The newest arrival seemed more solid, richer, and less transparent, and the difference worried him. He could think of no reason why most of the murders would leave pale spectres.

He sipped his tea and continued his notes until Dien said, "I think I found something." He handed Dubric both books. "Horace Mulconry of Myrtle. Sir Haconry paid him for 'services' several times."

"King be damned. Nice work." Dubric examined the

ledger listings Dien had marked, noting that Horace had received three payments of fifty crown. "What sort of 'services' would a bootlegging sheep farmer provide, especially one with such a lovely disposition?"

Dien yawned and stretched. "No way to tell, sir. But each was paid two days after mid-phase, matching Braoin's disappearance pattern."

"Mulconry, Mulconry," Dubric said, tapping his chin. "Is that not Pigshit Mul's surname?"

"Damn, I don't know. Is it in your notes?" Dien picked up Dubric's notebook and flipped back through it. He looked up, surprised. "I'll be pegged. It is."

Dubric retrieved his notebook and noted the information. "A bit of a coincidence, do you not think, to have two Mulconrys leading to Sir Haconry and being involved in the disappearances? Even if they are not brothers, they are surely family. Anyone connected to Haconry could be Devyn's 'wood colt bastard.' " He set aside his notebook and took a sip of tea. "Continue searching the ledger, and particularly note anyone else who may be related to Haconry. Nepotism in the Reach would explain a great deal. Also look for anyone who received similar payments that may coincide with the disappearances."

"Yes, sir," Dien said, returning to Calum's books.

Dubric stood and stretched. "Do not stay up too late. We are leaving again at dawn." Yawning, he went to prepare for bed.

"Ah, rain at last," the thing in the dark said, grinning its yellow teeth grin.

Otlee whimpered, shaking his head, as tendrils spewed from the thing's mouth and skipped along

Otlee's bare and bleeding flesh, drawing fresh blood, making him scream. He was bound, hand and foot and throat, unable to struggle or escape while the dark explored and cut and ravaged him. Up close it stank of rot and nutmeg and clove, a sweet, dead smell. Otlee would have vomited, but he had not eaten. Nor had he slept. He dry-heaved, tasting bile.

"He pleases you?" Otlee heard someone whisper. He saw nothing but dark and red eyes and yellow teeth, nothing but the apparition that tormented him.

"He will do. For now." The dark laughed, then it leaned close for a taste.

CHAPTER

21

†

As morning approached, Dubric sat in the kitchen while Maeve washed their breakfast dishes. He reviewed his notes and sipped tea as he tried to plan his morning and Haconry's interrogation. Six names repeated in Calum's ledger, each with multiple payments of fifty crown, corresponding to the dates Braoin had calculated. Did Haconry pay others to take the boys? To dispose of bodies? To turn a blind eye? Whatever the reason, Dubric intended to tear the manor house to its foundation if need be. King help Haconry if Otlee was within its walls.

Four ghosts stared at him. The newest arrival had ceased his terrified wail and instead glowered like a foul-tempered dog. He wavered, fading to mist then strengthening again, while the others maintained their glowing green transparencies. Braoin's hue was especially intense, the color of dandelion greens, while Calum was the grayed color of rye going to seed.

Dubric considered Braoin's intense hue, finally deciding that it was due either to his being at home or to his having been an artist. Only the new arrival seemed solid and three-dimensional, like Stuart, whom he had not seen since leaving Lars on the farm the day before.

Braoin, Calum, and Eagon looked like reflections of smoke.

Maeve finished the dishes and dried her hands before pulling the teakettle from the stove.

"Tell me about your wife," she said as she poured.

Dubric wrapped his fingers around the mug to warm them. "There is nothing to tell. She has been gone a long time."

Maeve sat. "What do you remember most?"

For the first time in recollection, Dubric felt a blush brighten his cheeks. "It has been so long, Maeve, truly, there is little to recall."

Maeve sipped her tea and sadly contemplated him over the cup's edge. "Yet you hold on to her memory like it's a gift. That's an amazing thing. A wonderful thing."

He lowered his head and stared into his tea, smiling at the first memory that sprung to mind. "She liked picnics. In fact, that is how we met." His hands tightened around the cup. "She was assigned to Tunkek Romlin's army as their Mage Killer. It was a difficult post to fill, for any army, but especially for Tunkek's. They were the largest battalion and were often sent to face the powerful mages. Oriana was good at her job. She understood the risks involved but faced them anyway."

Maeve touched the back of his hand, and he looked up, into her eyes.

"Oriana was an assassin for Malanna's church," he said. "That is what she did. Sneak in, get close, and kill mages. By the time I met her, she had killed four, if I remember right. But I did not know that at the time. After nearly a moon of tracking our quarry, my army and Tunkek's met up in Lattalok. Our respective mages had run aground, seeking shelter in the caves. They were trapped, and it was only a matter of going in and getting them. While my men were taking a couple of bells to prepare, I wandered off on my own to eat. I saw a woman walking alone in a barley field. She was singing and I was downwind. I heard her long before I saw her."

"Singing?" Maeve asked, surprised.

"Yes. Before the war she was a bard, but she showed a resistance to magic and was pressed into service."

Maeve sipped her tea. "Go on."

"I noted she wore Tunkek's colors, and I asked why she was so far from her station. She lifted her ration sack and said she was looking for a quiet place to eat." He smiled and took a sip of tea. "Then she looked at me, looked right through me, it seemed, and asked what *I* was doing so far from *my* station."

Maeve smiled, watching him.

"As luck would have it, I was on the same quest. We ate our rations together in that barley field. Once the mages were dispatched, our armies separated again, but Oriana and I corresponded. One officer to another, our messages tucked in with official orders, but soon our letters became more personal.

"Several moons later, Tunkek and I tracked mages to Felder. Different regions, but the same province. I left my lieutenant in charge and went to see her. She was not with the army. Once again she had wandered off to find a peaceful place to eat. I found her on a rocky hillside, out of uniform." He felt blush on his cheeks again. "She was waiting for me."

"Why would you say that?"

"Because she had food for two."

"Ah," Maeve said. "What then?"

"Nothing," he said. "Neither of us wanted to shirk

our duty, and I did not want her to transfer to my command. Not only would it have been grossly inappropriate, but how could I send her to face a mage alone? Our correspondences faded off after that. She started seeing someone else, and I . . . I would meet a girl here, a girl there. Nothing serious, but enough to help me try to forget her." He sipped his tea. "We were both very young."

"But that's not the end of the story," Maeve said.

Chewing his lip, Dubric stared into his tea again. "I could not forget her, no matter what I tried. Summers passed, and the war ended. I found her in Waterford, of all places. She had returned to the city phases before I had, to look for me. We made arrangements to meet for dinner at the castle gardens."

He looked up. "She brought a basket of food, enough to feed six hungry soldiers, for the two of us, and we sat amongst the apple trees while we ate and talked. It felt as if we had been apart a few days at most, not several sets of seasons."

He closed his eyes, remembering. "I can still smell the trees, the ripening fruit, hear the birds. We sat on a blanket on the grass. Her grandmother had made it, she said, and it was a cloudy day, breezy and cool. She joked that she picked that particular blanket because it was warm. Just in case.

"We fell quiet then, barely talking, only looking at each other, and I felt something on my hand. It was a spider, a black, furry one. A hunter. I was about to flick it away, or smash it, I do not remember for certain, but I do know that she grasped my hand. 'I've seen enough death,' she said, and she picked the spider up and cupped it in her palm, whispering to it as she carried it away. She put it in the grass well away from us then came back to me, laughing about how silly she was. I kissed her then, for the first time. That night, when I walked her home, I asked her to marry me and she said yes."

"Oh, Dubric, that's a lovely story."

"I wish it had a happier ending," he said. "We courted for three moons before the wedding, and she died three moons after. I have spent a lifetime looking back to the more than two summers we missed, all the wasted time when we knew we wanted to be with the other, yet were not. All the time we lost. We could have had nearly three full summers. Instead we had six moons. It wasn't enough."

Tears stung and rolled down his cheeks. "Forgive me," he said, standing. "Even old memories fester." He took a shaky breath and left the kitchen, hurrying through the porch to the darkness and his waiting horse.

Dubric and Dien left before dawn and rode northward, to Wittrup. They crossed the Casclian at the ferry and Dubric sighed, rubbing his eyes and wishing the ghosts would leave him at peace. Dien leaned against the ferry rail and glowered. Neither spoke beyond polite pleasantries, but the ferryman chatted a great deal.

Dubric's thoughts churned. In the few days he had known Maeve, he had brought her nothing but death and blood and sorrow. No happy memories, none at all. No picnics or sunshine or hope, only a dead son and worries over his own missing page. He took a deep breath and looked over the water. *At least Otlee lives, and there is no war. Maybe things do not have to be perfect. Maybe I still have hope.*

Once off the ferry they headed east, toward Tormod, and into the rising sun. "We need a break, sir. Somehow," Dien said.

"We are beginning the third day," Dubric muttered. "I am certain that we will find the man responsible, but how long can Otlee survive?"

Dien drew a heavy breath, then stopped, his head tilting. "Do you hear that?"

Dubric leaned forward in the saddle, listening. He heard a ruckus of some sort up ahead. Heeling his charger to a trot, he rode around the bend with his hand on his sword.

Glis Sherrod, the constable of Tormod and a prominent name in Haconry's ledger, climbed over a mule cart and looked up at Dubric's arrival, while several village men milled about the road and talked loudly in their excitement. "Lord Castellan!" Sherrod said, jumping down. "What a pleasant surprise. You'll be pleased to hear that we've captured the criminal just this very morning. Your work here is done."

Dubric reined his horse in and it pranced to the side, turning toward the cart. "You have? How?" The mule cart was made of plain, unpainted wood—a workingman's cart—and it carried the body of Dubric's latest ghost in the back. Half naked, he lay faceup with his privates missing and black rope wrapped around his throat. His legs hung off the edge, dangling, with his pants wadded around his ankles, above his grimy boots.

Sherrod nodded toward the body in the cart. "Some kid saw the other being mauled last night and bashed the bastard on the head. He's on his way to a cell as we speak."

Dubric dismounted; Dien did the same. "That's no lover's quarrel," Dien said.

"No, it is not," Dubric said. He walked to the back of the cart to find the wounds rinsed clean by rain and the ground beneath his feet partially washed smooth, but blood lingering where rain did not reach. The young man's penis had been torn away, but his testicles remained. His eyes bulged open, staring at the sky from a swollen and bluish face, and the undersides of his arm and back were purplish green. *The severed penis did not bleed enough to cause death. His lower parts are too discolored from settling blood. Likely death by strangulation.* Dubric leaned forward to close the boy's eyes.

"This happened last evening, you said? Why did no one come until morning?" Dubric sketched the placement of the body, the work pants puddled around his ankles, the arched back, and the partial bare footprints and blood beneath the cart.

"I'm surprised you aren't asking who did it," Sherrod said.

"It is not the same man." Dubric climbed into the cart and stood over the body. "Has he been moved at all since he was discovered?"

Sherrod grasped the edge of the cart, smoothing away a burr with his gloved hands. "Not that I'm aware of. What do you mean it's not? I saw that kid pulled from the river last phase. His prick was gone; he'd been strangled. It's the same man."

Dubric tossed Dien his notebook and knelt beside the body. "What is the victim's name?"

"Rao. He doesn't have an after name, at least not that I know of. Just a street thug from Wittrup."

The name sounded familiar. Dubric looked up and Dien nodded, flipping through the notes.

"Worked for Jak is all I see here," Dien said. He took a breath and glanced to the northeast, toward the farm.

"What can you tell me about him?" Dubric asked as he lifted Rao's head. *No puncture wound, no string.* He looked at Dien and shook his head.

Sherrod leaned forward, one arm resting on the cart's edge, and stared at Dubric. "Like I told you, he's a street rat from Wittrup. Been in trouble now and then. We got Jak without a bit of fuss and he's on his way to the gaol, milord. It's over."

"No, it is not over," Dubric said, rolling Rao's body to the side. "This is a copy. Not the same at all. And an inaccurate copy at that." A hammer hung between Rao's shoulder blades, the black cording wrapped round and round the handle and broken steel head as a mechanism to tighten the pressure on his throat. Dubric unwound the hammer and pulled the cording free. Made of braided black silk, it was as thin as the marks on Calum and Eagon's wrists and ankles. "May I keep this?"

"Keep whatever damn thing you want. You're wasting your time. Jak did it. He's been captured."

Pocketing the cord, Dubric returned Rao to his back and examined the nearest hand. The fingernails, while filthy and ragged, were free of struggle cracks and scraped skin fragments. He had no bind marks anywhere except his throat. "Jak may have killed this boy— only time will tell us for certain—but the man stalking the Reach's children did not." He opened Rao's mouth and frowned. Every tooth was in place.

"How can you be sure of that?" Sherrod asked, his eyes narrowing.

Dubric climbed from the cart. "Several ways. This boy wasn't tortured extensively, nor was he bound. Yes, he was raped, and his genitals were ravaged, but he died by strangulation, not from being stabbed in the head or from the effects of torture. He has all of his teeth. Shall I continue?"

"It's the same man."

Dubric took the notebook from Dien and added his own notations before returning it. "No, it is not. I do not have time to debate this with you. Where is Jak? I must speak to him, and to the boy who witnessed the attack."

Sherrod stood a bit taller and yanked off his leather gloves. "Jak is currently bound and unconscious in a barred cart. He's not going anywhere. The boy has been delivered to his father."

Dubric nodded and walked around the mule cart, looking for potential dropped clues, but fresh footprints and a large indentation marred the mud. "When is Jak's judgment hearing?"

"Tomorrow. We'll hang him the next day, most likely."

Dubric stood straight and stared at Sherrod, unable to believe the brutal speed of punishment in the Reach. "Are you not going to investigate this further? There is no reason to hang him so quickly. If you are so certain that he is ultimately responsible, he should be tied to the other disappearances. We must not leave any room for doubt."

Sherrod rolled his eyes and started to walk away. "The kid saw what was happening and bashed him on the head."

"Who is the witness? I must speak to him."

"The witness is scared out of his wits and is resting on his family farm. I will not let you turn this into a gypsy circus. There isn't any doubt, and there is no 'we.' Jak is my prisoner and my prize witness is safe. You are finished here, Lord Castellan. Go back to your castle."

Sherrod climbed onto the driver's seat and lifted the reins, but Dubric grabbed the mule's bridle to hold it still. "You are making a grave mistake. This was a copy. A mimic. Jak is not the real killer. You must have patience."

"I've had ample patience, sir," Sherrod said, "Nearly three summers of patience. It's time someone paid for these crimes."

Sherrod yanked on the reins and the mule jumped back a step, breaking Dubric's grasp on its bridle.

Dubric stepped aside and let them pass. "Take statements from every man here," he said to Dien, striding to where the cart used to be. While Dien talked to the village men, Dubric knelt beside the footprints that had been under the edge of the cart. He pulled his measuring string out of his pocket and set to work, discerning every possible detail he could before time and weather obliterated them.

Jess pulled a skirt from the washtub and set to scrubbing while, beside her, Fyn did the same. They sat in the sun on a grassy patch behind the house, a large basket between them, rapidly filling with soapy, scrubbed clothes. A massive pile of dirty laundry waited nearby.

"I can't believe she hasn't done a lick of laundry all phase," Fyn said, scouring a pair of their grandfather's trousers into the washboard. "Didn't Mam tell her days ago to get it done, or else? For Goddess' sake, I've worn the same filthy blouse two days in a row now. I'm tired of smelling like puke."

Jess sighed and nodded, pulling her mother's skirt from the wash. She dropped it in the basket and reached into the wash pile, pulling up a pair of Lars's pants. Seeing where her hands were, she blushed. *It's just laundry,* she reminded herself, *but Goddess, I will absolutely die of embarrassment if I have to scrub his underdrawers.*

She'd scoured one knee clean and had begun on the other when Kia trudged up behind them. She said nothing, just dropped an empty basket beside them and picked up the full one, then lugged the heavy, soapy mess down the hill to the creek.

Fyn looked up to watch their elder sister walk away. "She sure is quiet today."

Jess shrugged and continued to scrub Lars's pants. "She was quiet last night, too."

"Good," Fyn said, dropping Grandfather's trousers into the empty basket. "It's about time." She pulled one of their father's shirts from the water and set to work while Jess shifted her grip on Lars's pants.

Something was in the pockets and Jess paused to empty them. She already had a small pile of coins and thimbles and things beside her hip. The little stuff people just carried around. Pocket sludge, Fyn called it. Jess was curious about what sort of pocket sludge Lars had.

A scrap of paper with a diagram of some sort. Two crown, three scepters, and a few pence. A broken buckle. A nail. And a tooth.

She held the tooth between her fingers.

"What's that?" Fyn asked.

Jess showed her the tooth. "Weird. Looks like it came from a dog or something. Why would he carry it around?"

Fyn shrugged. "Heck, I dunno. Maybe he secretly wants to tend teeth. Next time he brings us water, why don't you ask him?"

Jess blushed and put the tooth beside her hip with the other pocket sludge. "I can't."

Fyn chuckled and shook her head. "You have to talk to him sooner or later. You are living in the same house."

"Just for a few days. We'll be going home soon."

"I wish," Fyn sighed, scrubbing the shirt. "We never leave until after the Planting Festival. Why do we have to come every damned spring?"

"Because we have to help sell hats," Jess said. "Besides, the festival's tomorrow. We'll be home before you know it." She looked up to the brilliant morning and wondered if her dad was having any luck finding Otlee.

"So many. Dubric said twenty-four dead," Lars mumbled, reviewing Otlee's notes while he tried not to seethe. Someone had thrown his gear around during the night, scattering his clothes and papers and books across the house. Fyn had risen early and tried to tidy the mess, but Otlee's clothes were mixed with his, papers were rumpled and torn, and Jess had found his boots in the stove.

Sarea set a plate of sweet biscuits before him, patting Lars on the back as she moved away, and he thanked her before returning to Otlee's notes.

A number of small things had gone wrong for him

since he got back to the farm, and they had to be more than coincidence. His belongings were often moved, lost, or damaged. He'd stumbled several times when he shouldn't have. Once, he even thought someone had pushed him when he went to the barn to talk to Dev. When he turned around there was no one there, but the barn was a dark place, full of hiding spaces. Someone—someone jealous and angry, he'd guess—was trying to make life difficult for him.

I bet it's Kia and one of her jealous games. Damn.

Lars took a deep breath and refocused on the case. He grabbed a biscuit as he read through autopsy notes for Calum. *So he likes it. He's not doing it to prove anything, not anymore. It's a compulsion.* Raped, bound, cut, stabbed. *Goddess, what kind of monster would do things like that?* Lars ate his biscuit and read, glancing up as Fyn and Jess came in from washing clothes. He smiled, certain they hadn't trashed his things. They'd helped clean up the mess while Kia remained in their room. *Damn her.*

"What are those marks on your map?" Fyn asked as she set a handful of trinkets on the table.

Jess hesitated, then walked to the other side of him and looked at the map, too. "Something about Dubric?"

Otlee's notes had mentioned Dubric falling twice and holding his head, one of the few things Lars could count as notable evidence, but he hesitated to tell the girls Dubric's secret. "There's a phenomena that, um, happened in those places, and I thought it might be important."

Fyn stepped back, concerned. "Like just this side of the cemetery? Isn't that where you two saw that monster?"

"No," Lars said, standing. "We were on the village side of the cemetery when we saw him."

"But he wasn't," Jess corrected, as he walked around the table. "He was on the other side."

"Hey," Fyn said, pointing to the map, "isn't that where Dad said Dubric almost fell from the saddle? Twice?"

"Yeah," Jess said. "He was worried Dubric couldn't take the strain of the investigation." She looked at Lars. "Is that it? Are the other marks the same thing?"

"Yes. Dubric gets bad headaches sometimes," Lars said, his voice lowering.

"Oh, we've heard all about that," Fyn said, marking the map just north of the cemetery. "Whenever there's a murder, Dad gripes about Dubric's headaches making him pissy."

"Fyn!" Jess said, covering a laugh with her hand. "You're going to get Dad in trouble."

Lars smiled, relieved. "Your dad's right. Dubric does get pissy with the headaches, and murders."

All three looked at the map again. Jess said, "Look, they follow a curve."

Lars traced the marks with his finger. "Are you sure?"

Fyn walked to the kitchen cupboards and returned with a bowl and small plate. "Let's see," she said.

Lars smoothed the map and Fyn set the bowl on it. It touched two points, but arced away from the third. "Something bigger," she muttered, trying the plate. Too big. Fyn returned to the bowl and frowned. It simply wouldn't fit.

"Can you move in a bit, make it equal distance from all three?" Jess asked as she hurried away. "I have an idea."

Fyn slid the bowl to the left, and, sure enough, it followed inside all three marks.

Jess returned to the table with a spool of thread. "Pencil?" she asked Lars, her eyes twinkling. He handed her one—broken the night before—and she tied the end of the thread to it, then lifted the bowl.

"A lot depends on how accurate your map is," she said, setting the pencil tip on one point while spooling thread toward the village of Wittrup. "And how accurate your points are."

"It's a circle, I'm sure of it," Fyn said, grinning. "We did an exercise a lot like this in class not two moons ago." Jess held down the thread and lifted the pencil, moving it to the next point. It didn't quite reach, and Fyn said, "Try moving the center a bit north, maybe west."

Jess did, and the point lined up. She returned to the first one and made another adjustment, then moved to the second point, then the third. "Want me to draw the whole circle?" she asked, looking up at Lars.

"Sure," Lars said, nodding. "And will you mark the center, too?" *That's my girl,* he thought, beaming with pride, *and I'll be damned if Dubric doesn't have a range for his ghosts.*

The circle drawn, both girls stepped back and smiled while Lars examined the map.

"It's just geometry," Jess said, shrugging, when Fyn nudged her in the ribs.

Sarea walked over and looked at the map. She frowned at Lars and said, "Girls, go on and check on your sisters. See that they finish hanging the laundry."

"What does this mean?" Sarea asked after the girls left, pointing to the center mark, on the peninsula west of Wittrup. "And don't dodge around that 'might be important phenomena' business. I'm a mother; you can't lie to me. I know when you do."

"Dubric gets headaches during murders," Lars said. Sarea nodded. "I know that."

"The marks are where his headaches stopped or started, suddenly. I thought it might mean something."

Sarea lifted her hand to see the whole map then touched the peninsula again. "Dien always thought Dubric just knew when people died. So you think that whatever's happening is inside this circle? Maybe at the middle?"

"Or near there," Lars said. "Maybe. There's no way to tell, unless we search the area." Lars looked into her eyes, imploring her. "It might not mean anything, I know that, but I'm trying to help find Otlee and we're running out of time."

Sarea took a step back, her eyes wide. "No, you can't go."

"I have to. Please. I have to try. I'll be fine. Maybe the girls are right and he's somewhere near there."

Sarea's face paled. "No. Not you. I can't take the chance."

Lars held her worried gaze before looking at the map again. "I have to. It's my job. Maybe I can save him."

Sarea said, her voice shaky, "Both bodies were in the river near Barrorise. That's a long way from Wittrup."

Lars sighed and sat, examining the map. "But both were downriver from Wittrup. Even though Eagon was found a bit north on the lower stretches of the Tormod, there has been a lot of rain. Maybe he washed upriver? In the flooding?" Lars asked. "It's only fifty, seventy lengths from where it feeds into the Casclian."

"And we're still seeing runoff from spring thaw up north," Sarea sighed. "The few days before you boys

came, all the rivers and creeks were swelled with it."
She looked at the map and frowned. "Oh, damn."

"I have to go, Sarea. Please."

"Lars, no."

"I could stay to the riverbank. Take my horse." Lars
traced along the stretch of river between Wittrup and
the far side of the peninsula. "That's only a mile or two
of bank, surely."

"I don't know, Lars," Sarea said, backing away. "I
can't make decisions like that."

"Dubric and Dien could be anywhere, following
their own clues. Every day, every bell we waste could
mean Otlee dies. I've been here, hiding on the farm all
this time. Let me do this, let me help. Please."

Sarea stared at the map and chewed on her lip. "You
really think he might be there? On the riverbank?"

Lars looked at the map before meeting Sarea's worried gaze. "Honestly, it's a long shot. He might be near
the river, or anywhere on the peninsula, or somewhere
else. There's no way to tell, not until I look. But I might
get lucky. I also might only get muddy and wet."

Sarea hesitated.

"Please," Lars said. "It's the best clue I've got for
where Otlee might be, and we're running out of time. I
have to try. Even if I only find him dead. Please. There
might be a path, might be *something* I can tell Dien and
Dubric."

Sarea sighed harshly and nodded. "All right. But you
be back before dark. I don't care what monster you see
or how many storms blow through, or if you break your
damned leg. You get home, you hear me? You stay on
your horse and if you run across the least bit of trouble,
you get back here. No heroics, no damn 'duty to
Faldorrah' nonsense. You're out there to look for Otlee.

That's it. You're not investigating squat or looking for a single damned clue, and if I find that you've taken any risks I'll tan your hide myself. Do we have a deal?"

"Yes, ma'am," Lars said, bowing. Grinning, he ran from the house before she could change her mind.

Dubric stomped into the office of Tormod's constable without bothering to knock mud from his boots. Sherrod leaned behind his desk talking to Dwyer, the shoemaker from Barrorise.

"Did ye hear, milord?" Dwyer asked, turning, his face bright with excitement. "Everyone's talkin' about it. They caught him!"

"Yes, I have heard," Dubric said, while Dien's bulk filled the doorway behind him. Ungus Dwyer's name had appeared twice in the ledger, both for "services," and not for the purchase of shoes. Dubric could barely stand to look at either man. "Constable, I must speak with the accused," he said, hoping he was not grimacing.

Sherrod leaned forward, staring at Dubric. "He is my prisoner and the Reach will repay him for his crimes. I've already told you this isn't your concern, Lord Castellan."

Dubric took a step toward the desk and said, "I will not ask again." Behind him, Dien moved, and Dubric heard the sleek sound of steel being drawn, just far enough to deliver the message.

Dwyer fled the building and Sherrod stood, bristling. "You dare to threaten me? Do you know who I am?"

"A man missing his right arm if you do not let us pass," Dien said. "Nothing else means piss to me.

Dubric wants to talk to Jak, and he will, whether you like it or not."

Sherrod stared at Dien. "I should have you both gelded for this."

Dubric walked past him and opened the door leading farther into the building.

Dien said, "Difficult to do that with one arm, but you're welcome to try. Where are the cells?"

Sherrod sat, staring at Dien. "Through the left side door."

Dubric nodded and turned left. Dien followed him.

The door opened silently to a room filled with straw and stink. Old devices of torture stood clustered about, and shackles hung from the walls, five of which held limp men upright. All but one had messed themselves; two were naked below the waist, with their filth dried and caked to their legs. Even the sunlight slanting through the high, barred windows seemed to be stained with piss and feces.

"Barbaric," Dubric muttered, striding through. He found Jak easily enough—he was the only prisoner not stewing in his own filth—hanging by the wrists against a dank, chipped wall of rough-hewn stone. He was unconscious, bleeding from behind his right ear, and he wore all of his clothes, even his work boots.

"Wake him," Dubric said. "I have a feeling he may be innocent."

"How so, sir?" Dien asked.

"The man who killed and raped that boy was barefoot at the time. Jak is wearing his boots, and the front of his trousers is just as dirty as his shirt and face. I would wager my best horse his trousers were up and fastened when he fell to the ground."

Dien tapped Jak's cheeks with his palms without effect. Shouting, too, brought no response from Jak, but two of the other prisoners groaned and told Dien to shut his frigging yap.

"Water," Dubric said, examining the wound on Jak's head. "If you can find it." The back of Jak's head felt soft and spongy. Swollen. Dubric sighed and let the big man's head droop again. *Can we wake him at all?*

Dien located a bucket among the winches and spikes, and he frowned as he carried it to Dubric. "I'll be damned if I stand aside while an innocent man is tortured and hanged." He sighed and shook his head, staring at Jak as he hefted the bucket in both hands. "It's water, sir, and not too rancid. Have you seen all you need before it's washed away?"

Dubric nodded and took a step back. "He needs to wake before he never wakes again."

Dien took a breath and threw the water, slamming the entire bucketful on Jak's face. Drenched and dripping, Jak spluttered and moaned, twisting in his shackles, but he did not wake.

"Find another," Dubric said. He approached Jak again and slapped his cheek. "Wake, damn you."

Fluttering eyelids, a low moan, and Jak drew his face away. Dubric slapped him again, harder. "Wake up!"

Dien returned with another bucket. "There was a frog in it, sir, and some dead bugs, but it should do."

Dubric nodded and stepped back while Dien threw the water.

Jak awoke with a start, screaming a low warbling wail. "What happened to my head? Where am— You!" he said, his attention settling on Dien. "Where are my boys? What am I doing here?"

Dubric took a step forward and pulled his notebook

from his pocket. "Look at me," he said, watching Jak. "What is the last thing you remember?"

Jak's head rolled to the left as if on creaking hinges and he spat. "The farm boy, page, whatever he is, just kicked the life out of my work crew for tormenting the master's daughter."

"What in the hells happened to my daughter?" Dien snarled.

Jak cowered back and said, "My boys admitted grabbing her, scaring her. But your daughter's all right, I swear on my life. Your farm boy made sure of it."

"Of course he did," Dien said, stepping back. He cursed and paced behind Dubric.

"What happened on the road?" Dubric asked.

"I sent the lads home," Jak said. "Two were upset over being dismissed, and they set out on the road alone." He took a deep breath and struggled against his chains. "No matter what they'd done, I couldn't let them brave the dark, so I went after them."

"Go on," Dubric said, wishing Otlee stood beside him. The boy never missed a word when taking notes.

Jak swallowed, winced, and said, "It was just full dark when I found Rao walking the road alone. But as I tried to talk some sense into the boy, something hit the back of my head. I fell."

He winced again. "I woke in a barred cart, seeing sky through the bars, but I couldn't move. Next I knew, here you are." He paused, staring at Dubric. "What's happening? Does Elle know what's happened to me? Where are my lads?"

Dubric looked Jak in the eye. "You're accused of murder because one of your 'lads' is dead, killed in your work cart."

Jak slumped. "No. Not another one of my boys. I

take them home, for Goddess' sake! I don't let them go anywhere alone after dark!"

"Did you see who hit you?"

"No, milord."

"Do you remember where you were when you were hit?"

"Beside my cart. Up by my mule, I think."

Dubric rubbed his eyes and sighed before adding the information to his notebook. The body-shaped indentation in the mud matched Jak's explanation.

Dubric looked to Dien. "Check his feet."

Dien knelt before Jak to remove his boots. Well-maintained socks with only a day's worth of sweat and boot grime covered an unremarkable, callused pair of clean feet.

"What other boy left angry besides Rao?"

"Flann," Jak said. He turned to look at Dien. "I'm sorry, sir, but they were responsible for what happened to your lass. The other two just got caught up in it, but Flann and Rao . . . 'Twas their idea, their doing. I dismissed them, sir. I can't do much to atone, but I swear it won't happen again. Not with my crew."

Dubric asked, "You did not see Flann on the road with Rao?"

"No, milord." He looked up to the shackles and said, "Can you let me out of these? I won't cause trouble."

"They are not mine to control," Dubric said. "You are in the constable's gaol. Until I investigate this matter further, you must remain here."

"I didn't kill anyone, milord, I swear. I've never harmed a soul my whole life." He glanced at Dien and added, "I know the master there worried over me talking to his farm boy, or page, or whatever he was, but, see, milord, the boy didn't have anyone, and that's a damn dangerous thing here in the Reach for a lad his age. I took in every one I could, made sure they was fed and sheltered. It's not safe for a lad alone in these parts. Not safe at all."

He stared at Dubric. "He takes boys, milord. And they never come home. Especially the nice-looking ones, the young lads with light and fire in their eyes."

"Who?" Dubric asked, stepping forward. "Who takes them?"

"I wish I knew, milord," Jak said, tears streaming down his cheeks as he looked up at his chains. "I used to pray that I'd find him skulking on the road after I took my lads home. I used to pray that I'd kill him myself. Isn't that a damn fine thing for a peaceful man to pray for?"

PART 3

CUT

CHAPTER

22

†

Seething, Dubric rode from the constable's office down the road to Barrorise. The ghosts left him without warning, and he clenched the saddle to keep from falling.

When Dien looked at him, concerned, Dubric asked, "Do we have any hope that Haconry will agree to have Jak released?"

"Not much, sir," Dien said. "What little I know of the wretch isn't encouraging."

"I agree." Dubric glimpsed Haconry's estate on a hilltop ahead. "He is a most vile and aggravating man."

"He's not a man, sir," Dien said, looking ahead at the tiled rooftop. "Men don't do things like that to children. It amazes me to no end that the people here allow him to be steward at all, let alone permit him to touch . . ." Grumbling, he shook his head and stared at the road. "Isn't my place, sir. I gave an oath to uphold the laws of Faldorrah, even the loathsome ones, and I don't live here, but, pegging hells, this is just wrong. Law or not."

Dubric said, "He is involved, somehow. I may be in the midst of an investigation and am therefore forced to endure various uncomfortable circumstances to make headway into the particulars of the case, but my pages will not be compromised. By the King, they will not. Haconry threatened Otlee with depraved intent more than once. He will pay for that, and pay dearly, whether he has a hand in harming the boy or not."

Dien glanced at Dubric. "What kind of filthy shit would threaten Otlee?" He took a deep breath, and Dubric saw the big man's hands tighten on the reins. "A dead filthy weasel, that's what. I'll crush his pegging skull."

Dubric frowned, remembering his ghosts' icy weight. The thought of having Haconry follow him, perhaps for all time, turned his stomach as much as the thought of Haconry touching Otlee. "Let us hope it will not come to that," he said. "Sometimes there are worse punishments than death."

"Like castration," Dien said, heeling his horse to a gallop.

"Ungh." Flann lay on a ratty mattress, a blanket tangled around him, and groaned, covering his mouth and nose against the stench.

Aggravated and cursing, he sat and looked blearily around him. Red worms crawled on the stained floor, some spinning cocoons in corners or in holes, and everything was filthy. Rotting food, splattered mud. Old blood. The place stank of urine and shit and things long dead. It was his job to clean it up.

Flann fell back to the mattress, his blood-spattered arm over his eyes. Sherrod had told him to hide on the farm, be quiet for a few days, and get rid of the mess; some old prick named Byr was getting close. The old bastard had everyone else running in circles, but not Flann. He wasn't worried. Hells, no. Once he was

Foiche, he'd do anything he wanted—including slowly killing that arrogant puppy on Dev's farm—but right now he wanted to doze, not scoop up worms and bones.

He tried to breathe, tried to relax, but his eyes remained open. He was awake. Daylight was wasting. And that corpse wasn't getting any fresher.

He stood, kicking aside the blanket, and stomped from the room, cursing all the while.

Dubric held out a hand to slow Dien as they came around a curve in the road. "Do you see what I see?" he asked, pulling his horse to a stop. Ungus Dwyer hurried away from them and opened Haconry's outer gate, taking time to wipe his brow before scurrying up the lane.

"That's the same swine who was in the constable's office when we arrived. What's he doing here?"

"I would wager that he is delivering a message," Dubric said, easing his horse backward. He dismounted and led his horse to the ditch, then crept ahead again to hide in the bushes. "I do not think that he heard us."

"No, sir," Dien said, kneeling beside him as Dwyer ran up Haconry's stairs. "He never looked back. Who is he?"

"A common shoemaker, from Barrorise. He is on the list for payment for 'services.' "

"Bribes and a quick check-in with the boss. It can't ever be simple, can it, sir?"

"No. With twenty-six murdered, simple is not an option." Dubric rubbed his aching eyes. "We shall wait for Dwyer to leave, and converse with him privately. I want to know as much as I can before facing Haconry."

"Doesn't look like we'll have long to wait, sir."

Dwyer stood before the door for moments before it was opened. He spoke briefly to whoever answered, then descended the steps while the door closed behind him. He took a deep breath and glanced at the sky, seeming to relax as if losing a mental burden.

"The message has been delivered," Dubric said, releasing the peace bond on his sword. "Perhaps we should deliver one of our own."

"Damn right, sir."

They crept forward, hiding behind brush, as Dwyer walked down the lane to the gate. He glanced furtively in both directions and, apparently assured of his solitude, stepped onto the road.

He had taken fewer than ten steps south when Dien came up behind him. He spun Dwyer around and grabbed him by the throat.

Dwyer panicked, but Dubric said, "I suggest you remain silent for the time being."

Dwyer nodded, trying to talk, his eyes rolling to look at Dubric.

"Shh," Dubric said, leading them into the brambled cover.

"Are ye gonna kill me?" Dwyer asked when Dien slammed him to his knees. He looked up at the pair, his lower lip quivering while his eyes darted between them.

"That depends," Dubric said. "The more you tell me, the greater the likelihood that you will see the morrow."

Dwyer nodded, glancing at Dien before returning his attention to Dubric. "I ain't killed no one, milord, I swear. I ain't had nothin' to do with that part. But I did take two boys."

"You what?" Dien asked.

"I had to, I swear. If I didn't, they swore to put my son on the list and . . . I had to! I never harmed 'em, though, not once. I tried to ease their pain and fear."

"You stole other men's sons?" Dien asked.

"No," Dwyer said, shrinking. "The two I took didn't have no fathers."

"Which two?" Dubric opened his notebook and licked his pencil.

Dwyer swallowed, shaking. "I can't. They'll kill me."

Dien growled, pulling Dwyer's head back and putting his knife at his throat. "I'm a more imminent threat. Perhaps you'd best keep that in mind."

Dwyer panted, tears streaming down his cheeks. "I didn't hurt 'em, I swear. Just put the cloth over their face 'til they quieted, then took 'em to the tower. I never hurt 'em!"

"Who?" Dubric asked again. "Which boys did you steal?"

Dwyer winced as Dien's blade broke the skin. "Some nameless street rat in Tormod, and Braoin Duncannon! Please!"

Dien fell back, astounded, and dropped his knife. "You goat-raping bastard! You kidnapped Bray?"

Dwyer swallowed and lowered his chin. "He'd topped the list fer so long. We was all looking fer him, the top prize. I just got lucky."

"Why?" Dubric asked. "Why Braoin?"

Dwyer shook his head and stared at his knees. "I can't. Please."

"Yes, you frigging can," Dien snarled, backhanding the smaller man and knocking him aside. "That boy was my cousin and a damn fine lad. Because of you he's dead."

Dwyer cowered away, mewling, but Dien lifted him by the hair and hit him again, cracking his cheekbone and knocking teeth from his mouth. "Talk to us, you pustule on a sow's ass, before I rip out your throat with my bare hands."

Dwyer burbled through the blood, trying to hold up his hands, but Dien threw him like a wet rag into the bramble.

"Hold," Dubric said through gritted teeth. "Let the man talk."

His teeth bared, Dien pulled Dwyer upright and slammed him onto his knees.

Dywer babbled, "Braoin was too curious, he asked too many questions, and he was wily, slippery, clever. No one could catch him alone on the road. Anywhere. Then, one afternoon, I was standin' by my cart, takin' a piss, and he comes outta the brush. He barely looked at me before hurryin' across the road, and he was gone again. I thought if I could catch Braoin, maybe I'd never have to get another, so I followed him. I'm so sorry." Dwyer fell forward, landing on his forearms as he spat blood. "Milord, please. I never meant to harm no one. I didn't want 'em to die."

Dubric stood over him. "You knew what would happen, yet you did it anyway. Why didn't you take your family and leave the Reach instead of selling those boys?"

"I didn't know!" Dwyer cried. "Not 'til I saw those two from the river. I swear, milord, I didn't know what he did to them. When I left they were alive, I swear on my life!"

"Who?" Dubric asked, pulling Dywer's face up so he could see the man's eyes. "Who is killing them?"

"I . . . I dunno! I never saw him, not really. I only brought the two boys, and the first . . . I dunno when he came, but I left the boy alone in that dark place. He hadn't come yet."

"And with Braoin?"

Dwyer swallowed and shook his head. "Please, ye have to understand."

"We understand shit!" Dien said, kicking the man in the ribs.

Dubric nodded slowly as Dwyer's pained gaze met his. "Next time, break something, then remove it."

"Yes, sir," Dien said grimly.

"Braoin woke up!" Dwyer screamed, curling on the ground. "And he struggled. I couldn't finish quick enough, and he came, he did, but I left right away. To look on him is forbidden. He woulda killed me."

"So instead you allowed him to kill an innocent boy. Several boys. Who was it? Who?"

"I dunno!" Dwyer panted, braving a glance. "Truly, milord, I dunno. I just took the boys to the pit, stripped and tied them, then left. I swear."

"You were paid for this service?"

Dwyer nodded, whimpering. "Yes."

"How? By whom?"

"Both times, I was paid by Glis Sherrod, the constable in—"

"I know who he is," Dubric snapped. "Did you tell him or anyone else who you 'acquired' before receiving payment?"

"Just went to his office, told him who and when, then he paid me. He had the money in his desk."

Dubric noted the information. "You mentioned a list. What list? Where did it come from?"

"The constable gave it to me. I got a new one today when he told me to tell Sir Haconry about capturing Jak. Here. Take it." Dwyer reached in his pocket and pulled out a scrap of parchment with a bloody hand and gave it to Dubric. "When ye came to the Reach, and then I heard that Jak was caught, milord, it was such a relief. I thought the madness was over. But—but if Sherrod gave me a new list . . . it ain't done yet. Is it?"

Dubric looked at the list, and clear, cold anger slipped into his heart. "Tie him, gag him. Hells, ghost or no damned ghost, kill him if you must. But try to remember he is not the beast, merely one of its claws."

"Sir?" Dien asked, dragging Dwyer to his feet with one hand while pulling a loop of rope from his hip with the other.

"Lars heads the list," Dubric said. "And he is marked at five hundred crown. The bastard put a bounty on him."

CHAPTER

23

†

Lars urged his mare to a fast canter. It felt good to be investigating again, even in a limited capacity. Every sight was a new experience, every person he passed a new face. Even the muddy road was new.

He rode west, intent on reaching the peninsula before mid-morning; he had a lot of shoreline to cover before dusk. After passing the ferry he slowed, turning his horse to the undergrowth.

Riding soon became impossible, and he dismounted to lead his horse through brambles and muddy thicket along the bank of the Casclian River. Little more than rocks and mud, it was the sorriest soil he'd ever seen.

He walked along, looking up the bank then down to the water every few steps. He yelped as a clump of rocks gave way beneath his feet and fell down to the river. *Better move inland a bit before I get soaked.*

He climbed uphill, rounding a blackberry tangle, then continued south, but he soon discovered he couldn't see the water's edge. As he tracked back toward the bank, a group of baby rabbits scurried from beneath the ground cover, startling him and his horse.

He squinted through budding branches to see the sun. After a few more steps, he stopped, sniffing.

Lars turned his head and tried to follow the

unpleasant scent, breaking a trail uphill and deeper into the brush. "Goddess, that stinks," he said, grimacing. He looked uphill to brush and rocks and brambles tangling into an impenetrable dark mass. Somewhere, in the distance, he heard a door slam, followed by an obscenity.

He turned and looked down to the river. He'd climbed a good forty, fifty lengths up the hillside. Debating his options, he looked back up to the stink. At last he sighed and led his horse downhill. He'd given his word to Sarea that he would stay by the bank, and stay safe. Besides, it was probably just some livestock that died over the winter. Goats, perhaps.

Winter-rotted goats. Now, that's disgusting. He worked his way back to the bank and continued south, looking for signs of Otlee or bodies in the river.

Dubric paced along the road as he waited for Dien. He opened his hand to stare at the crushed bit of parchment and a single familiar name.

Lars Hargrove—castle page/farm boy, tallish, blond hair, N. of Tormod, use caution—500CR

Other names were listed below, names of boys he had never seen or heard of, but his gaze remained on the listing for his page. *How did they discover his name?* he thought, pacing, while Dwyer's screams faded on the breeze. *Would Lars advertise his identity? How in the seven hells could they know? Why is Lars considered dangerous? Is it because they have already caught Otlee? Or something else?*

"Sir?" Dien asked, breaking Dubric's spinning thoughts. "He's bound to a tree and gagged, but I broke both of his hands. Even if he could reach the knots, he'll never unfasten them."

"That is fine," Dubric said, handing the parchment to Dien. "How could they know Lars's name?"

Dien read the list, his eyes hardening. "The peddler came by the farm, and I think one of my girls mentioned Lars's full name to him. You've met him, he's a terrible gossip. And Lissea's walked to Tormod several times, so it's possible that she might have said something. Jak might have heard his name mentioned around the farm. You know how quickly gossip can spread. I'm sorry, sir, but it's probably my family's fault."

Dubric accepted the list, looking at it one more time before putting it in his pocket. "Haconry certainly has not cooperated in the investigation, and has shown undue interest in Otlee. I do believe it is time to put a bit of fear into the steward of the Reach, if not snap him in two. But I want him alive."

Dien nodded and took a deep breath. "Alive, I can do. I can't guarantee one piece."

Side by side they walked to the gate and opened it, continuing to the manor's steps.

Lars stood at the edge of a long, cracked stretch of rocks and mud that threatened to collapse into the river. Great slices of it had fallen away, leaving ragged gaps, and the cracks streaked like claw marks up the naked hillside. All of the vegetation had long since washed away, leaving only a desolate and crumbling mire. *Maybe this is a good place to turn back,* he thought, squinting at the sun. *I don't want to cross that.*

He turned his horse around and started the long trek back to the road, his shoulders sagging. He'd found nothing but thornbushes and prickle burrs, and had seen no signs of any people except himself.

A short distance ahead, a group of starlings flew from the trees, and he paused to admire the flock over the river, twirling through the air, switching direction, and folding onto itself like a scrap of fabric floating on the breeze.

He took a dozen steps, then jolted to a stop. "It can't be." Lars tied his horse and crept to the bank's edge.

Fifteen or so lengths below, a mud-smeared corpse lay half in and half out of the water, and fresh gouges led up the bank's crumbling face. *I'll be damned. I was just here a quarter bell ago, if that.*

He stood straight and assessed the scene, checking for cover, movement, anything out of the ordinary. Carefully, he moved along the bank toward the corpse and glanced uphill.

Another look down to the river and the nude corpse on the bank. *This is impossible. I was just here.*

He squinted into the trees, but saw nothing. No movement, not even birds. The air stank of rotten meat and nutmeg. It made his skin crawl.

Something rustled up the hill. He heard wet, rotted leaves shifting, then utter silence.

Slowly, his eyes and ears searching for movement, Lars pulled his sword.

Listening, he looked down at the body. Male, older and bigger than Otlee, the body lay in the mud, one arm pinned beneath his chest and the other floating on the water. Bruises marked the purple-green back, lacerations crisscrossed the anus and buttocks, and Lars saw ligature marks on the wrists and ankles. Two fingers were gone, and the corpse's hair was blood-soaked. A hinged wooden clothespin was clipped to its ear.

He heard another crackle of leaves or rocks. He turned, sword in hand, and stared up the hill, his gaze steady and hard. *What am I going to do? I gave my word I'd stay to the bank, but, damn, I'm so close! How many are up there? And, hells, they have the high ground.*

He took a breath and watched for movement. *It doesn't matter if there's only one of you or a dozen. If you've dumped a body, you've got Otlee, and you can't have him anymore.*

Lars kept his attention focused uphill, and he turned his head slightly at the sound of one branch shifting against another.

C'mon, you bastard, make another sound. Give me an excuse to go up there and leave your guts in the mud.

There was another rustle of movement. Lars shifted his stare, easing his body to the right. *Tighter, tighter. Where are you? Aah!*

A footprint led up the hill, deep and gouging where the bare toes must have dug into the mud for purchase. Following the path with his eyes, he saw another bare footprint a step away, then some disrupted dead leaves, a smashed bush, and a muddy path broken through the tangle. The markings stopped and his gaze settled on a blackberry bramble, the twigs reddish against the overall gray-green of the surrounding vegetation. While he stared at it, the bramble moved, trembling in the air.

There you are. He took a step up the broken path, and another, his gaze never leaving the bramble. He saw movement, a bit of blue behind the red twigs and tiny leaves, and he smiled, licking his lips. *Let's put an end to this.*

With a crash and a thunder of the bush, a man in a

blue shirt and grimy brown pants scrambled into view and fled, disappearing into the brush far above. Lars gave chase.

Dubric stood in Haconry's entry hall with Dien beside him. Haconry's housekeeper, Vidulyn, shuffled down the hall toward the far door as if her life depended on it.

"She seems a bit flustered, sir," Dien said.

Dubric checked his sword and rocked back on his heels. "You *are* covered in blood."

Dien coughed, smirking. "Good. Then I don't have to worry about him making a bigger mess."

Vidulyn opened the far door and stepped aside.

Haconry burst past her, tying a robe around his waist. "Lord Castellan!" he called. "I hear congratulations are in order."

Dubric forced a smile. "You are mistaken."

"Tsk, tsk. Do not be so doubtful. Jak the carpenter was caught, shall we say, with his pants down, was he not? Surely that is cause for celebration." Haconry appraised Dien with a knowing smirk. "You have astounded me yet again, my Lord Castellan. I expected you to replace the delightful, fiery lad with another choice specimen rather than this aging brute."

Dubric held out a hand to halt Dien before he could tear the steward to tatters. "I have not come here to exchange pleasantries."

"Oh?" Haconry said, tilting his head. "So this is not a social visit before your return home?"

"No. I have come to give you an opportunity."

Haconry's smirk remained. "And what 'opportunity' might that be?"

"An opportunity for you to escape a hangman's noose. I will offer it only once."

"My Lord Castellan! Surely you cannot be serious."

Dubric pulled Calum's ledger from his coat pocket. "Deadly serious." He opened to a marked page. "Would you care to explain for what 'services' you paid Ungus Dwyer fifty crown?"

Haconry's eyes rolled, amused. "I purchased shoes. There is no crime in that."

Dubric sighed and rubbed his aching eyes. "We have already spoken to Dwyer, and you have just chosen the noose. My offer of mercy is withdrawn."

"Congratulations, dung heap," Dien said, reaching for the steward. "I've waited a long time to see you twitch in the breeze."

Haconry stumbled back as Dien gripped his robe. As he struggled, the fine silk tore, splitting the robe in two. Naked, Haconry broke free and ran, Dien on his heels, and both disappeared through a door.

"Why must they always run?" Dubric muttered. He picked up the ruined robe from the floor and searched the pockets, finding them empty.

He heard movement, and looked up to see Vidulyn approaching him, crushing a dark kerchief in her hands. "What do you know of the kidnappings?" Dubric asked, struggling to fold the slippery silk of Haconry's ruined robe. "Have you any idea how many are involved, or who they may be?"

"No, my lord," Vidulyn said, stepping aside. "It is best if I do not see what he does. May I fold that for you?"

He tried to meet her gaze, but she stared at the floor, even as she took the robe from him. He wondered if

Haconry abused her. "My page, the boy I brought with me several days ago, have you seen him?"

She shook her head and smoothed the silk. "Of course not. Not here."

A crash filled the air, followed by the tinkle of broken glass. Dubric moved past her, toward the open door

Haconry fell through and landed facedown on the floor. Dien stomped through, sword in one hand and a busted chair in the other. "I've had about as much of this as I can take," he snarled, slamming the chair on Haconry's back. "You're finished, so quit arguing about it."

Dubric stepped aside to let Dien bind Haconry's hands. The steward lay on the polished floor, bruised, battered, and bleeding, with an oozing slash low on his back. "I see he still lives."

"Yeah, and it's a damn shame. Think he might lose that kidney, sir?" Dien asked, yanking the steward to his feet.

"It does not matter," Dubric said. "He chose to keep his appointment."

Lars felt amazingly calm, his mind clear and sharp. While his quarry had run through the woods and over rocks in a random path, he had followed at a steady pace. *Show me where you've hidden Otlee, you weasel,* he thought.

The fugitive burst onto open ground and stumbled into a barnyard. His feet tangled beneath him and he fell, sprawling in the mud. Scrambling upright again, he tore toward the shed.

Lars recognized Flann and snarled, baring his teeth.

"I kicked your filthy ass once," he hollered, following. "Gutless coward! Where's Otlee?"

Flann disappeared into the shed, slamming the door behind him.

Lars coughed. Death and rot hung heavy in the air, close and putrid. The shed was perhaps eight lengths on a side and well built, but in need of fresh white-wash. Something crashed within. Lars took a slow breath, taking time to assess his quarry's cover.

Only one door, hinged. Probably dirt floor—

The door burst open and Flann came through swinging an axe. Dried blood covered his left shoulder, a relic from his fight with Lars the day before, and he held the primary weight of the axe in his right hand. "Hey, piddle pup," he said, grinning as Lars jumped back. "This time I'm gonna cleave your pegging skull."

"Try," Lars snarled, ducking the wild swing and pulling a dagger with his free hand. *Be careful—I'm injured and he's got a longer reach with no control. Watch him, watch him . . .*

Lars moved in closer, but Flann knocked him aside on the backswing and waggled his tongue. "After I'm done with you, I'll grab your girlie again. She was mighty tasty."

"Where's Otlee?"

"That your girlie's name, piddle pup?" Flann swung, just missing Lars's belly. "How's it feel to know I had her first, eh?" He blew Lars a kiss and swung again.

Right leg. Right leg. Lars ducked, lunging close, and drew blood with his sword before he rolled away. He hoped he hadn't popped his stitches.

Flann howled, right hand falling to his bleeding thigh while he switched the axe's weight to the left. "By Foiche! You cut me!"

And I weakened you, but you don't notice that, do you? "That's for Jess," Lars said, staying just beyond Flann's loose and uncontrolled swings. The piercing on Flann's shoulder bled anew, soaking his shirt, and blood ran down his arm to the axe handle.

Flann brought both hands to the axe and pulled to the side to swing. Lars lunged close, letting Flann's arm bend around him. Flann fell backward, falling over his bleeding leg, with Lars half caught in his bloody embrace.

Shift, twist, and Lars's dagger found flesh, a belly wound. He rolled off and out of reach. "You are hereby charged with murder, so drop your weapon. It's over. Where is Otlee?"

Flann snarled, drawing to his feet and dragging the axe with him. "Peg you, piddle pup. I ain't dead yet."

"I don't want to kill you," Lars said, approaching slowly. Three solid wounds, none life-threatening, bled vigorously, soaking Flann's skin and clothing. He looked woozy and about ready to drop. "Where's Otlee?"

Flann panted, cowering back. "Who in the hells is Otlee?"

"My friend," Lars said, watching Flann's eyes as he circled to the right. "He's been missing for three days and I want him back."

"Three days gone, he's cut to hells, raped, and half dead. Taken it up the *ass*, piddle pup. Even if he lives he'll never shit right again. You're better off letting him finish it."

Oh, crap, he's gonna faint. "Him who?"

Flann stumbled back, holding his belly with his right hand, and Lars rushed forward to grab him. Flann grinned and swung low, at Lars's legs, left-handed and loose.

Lars jumped up and forward, trying to escape the swing, but the axe hooked his ankle and yanked his balance away, throwing him to the ground on his back, knocking away his air.

While Lars struggled to breathe, Flann laughed and swung downward, missing Lars's head by mere finger widths. Lars tried to roll, but Flann slammed his foot on Lars's chest and drew back for another swing.

Trying to force air into his lungs—Not again! Goddess, it hurts!—Lars heaved like a flopping fish and pulled on Flann's weak leg, knocking him off. Flann fell backward, startled and yelping, to land on Lars's feet.

Lars kicked him away and rolled, choking, dragging air past the constriction in his chest, as he scrambled upright. "Enough!" he coughed, staggering aside. "You are accused of murder and are going to be my prisoner if I have to hamstring you to do it!"

Flann said nothing.

"No!" Lars said, scrambling to him. Flann lay on his back, thrashing, his chest oddly swollen and blood leaking from his mouth. The axe handle lay at a crooked angle beneath him, while blood flowed on the mud.

"Don't you die!" Lars screamed, grabbing him by the shirt. "Not until you tell me where Otlee is!"

"Peg you," Flann said, and spat.

Bloody spittle dripping down his face, Lars shook the boy. "Where is he? Who took him? What did you do to Otlee?"

Flann grinned, his breathing becoming rattly and slow, then he died.

Lars shoved the body away. He staggered back, turning in the echoing yard, with the scent of death whispering around him and fresh blood on his hands.

With Haconry securely trussed in the main hall, Dubric and Dien had gathered all members of the staff, taking their statements before dismissing them for the day. He and Dien had found no other souls in the entire manor, no boys, no prisoners shackled in the cellar, and no Otlee.

Assured that they could reexamine the residence and its contents at leisure, they dragged Haconry over the haunch of Dubric's horse, then retrieved Dwyer, draping him over Dien's gelding.

"We need another horse," Dien said as they rode to the south. "Or Pigshit Mul will have to walk."

"The exertion might do him good," Dubric said. They crossed the bridge into Barrorise and ignored the curious stares of the villagers. They dismounted before Mul's house of torture, and Dien kicked the door in.

They heard a startled scream and rushed down the hall to see a half-naked girl run toward them, clutching her dress against her bare chest with one hand and covering her mouth with the other.

"What in the seven hells?" Mul snapped from within the room. "Get your ass back here! I washed it! We made a fair trade!"

Dubric and Dien stepped aside to let the girl escape, then both pulled their swords. "We can do this the easy way or the hard way," Dien said as they stood on either side of the door.

Mul snatched it open, naked and odorous. "Who are you? Do you have any idea what I had to do to get a blow from—" He saw Dubric and his face fell. He backed away, his hands held up before him. "By the ghost of Foiche, I can explain."

"Where is my page?" Dubric snarled.

"Page? What page?" Mul asked. He yelped, startled, when he backed his bare backside against his desk.

"The boy I had with me when we first met," Dubric said, trying to ignore the red haze of rage teasing the edges of his vision.

"I . . . I don't know what you're talking about."

"Where is he?" Dien stabbed his sword tip into the loose fat of Mul's belly, then yanked it free. "Next time it's your balls."

"I don't have anything to do with that!" Mul shrieked, cowering, his hands over his privates. "I disposed of the one body, just the one! I'm not part of this!"

Dubric loomed over him, grinding his teeth. "Which body?"

Mul babbled, tears streaking down his cheeks. "That first one, the one you looked at here. I was supposed to just let it rot and toss it away, but you came. They made me get it back, made me throw it away again."

"Who?" Dien and Dubric said in unison.

"I don't know! Martaen said to do it for Foiche or he'd take my practice away! It's all I have! Please!"

Dubric shoved the tip of his sword against the base of Mul's throat. "Foiche? I killed him fifty summers ago."

Mul wailed, "He's not dead, not anymore. He has family, I don't know who, I swear, who want him back. They made me take a blood oath to serve. Made all of us!" He looked up at Dubric and said, "I never knew who, but all us Conrys took the oath, back when we were kids, back before they tried to turn that crippled kid into Foiche."

Dubric narrowed his eyes. Tucker Conry had been Foiche's most trusted advisor and right-hand man. He, too, had died in the war, but had his children survived? Both sons were killed, but his daughters? For the life of him, Dubric could not remember what had become of the three daughters. "Stuart," he asked, afraid of the answer. "What do you know about Stuart?"

Mul shook, pleading. "They'd teased him for phases, having the red worms crawl over him, bite him. He'd cry and run home, but they'd grab him again a couple days later. Then they took the cloth and tried to . . . to make Foiche live in his body."

"Who?" Dubric snarled, leaning close.

Mul swallowed, scrunching his eyes shut. "Didge and Bilton Haconry, and Tropos."

Dien blinked, shaking his head. "There *were* three? Dammit! Who's Tropos?"

"I can't," Mul said. "Word is he's back. He'll kill me."

Dubric growled and shifted his wrist despite Mul's screams. He slowly shoved his sword through the slope of Mul's shoulder and into the wood desk. "I'm going to kill you if you do not talk. Who is Tropos and where is my damned page?"

"I don't know!" Mul shrieked. He threw his head back and wailed. "I was a kid. Never met him! They don't tell me anything! I swear! If I knew I'd tell you! No one tells me anything!"

"They?" Dien asked. "They who?"

"Tropos, I think, and someone else. There's two, maybe three of them, I think, but there might be one or seventeen or six. I swear, I honest to Goddess swear, I don't know who or where or anything. Haconry told me to destroy the body. Then, when I let it go, he made me get it from the undertaker again, and that's the Goddess' truth! That's the only thing they've trusted me with and I failed!"

"Is a farmer named Horace involved in this?" Dien asked.

Mul hesitated, then nodded. "Probably. He's a Conry, too. My brother."

"Constable Sherrod?" Dubric asked.

"Half brother," Mul whispered. "Mayor Liconry of Wittrup, too, and I have cousins in Oreth and Tormod and Reyburn. Nap's Folly, too, but he's just a kid. Fourteen, maybe fifteen summers."

"Peg my mother," Dien muttered. "A whole frigging family of kidnapping, murder, and treason."

"It's not treason," Mul said, raising his chin. "We Conrys ruled this land for Foiche before the war stole it from us. We're taking it back. Foiche will reign again."

Dubric pulled his sword free. "Over my moldering corpse," he said, yanking the physician to his feet. "Put some pants on. I do not want to lose my breakfast."

Bare-chested but privates covered, Mul staggered from his office at sword point, and they lashed him to Dien's horse.

Lars had found nothing on the farm but bugs and bones and filth, all of it stinking and vile. *How many dead?* he thought, staggering down the bank to the river. *And how was Flann involved?*

Partway down he stopped and turned, looking back the way he had come. *Movement? Wind? Some animal?* He listened, not moving, his hand resting on the hilt of his sword and his heart thudding steady and slow.

Silence, nothing more than the breeze through budding trees and occasional birdsong. He smiled and relaxed when the brush shifted and a scrawny raccoon scrambled up a gnarled, old tree.

He continued down to his horse and pulled a coil of rope from his saddle. He wrapped one end around a tree three times, tied it, and let the rest fall to the ground.

Returning to his horse, Lars pulled a pair of rolled blankets from beneath the saddle straps. He looked down at the body and dropped the blankets to the rock-strewn mud beside it.

He grabbed the rope and checked the knot at the tree, then backed away, measuring and keeping the rope taut. Satisfied, he threw the loose end toward the river and stood at the edge of the bank with his heels hanging over the rim.

A quick prayer, and Lars jumped over the edge and down to the body.

"Rabbits!" the crone snapped, stomping through her house to a worn cupboard. "Haconry is a bigger coward than I thought, and Mul, too!" She yanked the door open and knocked aside little glass bottles until she found one she sought. She squeezed it in her fist and spat on it before she dashed it against the wall. It exploded in a shower of glass and left a black smear behind.

Muttering again, she returned to the cupboard and resumed her rabid search. Her fingers closed around the vial and she shook it in her fist as she stomped across the room. "Imbecile! Coward!" She glared into the vial. "Do you feel this? Damn you, you putrid wasp, do you feel? One pegging word to the Byr and you're dead."

The vial in her hand cracked and black fluid oozed between her fingers. A drip fell to the floor, hissing and burning through. From the cellar, a boy screamed.

Haconry flailed and whined the entire journey to Tormod, but Dwyer remained nearly silent, with only an occasional grunt to denote his existence. Mul just wept. Dubric winced when the full onslaught of ghosts waited for him on the road, but he had endured their arrivals and departures before, and, King willing, he would not have need to endure them much longer. The newest ghost, the boy he had found in the cart that morning, was gone.

They reached the constable's office without incident or clamoring crowds, and dragged their charges inside.

Sherrod lurched upright when they strode in, paling at the sight of Haconry and Mul. "What have you done?" he asked, slumping into his chair. He stared at Haconry, who fell like a bloody pile of laundry upon the floor.

"We have begun the final phase of my investigation," Dubric said while Dien left to retrieve Dwyer. "And I shall give you the same choice I gave Haconry." He stared Sherrod in the eye. "This is a one-time offer. Life or the noose, and it is not negotiable. One lie, and you choose the noose. I shall never offer life again."

Sherrod blinked, paling, as he stared at Haconry.

Dubric pulled his notebook from his pocket. "How many people have you paid for kidnapping?"

"Six," Sherrod said, his hands shaking. From behind Dubric, Haconry squealed and thrashed.

"Who?"

Sherrod listed Dwyer, Horace, Flann, and three unknown men.

Dubric's pencil stood poised over his notebook. "Where did the money come from?"

Haconry squealed again, but Sherrod lifted a quaking hand and pointed at him.

Dien came through the door, half dragging Dwyer, whom he shoved on a chair. Sherrod's shaking intensified, moving from his hands to his arms, then his shoulders and neck. He shook his head rabidly, looking between the prisoners. "Please, milord, have mercy. I don't want to die."

"Yet you participated in the ritualistic molestation and execution of more than a score of young men."

Haconry wailed and writhed against the floor, but Sherrod nodded, his shaky gaze loosely holding Dubric's. "I did, yes."

"Who decided to frame Jak the carpenter for the crimes?"

"I . . . I don't know. I received a note to go to the road, and there he was, bound, with the dead boy in the cart."

"Who delivered the note?"

"I don't know. It was here, on my desk, when I arrived."

"Who killed the boy in the cart?"

Sherrod paused, scrunching his eyes closed, while Haconry's fit intensified. "They'll kill me, milord." He opened his eyes again and stared at Dubric. "But one word, and I'll fall down dead. Please, I beg of you."

"Sir, I think you need to see this," Dien said.

Dubric turned. Haconry convulsed on the floor. Raspberry-colored goo leaked from his ears and nostrils, streaming in bright rivulets on the black slate floor. Mul threw his head back and wailed, his ears and nose leaking. The ghosts all stared at the sludge with horrified expressions. Eagon ripped at his face in terror and Braoin wailed, trying to pull Calum away.

"You see?" Sherrod whispered. "They're watching, and I'm already dead."

Dubric swallowed back the acrid taste in his throat. Even after fifty summers, he had not forgotten the utter mess of a Shadow Follower dying, or the rancid nutmeg stink. "You have aligned yourself with a dark mage?" he asked, turning.

Sherrod nodded and wiped his nose with a shaking hand. A thin line of brilliant red streaked down his finger. He stared at it, horrified. While Dubric watched, Sherrod's forehead split open in a thin line of red that oozed toward his eyes.

"Hurry!" Dubric said, slapping his palm on Sherrod's desk. "Who is the mage? Who is responsible for this?"

Sherrod's head shook, the line on his forehead cracking open to his ears. "I can't."

Dubric glanced at Dien. "Get Jak, and any other prisoner you can. Get them out of here." His attention flicked to Dwyer. He saw no red ooze. "Remove him as well."

"Yes, sir," Dien said, then lumbered to the back hall.

Sherrod's forehead slipped down, slumping onto his eyebrows. The oozing flesh twitched then peeled away, falling onto Sherrod's lap.

"Listen to me," Dubric said, leaning over the desk. "I cannot do anything to aid you, but no more innocent boys need to die. I need your help to save them. Who is killing them?"

Sherrod rocked fore and back, banging his head

against the wall and leaving a red, slimy smear. His hands clenched into fists and pounded his thighs. "I can't. I'll die."

"You are already dead," Dubric said. "The mage has called your due. Please help me before more boys die."

A warble started in Sherrod's throat, fluttering and fluid, and the smear on the wall grew. "They don't tell me, they don't tell anyone. But he dyes them."

"I know he kills them," Dubric said, wincing as Sherrod's left eye burst.

"No," Sherrod moaned. "He dyes them, to color the thread."

Sherrod fell face forward, his head splattering when it hit the desk, and his hands ceased pounding.

CHAPTER

24

✝

Dusk had fallen by the time Dubric and Dien reached the lane to Devyn's farm. They were exhausted and filthy, reeking of rancid nutmeg and stained with brilliant red goo. Dubric wanted no more than a cold ale and a hot bath—preferably together—but he had a good two bells' ride ahead of him. He doubted if Maeve had any ale, cold or not, or if he could sleep. *Where is Otlee? How can I find him when all my witnesses are dead?*

He stretched and followed Dien to the porch, intending to remain outside.

Sarea looked up when the door opened and, bawling, she staggered to Dien. The girls sat at the table, sniffling, and Stuart's ghost moved from his perch on the corner chair. Dubric heard the baby cry from somewhere within the house.

"Where's Lars?" Dien asked, pushing Sarea back to look at her face. "Which of the girls is hurt? What the peg happened?"

"Jess is fine and Lars is in the barn," Sarea said, dabbing at her eyes. "With Braoin."

"Braoin? How in the seven hells—" Dien said, but Dubric did not wait to hear the rest. He turned and leapt from the porch, then ran to the barn.

His heart slamming, Dubric opened the door. Lars sat on the side of a stall beside a lantern. His clothes were stained with mud and he stared down at whatever waited inside. He did not look over as Dubric approached.

"Are you all right?" Dubric asked.

"Yes, sir," Lars said, still staring downward. "But I didn't find Otlee. I failed. Do you still have ghosts? Did I at least kill the murderer?"

"My ghosts remain, save one. What happened?"

Lars took a shaky breath. "Your ghosts have a range, sir. Approximately five miles, according to the map. Jess and Fyn saw the marks Otlee made where you encountered or lost them, and it was easy enough to figure out where they came from, or originated, or were killed at. However you want to describe it."

He swallowed and took another breath. "So I went, hoping to find Otlee along the river. I found Braoin instead, but I guess you already knew that."

Dubric heard movement behind him, and he held up a hand to slow Dien. The big man looked ready to break heads.

Lars chewed his lip, his gaze never leaving the stall. "I caught Flann there. He was one of the guys fixing the barn roof, and he'd attacked Jess, picked a fight with me. He'd just dumped the body, and I tried to question him. We fought and he died. It was an accident, I swear."

His breath hitched. "I hope you can forgive me, sir, and I hope Otlee can forgive me."

"There is nothing to forgive," Dubric said.

"Yes, there is. If Otlee dies, it's my fault." Lars paused for a heartbeat, then said, "I hear Braoin was an artist, that he was betrothed, that he was a good man. Ever since I came here, the girls and Sarea have said only nice things about him. And yet . . . this happened." His shoulders slumped. "What did anyone do to deserve this? And why didn't I find Otlee when I could? Why? Flann knew, damn him, yet he wouldn't tell me."

"Sometimes bad things happen and there's nothing we can do," Dubric said. "There are so many people involved. This is not a simple murder. Be thankful you are alive."

"I read Otlee's notes, and they don't do this justice. I've seen murders before, sir, but this . . . this is a whole new category of perversion. I made everyone stay inside while I took the survey of injuries and evidence. Goddess, I hope Otlee . . ." Teary-eyed, Lars glanced at Dubric and jumped down, into the stall.

Dubric rounded the stall, Dien following him. Lars wiped his eyes with the back of his wrist, then opened his notebook. "I found him beside the riverbank west of Wittrup at roughly two bell in the afternoon. I estimate his exposure to water at less than a quarter bell. The killer was still in the area when I found him and I promptly returned to the scene. Sarea identified the body as Braoin Duncannon. I did not allow the girls to see him."

"I wish you hadn't allowed my wife," Dien muttered.

"Me, too," Lars said, nodding as he looked over to Dien, "but I wanted to be sure I'd found who we were looking for."

Braoin's naked body was awash with bruising, blood, and assorted cuts. A sharp bit of rib poked through his bruised side. His left chest, thighs, scrotum, and penis were lacerated, flayed into strips and covered with dried blood and flies. Bloodless, curling lines were carved into the flesh of his belly, and some of his fingers were gone. His cheeks had been cut apart, then crudely sewn together to form a grotesque pucker of his mouth. Ligature marks crossed his throat, and his eyelids sagged over empty sockets. White film caked his mouth, cheeks, and chest, and had dribbled into his eye sockets. An old clothespin was clamped on the lobe of one ear; the other ear was half torn off, tangled in a mess of black thread that originated at his temple. His nose had been sliced away and sat beside his head. He stank of rot and semen.

As Dubric entered the stall and knelt beside the body, Lars cleared his throat. "I have left the deceased as he was when I unwrapped him. His nose was originally within his mouth but fell out during transit. The knife remains."

"Knife? What knife?" Dien asked, kneeling on the blanket beside Dubric. Both men swallowed and looked up at Lars.

"The one in his anus," Lars said, his hand shaking as he turned a page. "At least I believe it's a knife. The handle protrudes perhaps a finger width."

Dien raked his fingers through his hair and muttered a curse.

Dubric reached into his pocket and pulled on the spare gloves Piras had given him. He gently pulled Braoin's mouth open and noted that his front teeth had been forcibly removed, leaving gaping, crusted sockets. His mouth contained copious amounts of thick, malodorous slime.

Lars coughed once and began reading. "The deceased was found facedown on damp river clay. He lay on his left arm, but the right floated in the water. I assume water rinsed blood and semen from the anterior of that arm and the right anterior chest, because they're cleaner than the rest of his body. Height five lengths, nine fingers. Brown hair, indeterminate eyes, old scar left of his spine above the tenth rib. Broken wrist. Flecks of paint on both hands, his left collarbone, and under his fingernails. No other identifying marks apparent, no combative or self-defense injuries. Lacerative wounds to his privates, thighs, chest, and anal region bled extensively. Presumably they came premortem, as did the removal and partial severing of fingers. Several wounds show extensive clotting and scabbing. Black cording remains from strangulation and binding. The twine is frayed, probably from being cut with a dull knife. I found similar twine hanging from beams on the site."

Lars paused and stared at Dubric. "How long was he gone before he died?"

Dubric leaned back. "Four days, to the best of my knowledge."

"He endured four days of this?" Dien whispered.

Dubric nodded, swallowing the acidic tang of disgust from his mouth. *I should have done more to stop this. Somehow. I should not have allowed this to happen. And Otlee's gone.*

"He was tough," Lars said, lowering to his knees. "And he didn't deserve to die this way. Neither does Otlee." He paused then looked at the two men. "Punish me if you have to. Hells, dismiss me from my post. I don't care. I'm glad I found him. Someone needed to, before all these details were lost to fish and rot. Someone needs to avenge him, and the others that died before. Someone needs to find Otlee. This madness is going to stop, even if I have to personally chase that bastard to the ends of the known lands and into the pits of the abyss. I'll shove my whole pegging sword up his ass if he's done half of this to Otlee."

He looked at Dien then, staring him straight in the eye with a conviction that made Dubric proud. "Come daybreak, I'm tracking him whether you like it or not, and I will catch him and kill him. Either you can help, or you can get out of my way."

"You need to stay here, pup, where it's safe. Dubric and I can find him."

Lars did not blink or raise his voice. "No. I'm not a kid anymore, and there is nothing you can do to keep me hidden on this farm. I'm going, with or without your approval."

Dien started to say something, but closed his mouth. At last he nodded, releasing his breath in a deep, shaky sigh. "All right. You can come. If you're ready when it's time to go." He nodded again, surer this time, and patted Lars on the back. "Good to have another man on the team."

Dubric opened his notebook to his private notes in the back. At the top, he added a reminder to have Lars promoted to squire once they returned home. That done, he returned to the middle of the notebook, to the first empty page, and began Braoin's autopsy notes.

They examined the clothespin first, carefully unclipping it from Braoin's ear. A small, rusty spring near the middle ensured it remained tight when closed. Dubric saw no blood anywhere on its wooden surface, but it was stained and spattered with dark grime. Curious, he opened and closed it a couple of times, wondering who in the Reach would purchase, then discard, such a novel clip. Most laundry pins were simple U-shaped bits of carved wood, and he had only seen hinged clips once or twice in his entire life.

He held the pin in the light to examine it closer and opened it again to peer inside. Something was tangled in the spring. "Lars, I have forceps in my saddlebags. Fetch them and a clean, white cloth."

"Yes, sir," Lars said, and he left the stall running.

Jess sat on the porch steps with her head on her hands and stared at the barn. It was all true. Braoin was dead, killed by a sick, demented man. A man who still had Otlee. But she had faith in her father, in Dubric, and in Lars. They would catch him and make him pay.

The barn door flew open and she sat straight, curious, then smiled when she saw Lars. She stood and smoothed her skirt as he ran over to the horses. "Making any headway?"

"Some. I hope." He reached Dubric's horse and rooted through its pack.

She hesitated before walking toward him. "How bad is he?"

"Horrible." Lars stopped his search and turned his head to look at her. "Broken bones, stab wounds, missing teeth. He's a mess, Jess. I'm sorry."

She nodded and looked at her hands. "I'm sorry, too."

Lars resumed his search while Jess lingered nearby. Nervous, and reluctant to go back to the house, she said, "Speaking of teeth, I found one today, in your pants pocket. Weird, huh?"

He turned to stare at her with a concerned

expression on his face. "Goddess, I forgot all about that. Do you still have it?"

"Yeah, it's in a bowl with all the other pocket sludge. What's wrong? It's just a dog's tooth."

"It's a human tooth," he said softly. "I found it in your granddad's barn a couple days ago."

She wanted to ask how a human tooth could be in her grandfather's barn, but he grasped her shoulder before she could speak. "Can you get it? Please? It might be important."

She backed away, afraid she might vomit. "Sure. I'll be right back."

"Jess? What's wrong?" her mother asked as she ran into the house.

"The tooth," she said, glancing at Fyn. "Lars needs it back."

"A tooth?" Lissea asked. She paused in her rocking of baby Cailin as Jess opened the cupboard door.

Kia flounced from their bedroom. "Someone swiped my perfume again, and what tooth?"

"It was just in Lars's pocket," Fyn said. "It's nothing."

Jess found the bowl and fumbled through it, searching. She refused to consider that she might be looking for a piece of a human being. *It's just a dog tooth.*

"Why's he need it back right now?" Lissea asked. She stood, patting the baby on the back.

There it is! Near the bottom of the bowl, beneath string and coins and a little wooden figurine, she saw a flash of white. She snatched it into her fist and turned toward the door. It felt hot and hard, strangely alive, and her stomach did a slow roll. *Don't think about it, where it came from, whose it might be. Just get it to Lars.*

"I don't like this," Lissea said, giving Jess and

Sarea appalled glares. "That boy carries *teeth*? In his pocket?"

"He's fine, Mother," Sarea said as if she'd belabored this same point a million times. "Stop worrying."

Jess didn't hear the rest of the discussion. Lars waited at the bottom of the steps for her and she dropped the tooth in his palm. He smiled at her, nodded in thanks, then turned and ran for the barn. When Jess let her breath out and returned to the house, her mother and grandmother were still arguing.

"What took so long?" Dien asked as Lars came back through the stall door.

"I'd completely forgotten about this," he said, opening his hand. "I had Jess get it for me."

Dubric lifted the forceps from Lars's palm, then the tooth. "Where did you find it?"

"Here, in the barn. It was stuck in Sophey's shoe, a couple of days ago."

Dubric examined the tooth, rolling it between his fingers. "And you had not taken her anywhere?"

"No, sir. I think Soph was limping the morning after we met that man . . . Foiche . . . on the road. I hadn't ridden her anywhere since we arrived, not even around the barnyard."

"One of the workers could have lost it," Dien said.

"Perhaps," Dubric said, "but who would discard, let alone pull, a perfectly healthy tooth?"

All three men looked at the corpse at their feet. "This just gets better and better," Dien said, raking his fingers back and forth over his head.

"That it does," Dubric said. Squinting, he opened the clothespin and reached into the spring workings with the forceps, then slowly removed the obstruction. "And what have we here?" he asked, holding the warped and curly strand in the light.

Lars held out a white handkerchief and Dubric placed the strand on the fabric. About as long as the two tip-joints of Dubric's index finger, it curled and kinked in random directions and threatened to drift off the cloth.

"That's not the same thread," Dien said. "It's too stiff. And it's gray, not black."

Lars felt heat on his cheeks. He cleared his throat, then said, "It's a pubic hair."

Dubric smiled. "I do believe the boy is right."

Dien leaned closer, squinting, and he nodded. "I'll be damned. How did that get up by Braoin's ear?"

"Or in a clothespin?" Lars asked. "As much semen as we found on him, I can accept that our killer left a few hairs behind. But *inside* the clothespin? What did he do? Snap it to his penis or balls?"

Dien and Dubric looked at each other and shrugged. "Seems as likely as anything else," Dien said.

Lars grimaced and held the cloth toward Dubric. "That is absolutely disgusting."

Dien shuddered. "And probably rather painful."

"Let us hope we never find out firsthand." Dubric lifted the hair again and turned it in the light. "You were right about the color. It is definitely gray. Our friend is not a young man."

Dien spat in the corner. "I've told you before, sir. He's not a man at all. He's a deranged freak."

"Stuart?" a whisper said, hot breath on the back of Lars's neck.

Lars turned and saw Devyn stretching to peek over

the wall. "You can't be here," he told the old man. "This is an official investigation. Secret."

Devyn held a gnarled finger to his lips. "Shh, Stuart. Our secret." He grinned and patted Lars on the cheek. "Rabbits and wasps, you're a good boy, Stuart. Braoin saw the wood colt, but not you."

"Speaking of deranged freaks," Dien muttered, lumbering from the stall. "Not now, Dev. Not tonight."

"No!" Dev cried, clawing at the wall, reaching for Lars. "Rabbits and wasps! Secrets! They'll see! Stuart!"

"No one's seeing anything," Dien said, dragging his father-in-law from the barn.

Lars took a deep breath before turning back to Dubric, and he jumped when the barn door slammed behind Dien. "Sorry about that, sir," he said. "Devyn seems to think I'm his dead son."

Dubric frowned, his gaze flicking past Lars to the corner of the stall. "An understandable error. There is a fine resemblance."

"You see his ghost? Still? After all this time?"

Dubric nodded and tucked the pubic hair into his notebook. "I am afraid so, and he is connected to this mess." Notebook put away, he retrieved the tooth. "Now let me see your teeth. I know next to nothing of dentistry but I need to identify the placement of this tooth."

Lars let Dubric tilt his head in the light. "Upper, second to the left," the old man muttered before releasing him.

Dubric knelt beside Braoin's body and pulled his dagger from its sheath at his hip. A quick cut, severing the crude stitches on the dead man's cheeks, then Dubric rocked Braoin's head back and opened his mouth.

Dien returned, glowering as he came into the stall, and he paused to watch Dubric feel along Braoin's upper jaw. "Well?"

Dubric leaned back. "Once past the resistance of his gums, it slid into the socket cleanly. I cannot say for certain, but I do believe we have a match."

Lars took a step back, but Dien grumbled and rubbed his head. "How is that possible?"

Dubric shook his head. "I have no idea."

"Maybe Flann dropped it in the yard," Lars said. "Or through a hole in the roof?"

Dien looked up. "Yeah, I can see that. Damn, it's been a long day."

Dubric agreed. "And we still have much left to do."

Working well into the night, they counted and cataloged every bruise, puncture, and laceration, noted the broken ribs, wrist, and dislocated hip, and diagrammed every smear of seminal residue, vomit, or blood as they discussed the likely timeline of Braoin's torture. They examined the knife last.

It was very sharp, and nearly as long as Lars's forearm. Its old, worn wood handle bore the pits and scratches from summers of use, and the blade had been honed to a paper-thin edge. Lars guessed that nearly every kitchen in the land had a similar tool for butchering game or livestock. He carefully wrapped it in a bit of blanket before setting it aside.

Lars yawned, blinking to stay awake, and trudged to bed when they finished the examination.

The crone opened her eyes. Someone was in the house. "The pegging Byr," she whispered. Her hand crept beneath her thin pillow, and she wrapped her fingers around a knife. She slipped from the bed, wearing only her blood-flecked nightdress. She shivered and took a slow step, then another. She saw no one, but she heard breathing. A man.

A grunt and a whine, and the cellar door flipped open. Her fool son climbed out, stark naked. "Nice dyer."

"He's not for you," she said, tossing the knife aside. "Get out and find your own."

"I can't," he said. "Flann's dead, killed by the Byr's pet, there at my house, and he found the last dyer and took it away."

"You let one of the Byr's pets kill the chosen Foiche? See a dyer? Have you lost all sense?"

"He was too alert, on open ground. I had no chance to sneak up on him."

She paced, frantic. "The Byr sees everything, and now he has a fresh dyer? He's taken Haconry and Mul. He'll find us, and for what? Foiche is free, but we have nowhere to put him! You should have caught the Byr's pet and set him to dye."

"He was armed, a killer. And he's Hargrove's son."

She stopped pacing. "Hargrove? You're sure?"

"Yes, mama, I'm sure."

She grinned and stepped back. "I must think about this. Decide what to do. To have a young royal within our grasp, think of the power Foiche could pull."

"Mama?"

"Go, go," she said, flicking her fingers toward the open cellar door. "Play with him however you wish, but do not kill him. He will not be set to dye."

He hurried to the open door. "Yes, mama. Whatever you say."

She climbed back into bed and stared at the ceiling. *The boy may work as a vessel. I could beat the Byr. Have my revenge. Feed his royal pet to the Foiche.*

Screams rattled the floor and she smiled, drifting to sleep.

CHAPTER

25

†

Lars woke early, well before dawn, to the familiar rumble of Dien's snores. They were not going to leave him behind, not this time, not unless they strapped him to the house's foundation.

He washed and dressed, even polished his sword to the light of a single candle, and he settled in to wait.

Time dragged.

He yawned and reached for Otlee's pack, intending to review his journal, but the bag was full of scissors, glue, and hat scraps, and the wooden plank with Devyn's painting of his son.

"What the heck?" he muttered, searching through the mess without luck. "How did this stuff get here? I put Otlee's journal here last night, before I went to bed."

Someone else strode to the hall—not Dien, the snores hadn't stopped—and Lars looked up. He heard a creak, a giggle, and Aly's cart rolled to the kitchen on three wheels, then crashed against a table leg.

"Aly?" he asked, standing. No one answered. Movement to his left. A small mirror stood on the mantel and his own reflection stared back at him, terrified and blinking. He looked away.

He swallowed and took a step toward the hall,

candle in hand. The cart backed away from the table and slammed into it again. And again. Then it fell still.

A heavy hand landed on his shoulder, and Lars nearly screamed. "Stuart's here to help sell hats," Dev said. He held out Otlee's notebook. It was muddy and damp. Dev grinned, every breath a noxious metallic cloud.

"That's Otlee's, not mine," Lars said, taking it from him. "I'm not helping sell hats today."

Dev's smile widened. "Not *you*," he said, pointing to the broken cart. "Stuart." He knelt slightly and held his arms wide. "Stuart!"

The cart skidded across the floor and deep, chilling cold pressed through Lars, nearly knocking him aside. He backed away, shaking his head. *Stuart's ghost is really here? Goddess, how crazy is Dev, really? Is he just trying to be a father to a ghost?*

Dev hugged the air, then stood again. "Soon, Stuart," he said, walking to the front door. "I'll get hats. You stay."

Devyn opened the front door and stepped through. It slammed shut behind him, although Dev had done nothing to close it.

A faint giggle broke the icy silence, and Lars felt cold fingers tug at his clothes.

"Can you talk?" he asked, astounded. None of Dubric's ghosts had ever made a sound, as far as he knew.

He heard a whisper of a laugh, and felt a cold hand tugging him forward until he faced the mirror on the mantel. A cold nudge on his back, then another.

"You want the mirror?"

Movement away from him, and the painting slid from Otlee's pack. It turned, twirling, to confront him with a face so like his own. "Yes. I know we look the same."

Stuart had been nine when he died, still a small child. *He looks like me, maybe wants to play. Maybe I can make contact, learn something.* "Okay," Lars said, taking the mirror from the mantel. "We can look in the mirror. Maybe find your reflection." He sat on the settee and held the mirror before him, gazing into it. His own face said, "Can you see yourself? Can you show yourself to me?"

The settee beside him shifted, and he felt cold against him, the weight of a child climbing over his back. He smiled at the chilly but familiar sensation and tilted the mirror. "Can you see?" he asked again, then his breath caught in his throat.

Green haze shimmered beside his right ear in the reflection, a whispered image of a little boy's face much like his own. Slashed, ravaged, and bleeding, it grimaced, solidifying, and the weight on his back grew heavier. "Goddess, you do look like me. We could be brothers."

Stuart bled from his throat and his cheeks were cut open, much like Braoin's. One ear was gone and a diamond shape was gouged into his forehead, sending blood dripping into his eyes.

"What happened to you?" Lars asked, reaching up to touch the poor ghost's face. Stuart screamed, a high-pitched wail barely within Lars's hearing, and disappeared.

The settee shifted as Stuart fled. "Wait!" Lars said, setting aside the mirror. "I'm sorry, I didn't mean to scare you." But there was no sign of the ghost. Aly's cart remained still. *What do I do now?*

His shoulders sagged, and he stood. "Stuart, I'm

sorry. Can we try again? I want to help you, help your dad."

Otlee's pack upended, spilling everything to the floor. Lars turned and saw Jess's book sitting on a small table near the rocking chair. It flipped open, then flew against the wall. Stuart's portrait slid past his feet. The table fell over, landing on Otlee's pack. Lars sat on the settee, watching as the scissors clattered across the floor and Otlee's journal skittered away. Felt scraps fluttered through the air. Things fell still.

"Stuart?" Lars looked around, but nothing moved and he heard only Dien's snores. The settee shifted, someone climbing up beside him, and he turned, taking the full brunt of a wooden plank across his face. He fell back to the settee, everything fading to black.

Dubric knocked softly before entering the house, and Dien opened the door. "Shh, sir," Dien said, beckoning Dubric to enter. "He's still asleep."

"We were up rather late," Dubric said, smiling fondly at Lars. He lay fully dressed, facing the back of the settee with his arm over his eyes, sound asleep while the rest of the family ate breakfast. "He will not like being left behind."

"Should I try again to wake him, sir? I haven't had much luck."

"Let him sleep." Dubric looked to Sarea. "Tell him we could not wait any longer and he is ordered to remain with you."

Turning away, Dubric followed Dien from the house and into the dawn.

*　*　*

Sarea winced as she entered her parents' bedchamber to change bed linen. The room smelled like old metal; she had always hated the stench. Her blossoming headache didn't help.

"You okay?" Aly asked, jumping on the bed.

"Yes, honey," Sarea said. "Of course I am."

Aly didn't seem to mind the stink. She had a bed to jump on, after all. "I hope Lars is gonna waken up soon."

"You hope Lars will wake soon," Sarea corrected.

"Yeah. Then we can wrestle!" Aly bounced on her butt then up to her feet again, and the headboard pounded against the wall. "I like wrestling Lars. I win and it's fun."

Sarea set the linens on a chair. "I know, honey. Quit jumping on the bed, okay? It hurts your mam's head."

" 'Kay." One more bounce to her butt, a pound from the headboard, then a *thud* beneath. Aly stopped, still as a stone, and her eyes grew wide. "I didn't mean to break it!"

Sarea winced. Just the thought of kneeling to look under the bed and see what had broken loose made her aching head feel like it would crack in two. She almost called for one of the other girls to come look, but instead she said, "Come on now and get off there," then lowered herself to her knees.

No dust clumps, just her mother's slippers, an ancient apple core in the corner, and a book beneath the headboard. One cover and a few pages lay on the floor, but most remained stuck between the headboard and the wall. Sarea tried to reach it, but a sharp spasm in her shoulder made her cry out.

"Mam?" Aly asked, kneeling beside her.

"I'm all right." Sarea pulled back to kneel beside the bed, rubbing her shoulder and rolling her aching head to get the muscle to relax. "There's a book under there. I think it's what fell."

"I'll get it," Aly said. She wriggled under the bed frame and kicked as she tugged, making the bed shake. She crawled back out with a battered old book in her hands. "It's heavy!"

"I bet it is," Sarea said. The book was as thick as her palm was wide, with a leather cover and parchment pages.

Aly handed her the book backside-up, and Sarea turned it to see the cover. *Official Record* had been tooled into the leather and gilded with silver.

"Why did Dubric leave it in here?" Aly asked.

"Dubric?"

Aly nodded and climbed onto her mother's lap. "Yeah. It was in his saddle packs. On his horse. I saw."

Sarea opened the cover to see birth and death notations from three hundred summers ago. "Are you sure, honey?"

Aly nodded. "He said it was a 'vih-dance.' What's vih-dance mean?"

"Evidence," Sarea corrected. "That means it's a clue they've found." She skipped forward, watching centuries pass in a blur. Scores of people were born and died. *What does this have to do with the missing boys?*

"To find that bad man?"

Sarea nodded, enthralled. She recognized some surnames, ancestors of people she knew when she was young, many who lived here still. Time flipped beneath her fingers, marching ever forward in its unrelenting thread, and she saw her father's name:

42396: Devyn Ignatial Paerth (liv. male)
b. 5–26–2210; m. Kialyrre (Janner) Paerth
(41972); f. Hidde G. Paerth (41914); d._____

"What does it say?"

Sarea touched her father's name. "It's Grandpapa. It has his name, his birthing day, and his parents' names."

"Am I in there?" Aly asked. "I was borned here, right?"

"Yes, you were, so let's see." Sarea flipped forward, watching the dates, and, sure enough, Aly's name.

44226: Alyson Mira Saworth (liv. female)
b. 8–12–2258; m. Sarea (Paerth) Saworth (42871);
f. Dien Saworth (n/a); d._____

Sarea read her the information, pointing to each piece as she read it. "What about Kia and Fyn and Jess? Baby Cailin?"

"Fyn should be here," Sarea said, flipping back. "She came early."

"Did I come early?"

Sarea smiled. "No, punkin. You came right on time. Granddad was sick and I had to help. I was here longer than I'd intended, and you came before I could go home."

She found Fyn's name and read it to Aly.

"What about you? Where's your name?"

Back farther, to line number 42871. Sarea stopped, her vision swimming.

42871: Sarea Lyrre Paerth (liv. female)
b. 2–31–2229; m. Celeste (Newbush) Paerth
(42389); f. Devyn I. Paerth (42316); d._____

"Mama? What's wrong?"

Sarea stared at the unknown name. Celeste Newbush Paerth. *What in the seven hells? That can't be right.* She flipped back a few pages, to line 42389, reading the names of people she had never heard of before. Celeste had died in the winter of 2231, when Sarea was two and Celeste was seventeen. She'd had no father, and her mother, Tyne Newbush, had died the same day Celeste was born. Tyne had been fourteen summers old and had no parents listed, only the date of her birth and death.

"Orphans," Sarea whispered, touching her name on another woman's listing. "Both of them."

"What's an orphan?" Aly asked.

"A child without parents. Sometimes their parents die, sometimes they leave."

"Oh." Silence, then, "I'm not going to be an orphan, am I?"

Sarea hugged her daughter and closed the book. "No, honey, not if I can help it. Let's finish making the bed, okay?"

Aly climbed off Sarea's lap and helped pull the old linens from the bed.

Lars rolled from the settee and held his aching head. "What happened?"

Kia flounced past him. "Your face is all red. Looks like you had a wild night, left us a big mess to clean up. You steal some of Granddad's liquor?"

"No," he said, staggering upright. "I haven't even had an ale." He ran his hands over his cheeks; all his facial features were attached, if sore, and seemed to be functioning. Stuart's mess was gone and things were put back in their proper places. "Where's your dad?"

She snorted. "He left, almost a bell ago. You overslept."

They left? Without me?

"Lars!" Aly cheered, running to him. "You're awake!" Her broken cart skittered across the floor and tangled in her feet. She fell with a shriek, holding her knee.

Lars saw the cart move on its own and rushed to Aly. *Stuart, don't.*

Jess hurried down the hall in her chemise. "Someone tore my favorite blouse. Fess up, Kia."

Before Kia could retort, Jess's gaze landed on Lars and she shrieked and ran for her bedroom. Kia stomped after her and Lars heard the raised voices of the three elder girls arguing in their room. Their door slammed, opened, then slammed again.

Jess! Lars swallowed, watching the door, but it remained closed. *Aw, crap, they'll be going home tomorrow. I almost forgot.* Today was his last chance to ask Jess to the castle faire. He scooped Aly up and carried her to a chair, looking up at Sarea as she trudged into the room with a large book in her arms. She looked like she wanted to cry.

"Aly banged her knee," he said, but Sarea barely seemed to notice. She slumped in a chair and stared at the book.

Cold fingers tugged at Lars's hair. He batted the spectre away and looked up to see Dev frowning at him. "Stuart's coming!" Dev tittered. "Stuart's selling hats!"

Sarea sighed, her head in her hands. "Dad, please stop calling him Stuart." She looked to Lars and said,

"Since you overslept, you're supposed to stay with me today."

Aly's cart banged hard against his leg and he put his foot on it to hold it still. Dubric and Dien would be searching Flann's farm for Otlee, and he had little hope of catching up with them now. He thought, too, of Jess's torn blouse, Aly's knee, and his own aching head. Stuart was capable of breaking things, of hurting people. But why? What had he done to the poor dead little boy that he could show such malice?

Across from Lars, Dev sat by the table and mumbled under his breath, a rapid-paced conversation with himself. Lars stared at him. Devyn, Stuart's father, who got confused so easily and thought Lars was his son. *Maybe the jealous person who'd been tormenting me wasn't Kia at all, but Stuart, because I'd taken some of his father's attention.*

I don't know how I can stop Stuart from causing trouble, but I have to try. Goddess, Stuart could do anything and no one could stop him. What would happen to the girls if I just left? Cold fingers reached up his pants leg and pulled hairs. "Sure. Let's sell hats," he said, wincing.

How can I control a ghost?

"Dammit, Kia, hurry up!" Sarea hollered. "Everyone else is ready to go!"

Fyn leaned against the wall and burped. "All the primping in the world isn't going to make her look any better."

Jess gave her sister a sideways glance. "You're going to get us in trouble."

Fyn rolled her eyes, but remained silent as their mother hurried to the porch.

Jess fidgeted and looked out the window. Lars loaded the handcart while Grandpapa fussed over the hats. "I'd rather stay home," Jess said. "I've almost finished scrubbing floors. Only the sitting room's left, and I might actually get it done if everyone else is gone."

Giggling, Fyn nudged her. "What? And miss the fun and excitement of selling hats?"

"What are you two whispering about?" Kia asked as she flounced through the door in a perfumed cloud. "Whatever it is, stop it. You're making us late."

"We're not making anyone late," Fyn said, following her sister from the house. "That dubious honor falls to you."

Jess closed the door and followed her sisters down the steps. While Fyn and Kia argued, she grabbed the food basket from the porch. Sarea gave all three girls a withering glare, then Devyn lifted the handles of the handcart. With Lissea bringing up the rear, and Fyn leading three young goats, the family walked down the lane toward town.

"It's going to be a nice day," Lars said, falling in beside Jess. He carried a burlap sack that held five hens and a young rooster, extras from the coop.

Jess looked up at the sky, to the thin, high clouds against brilliant blue. "I hope so. And I hope we can get a decent place to set up. Couple of summers ago, all we could find was near the alehouse. It was loud and smelly."

He smiled and watched Aly skip beside them. "I'm sure we'll find something."

They walked in companionable silence for a while,

then, "I didn't expect you to come today. Thought you were looking for Otlee."

Lars shifted the bag over his shoulder. "So did I." Silence again, then, "Dubric and your dad can manage without me."

Jess blushed and braved a glance. He smiled at her; she smiled back. *Maybe selling hats won't be so bad after all.*

Dubric knelt to touch cart tracks on the second trail leading into the peninsula. Rain had smoothed the ground, softening the edges of the grooves. Footprints marred the dirt between the tracks, coming and going, and most were fresh, within the past two bells or so. "The cart tracks are at least a day old," Dubric said, dusting off his hands before climbing back into the saddle.

They rode on, looking for other footpaths and trails leading off the main one. Following where the paths took them, they visited farms and fishing holes, orchards and peat pits, but found no bodies, no likely suspects, and no further clues. The ghosts lingered, barely of substance, yet so very heavy.

The main path petered out to no more than two wheel grooves in grass and an occasional bare footprint. They followed the trail across a meadow and thicket, barely speaking, until Dien said, "Do you smell that? I think we're getting close."

They stopped and sniffed the air.

"I do not smell anything unusual," Dubric said. The cart tracks led over the slope of a grassy hill. He eased his horse forward again but once he crested the hill and started down the far side, he stopped. "I will be damned," he said. After summers of war and decades of tracking murderers, Dubric could never mistake the gassy odor of rotting human flesh.

"Guess the pup was right about the stink." Dien faced the stench without obvious repulsion.

"Let us see what we shall find."

Mouths set tight, they urged their horses down the hill.

The crone let her worthless son help her into the cart. "Don't touch me," she said, yanking her hand away once she had climbed aboard. "And don't you sass me, either. We're doing the damned festival, you hear? People will notice if we don't. The Byr will notice if anything's amiss, if people whisper that we're gone."

"Yes, Mama," he replied, staring at the ground. "But do we have to take the vessel? Can't we come back for him?"

She slapped his face. "That wily little boy's almost escaped *twice* already, and you want me to leave him in the cellar alone? We're so close, you fool. We can't take the chance he could slip away, not with the Byr sniffing around, not now that Foiche has prepared him himself."

"Yes, Mama."

The useless sack of meat she had long ago pushed from her loins climbed onto the seat beside her. She looked away. He lifted the reins and clucked to his scrawny mule.

"I will see the bastard Byr dead," she said as they lurched away. "He will pay for his crimes, even if it takes the rest of my life to see it done."

Once they had left sight of her hovel, she took a deep breath and smiled. Today was Planting Festival day, and she intended to enjoy it. Even if she had to endure her worthless son.

"Stuart! The red one!" Devyn called over his shoulder.

"Got it," Lars replied, jumping as Stuart stomped his foot. He pulled a red felt hat from the rack and handed it to Devyn before wiping his brow with his forearm. They had found a good place to showcase their wares, along the main road on the southern side of the town well, but there was no shade, no breeze, no escape from the heat. Stuart's freezing cold fingers poking him didn't help improve his mood.

Sarea and Lissea handled the money. The girls barkered the crowd and modeled hats. Devyn, however, made most of the sales. Even in his madness, he knew his hats, and his customers.

The red hat came back with instructions to try the brown one with pheasant feathers, and Lars pulled the new hat from the display rack and replaced the red one.

Behind him, Sarea said she needed a man's leather band with carved birds, and Lars rummaged through the band box to find it.

He found Sarea's band and gave it to her, accepting two discarded hats while Lissea gave three to Devyn. Six more patrons waited in line, some with old hats, some with bare heads, all clamoring for service. *No wonder they all come for the festival. Dev and Lissea could never keep up with this madness.*

In the midst of the crowd, Jess tilted her head, laughing, her current hat perched at a flirty angle. She twirled, switching hats, and found a different pose. *Goddess, she's beautiful.*

"Stuart! Pull your head outta the clouds and get me that hat!"

"Yessir." Lars looked over the racks, seeking the hat Devyn had requested, but before he could spot it the old man reached over his shoulder and plucked it from the rack, smacking Lars with it as he pulled away. Stuart smacked him with a hat, too, but Lars snatched it and put it back. No one seemed to notice, but Lars vowed to remain on task and not get distracted again.

They sold twenty-six hats the first bell, along with two chickens, one goat, and a score or more hatbands and feathers. The crowd thinned to a trickle, then disappeared completely, giving everyone a chance to catch their breath.

Sarea said, "Girls, come back here and help Lars fill the racks."

Lars stepped aside for Fyn, passed a nod with Jess—he was afraid to look too long for fear he'd start to stare—then knelt to open a fresh box. Stuart yanked hard on his ear, but Lars pushed him away and whispered, "Stop it. We're working!"

"Did you say something?" Jess asked.

Lars shook his head in reply and didn't look up. *I just need to keep busy,* he thought, handing hats to the girls. *Think about something else, anything else, besides asking Jess to the faire. But today's my last chance. They go home first thing tomorrow and I have to stay here.*

I have to ask her. Today.

Stuart pinched his forearm and Lars tried not to wince.

*   *   *

Dubric knelt beside the dead body in the yard. Birds had already pecked away the victim's eyes. Ghosts lingered nearby, oblivious to everything except their own anguish. Rubbing his aching eyes with one hand, Dubric pulled his notebook from his pocket with the other, then took a deep breath before adding to his notes.

"Just like Lars described, sir. Three outbuildings and a barn, besides the house," Dien said, returning from his inspection. "The stink's coming from the barn, and there are clothos worms at the door."

Dubric stood and found his tub of myrtle and mint. "Let us start there. Fetch torches. I want to kill those worms."

Dien nodded and walked to the horses.

Dubric steadied himself before he opened the barn door. Even with the mint smeared beneath his nose, the stench in the barnyard was indeed horrid, but it was a blossom-filled spring morning when compared to the insidious, putrid syrup that poured from the barn. The rotting fumes were a physical thing, hard and heavy and hot, filled with rustling wings and gnawing mandibles.

A skull lay just inside the door. Completely stripped of flesh and missing its lower jaw and left cheekbone, it stared up at them as if surprised. Beside it lay three vertebrae, connected by dry and cracked nerves, and one lone rib that peeked out from beneath a board. A fat moth fluttered over the rib, landed, then continued on to the skull. Once there, it crawled to an eye socket and proceeded to lay eggs.

Torch in hand, Dubric stepped onto the board and

heard bones crush underneath. A pathway of old boards led past a plain and humble chair to a low box. Between the chair and the box hung four long lengths of black twine. Noting the roughly cut lower ends, he looked up to see the upper portions tied around the barn's main beams. Blood smeared the closer beam near the twine. Metal and glass shards along the upper surface glinted in the torchlight.

"They were kept and tortured here," he said, taking another crunchy step. "Bound hand and foot."

Worms and moths writhed on either side of the board path, but few clamored to get to him. Black cocoons hung from the walls, posts, and chair, and clumps of grayish eggs lay clustered in gaping eye and hip sockets. He swung his torch toward the insects and they scurried away from the heat, the stragglers popping as they incinerated. *Good*, he thought. *They are not yet immune to fire.*

Assorted phallus-shaped horrors lay on the ground, some of wood, others of metal; one was made of tightly twisted rope. All were stained with blood and feces. A broken bottle of sweet vitriol bore similar stains, as did a whiskey bottle.

Dien looked ready to rip someone apart. "Did that pegging bastard cram those things . . ." Snarling, he bared his teeth.

"I believe so, yes," Dubric replied. He pulled a handkerchief from his pocket and knelt beside the nearest phallus, a wooden monstrosity nearly as thick as his wrist and as long as his forearm. He turned it over, grimacing at the blood smeared along the length, then dropped it back to the ground.

Bones lay in the wretched soil everywhere he cared to look, with most surfaces scoured clean of muscle, tendon, or skin. Only a few harbored lingering bits of flesh and gristle, and they were covered with swarms of insects. He counted fifteen skulls from his vantage point near the door, but saw several separated pieces. The insects had ripped the sutures and joints apart, disassembling the corpses like children's puzzles.

"Burn it," he said, turning back to the door. "They have eaten any possible clues, and we can sort through the scorched bones tomorrow. We dare not take the chance any worms or moths escape."

"What about the rest?" Dien asked. "There might be something we need, something that could lead us to Otlee."

Dubric paced, his heart thudding and a metallic taste tainting his mouth. "The worms must be killed, and fire is the only way. We can't risk leaving them any longer."

"Aye, sir," Dien said. Once Dubric had walked clear, Dien threw a torch into the middle of the barn. While the flames caught and spread, Dubric strode to the house, Dien right behind him.

CHAPTER
26

†

Dubric looked through the open window to the burning barn and twirling smoke. "Have you gathered everything?"

"Yes, sir," Dien said. "Three black threads, two red ones, a dead moth, and some bloody clothing. No sign of Otlee."

Dubric let the filthy curtain fall. "And the needle?"

They had found a corroded steel needle as long as his forearm on the floor in the bedchamber. Dubric's ghosts had stared at it with hatred and alarm, the only notice they had yet paid to anything outside of their own torment. Never had he seen a ghost notice its killer, nor had a ghost ever ignored the instrument of its death. A most perplexing dichotomy.

"Yes, sir. It's wrapped and in its own sack. I've already put it in my saddlebags."

Dubric turned away from the window and gave Dien a sad smile. "When we gather bones, we shall compare it against head wounds. I expect it will be a match."

"Yes, sir," Dien said, watching him expectantly. "And we'll ask the neighbors who lives here. We'll find him."

Dubric looked away, to the wretched, urine-stained bed, the tattered clothes, the empty whiskey bottles. He lingered, staring at the filth, while rancid smoke teased his nostrils. Something was wrong; he felt it nibble at the back of his brain like a rat worrying a rope. A piece of information eluded him, perhaps in this very room. "Review my notes," he said, his gaze resting tiredly on the urine stains. "We are missing something."

He heard Dien open the notebook. "Suspect's home searched. Three rooms. Two sleeping. A kitchen. Storage and livestock shacks outside. Entire area chaotic, poor. Many empty crates. Kitchen has a variety of knives, apparently for cooking. None seized. Rotting food, crusted dishes, leaking pots. Furniture broken, possibly due to repeated physical struggles of kidnapped boys."

Dien cleared his throat and continued reading, his words falling to a low drone.

It is here, in this room. His sanctuary. Dien's voice calming his mind, Dubric leaned over to look beneath the bed. He saw a metal ring on the floor, far back and partially hidden by filth. *Cellar access?* Grunting, Dubric pushed the mess aside and tried to reach it. It was too far away, nearly to the wall.

He rolled back and examined the bed. A simple wooden frame, slat supports, and a bare straw mattress. Surely it was light enough to push aside. "We are moving the bed," he said, standing.

Dien ceased reading. "Yes, sir."

Dubric grabbed the mattress, wincing at the fleas that leapt to his hands, and lifted it.

Beside him, Dien said, "Sir, it's hinged."

"So I see," Dubric said. The closer edge lifted with a comfortable creak; he pushed the bed up to lean against the wall.

"There's a nest of live worms," Dien said, pointing.

"I see them." A score or more worms crawled over a desiccated rat corpse behind a box. He pulled the box toward him, leaving enough room behind it for his feet, then crushed the worms and the dead rat.

The box was as long as his arm, and nearly a length tall and wide. The wood appeared to be fine maple, carved in intricate diamond patterns, but it had been exposed to wetness, leaving the wood stained with gray mold and water lines. The hinges and lock were corroded, perhaps once made of shining brass, and iron plates protected the corners. It was very heavy.

Dubric tried to lift the lid, but the box was locked. Hopeful, he glanced at Dien. "Have we found any keys?"

Dien checked his notes. "No, sir."

Dubric grumbled and pulled his dagger. A few hard slams, and the lock popped open.

Beside him, Dien whistled. "Stolen booty?"

"Stolen is a distinct possibility," Dubric said.

The box was full to heaping with gold stars, coins of a vintage from before the War of Shadows. He lifted one to examine it in the light. It twinkled in his fingers and sent shivers down his spine. He had not seen a gold star in nearly fifty summers, and had hoped that he would never see mage money again.

"Keep one as evidence," he said, standing, "I do not want to carry a case of the filthy things. One soul died for every coin; I bear enough ghosts." He rummaged in his pocket for a small evidence bag and slipped the star inside before giving it to Dien.

"Let us see what awaits us in the cellar." He pulled on the ring. A ladder led into the darkness below and it smelled of wet dirt and rot and earthworms.

"I've lit a lantern, sir," Dien said, handing it over. "Want me to go first?"

Dubric shook his head and lowered himself to the ladder. Dien's lantern in hand, he descended.

Jess held her hand above her eyes to shield them from the sun, while she tried not to look as bored and tired as she felt. Once the initial rush had passed and the hats were organized again, there was nothing to do other than tend the baby. Cailin was hot, tired, and cranky, needing to be walked or put down for a nap, but there wasn't a good shady spot, other than beneath the tables. Jess wondered if the intermittent bouts of crying had scared off some customers. She stifled a yawn.

"Why don't you kids go have some fun," Sarea said, glancing back at Jess. "But watch over your little sister, and come back in a bell or so, okay? We brought lunch."

Aly cheered and started skipping in circles. Kia rolled her eyes and sauntered to the road, flicking her hair as she walked away. Fyn shook her head. "I don't feel so good," she said. "Light-headed. I think I might lie down in the shade somewhere."

Lars looked up, staring worriedly at Fyn, and Jess said, "I'll take Cailin, Mam. If you want. You need a respite, too."

Sarea looked between Jess and Fyn. "It's not fair to stick you with both of your little sisters, and you've been watching her for the past half bell."

"It's okay," Jess said, shrugging. "Better than having her crying here." Once her mother agreed, she grabbed the diddy bag and carried Cailin out into the festival.

"Here, I'll take her," Lars said. "Fyn going to be all right?"

He held out his hands and Jess obliged. Cailin got heavy after a while and she was happy for the reprieve. "Yeah, I think so. I just wish she'd tell Mam what's really going on."

He was silent for a long time, and when he spoke, he whispered. "You know?"

Jess watched as Aly stopped to examine a basket full of dolls. "I have a pretty good idea." Fyn had missed her courses—again—and pined almost constantly to see Gilby. Add nausea and fatigue to the other evidence, and not many possibilities remained. After Cailin's recent birth, Jess knew what pregnant, even the early stages, looked and acted like. "You know, too?"

"I want a candied apple!" Aly said, dancing around them. "Please, please, puh-lees?"

Lars met Jess's gaze as they worked their way to the apple stand. "Yeah. She told me, that time in the cellar. That's what we were talking about for so long."

"Why didn't you say anything?"

He shrugged as they walked to the end of the line. "Because she confided in me, and, as her big brother . . ." He shrugged again, nervously. "She promised to tell your folks once she had a chance to square things with Gilby. I started to tell your mam, but I couldn't. I guess I figured that a few days wouldn't make much difference." The line moved forward and he turned his head to look Jess in the eye. "Sometimes secrets need to be kept, at least for a little while."

"I guess so," she replied, lowering her gaze.

The line moved forward again. "Speaking of secrets," he said, looking away, "can I talk to you about something later?"

"Sure." Jess started fishing coins from her purse.

"I've got it," Lars said. He stretched to look over the farmer in front of them. "You girls want toffee apples, pears, or just toffee?"

"Toffee!" Aly said, jumping around him.

The farmer received his apple and moved away, leaving them to face the tired-looking farm girl. "Whatcha want?" she asked.

"Jess?" Lars asked, glancing at her as he balanced Cailin against his shoulder and counted coins.

"An apple," Jess said.

"Two apples and a small bag of toffee," he said.

Jess watched the farm girl swirl the apples in their sweet coating. Lars paid, and she handed Jess the apples and sweets. Jess gave Aly the bag of toffee as they walked away.

A boy with a goat cart rattled toward them, and Lars herded Aly from his path. Cailin had fallen asleep; he smiled at her as they walked on.

"Any idea who killed Bray?" Jess asked.

"Not really." He sighed.

"Me, either," Aly said, reaching into the bag for another toffee.

Jess ruffled her hair. "You don't even know what's going on."

Cailin tucked in the crook of one arm, Lars accepted an apple from Jess as they walked toward a patch of grass near the minstrels.

Kia walked past on the arm of a young merchant; she tossed her head and smirked. Jess ignored her.

"Lars, Jess!" Aly cried, pointing across the square from the minstrels. "Mister Atro's puppets! Can I? Please?"

Lars swallowed his bite of apple while they all

looked toward the puppet stage and the crowd settling onto the benches. "I don't know. It's awful crowded."

"But Laaaars," she whined. "Please? It's just puppets."

Lars looked to Jess. "Would you like to see the puppet show?"

Jess sighed as Aly jumped all around. "Not especially, but I don't think we have much choice."

Lars nodded and Aly squealed, running to the crowd. "Stay with the other kids!" Jess called after her.

Lars fidgeted. "Just us, then?"

She nodded and braved a glance. "Yeah, I guess so."

They walked to the benches, not talking, until they reached an open spot behind a teeming gaggle of children. Jess laid Cailin's blanket on the ground, smoothing it, then Lars set the baby down. He sat, feet on either side of her, while Jess kicked off her shoes. Dulcimer music twinkled from nearby minstrels and Jess smiled. She saw Aly scampering with another girl about her age. She braved a glance at Lars. *Maybe this won't be so bad.*

Lars took another bite of his apple. "Aly seems to be having fun."

"She'll be fine," Jess said. "I hope Fyn's okay. I think Mam's getting suspicious."

"At least you're going home tomorrow. I'm sure your dad is going to want to talk to Gilby."

She shuddered. "Kill him is far more likely."

A long silence, then, "Jess, speaking of going back to the castle . . ."

She glanced over to see Lars blushing. "What about it?"

"I'm not going back, not till this is through."

She nodded, her fingers clenching against the

bench. "I know. You have a job to do. You have to help Dad and Dubric find Otlee and finish the investigation."

The show started and people clapped and cheered. "Yeah." He looked at the crowd, then down to Cailin. "I need to ask you something before you go home, if that's okay."

"Sure."

She'd never before noticed how long his fingers were, or the crooked scar running from his ring finger to his wrist. He'd been Dubric's page for six summers. How many times had he been hurt?

He said, "I know the castle faire is coming in about a moon, and I also know Moergan and Trumble are probably planning on asking you to go."

She looked up, startled. "They are?"

"Yeah," he said, glancing quickly at her. "Maybe Serian and Deorsa, too. Lots of boys."

"Oh," she said, not sure what else to say. He fidgeted beside her and she tried to watch the puppet show. She barely saw it.

A long pause. "But, see, even though asking day isn't until the new moon, and I know that your birthing day is a couple of phases after that, and I should wait until then even though you'll need time to get a dress and all, but I'm probably going to be stuck up here, and, well, I thought maybe . . ."

She looked at him, afraid to trust her voice.

He swallowed. "I just wanted to ask you if you'd like to go to the castle faire with me, if you want, if I'm back in time to take you." His face reddened and he said, "Instead of Moergan or Trumble or whoever. If you want."

She closed her mouth.

He nodded, still blushing, and lowered his head. "If you don't want to go with me, considering all that's happened lately, I understand. It's okay."

He started to lean away but she touched his hand. "Yes."

He stared at her. "I can take you to the faire?"

She nodded.

"Really?"

She smiled and tried to breathe. The puppet show and the crowd around them disappeared. They could have been sitting in a field of daisies.

"We can go to the dance, too, if you want. I know some of the boys won't dance, but I don't mind."

"Sure," she said, trying to sound like she'd been asked to faires and formal dances scores of times.

His face returned to its normal hue. "And, maybe, if we have fun at the faire and it all works out okay, we could eat supper together sometimes, maybe see the minstrels in town, or take walks? Do you think maybe we could?"

Abruptly aware it had fallen open, she closed her mouth again. "Are you asking to court me?"

His pinky finger touched hers, sending a jolt through her. "Yeah, I guess I am. With the most honorable of intentions, Jess, I swear. If that's all right."

She nodded, nervous. "It's fine."

"Great," he said, and his pinky finger hooked hers, bringing another delightful jolt with it.

As she looked into his eyes she thought about how many times he'd touched her hand. He had helped her stand, had handed her things . . . but not once had she felt a tingle before.

He cleared his throat and drew his hand away, shaking his head. "I can't believe you said yes."

"I can't believe you asked me."

He smiled and looked away. Side by side, they ate their apples and occasionally braved glances as they listened to the puppet show. Jess could not remember ever being so happy.

Dubric held the lantern before him and let his breath out slowly. Dark things floated in the air, shadows hovering at chest level. At first he thought they were bound birds or even the desiccated corpses of infants, but as he stepped away from the ladder, and heard Dien come down behind him, he saw they were not babies at all. They were puppets.

The nearest was nude and male, made of wood, with slashes across its chest and thighs. Its little puppet penis was gouged, and its eyes carved out. Curly brown hair was glued to its silently wailing head and it hung faceup, bound wrist and ankles, on black string. Holes, wide and deep enough to insert a finger, were drilled in its hips and mouth. Crusty film coated the holes and dark blood or paint oozed from the carved wounds.

Dubric wanted to vomit. *He made trophies, something to remember the boys by.* "How many are there?" he asked, choking back bile.

Dubric walked to the next closest, a blondish version with flayed calves and sliced hands, while Dien ducked through the floating, wooden horrors.

"I count twenty-three hanging, sir," Dien said, turning with a lantern in hand. "There's another on a table. It's in pieces."

Dubric took a deep breath and lowered his head, grimacing. Instead of fighting the presence and pain of his ghosts, he let them come, gasping at the chills teeming around him. Transparent green spectres crowded around him, and he soon found a boy resembling the nearest puppet. Features and wounds were similar and frightening. Another puppet, another ghost, each turning Dubric's stomach.

"The one on the table," he said, rubbing his eyes and sending most of his dripping green horrors away, "does it resemble Otlee?"

Dien moved toward the far corner. "No, sir," he said, looking back. "Braoin."

"Where is Otlee?" Dubric ripped the nearest puppet from its strings and dashed it to the dirt floor. "Where is he?"

He looked at the puppet sprawling at his feet and tilted his head. *I have seen this before. A puppet on the ground. Who? Who had them? A box full, in a mule cart. I remember children . . . A gray-haired man telling them to leave the puppets alone . . .*

He stood straight and took a breath. Atro. A big, strong-looking man, he traveled the Reach all hours of the day and night, giving him plenty of opportunity and easy access to children.

The gray pubic hair. The name "Tropos" could be a child's shortening of Atropos. And a peddler would have access to medicinal concoctions, strange sexual devices, and clever clothespins. He would also know the shortcuts, the hidden places, all the secrets of the Reach. The boys were bound like puppets, hung and tortured until they died. And he had a son on Jak's crew. Lars had killed a young carpenter outside this very house, and the boy had taken Rao's ghost with him when he died. "It is Atro the peddler," Dubric said, backing away from the floating puppets. "We must find him. Immediately. Before Otlee becomes a puppet, too."

"He's at the Planting Festival every spring," Dien said, hurrying to the ladder. "Aly is crazy for his puppets."

Dubric climbed. "Then praise the King he has no appetite for little girls."

The show ended and Aly clapped.

Other children ran about, laughing or sulking or begging for treats, but she happily munched her toffee and climbed on a bench to look for Jess and Lars.

They sat a few rows back, talking. They probably didn't even notice that the show was over.

Aly grinned. Then they wouldn't notice if she snuck backstage for a peek at the puppets. She jumped from the bench and ran toward the stage. Skipping, she followed the path around to the back.

Atro's cart and mule waited in the shade, and he was laying the last of his puppets in the box. Aly was about to call out, but he tossed the box in the cart and walked away from her, toward a privy. An old woman watched him go, saying something Aly couldn't hear, but he kept walking away.

The cart door stood open. Aly crept forward and quietly climbed inside. "Just a peek," she whispered, reaching for the box waiting beneath a black robe. The lid creaked open, and she grinned. Atro had brought the good puppets for the show, the ones with real fur and sparkly glass jewels. They lay faceup in the box, their control handles strapped to the lid. She couldn't help but touch them. They seemed so alive.

She heard a muffled cry and a tap as something in

the cart with her shifted. She looked up, squinting into the dark as it tapped again, and the upper planks of a bench box creaked.

A darkly smeared lock hung from a battered hasp, fastening the top to the front. Puppets forgotten, Aly crawled toward the box; it creaked again, the lock jiggling as whatever was trapped inside tried to get out.

Aly glanced out of the cart but saw no one near. She turned back to the box and eased closer. "Hello?" she whispered into the crack between the top and front. "Is someone in there?"

She heard a muffled squeal calling for help and more frantic movement from within the box.

I should get Lars, she thought, shifting back, but her gaze lit on a display tray of small implements and tools glistening in reflected sunlight. She looked back to the bench box and the lock with its dark smear.

"I opened the crypt for Lars's granddad. I can do this by myself," she whispered.

She plucked a fine metal file and an awl from the display box, then peered into the lock. It was newer than the lock on the crypt and looser, easy to spring, and she quickly tugged it off the hasp. The smear was damp and red and tacky. Blood. Grimacing, she wiped the mess on her skirt.

She dropped the lock and lifted the lid. A boy, naked and bleeding and gagged, stared at her, his eyes glistening. He looked broken and twisted, like a discarded toy. He struggled to sit, but his binds held him fast.

"Otlee?" she gasped, helping him upright. He was heavy and weak and she had to stand to get leverage, but she dragged him up until he sat in the box. "Everyone's been looking for you."

His eyes grew wide and he cowered back, shaking his head. Aly froze.

"What have we here?" a woman's voice said. "A stowaway? A thief?"

"I'm not a thief!" Aly said, turning. "He's my friend."

The old woman in the doorway grinned. "No, he's my new Foiche." She reached for Aly, her arms crawling with red worms with tiny, snapping bug mouths. "I think he'll find you tasty."

Jess stood abruptly. "That's Aly."

Lars lurched to his feet beside her, his hand falling to his sword. "Grab the baby."

He started at a trot, then broke into a run when he heard Aly scream in pain, the sound diffused and misdirected by scores of milling people. The puppet show had ended, and he saw the empty stage, the empty benches, but no sign of Aly.

Confused, he stopped in the middle of the path and turned around, listening for another shout, but he could hear little over the terrified thud of his heart.

Jess ran to him, Cailin clutched to her. "Where is she?"

"I don't know. I can't see her."

"Me, either. But she was right here!"

"Where else would she go? More candy? Toys?"

"I don't know," Jess said, her eyes wide and terrified.

"Goddess, I hope she's okay." Lars looked all around again. "Can we be fairly sure she watched the whole show?"

Jess nodded. "Yes. Aly loves puppets."

"Let's look here first, then. The show just ended a few minutes ago. She couldn't have gone far."

Hurrying, they found only empty benches and discarded food. Lars looked at the ground as he walked, searching for footprints, for clues, but it was all a mishmash from scores of people, until he worked closer to the stage.

"I think this is Aly's," he said, kneeling. One clear print lay above the others, from a small girl's shoe. Jess beside him, he followed the trail around the stage, and saw additional prints leading to the shade.

"Why did she come back here?" Jess asked.

His head down, Lars followed the trail. "Maybe Aly wanted to see the puppets closer." *I should have been paying attention. I should have been watching her.*

"Oh, no," Jess said, breaking into a run.

Lars stopped, snatching up his head, but his hope fell, making him stumble. "What? Oh Goddess!"

Jess lifted a bloody lock from the ground. "What's happening?"

Panicking, Lars ran to her. "Don't move." Quickly, he examined the thick and cracking mud, noting the tracks before they were lost. "It's her. Two adults. And a cart." He knelt, his fingers touching a curved gash in the earth, a cart track so much like one he had seen in the road the night he arrived in the Reach, and the toffee lying beside it. He stood and pulled his sword, following the trail to an alley between two buildings, and he picked up an empty whiskey bottle. He sniffed it, grimacing at the hard, alcoholic stink, then threw it to the ground. "Get your mam. Now. Tell her what happened."

"But, Lars! You can't go alone!"

He paused and turned to look back at her. "If I don't, we could lose her. Go!"

Jess stumbled away, taking the lock and the baby

with her. Lars turned back to the cart tracks and ran, sword in hand, and disappeared into the shadows.

"What's put ye in such a temper?" Lissea asked.

Sarea shrugged and arranged hats by size. "It doesn't matter."

Lissea laid out a selection of hatbands, smoothing them on the display table. "It must. Ye've barely spoken all day, other'n to send the kiddies away."

"It's nothing."

"Don't fib to yer mother."

Sarea turned, her hands clenching. Her father had gone to get an ale, and there were no customers looking over their wares. She tried to stop herself, but it came out anyway. "You're not my mother. You've never been my mother. You don't even look like me."

Lissea stared at her, her mouth working noiselessly. At last she turned away and resumed straightening hatbands.

"At least you're not trying to deny it." Sarea slapped a hat into the rack.

"No, yer right."

They worked in silence until Sarea asked, "Why didn't you ever tell me?"

"Just weren't never a good way. I tried once, when ye were little, but ye wouldn't hear of it. Ye said I was yer mam and I never mentioned it again."

Sarea's shoulders slumped and she turned. "That must have been difficult, I guess."

"It was. Everythin' 'bout it was hard. Yer mama died when ye were 'bout two summers old, and I was sent to help yer daddy take care of things. I was just a skinny little girl, but ye latched onto me and wouldn't let go."

"'Take care of things'?" Sarea asked.

Lissea took a deep breath. "Devyn needed someone to tend the house and his child. I was traded to him. Fer a few hats and some sheep, if I 'member right."

Sarea stared at her, horrified. "You were sold? Goddess, why? How?"

Her eyes lowered, Lissea said, "My folks died in the war. I was just a baby, a few moons, maybe only a few phases old. Some folks took in war orphans fer servants, others kept 'em to make money. Mister Duncannon worked fer my daddy afore the war. He took me in, but was greedy and traded me several times afore Devyn. Fer money, fer whiskey. Fer a few days or a couple of moons. When I was fourteen he got a girl pregnant. I was just glad it wasn't me. Maeve's mama and I didn't get along and she sold me to Devyn fer two summers. Devyn was good to me, so I never went back, even after my time was done." She looked up. "No one came fer me. They'd forgot all 'bout me."

"I'm sorry," Sarea said, her stomach churning.

"What's past is past."

"You didn't have any other family? No one?"

Liss laughed harshly. "Besides a baby girl who thought she was my sister? I had a cousin. A crazy aunt. I was better off sold."

"But . . . the things you must have endured."

Liss grabbed a few more hatbands. "What don't kill ye makes ye stronger." She took a deep breath and turned away. "I did everythin' I could to make sure ye didn't suffer the same fate. That ye weren't forced to lie with strange men fer a bottle of whiskey, or toil in the fields until yer hands bled. That ye never felt a whip on yer back or a knife 'tween yer legs. That ye'd grow up with a future."

Sarea wrapped her arm over her mother's narrow shoulders and hugged her. "I'm sorry. I didn't know."

"I tried to tell ye, I did. But I couldn't. And when ye grew up, married, moved away, I thought that maybe I did all right. Ye were happy and married to a good man. Ye weren't a servant, a piece of meat gettin' passed round. Ye weren't beaten or raped. Not like me all those summers afore yer father bought me."

"Dad would never have let them take you back," Sarea said, squeezing her again. "He loves you."

Liss glanced at Sarea. "He don't love me. He never stopped lovin' yer mama."

"But he married you. That's—"

Liss's voice fell flat. "He married me 'cause of Stuart, not fer love. Ye've no ken how lucky ye are. No one's ever loved me. 'Cept ye."

Sarea drew away, confused. "Dad, and you . . . He forced you to . . . ?"

"He never forced me to do anythin', not once in all the summers I've known him." She turned to stare Sarea in the eye. "He never touched me neither, not 'til after Stuart was born, and I was his wife then so it didn't matter."

"What? No!"

Liss shrugged and resumed laying out hatbands. "Ye wanted the truth. Now ye know. I was his servant. A surrogate mama fer his daughter. Nothin' more."

"Then Stuart wasn't my brother at all?"

"No. A boy came passin' through and spent the night in the barn. I don't even 'member his name, if I ever knew it at all. I tried to stop the baby, but it didn't work. Yer father found me bleeding, and he married me so no one'd think he'd fathered a bastard with a servant. He was an elder in the temple, after all. A businessman."

Sarea wanted to fall to the ground. "Goddess, I think I remember a wedding. I was so happy picking flowers, getting a new dress . . . But it was for appearances?"

"Ye were six," Liss muttered. "All little girls like weddin's. And ye liked having a baby brother, even though he was damaged." She took a deep breath and shook her head. "I've never forgiven myself for what I did to Stuart. It's all my fault what happened. All of it. And yer father loved him from the moment he saw him. He didn't care he was a bastard."

Sarea tentatively approached her. "You were young. You were scared. It was an accident. You don't have to blame yourself."

"It were no accident," Liss said, wiping her nose with the back of her hand. "But after what yer father did fer me, I can't go. I know he's crazy, and it's hard sometimes, but I can't leave him." She sniffled as Sarea drew her into her arms. "I've wanted to tell ye fer so long. How sorry I am fer what happened. How sorry I am fer Stuart."

"It's okay, Mam," Sarea said, hugging her tight. "It's all in the past now. Everything's forgiven."

"Not everythin'," Lissea said, hugging back. "But I've done as best I can. It no longer has a hold of me and it's out of my hands at last."

"Good," Sarea said. One last squeeze, then she saw Jess running to them in a panic.

"She's gone! They're gone!"

"Jesscea! Calm yourself!" Sarea said, taking the baby away and handing her to her mother. Jess flailed about, and Sarea struggled to keep her daughter rooted to the ground. "What happened? Who's gone?"

"Aly! Lars went after her. We have to do something! Now!"

"Where did she go?"

"I don't know!" Jess cried, shaking a bloody lock near Sarea's face. "She's gone! Disappeared in some-one's cart! Lars is chasing her!"

"Who took her, Jess?" Lissea asked, her voice soft and shaking.

"I don't know!" Jess wailed. She fell to her knees, dragging Sarea down with her. "We were at the puppet show and Aly just disappeared! Lars went after her. That's all I know."

"No! That's not possible!"

"Mam? Grandmama?" Fyn said, hurrying over. "What's wrong?"

While Sarea struggled to remain coherent, Lissea grabbed Fyn by the chin. "Get yer grandpapa. He's at the Hog Leg. Run, girl. Now."

Fyn stumbled away then ran, disappearing into the gawking crowd.

Sarea cried, "Aly! Goddess, no!"

"Get up," her mother said. "Keep yerself together, Sarea. Ye have to."

"But my baby, my baby . . . Someone stole my baby!"

"I'm sorry, Mama," Jess cried, reaching for her, but Sarea batted her hands away. "I'm sorry! It's all my fault!"

"Someone stole my baby!" Sarea screamed.

Lissea grabbed Sarea by the armpits and hauled her upright. "Stop it. Damn ye! Stop it!"

Sarea struggled in her mother's hard grip. "You were supposed to watch your little sister!"

"We just sat behind the kids," Jess blubbered, "with Cailin. We could see her, and I thought—"

Sarea sagged. "How could this happen? Where's my baby?"

"Lars will find her, Mama," Jess cried, reaching for her. "He will. He promised."

Sarea nodded, struggling to breathe. Lars always kept his promises. She reached for her daughter and sobbed. She heard a crash behind her and she turned. A box of hats lay busted on the ground, but no one was near. A shiver tingling up her spine, Sarea held Jess and cried.

Lars felt certain that his heart would burst from his chest and run ahead of him down the road. He wanted to stop and catch his breath. Hells, he wanted to drop down dead. But Aly was still in that cart—a cart he could see on the road ahead—and he would keep running until the Goddess herself stole his life away.

Lars vowed to leave Atro's guts in the mud. He would have spoken the vow, screamed it to the sky, had he been able to talk. Instead he screamed it in his mind and ran, holding his side as he slowly closed on them.

The road was a thick and treacherous clot of mud and half-dried ruts. He tripped, cursing, but kept on. He wondered how far he had come—One mile? Two? Five?—then brushed the question away. The distance was immaterial. He was a page, not a courier, and while a quarter-mile trot to the village south of the castle had never posed a problem, an endless mad dash over uneven terrain was another matter entirely. He had already run farther than he ever had before, and would run ten times more if it meant saving Aly.

Assuming his heart didn't explode before he got there.

He crested a hill and forced air into his lungs, noting the cart starting up the next muddy hill. As it clattered up the slope, the back door swung open and he saw a blond head moving toward the door, then being pulled into the dark again.

"Aly!" he cried out, his voice little more than a whoosh of air and pain.

She's alive, he thought, throwing himself down the hill. *And I will get to her. Failure is not an option. I can't. I won't.*

The cart climbed the hill, its back door swinging open. Lars followed, close enough to see Aly struggling with an old woman inside.

"Lars!" Aly screamed, wrenching free. She held on to the door frame and looked down at the rutty road, then at him. "Otlee's here, too! He's hurt!" She had a bloody nose and a bruise on her cheek, and she appeared both terrified and furious.

"Jump!" he cried out, lunging as fast as he possibly could, reaching for her even though she was a good fifty lengths away. "For Goddess' sake! Jump!"

Aly nodded but the old woman moved behind her and pulled her into the shadows again.

"Let her go!" he screamed.

He saw a struggle, heard Aly squeal, then the old woman appeared in the open door, holding Aly by the hair. "Take the little bobcat if you want her so bad!"

Aly clutched at her throat, her eyes wide and terrified. The old woman snapped her up then down, and Lars saw she didn't hold Aly by her hair, but by black twine wrapped around her throat.

Aly kicked, struggling, and the old woman grinned at Lars as she dropped Aly into the mud.

She rolled, head over foot, and he scrambled to her even as the cart rattled over the hill.

"No!" Lars cried, reaching her, falling to his knees as he tried to rip the twine from her throat. She fought, her face turning blue, her eyes bulging, and fresh blood trickled from her nose.

The cord was knotted, wrapped several times around and digging into her flesh. He ripped his dagger free and cut it off, gouging the muscle on the side of her neck. He yanked the cord away and threw it aside, trying to catch his breath, hoping against all reason that she'd be able to walk. Otlee remained on the cart, getting farther away by the moment. *Oh, Goddess, please help me!*

Aly writhed, clutching at him and struggling to breathe, her face still blue and a low squeal escaping her dented throat.

"No!" he screamed, his fingers dancing across the indentation. "No, Goddess! No!"

Despite her struggles, he tilted her head back and heard a whistle come from her. Her kicking faded, and the lurches in her chest slowed.

"Stay with me!" he cried, trying to breathe into her, trying to get her some air, any air. "Dammit, Aly! Don't you die!"

He leaned over her, his mouth locked over hers, and he blew, harder, *harder*, but it was like blowing into a goblet. There was nowhere for his breath to go.

"Oh, Aly," he cried, trying again. "Don't be broken. Hang on, honey, we'll fix this. I'll fix this. I swear I will. Breathe, just a little, please, for the love of the Goddess, breathe!"

She twitched, looking up at him, then twitched

again. Her hand released its grip from his shirt and fell loose and limp across her chest.

He felt warm wetness soak into his lap as she sagged in his arms. Crying, he tried again and again to get air into her, rocking her and pleading with the Goddess. "Take me. Don't do this, not her. Please don't take my baby sister. I'll do anything, just please, please . . . Please, Aly, breathe. I'll do anything."

But he knew there was nothing more he could do.

Crying, he smoothed her hair, holding her close. "Why?" he asked the sky. "What did she ever do to deserve to die?"

He looked down at her face, his Aly, and he saw his tears patter on her bluish skin. Wailing, he staggered to his feet and tripped over a rut in the road. He held her against his chest as he stumbled and tried to find his balance. His legs quaked with exhaustion and threatened to send him sprawling to the mud.

He wanted to cry, wanted to grieve, but instead he looked up the hill. *Atro and the old bitch still had Otlee.* No longer able to run, and refusing to leave Aly by the side of the road, he climbed the hill and prayed he would not be too late.

They had almost reached the main road when the hated weight of a ghost fell behind Dubric's eyes. "No. It cannot be." He cried out, clenching the saddle.

Tears streamed down his cheeks. He could think of no connection between Alyson and the dead boys, but neither could he see how she would be the object of a random murder, not while he had two dozen other ghosts. He reached for Dien.

"I am so sorry," he said, barely able to speak. "So damned sorry."

Dien turned ashen. "What is it, sir? What happened? Are we too late to save Otlee?"

"Not Otlee. Alyson."

"No," Dien said, looking up the road and kicking his horse to a faster gait. "That's a lie."

Dubric glanced at her ghost and said, "It is the truth. I do not know how, nor why, but she is dead."

"She's with my pegging family! With Lars!" he screamed. "I don't care what you think you see, my daughter is not dead!"

They galloped on in anguished silence, Dubric berating himself for not considering Atro earlier, and for not believing magic survived in the Reach. They had killed Foiche and his underlings in the war, exterminated them like the vermin they were. Could one have escaped?

No, he decided, looking to the horizon. *We captured and killed every last mage, the acolytes, apprentices, adepts . . . any man or woman, even peasantry, that showed the slightest hint of magic was tested. None escaped, it was simply not possible. Not with thousands of soldiers, several armies. We caught every living soul in the Reach and questioned them.*

An old memory flickered to life.

After he had crawled from the suffocating tunnel, when he emerged into a landscape of flame and smoke, he had continued to chase Foiche, but he had found a girl—not a child, yet not a woman—cradling a baby in her arms and holding the hand of a boy who was barely old enough to toddle beside her. He had not captured the girl; instead, he had told her to run. To get as far away from the place as she could, for the armies were coming, and some were not kind to young girls without protection. He had not seen her in the internment camps, and he had been relieved, assuming she had taken his advice. And he had hoped he had saved one soul from torment and pain.

A shiver crawled down his spine as he tried to recall her face, but it was lost to the haze of time. Nearly fifty summers had passed since he saw a girl in the smoke and bade her to save herself and her children.

The girl had been fourteen, perhaps fifteen summers old, and she had stared at him with a mixture of hatred and horror; he had been nearly nineteen, gallant, and incredibly naive of women, even those who despised him.

I still am, he thought, rubbing his bald scalp. *Could I have seen a terrified young mother and been blind to her magic? Could an old woman, nearly my age, be immersed in this?*

He blinked, astounded, and almost pulled his horse to a halt. A boy staggered over the next hill, carrying a limp child in his arms. *Lars?* Dubric kicked his charger in the ribs. Dien screaming beside him, they barreled down the road.

CHAPTER

27

†

W e are coming!" Dubric called.

Lars staggered, fell to his knees, then hurled himself upright again, all the while carrying Alyson.

Dien screamed, anguish and pain and fury intermixed.

Lars stumbled but never dropped his burden. They rode close as he got his feet beneath him. He was wailing, holding poor Alyson to his chest while her arms and legs hung limply from his grasp. "I begged the Goddess to take me instead, but she wouldn't!"

"The bitch never does," Dubric said, dismounting.

Dien slid from the saddle. "Give me my daughter."

Lars nodded and held out the body, his arms quaking. "I tried to save her, but her throat's crushed. I tried to make her breathe, but she wouldn't, and she just . . ."

Dien fell to his knees, cradling his child. He shook, crushing her to him, then screamed at the sky.

Dubric turned Lars's face from the grieving father. "What happened? Start at the beginning. We do not have much time."

Lars swallowed, wiping at his leaking nose with the back of his arm. "Jess and I took Aly to see the puppets and she ran off. We heard Aly scream and went looking

465

for her. It's Atro the peddler, sir, and some pegging old bitch. She's the one that killed Aly. She tied twine around her throat." He swallowed and added, "They have Otlee, too, Aly said so, but the old woman strangled her, then threw her from the cart. I was so close, sir, but I couldn't—" His face contorted into a grimace and his hands balled at his side.

"You did what you could," Dubric said, patting the boy's shoulder. "But you have to set aside your grief for now. Did you see Otlee?"

"No, sir. Just Aly. She tried to get away, but that woman—"

"Pegging bitch," Dien snarled. "Goat-raping whore."

Not now, Dubric thought, turning toward Dien. *All this emotion will not help us face a mage.* "We have to save Otlee. He must not suffer the same fate as Braoin."

"He won't," Dien said, standing. "I'll kill the lad myself before I let that bitch and the boy-raping shit harm him again."

Lars took a shaky step toward him. "I'm so sorry. I tried to save her, I swear I did."

Aly draped over his shoulder, Dien pushed Lars aside and climbed onto his horse. Reining about, he said, "You let my daughter die."

"No! Wait, please, no!" Lars cried, stumbling after him, but Dien rode on, heedless to the boy's pleas.

"He is in pain and does not know what he is saying," Dubric said. "Let it go."

Lars hung his head. "No, he's right. It's all my fault. All of it."

He said nothing more as he climbed onto Dubric's horse, and they followed Dien down the road in sharp silence.

* * *

The cart had turned off the road onto the path leading to the tower ruins. The wheels left a clear trail, and Dubric led his men through the brush and weeds.

"Why here?" Lars asked, his eyes drawn to the holes in the ground and jutting steel beams.

Dubric guided his horse around a pile of concrete and glass. "This is where Foiche kept his prisoners, where he fed. It is likely the site of greatest power."

He barely heard Lars's question: "Where he *fed*?"

They reached the corner of the tower and Dubric dismounted, pulling his sword, while Dien gently laid Aly in the shade. "Magic comes at great cost. The Shadow Mages pulled life from living beings to cast their vile spells, often killing them in the process. Foiche was particularly adept at draining his people until nothing remained but dust."

Dubric followed Dien down the walled path to the entrance to the temple. Smoke stained the bricks, the tattered cloth, and the packed mud, but fresh prints marred the ground.

"You should wait out here," Dubric said, reaching for Dien. "You are grieving. It feeds her, makes her stronger. Your despair could kill us all."

Dien shrugged off Dubric's touch and stomped down the aisle. "I'm coming. That bitch killed my baby. She can't hurt me more than she already has."

Dubric hurried to keep up. "Dien, please, listen to me. She *wants* you upset. She has laid a trap and we cannot fall into it. You know what we might find in there, what might be happening. Strong emotions will not aid us; they will only get us killed."

Dubric reached for Dien. "Please. Think about your wife, your other children. Otlee. We cannot save them if we succumb to anger. We *must* remain calm."

Dien growled, low and rumbling, but stopped his furious trek. "All right, sir, whatever you say. But they are both dying today." He looked to Dubric and nodded once, slowly. "I won't wait for the hangman. Not after what happened to Aly and all those boys."

Dubric glanced to Lars and saw the boy's grim nod. A unanimous decision. "Agreed. Let me go first."

Dien stepped aside and Dubric entered the tunnel. Cold sweat beaded on his skin as the walls seemed to close in on him. He rounded the corner and paused, tasting fear and feeling Dien's bulk close behind. *We must all remain calm.*

"Ah, the filthy Byr has arrived at last," a woman said. Haconry's housekeeper leaned into the tunnel and grinned at him. "About time you got here."

Dubric stared at her, seething. "Where is my page?"

Vidulyn looked behind her, then back to Dubric. "I'm afraid your boy is a bit tied up at the moment, playing with my son."

Dubric heard a low whine. It made his skin crawl. "Give me my page," he said, easing forward again.

"Oh, I can't do that," she said, backing from the hole. "Your other pet killed our vessel. I'd prefer the Royal as a replacement, but this one will do. You've left me little choice."

Dubric inched closer, watching her eyes. "There is always a choice. Release him. Immediately."

"I choose to have my life back," she sneered. "Give me your sword."

He felt a tug in his head, slight at first then stronger. *I am ill prepared for this, I have not the protection, nor the strength. But with no distractions, no surprises, I may yet persevere.* "No. I will not."

"Oh, yes, you will," she commanded, reaching for the sword and curling her fingers. "I pulled a good bit from that rotten little girl before I let her go. She was so much sweeter than sheep."

The tug in his head did not strengthen; her command was weak at best, little more than a suggestion, a parlor trick. He looked into her eyes and hid his smile. He was no untrained farmer, but a soldier, and he had killed far stronger mages than her. Concentration would weaken her; he merely had to keep looking into her eyes, and once the thread that bound them had broken, he would slit her throat.

"You pegging bitch!" Dien snarled from behind. Dubric found himself being shoved forward and tumbling out of the hole.

"No!" he called out, trying to impede his progress, struggling to maintain his connection with the mage. "Not now! You have to stay calm!"

Vidulyn blinked and backed away, shaking her head. Dubric felt the thread connecting them snap as her will broke free of his. "You bastard!" she snarled, and kicked his sword away.

Dubric scrambled for his sword, feeling her try to snare his mind again, but this time he had no eye contact, no way to fight her, no defense. His vision darkened, filling and tangling with dark strands even as his fingers clenched around the hilt of his sword.

He panted, his head filling with pain, and he tasted blood.

Behind him, Dien screamed, and Dubric heard the heavy thud as he fell to the ground.

Vidulyn laughed, bringing agony to Dubric's head.

"Such a big man would feed me well. Think of the things I could do to you, Byr." He felt her touch on the back of his neck, slippery and dry like a snake. "But I believe I'll leave him for Foiche. A new Foiche must feed."

"Foiche is dead," Dubric said. He tried to lift his sword, but it was heavy, so damned heavy. "I killed him myself."

She laughed. "No, you killed the vessel. Vessels die, but the spirit remains. I only needed a way to transfer it, and the boy is adequate for my uses."

Dubric swallowed a mouthful of blood and felt more pour from his nose. "You will not corrupt my page," he said. "By the King, you will not."

"He is already corrupted. My son has seen to that. Soon his vessel shall be ready." He felt her breath on his ear. "I feared I had not made enough cloth, but it covers him nicely. I shall have Foiche thank you personally for the gift."

Dien had made no sound beyond low moans since he had fallen, and Dubric could not hear Lars at all. Was the boy all right, or did he, too, writhe on the floor while a Shadow Mage pulled from his mind? *For King's sake, lad, if you have any sense, run.*

Vidulyn's breath moved away, but the pain in his head remained. "Cut him, you worthless swine," she called out, "like I'd—"

Then she screamed.

Lars hung back after Dien pushed Dubric out of the tunnel, tasting fear in the back of his throat. The place stank like ash and old blood. He heard Otlee moan, heard cutting sounds and Otlee's weakening screams. *Not Otlee. Please, Goddess, no.*

He inched forward, clinging to the shadows. He could see Dien writhing on the floor and, beyond him, Atro laying fabric across Otlee's back, then slicing though and sopping the blood. "No, no, no!" Lars whispered, over and over, and all the while Dubric and Dien moaned on the floor, helpless and bleeding from their ears and noses. The old woman stood over Dubric with a long knife, saying things he didn't want to hear—just listening hurt his head—so he turned his attention to Atro and Otlee. *I can save Otlee. I have to. Please, Goddess, please.*

Lars swallowed his fear and slipped silently from the tunnel. Dagger in hand, his eyes focused on the back of Atro's head and the slight hollow between his shoulders. Lars moved as quickly as he dared, stepping lightly with only a whisper of sound.

Then he bared his teeth and slit the bastard's throat.

Atro fell back, gurgling and clutching at his gaping neck, with Otlee's blood smeared over him.

Lars shoved the body aside and pulled the repulsive diamond silk from Otlee's bare back and head. He was awash with bruises and little punctures or bites. Lars winced at the blood flowing from his anus and innumerable gashes on his back and legs. "I'm here. Hold on." Lars ripped off his shirt to cover Otlee's nakedness then knelt to cut the binds. Black twine had bound Otlee wrists so tightly his fingers were gray. Lars cut all of it and tossed it aside.

Hearing a scream and sensing movement, he turned and scrambled back, away from the screeching woman and her knife.

*   *   *

The pull on Dubric's head snapped free with a bright jolt of pain, then was gone. He blinked, thrusting his weight up from the cold ground to his hands and knees, and heard Lars's startled gasp.

"Get and maintain eye contact," he called out, struggling to roll upright. "No matter what she does, keep eye contact."

"That's impossible!" Lars cried.

Vidulyn screamed in pain, then snarled, "You stabbed me, you filthy bugger!"

"Do it!" Dubric commanded. "She is not strong enough to control you if you stare her down." His vision began to clear and he saw the green shimmers of his ghosts in the gray haze.

A yelp from Lars and a crash, then Dubric got his feet beneath him and stood, still half blind and his head sloshing. He wiped wetness from his nose and staggered toward the noise, then he fell to the ground again, tripping over Dien.

I am too old for this, he thought, once again struggling to stand. The haze thinned to a soupy fog and he saw Lars grappling with Vidulyn while Otlee lay limp and facedown over the charred altar, blood dripping down his bare legs. Atro was sprawled on his back nearby, with his throat gaping open. A strip of red-and-black cloth lay wadded just beyond Atro's head, shimmering viciously.

The ghosts all stared at the cloth, even Aly.

"You will not harm my pages," Dubric muttered, stumbling forward. "By the King, you will not."

Lars's eyes briefly flicked away from Vidulyn's, meeting Dubric's before they clouded over in pain. A thin trickle of blood leaked from his nose. She laughed and threw him against the wall. She plunged the knife into his chest and Lars slumped, screaming.

"You will not harm my pages!" Dubric screamed. Vidulyn turned, startled, and he swung his sword. It struck her along the slope of her shoulder and sliced down.

She snarled, raising her arms. He flew back and slammed against a rusted beam, cracking his ribs and his head. He slumped to his knees, dizzy, and tried to see, to think, but pain slid into his head and twisted, wrenching his face up to look at her.

"Pegging Byr," she snarled, pulling his sword from her shoulder. "So pious and superior, but look at you now, bowing before me." She tossed his sword aside and it clattered away. The wound on her chest glowed red, then closed slowly. "You killed my father, you son of a swine! And then you have the balls to tell me to run?"

She paced before him, snarling, each step bringing agony to his head.

"Mages must die," he said, gritting through the pain. He tasted blood again as red drops pattered on his hands. Someone moved to his left, someone big, and he heard the sleek whisper of drawing steel.

"The Byr must die!" Vidulyn sneered, intent only on Dubric. "You took away everything I had except for a few half-dead worms. I've spent a lifetime fighting to get back what you stole."

"You are the thief, taking lives, stealing souls. Not I. I freed the Reach," he said, struggling to meet her gaze. "I steal only your darkness, destroy only the pain you create. You harmed my pages, and for that you will die." *If I can keep her attention, hold her . . . maybe . . .*

She laughed, and fresh blood surged from his nose.

"Pitiful, your attempts to hold me. I am above your abilities now, Byr. And to think I feared you all this time." She did not see the shadow moving behind her.

"Shut up, bitch!" Dien growled. Blood leaked from his nose and ears, and he wavered on his feet, but he stood under his own power and swung.

Vidulyn turned, startled, just as her head separated from her shoulders, flying aside like a child's ball. As she fell, most of the pain of Dubric's ghosts left him. Dien fell, too, retching and holding his head.

Dubric scrambled through the lightness—*They are gone!*—and stumbled to Lars. "Hold still," he said, laying the boy flat on the ground.

"Save Otlee," Lars gasped, shaking his head and batting Dubric away. "Just let me die."

"You are not going to die. The wound is too far above your heart for that. I doubt the knife did more than slice muscle." Dubric pulled his cloak from his shoulders and cut a pair of long strips from the bottom edge.

"But Otlee! He's more important."

"Otlee is unconscious, and you are important, too," Dubric said. He folded one of the strips into a thick square. "Now hold still. This will hurt."

"Sir, please," Lars said, then he cried out as Dubric pulled the blade from his chest.

Dubric pressed on the folded cloth to staunch the bleeding, then helped Lars sit. "You did a brave thing," he said as he wrapped the long strip around Lars's chest. "Few men would face a mage alone, especially as exhausted as you are."

Lars looked past him to Otlee on the altar. "It wasn't bravery, sir. Just necessity."

"Bravery is not the absence of fear, lad, but doing whatever needs to be done even in the face of that fear," Dubric said as he tied the makeshift bandage tight. "You could have remained in the tunnel, or fled, and no one would have blamed you." He patted Lars on the uninjured shoulder and stood to check on Otlee.

Dubric lifted him, gently, then knelt to examine his injuries. Lars watched, wincing, as Dubric checked Otlee's privates.

"Is he going to be okay?"

Satisfied that no injury was life-threatening, Dubric wrapped Otlee in his cloak. "Physically? Yes, I believe so. Mentally, I have no way to know. Only time will tell."

"It was supposed to be me," Lars said, turning away. "I heard her. She wanted to use me. She should have."

"Do not say such things," Dubric said.

Behind him, Dien sat up, holding his head and wiping blood from his face. Growling, the big man lurched to his feet and stumbled to them. "Otlee?"

"He will heal," Dubric said. "How is your head?"

"Better than when the old bitch was laughing in it." He nudged her body with his boot. "Least she's dead."

"And we survived," Dubric said, standing, He handed Otlee to Dien and gathered up their weapons, while Dien carried Otlee through the tunnel and into sunlight.

As Dubric walked to his horse, he saw Stuart sitting with Aly's body. He was crying.

Dubric sent Lars and Dien to the farm, while he continued to Maeve's. Otlee woke, panicked and screaming, while they were on the ferry. No amount of assurance or coaxing calmed him. He screamed the entire width of the river before fainting dead away.

When Dubric rode to Maeve's shop, he dismounted without bothering to tie his horse. As he strode to the door, he wished he could return Otlee's innocence. "I have made them pay," he said to himself, cradling the boy in his arms, "but I do not know if that can ever be enough."

He felt tears on his cheeks, and he let them fall.

Maeve opened the door and ran to him. She said nothing as she looked at Otlee. She just stepped aside and let them in.

As he had the first night in the rain, Dubric carried Otlee through a house now familiar to him, while Maeve ran ahead to Braoin's room. No ghosts followed, but he felt Stuart's elusive ache behind his eyes. Its remnant worried him. All should have left with Vidulyn's demise.

"What do you need?" Maeve asked, stepping out of the way. "How bad is he?"

"I do not know, on either account." Dubric laid Otlee upon the bed, once again smearing the linens with blood. "I am merely relieved that he is alive."

"And those that killed my son?"

Dubric gently straightened Otlee's legs and covered him. "They are dead. But twenty-six boys have died, my other page is injured, and my squire has lost a child."

Maeve blinked, astounded and horrified. "One of the girls? Goddess, no."

"Alyson," Dubric said, sagging. "The deaths of two vile mages cannot balance all the pain they have caused."

"It is better than if they had lived," Maeve said, her hand squeezing his shoulder. "It's over now. No more boys will die. It may not be fair, nor just, but Otlee is alive, and other boys of the Reach will not suffer."

She wiped her eyes and smiled at him. "Thank you. I wish you had saved my Braoin and my grandniece, but thank you."

"You are welcome," he said. "I wish I could have saved them, too." He watched her go back to Otlee, worry tugging at his entrails at the thought of the one remaining ghost.

Dubric scrubbed all traces of blood and ash from his skin and reached for his clean clothes. Otlee slept soundly, Vidulyn and Atro's plans had come to naught, and he had one last evening in Maeve's home.

He had seen her smile for the first time since Braoin had died. Perhaps tonight would be a better evening. Perhaps he could get her to laugh. Perhaps he could kiss her.

The thought still rang in his head when he met his own gaze in the mirror. *What are you thinking, you old goat? You are far too old, and she too young. You are considering shadows, wishful thinking. Think of Oriana, think of your wife.*

Frowning, he shoved aside the thought and left the bath chamber.

I count bones tomorrow, he thought. *Charred bones of murdered boys. Think of that, not of a pleasant evening. I do not get pleasant evenings, nor days of rest, nor laughter.*

I do not deserve them.

He strode through the kitchen door, then stopped, looking around the room. Maeve was nowhere to be seen.

He called her name. No answer.

Worried, he went to her shop, her store, her bed-chamber, but found no sign of her.

His heart hammering and dread stinging his mouth, he ran through the back door and down the steps to see if she had gone out to feed Erline. Outside, barely visible in the gathering dark, he saw the cellar door standing open. It glowed faintly from within, and he released his breath in a rush.

"Maeve?" he called again, approaching the open door. "Is everything all right?"

"Yes, other than the fact that I'm too short," she replied.

Relieved, he descended the stairs to find her standing on a stool before a rack of shelves. Rows of tins and canned goods stood in organized groups. Apples and green beans and corn in glass jars, biscuits and salt and sugar in tins. Bins and barrels stood beside earthen walls, each with turnips or squash or potatoes, and salted meat hung from the ceiling beams. Dozens of boxes of fabric were stacked wherever there was room.

She turned to smile lopsidedly at him, and brushed cobwebs from her eyes. "I wanted to put tinned cherries on the ham, but I just can't reach them."

"I am delighted to get them," he said, helping her down from the stool. "Where are they?"

"Behind the tinned fish and the box of soda. Top shelf."

He stepped onto the stool and reached over the fish, stretching.

"Braoin put most of the food up last autumn. Evidently *he* could reach it."

"As can I," Dubric said, pulling the tin from its hiding place. He stepped down from the stool and placed it in her hands. "Are there any other . . ."

She had cobwebs in her hair and a light sheen of sweat on her brow. Her eyes closed slowly then opened again, taking his breath away. He wanted to whisper her name, wanted to brush the webs from her hair, wanted to touch her fine brow, but while he tried to decide what to do, what to say, she took a small step closer and put the tin on another shelf without ever dragging her eyes away.

She looked into his eyes, then kissed him, the softness of her breasts impossibly warm and inviting against his chest.

He froze, unsure what to do, amazed at his luck, and utterly entranced by the scent of her cheek.

"I'm sorry," she said, drawing away. "I thought . . ."

His mouth closed and he stared at her, barely able to breathe. *By the King, she kissed me!* "What? Why?"

"I shouldn't have. I'm sorry, I only thought . . ."

"No, that is not . . ." He reached for her, grasping her arms. "Why did you kiss me?"

"I thought you wanted me to. I'm sorry if I misjudged."

She kissed me! Damned, old, scarred me. "I am old enough to be your father."

"No, you're nothing like my father. You're different from any man I've ever known, and I just thought that maybe I saw—"

His breath dragged harshly into his chest and he felt unable either to draw her close or cast her away. "I cannot. I must not. My wife—"

"She's dead, Dubric, but I'm alive." A tear flowed down her cheek and he released his grip, wiping the drop away with his fingers. "And I don't want to be alone anymore. Not while I still have a life left to live. I thought you felt the same."

"Oh, Maeve," he said. Somehow he wrapped her in his arms and held her, let her cry against his chest. "Do not cry, please do not cry."

"I didn't mean to upset you," she said, trying to pull away. "I'll go cook—"

The touch of his scarred fingers on her chin silenced her. "Stay here," he said. "Please. For a moment, if you can."

"Oh Goddess," she whispered.

He stroked her cheek with the back of his fingers and a small sound escaped his throat. He said, so softly he could barely hear his own voice, "It has been so long, I do not know what to do."

She smiled and moved closer, her eyes growing deep and dark. "Neither do I."

He slowly drew her to him and whispered her name as he kissed her. He had forgotten how soft a woman could feel; her mature curves beckoned his touch. He held her close, his hands roaming with reverence over her back.

Hot fingers tugged at the laces of his tunic and he held her with one hand while reaching into a box of fabric with the other. He grasped something thick and warm, yanking it from the box and dropping it to the floor. His tunic disappeared over his head, landing King knew where, and he drew her down, taking her with him as he lowered himself to his knees.

He fumbled at the laces of her blouse. She brushed his hands away, undoing them herself while he tugged the blouse loose from her skirt. "Are you certain?" he asked, kissing her again. Urgent need he barely remembered surged through him, and he pressed her back onto the sprawl of fabric.

"I'm sure," she said, her hands on his bare back, his ears, his hips as he moved between her thighs. "You'll be gentle."

He opened her untied blouse. "I can be nothing else." He marveled at his hands on her silky flesh, and the sounds his touch drew from her. *Forgive me, Oriana,* he thought, lowering his head to kiss her breasts, *but I think I am falling in love again.*

A calm joy entered his heart, a moment of sweet remembrance that touched him, then departed, leaving him at peace for the first time in decades.

"What's wrong?" Maeve asked, wiping a tear from his cheek.

He laughed, nuzzling and nibbling her neck. "Nothing, nothing at all."

He grinned and she giggled, soft and warm and welcoming. He pushed aside their remaining garments. "Let us see if I can remember how."

He remembered, and later, after they staggered from the cellar to her bed, he remembered again.

Praise the King.

Lars stared at Dien's back as they rode to Devyn's farm. Dien held Aly on his lap, and he had not stopped crying, nor had he said a word since leaving Dubric at the ferry.

Silence clung near them while sounds from the festival echoed far behind and Lars felt shame clench around his heart.

"You're sleeping in the barn," Dien said, turning his horse toward the house.

Lars nodded, choking back tears, but Dien never turned to look at him, nor said another word as he dismounted and lumbered away.

Lars heard the porch door open, heard Sarea call out, then wail, then scream. He dismounted and hung his head. When he opened the barn door, he glanced back to the people he loved, to the light and the hearth and the hope he had once felt, and the pain of loss nearly sent him to his knees.

He didn't know how long he cried, but he finally pulled himself to his feet, wincing at the stab of pain in his chest, and grabbed the horse's reins. Sorrow or no sorrow, he had work to do.

Once the horse was put up and fed, he ventured to the yard. Lights shone from within the house. He tried not to look, but the golden light called to him, cutting into his heart like a set of shears into worsted wool. He saw the family around the table, crying, talking, drinking tea, comforting one another. They were together in their pain.

"Not apart," he whispered, turning away. "Not like me."

He tried to settle in the hay, but his grumbling stomach didn't want to sleep. He'd eaten only a candied apple since breakfast, and his belly had become accustomed to regular home-cooked meals. He rolled to his side and shivered. He had no blanket, not even a shirt to warm him, and he wondered if the chill was in the air or his soul. He had been alone most of his life—since the day his father had banished him, if not before—but having once felt the warmth of acceptance made solitude that much harder to bear. He curled into a ball and cried.

* * *

Maeve came to the kitchen and poured herself a cup of tea. She kissed Dubric's cheek. "He's resting again."

"Good," Dubric said. Needing something besides Maeve and her bed to occupy his mind, he reviewed and clarified his notes, closing the investigation. "Did he eat much soup?"

"Most of a bowl," Maeve said, sitting. "I think he'll be all right. In time."

"I hope so." Dubric shuddered and set aside his pencil, unwilling to imagine Foiche taking over Otlee's life and body.

Maeve grasped his hand. "What about you? Are you going to be all right?"

"I always manage," he replied. He smiled and kissed her fingers.

"That isn't what I asked."

"I will. In time."

"As will I." She took a deep breath and watched him. "What are you writing?"

"Information about Foiche," he said, adding a paragraph about Vidulyn's magic.

She cocked her head and furrowed her brow, then shook her head and resumed drinking her tea. "These are strange days."

He glanced up from his notes. "What do you mean?"

"The name brought back an old memory."

Dubric's mouth fell dry. "What sort of old memory?"

"It's nothing, really. I always thought it odd that Lissea and Devyn would name their son after such a despicable man. It just made me think of him. I haven't for a long time."

"I thought their son's name was Stuart?"

"It was. Stuart Foiche Paerth."

Dubric stood and his chair fell, scaring Lachesis and startling Maeve. "You are certain?"

"Of course I am. I even remember asking Lissea why she'd do such a thing. She said it was a family name, and needed to be kept alive to the next generation."

Dubric closed his eyes and cursed.

"What?" Maeve asked, setting aside her teacup. "What is it?"

He swallowed, hoping he would not have to do the unthinkable. "I thought Lissea was your sister."

Maeve's response was instant and earnest. "She is. My father adopted her after the war."

Adopted. Not a blood relative, praise the King. I will not have to kill Maeve. "What do you know of her birth family?"

"Just that they all died. What is it? What's wrong?"

"Fifty summers ago, I let Vidulyn escape. She had a little boy with her—Atro—and an infant. She and Atro killed the boys to give new life to Foiche, but what about the infant she had? Who did it grow up to be? What if it is Lissea? I have already heard that Stuart was groomed to become Foiche, and now you tell me that was his name? If Lissea was that infant, if she possesses shadow magic, or killed her own son, my duty is clear."

Maeve stared at him, her hands clenched on the edge of the table. "But Liss would never harm anyone, even if she came from a family like that. She's a good person. For Goddess' sake, she's my sister."

"She may come from a line of Shadow Mages; her son died under brutal, unsolved circumstances; I have one remaining ghost, her son, Stuart; and Lars is at her home. Those are connections I cannot ignore." He turned and hurried to the sitting room for his cloak and sword.

"No, Dubric! Wait! You're making a mistake." She ran to him, reached for him. "You can't! She's my sister!"

He strapped his sword belt around his hips. "Family loyalty be damned, I will not risk Lars to a Shadow Mage. I am sorry."

"You can't just kill her because of the family she was born from or because of something she may have done nearly twenty summers ago!"

He looked into Maeve's eyes and wondered if she could ever forgive him. "I must deliver justice. I have no choice. But if she is innocent, she has nothing to fear. I promise."

He clasped his cloak over his shoulders and turned to go. "Watch over Otlee. Please."

Before Maeve could answer, he left.

Lars rubbed his arms in a vain effort to warm them. The wound under Dubric's makeshift bandage throbbed painfully. Jess and Fyn had come not long after he'd holed up in the barn. They'd asked him to come back to the house, but he had refused. How could he, after what had happened? How could he ever be welcome again? Afterward, he had dozed off, but had woken to faint drizzle on the roof and noises coming from Devyn's shop. He heard a rumble, a crash, then silence.

"Guess Dev found what he was looking for," Lars muttered. He rolled over and reached for sleep but heard the door between the shop and barn open, bringing light with it.

"Lars?" Lissea asked. "Are ye here?"

At least someone was still talking to him. "Yes."

A relieved rush of air. "Can ye help me? Dev fell and I can't lift him alone."

"Sure," Lars replied. Wincing, he climbed out of the hay and brushed off the chaff.

She stood in the open doorway, silhouetted in the light, a tiny, fragile woman. "What happened to yer chest? Are ye hurt?"

"It doesn't matter," he said. He noticed that she had been crying and he said, "I'm so sorry." He lowered his gaze. What else could he say? Aly was gone and Otlee was horribly hurt, all because of his failings. If only he'd been faster. If only he'd been more alert and kept it from ever happening at all.

Liss stepped aside to let him pass, and her voice caught. "I'm sorry, too. Sometimes things happen that we can't stop, no matter what we do. I tried to cast it away, but it came back. I'm so sorry."

He met her eyes again, seeing fear and sorrow and weariness, then the moment spun away and he walked into Devyn's shop.

Devyn writhed upon a fallen rack of shelving, hats and leather and felt scattered around him. The shop was in shambles, with workbenches overturned and hats lying on the floor. The vat of lye and hides bubbled over a low fire, and had congealed into a noxious, scummy goop.

Lars knelt beside Devyn. "Are you hurt? Can you walk?" he asked, trying to help the old man sit up.

"Stuart! Run!" Dev said, his voice no more than a creak and hiss of air through a stinking cloud of rancid metal. He pushed Lars away, knocking him aside, then he fell back and arched against the shelving.

"What's wrong with him?" Lars asked, trying to reach for Devyn while avoiding the old man's waving hands. "What happened?"

"It's Foiche. He marked ye in the cemetery, but the tooth sealed yer fate. I tried to cast it away, but ye found it. I'm so sorry. Ye just wouldn't leave, and now I ain't got no choice. Dien brought the sight cloth home. Don't ye see?" Lars heard Liss hitch a sob, but beneath it, crawling up his spine, he heard a low chuckle that stood his hair on end.

He started to turn, his awareness clarifying and bringing every sound, every sight into sharp relief, and his mouth fell utterly dry.

Liss was crushing shiny diamond cloth in her bony hands, but he barely looked at her. The thing in the far corner claimed his full attention.

He saw only red eyes and yellow corpse teeth in a slash of deeper shadow.

Lars stood, Devyn forgotten, and reached for a sword that was not there. He clenched his teeth, remembering that he had left it in the hay, and he squared his shoulders and stared into the shadow's eyes.

The shadow moved to Lars's right. "You are wondering how many times I have been killed. That is the wrong question. You should instead wonder how many times I have lived. How many times you will live."

Lars turned, never dropping his gaze. "Actually, I'm wondering how I'm going to kill you. I don't have two girls to protect tonight, but I'm also unarmed."

Foiche laughed, his blood-colored tongue licking his black lips. "You will not be unarmed for long, I assure you. I offer power beyond your dreams, and the means to wield it."

Lars blinked, his eyelids rising again sluggishly, but he pushed past the pain in his head and stared into Foiche's eyes again. "You don't know anything about my dreams."

"I know you want to *belong*," Foiche said. "You carried a dead boy's tooth in your pocket, a marker for death, and have a living boy's blood on your hands, a marker for corruption. You belong now, boy. You *belong* to me." He paused, dead corpse teeth grinning, then he said, "Show him his future."

"Please," Lissea said. "He's a good boy. He saved—"

"SHOW HIM!" Foiche commanded, his voice slamming against Lars's head like a war hammer against an apple.

Lars held his head and fell to his knees onto careening ground, struggling to remain conscious, let alone upright. He saw only blackness, heard Foiche laughing vile promises inside his head, and felt warm wetness leak from his nose.

He tried to wipe the mess away, tried to find Foiche's red gaze and lose the maniacal glee pinging in his brain, but he fell helpless into the dark with the red taste of his own blood weaving through the black. Syrupy sleek silk slid across his skin, over his shoulders, and around his throat, bringing flickering images of lost lives and torment and pain.

Countless souls sucked dry, scores of others taken and possessed, each adding to the tangled chaos, each adding to the tattered screams. Strung through the images he saw one single thread, a flash of power and hunger and vicious brutality weaving in and out, just a whisper, a hidden mark.

Foiche's signature.

From one life, one vessel, to the next he wove, wielding a body until it rotted away, then taking another, and another, gorging on flesh and lust and pain all the while. Young girls raped and blinded. Babies cut open and smeared along walls. Old men flayed and their flesh fried and fed back to them. Young men sucked dry, their lives drunk like sweet brandy. Bellies ripped open, then the entrails strewn about for hogs to eat while the people were still alive. An orgy of blood and delivered pain. Lars felt the pain, saw the torment, devoured the innocence and fear as if were heady wine. People who had lived before the ancients gave way to a terrified crippled boy who looked much like him. *Stuart.*

"CUT HIM!" Foiche's voice commanded.

He felt a slash across his back, low, below the waist, and he arched back as silk slid against it. The tangle of images changed with the feel of warm human touch. In it he saw Lissea, much younger and furious, throw a fistful of teeth at a snarling, middle-aged Vidulyn. He saw her pleading for forgiveness as she slit her son's throat, saw her tormented, tortured, raped. Saw her carried from a fire, saw her birth. Her conception at the malevolent lusts of a rotting corpse.

Her touch left, taking her sorrow with it and plunging him again into the maddening red-black horrors of Foiche's reigns.

Lars wailed and fell writhing to the floor, lost in the interwoven strands of murder and rampage and death.

He felt another slash across his back, between his shoulders, and he screamed as he endured the rape and devouring of a young mother and her two infant boys. He felt the babe's flesh tear between his teeth, tasted the salty sweet blood, all the while taking what he wanted from its mother. He saw bites eaten from her breasts, heard her screams of torment as he thrust into her, ripped into her, and he felt dark joy at the pain he wrought.

Another slash, another horror visited that he could not stop nor turn away from. Then another. And another.

"Do you hear that?" Sarea asked. She raised her head, looking blearily at her cold cup of tea. The girls had gone to bed, crying, leaving her and Dien alone. She wished she had some whiskey to add to her tea. Just something to help her forget, or to numb the pain for a few minutes. Aly was dead, oh Goddess, Aly was dead.

Dien pushed away from the table and honked into his kerchief. Someone pounded upon the door and he grumbled as he snatched it open.

Dubric barged in, knocking Dien aside as if he were no larger than Otlee. "Where's Lars?"

"Sleeping in the barn. Why?" Sarea said, standing. Lars had not saved Aly. The thought twirled in her belly, making her nauseous. Aly had died, and life as she knew it was over. *She's dead, my baby is dead*.

Dubric said nothing, just turned and pulled his sword. He shoved past Dien again, then disappeared into the dark.

"What the hells?" Dien grumbled. He grabbed his sword and followed Dubric.

Sarea staggered to the door, then paused as a scream slipped through the night. Thin and terrified, like an animal in a trap, it was unmistakably human and it clawed at her heart, thrusting an old, hazy memory to the front of her mind.

It echoed Stuart's screams when her father had brought him home, broken and ruined and bleeding. She saw the blood-soaked cloth, Stuart's frantic terror, her own father's determined fury.

She had buried those memories most of her life, but she winced as she recalled her father laying Stuart's bleeding body on the settee. He had ripped the diamond cloth away and torn it to shreds while her mother tried to stop him. Then Devyn had stood and had looked at her, not her mother, not even Stuart, and had commanded that she ride to the castle and get the authorities, because her mother had tried to get her brother killed. Then he turned and hit Lissea across the face, knocking her to the floor.

Sarea shook, her hand clenching at the door. She had run to the barn, to their mule, and had galloped south screaming and crying and refusing to believe that her mother could—

Another scream tore through the darkness and Sarea felt hands on her back, her arms, her shoulders.

"Mam!" Jess cried, shaking her. "That's Lars! What's going on?" Fyn and Kia stood behind her, clutching at each other and crying.

"She tried to kill him," Sarea said, barely recognizing her own voice. "And when I got back my father was lost to madness, my mother was beaten, my brother was dead. My whole family was gone."

"But Lars isn't! We have to help him! I told you we couldn't let him stay alone in the barn!"

Another scream, then Jess released her. Sarea crumbled, falling to her knees. The porch door slammed closed, long after Jess had gone through.

* * *

Lars retched as he relived eating chilled human brains with an iron spoon. That experience completed, he grabbed a girl by the hair and forced her head toward his lap.

"AGAIN!" Foiche commanded, his voice shimmery and red among the bleak visions in Lars's head. "FINISH IT!"

Somewhere beyond the red-black madness, Lars heard Devyn scream "Stuart!" and a door creak open, but he devoured the girl's struggles as he forced her to pleasure him. That vision changed to rutting with a bleating and struggling animal during a rainstorm, then everything turned black.

Dubric heard Devyn call out. He kicked the latch, breaking it, and the door slammed open. Lissea, gripping a knife, struggled with Devyn. Both ripped the cloth wrapped around Lars while the boy writhed and wailed on the floor. He had drawn his knees to his chest and he tore at his hair and the trampled earth. Blood soaked his hands and covered his face and back.

All around, Dubric heard a low chuckle that settled like rusty needles into his brain. Stuart appeared near Lars, between him and a dark and grinning shadow.

"I have to!" Lissea cried, pulling the cloth with one hand and slashing toward Devyn with the other. "My line, my people, can't die! I have a duty to my family, my blood!"

"Stuart!" Devyn screamed. A red line appeared across his belly and he staggered back, taking a long strip of cloth with him.

The titter in Dubric's head screamed, "FINISH IT! NOW! I DIDN'T BEGET YOU AND LET YOU LIVE TO FAIL ME, YOU GOOD-FOR-NOTHING BITCH."

Dubric tried to step forward, but the needles in his head spun and jabbed, countless stabs of bright pain, and he fell.

Liss turned to Lars again, the knife poised over a loop of fabric at Lars's throat, while behind her, Devyn shoved up to his hands and knees and reached for the cloth. He pulled, screaming in pain, and dragged Lars backward across the dirt. Lissea's blade missed its mark, plunging hilt-deep into Lars's arm.

Devyn collapsed, panting, and tried to pull again, but he succeeded only in adding to the ever-growing puddle of blood beneath him. He rolled, his arm and the cloth in that hand hissing in the fire.

Foiche shrieked, and the pins in Dubric's head faded, leaving the smell of charred silk behind. Fire teased the edges of Foiche's ghastly image, his hands, his elbow, his left foot, his hair.

Lars groaned and struggled to free himself from the cloth. Stuart knelt beside him and tried to help, while the flames drew ever closer, wicking up the fabric.

Dubric stumbled toward them, sword in hand, while behind him, Dien staggered to his feet.

"It ain't too late! Ye can live again!" Lissea screamed, plunging the knife toward Lars, but she stopped, gagging and gasping as Dubric thrust his sword into her belly. "Papa?" she said, dropping the knife. "Help me?"

"DO IT!" Foiche commanded, the flames turning his arms to ash. "HURRY! I CANNOT DIE!"

"Yes, you can," Dubric said, sagging as he pulled his sword free. "It is finished. Your line is no more."

Lissea blinked and slumped to her knees, then fell face forward beside Lars. Stuart, still struggling to unwrap Lars from the smoldering cloth, disappeared as if he had never existed.

Dubric dropped his sword. He pulled his dagger and cut the burning cloth from Lars's throat and tossed the charring bits into the fire. Foiche howled as the flames consumed him, until nothing more than smoke and ash and a few yellow corpse teeth remained.

Dien staggered past Dubric and pulled Devyn from the flames. Assured that Lars was safe, Dubric stumbled to where Foiche had lurked. A full complement of teeth lay in a wispy pile of ash. Dubric snatched up the mess and threw the teeth into the fire. They cracked and sizzled, turning to coals.

Jesscea ran through the open door, then stopped, gaping at the bodies on the floor. "Grandmama?" she gasped, moving forward again. "Lars? Daddy?"

Dien held open his arms for her. "It's over now."

"Stuart?" Devyn gasped, reaching for Jesscea but looking at Dubric.

"He is at peace," Dubric said. While Dien comforted his daughter, Dubric checked Devyn's injuries, wincing at the exposed and cut viscera.

Devyn swallowed, pained, and asked, "And . . . and Lars?"

"He is a strong boy. He will heal."

Devyn winced and smiled.

Then he died.

Mid-morning, two days later, Lars followed Dien's family to the cemetery. They walked from the house, along with a few people from Tormod, but Lars lagged behind, staring at the ground and doing his best not to cry.

The burns on the back of his neck still stung, but sunlight made them feel lit afire. He didn't care.

Dubric had called for the village barber to stitch the gashes on his back and arm. Seventy-three stitches in all, but Lars didn't care about that, either.

Aly was dead. Devyn. Lissea. All because of him.

And then there's Otlee, he thought, sick dread twisting in his belly. *That's my fault, too.*

They reached the grave site, three regular graves and a small one, and the family clustered together while the village priest gave his sermon. Lars stood alone, far behind them, his head down. He barely noticed Dubric standing with Maeve and Otlee, barely heard the priest's words, barely thought of anything but the images he had seen in Devyn's shop and the pain and shame tearing through his heart.

Dubric had offered to have him stay at Maeve's, but he had declined. What could he say to Otlee, how could he apologize for his failure? How could Otlee ever forgive him if he could not forgive himself?

But staying at Dev's had been an acute torture of its own. He had lived the past days in silence, spending most of his time sitting on the settee. He had not eaten, had barely slept.

Pain follows me everywhere I go, he thought. *Is it my curse to bear, like Dubric's ghosts?*

Maybe everyone would be better off if I were dead.

He took a shaky breath and looked up as the priest spoke of Aly, and he blinked away the tears welling in his eyes. *I was there, I should have saved her. Somehow, I should have saved her.*

Dubric held Maeve's hand, and each had a free hand on Otlee's shoulders, comforting him during Braoin's eulogy. Sarea and the girls clustered under Dien's big arms. The priest droned on, some nonsense about coming home to the waters of life. All Lars could think was that Aly had died, suffocating on a muddy road, and he should have saved her.

He lowered his head again and tried to endure the morning.

Something touched his arm, the barest movement, little more than a whisper on the wind. Jess stood there, watching him with tears streaming down her cheeks.

"It's going to be okay," she said, squeezing his hand.

He squeezed back, nodding, even though he didn't believe it.

She released his hand and stood beside him, turning slightly to let her head rest on his shoulder.

"I'm sorry, Jess, so damned sorry," he said, afraid to move for fear he'd scare her away.

"I know," she said, raising her head to look at his face. "You did everything you could." She sniffled and said, "Oh, Lars, come here. You don't have to face this all alone."

Shushing him, she drew him into her arms and held him while he cried.

Afterward, when the services finished and he and Jess had comforted each other as best they could, he raised his head from her shoulder. He felt Dien pat him on the shoulder as he walked past and Sarea grasped and squeezed his hand. Lars sniffled, nodding, then noticed Dubric watching him.

Dubric smiled sadly, and excused himself from Maeve and Otlee before walking to Lars. "Chin up, lad," he said. "Better days will come again."

"Are you certain, sir?"

Dubric glanced back at Maeve, then turned to smile at Jess. "Yes, I am. Even if you do not believe, it happens all on its own."

Lars reached for Jess's hand. "Yes, sir, I suppose it does."

He waited for the others to leave, then he stood beside Aly's grave to say good-bye. Still holding Jess's hand, he followed their family back home.

ABOUT THE AUTHOR

TAMARA SILER JONES started her academic career as a science geek, took up graphic design and earned a degree in art, and now writes forensic fantasy full time. She's an avid baker and quilter as well as a wife, mother, and cat wrangler. Despite the gruesome nature of her work, Tam's easygoing and friendly. Not sick and twisted at all. Honest! Visit her online at www.tamarasilerjones.com.

*Read on for a tantalizing teaser
of Tamara Siler Jones's next
chilling fantasy mystery!*

VALLEY
OF THE
SOUL

Coming in Fall 2006

VALLEY OF THE SOUL
Coming in Fall 2006

I stripped Sweeny naked, tied her to the tree, and started a fire as I waited for her to wake. Once I knew she had no choice but to see, I began. Livestock first, from baby chicks to full-grown steers. I killed each one in sight of her and threw the carcasses on the flames, some in pieces. The livestock gone, I killed and burned her grotesque abominations, then everyone who worked for her, starting with the children, adding each body to the fire. Then her family. One by one she watched them die, watched them burn. I burned her books, her papers, her furniture. Everything she had. Everything. When the flesh had burned down to ash and flame, I killed her and burned her with the rest. I waited, watching until there was nothing left, not even smoke or embers, nowhere for her filthy soul to go. Then, just to be sure, I burned the tree I'd tied her to.

I salted the earth and ash, released the villagers, and prayed for my sins and the innocents I'd slaughtered. Lastly, before sleep, I sent a messenger bird to Tunkek telling him that Fayre Sweeny, the butcher of Quarry Run, was dead.

Oriana of Fallowes, from her journal
Dated 4 32, 2221

CHAPTER

I

†

A cart rattled past the village of Quarry Run under the watchful eye of a waning moon. Some of the villagers were home abed while others enjoyed the revelry at the Twisted Cypress tavern. None paid notice to the cart or its contents, despite the heavy, rotting stench it left in its wake. As the cart rolled down the ravine road to the outskirts of the village, two dogs barked and pulled on their leads, emboldened by the stink. A third dog cowered against a door and whined, its white fur and one speckled leg bright in the moonlight.

The carter grasped the largest bundle. "Shut up, all of you. You don't want none of this." Wrapped in burlap, it was cold, much colder than the warm spring night, and heavy. The carter took a quick look around and heaved the thing into the ravine. It crashed into the brush and weeds.

The carter hoped this time it would roll a goodly distance and quietly rot away. The last bundle, tossed a phase or two before, had settled not ten lengths from the road. It had been found the following morning but, thankfully, Marsden had decided to bury it. Burying was better, hells yes, but burying took time and invited curiosity.

Better just to toss the extra bits and let fate take hold. There were no marks on the bundles, nothing to arouse interest or suspicion. It was just meat after all. Rotting, buggy meat. Could be anything.

Dubric Byerly, Castellan of Castle Faldorrah, saw no ghosts as he cautiously slid down a tree-clotted ravine. He grasped a sapling to keep his balance and hoped his quaking knees would not fail him.

Below, on a flattened bit of ground, Constable Calder Marsden stood beside burlap-wrapped remains and worriedly watched Dubric's descent. Flies buzzed all around him and spectators gossiped on the road thirty lengths or so above, their voices muffled to a low drone by the trees. Marsden looked ill. To the best of Dubric's knowledge, the man had never seen a murder before.

The burlap looked clear of blood. *No blood, no ghosts,* Dubric thought, frowning as he completed his descent, *but most certainly a murder.*

Cursed by the goddess, he had been haunted by death's unwilling victims for more than four decades. He could not recall a time in which a murder had left no ghost, no headache, nothing but a corpse. If he approached the place of their death, murders revealed their ghosts. Always.

"It's here, sir," Marsden said, glancing at the corpse as Dubric caught his breath. "But there's not much to her."

An adult female's hips and thighs had been wrapped in burlap and tied with twine, at least until animals had found the rotting flesh. It remained mostly intact, although some of the flesh had been chewed away and maggots roiled over the exposed meat and her privates.

The rotting stench had an undertone of an herb, perhaps a spice, pungent and sharp amidst the gassy decay. Dubric did not recognize the scent.

"Are any local women missing?" Dubric ignored the creak from his arthritic joints as he knelt beside the remains. His own discomfort could wait.

Marsden shifted on his feet. "No, milord Castellan. Least ways not that I've heard of. Folks are working while the weather is good. I suppose someone might have disappeared, though."

"I will require a census." Dubric pulled a pair of thin sheep-gut gloves from his pocket and drew them onto his burn-scarred hands, carefully positioning the stitched seams over his knuckles. He prepared to dictate his findings then paused, remembering. Otlee, his younger page, the boy who had taken his notes during two previous investigations, had stayed home at the castle.

Dubric looked up. "How well do you write?"

Marsden swallowed, staring at the partial corpse. "Not very well, milord. I can make my mark, cipher a little. I read a few words, here and there, but don't hardly write any. I pay Pitt to do my official papers."

"Then fetch one of my men from the road," Dubric said.

Marsden nodded eagerly and turned to climb the ravine, grasping saplings to aid his ascent.

Dubric sighed and set to work, surveying the immediate area. He examined the fresh and decayed leaves, looked under bushes and plants, but found nothing unusual, no unexplained footprints, no clothing, no apparent clues. Nothing but a woman's hips and thighs partially wrapped in burlap. He wiped sweat from his brow and looked up to the glints of sky peeking through branches of elm, sycamore and maple. *By the King, I am nearly sixty-nine summers old. Too old to keep facing this madness.*

He heard someone break through the brush uphill and he turned to wave. "I am down here," he said.

Lanky, limber and fifteen, Dubric's elder page, Lars, skip-jumped down the steep slope with no apparent hesitation or discomfort. "I've taken a statement from the fellow who found her, sir. Carpenter. Name's Gossle. Was out hunting mushrooms when he stumbled over her. Dien's finishing up the spectator listings."

"That is fine," Dubric said, handing Lars his notebook. "How is he managing?"

Lars flipped through to find an empty page. "He'll be all right, sir. It's good for all of us to get back to work."

"None of us need to return to this type of work just yet," Dubric said. Murders a moon before had ravaged his team. His squire, Dien, had lost a child and young Otlee had lost his innocence. Lars had nearly died and even Dubric had . . .

Had what? he thought, pulling back the edges of the burlap and frowning at the bitten and torn flesh. *Had I realized that I am not yet dead?*

Dubric took a breath and let it free. The past was past. Only the now and the future mattered, with or without ghosts.

* * *

Dubric reached the road to find scores of villagers and quarry workers standing in loose groups. All watched him warily and most took a step back as Lars came through the brush with a sack slung over his shoulder.

Dubric's squire lumbered toward them, raking his thick fingers through his shorn hair. Once a steady and solid brown, Dien's hair was now flecked with gray and his massive bulk seemed diminished. Dubric wondered if he ate much anymore, or slept.

Dien barely looked up as he spoke. "One of the workers found a hunk of meat near the road a couple of phases ago. He buried it to stop the stink."

"We will have to exhume it," Dubric said, watching as Lars carried the remains to his horse.

Dien took a deep breath and met Dubric's worried gaze. "What are we looking at, sir?"

"I do not yet know. We have a woman's lower torso. It could be anything."

"And the other?" Dien asked softly, staring into Dubric's eyes. "You're sure about the other?"

"Yes, I am certain. I neither see nor feel any ghosts."

Lars came up to them and all three huddled close. "I've been thinking. You have roughly a five-mile range for the ghosts, right? What if she was killed someplace else and just dumped here? The merchant's road is less than a quarter of a mile away. That's not far to detour, and if it's a traveling killer we'd have no way to track him. Merchant roads run all over the provinces. He could be anywhere by now."

"Sounds fine to me," Dien said. "I've had enough blood and death to last me a while."

"As have I," Dubric said, "but we must rule out any possibilities that the killer remains in the area. The village is nearby, as are the workers' shacks, and there are scores of nearby farms. Any of the regional inhabitants could have done this."

Lars nodded, frowning. "Yes, sir, I agree, but the ghosts. How can it be a local killer if you don't see any ghosts?"

Dien looked past Dubric toward the ravine. "What if it's one of the crazies? The sanatorium's just on the other side of the bridge."

"Insane or not, murder is murder," Lars said slowly.

"If the killer doesn't know what they're doing at all, maybe the Goddess doesn't consider it murder."

"They're still people," Lars said through gritted teeth. "And murder is still murder."

Dubric said, "I doubt that the sanatorium is involved. The patients have no means of transport save their own feet and not only is it fenced and locked, it is on the far side of the ravine. Not even a seriously demented man would carry a partial corpse down one side of a ravine and halfway up the other, assuming he could get it past the fence."

"That's true," Dien said. "Bodies get dropped downhill, not carried uphill."

"Could it have been tossed from the road?" Lars asked.

Dubric pursed his lips as he considered the idea. "I suppose so, but there is no way to know for certain. I saw no unexplained tracks, but discovery and retrieval have disturbed much of the undergrowth. It may have lain there for bells or days before it was found. We have only speculation at this point. No motive, no suspects, nothing definite to follow."

"Yes, sir," Dien sighed, opening his own note-book. "Thought you might want to know Tupper Dughall's among the spectators."

Dubric looked over his shoulder and searched the crowd. He found Tupper easily—the criminal watched their conversation with interest and a slight smile. He stared into Dubric's eyes, winked, then spat tobacco juice on the ground.

Lars muttered a curse. "That wretch? He's been out of gaol, what, two phases?"

"Almost three," Dien said. "I find it rather interesting that our most violent prisoner just happens to be at the scene of a murder investigation. Especially when he's not supposed to be here in Quarry Run at all."

Dubric turned back to his men. "Did he give you any problems during his release or today?"

"No, sir, nothing more than usual. Bit of a mouth, some attitude," Dien said.

"And you had told him to stay away from Quarry Run?"

Dien met Dubric's gaze. "Yes, sir. I specifically told him to stay the seven hells away from the village *and* from Arien when I dragged his sorry ass to the castle gates."

"Then he's violating two terms of his release," Lars said. "I had a woman named Arien on my list. She was one of the first people I talked to."

"She's here?" Dien asked, turning his attention to Lars. "What did she say?"

Lars consulted his notes. "Just that she was going to the hospital to get medicine for her son when she saw everyone standing around. I let her go on her way." He glanced at the sky then up the road to the castle and frowned.

Dien popped his knuckles. "Sir? Want me to drag Tupper's carcass in for further questioning?"

"We shall scare him but let us not maim him yet," Dubric said. "Lars, borrow a shovel and unearth the buried remains. Dien and I will question Tupper."

"Try not to bust the chair," Constable Marsden said as Dien tossed Tupper into the office. "My grandfather made it."

"I'll do my best," Dien said, yanking Tupper from the floor only to slam him onto the seat.

The wood creaked but held, and Marsden let out a sigh of relief.

"You're not supposed to be here, dung heap," Dien said. "I told you to stay gone."

"You might of said, but I never agreed," Tupper said, leaning back and crossing his tattooed arms behind his head. He stretched out his legs and yawned. "A man's got a right to make up his own mind. B'sides, I ain't done nothing."

Dubric opened his notebook. "You have broken the agreement of release."

"I never made no agreement." Tupper smirked, glancing at Dubric and Dien. "This is my home and y'all can just go agree with yourselves."

"What about Arien?" Dubric asked, ignoring the taunt.

"What about her?"

"Have you been bothering her?"

Tupper chuckled. "Depends on what you mean by bothering. I ain't been bothered enough to crawl back to her snatch, if that's what you mean."

Dien mumbled and started pacing, his hands

clenching and unclenching while Marsden smacked Tupper on the back of the head and said, "Watch your damn mouth! You're talking to Lord Dubric."

Tupper stared at Dubric. "I know who I'm talking to. A creaky old man who likes to think he's top dog. But he ain't, not no more. He's just a toothless old hound who'd rather sleep in the sun than tree a possum."

Dubric drew a slow breath and let it free, reminding himself that he had no ghosts and thus no murder, yet. "I will only say this once. If you do not follow these instructions I will throw you back into the gaol. I want you out of Quarry Run. In fact, I want you out of central Faldorrah. I never want to lay my eyes on your pox-scarred face again. You will leave, immediately, in the clothes you are wearing, with whatever monies you are carrying, and nothing else. You will pick a road and will start walking, in any direction as long as it takes you far from here. You will not attempt to speak with anyone. You will not come back. Ever. Agree or return to gaol."

"You can't banish me, old man." Tupper sneered. "My family owns these lands."

"They may own them, but I enforce the law. May I remind you that you do not have to return to my gaol in one piece or arrive there alive." Dubric glanced at Dien. "Agree or disagree, it is your choice, but the choice will be made now and I will hold you to it."

Tupper leaned forward. "I never touched Arien and I don't know nothing about no body!"

"I do not care. Leave Quarry Run or return to gaol."

"In crumpled pieces," Dien added, grinning.

"Damn you, I served my punishment. I want my pegging life back!"

Dubric sighed and stepped aside. "He is all yours."

Dien moved forward but Tupper scrambled from the chair and away. "No, wait. I'm going, I'm going!" he said.

Then he was gone, the door slamming behind him.

Dubric smoothed his tunic and turned to Marsden. "If he returns, and he likely will, inform us and we will remove him."

"Yes, sir," Marsden said. "But, milord, if I may, why such threats? Other men have beaten their women and been allowed to return home."

"Other men did not attempt to kill the child their woman carried," Dubric said, rubbing the back of his neck. It hurt; a thin, sharp pain across his spine.

"He damn near succeeded," Dien muttered. He scowled at the door. "Damn near killed both of them."

The pain in Dubric's neck moved forward and to the right, stabbing and sharp. He rubbed it, kneading the throbbing muscle. "Tupper spent more than five summers in my gaol and not once did he show the least bit of regret or sorrow for what he did, or for the trials he has ensured for his son. In fact, he frequently commented that he 'should have finished it' and often promised to do so. I will not grant such a violent man the opportunity to complete his threats."

"Tupper was released a couple of phases ago and now we have an unknown dead woman," Dien said. "That seems like a strong coincidence."

Dubric nodded, shifting hands as the pain traveled across his neck to the left. His eyes started to hurt, throbbing and cold. Like a ghost ache, but without the ghosts. "Where has he been living?"

"He stayed with his folks the first couple of days," Marsden said as he walked around his desk. "Spent a lot of time at the Twisted Cypress."

"And after the first couple of days?" Dubric asked. He tried to ignore the sensation moving through his neck. Was it a muscle spasm? Apoplexy? Old age?

Marsden sat, his fingers lacing together on the immaculate wooden surface. "He's been shacking with Winni, one of the barmaids, ever since."

His eyes watering, Dubric added to his notes. "Does she pay his expenses or has he found employment?" he choked out as his throat cramped up, the pain moving forward and cutting off his air. Dien gave him a worried look.

"Oh, he's working," Marsden said, apparently oblivious to Dubric's discomfort. "Same thing he did back before he busted up Arien: driving the rubble carts. Nights, mostly. He ain't been near Arien, though. I check on her and Haydon every couple of days."

The three men looked over as the door opened and Lars peeked through. "Sir, I found something."

As suddenly as it appeared, the pain in Dubric's throat disappeared. The cool ache in his eyes remained. Rolling his head a little to loosen lingering muscle cramps, Dubric closed his notebook and strode to the door with Dien and Marsden on his heels.

Lars returned to his mare and nodded briskly

toward a reeking bundle strapped to the animal's back. "Burlap-wrapped remains again, sir, and it's human. The man thought it was part of an animal."

Dubric looked all around him. He saw no ghosts. Even his neck felt fine. It must have been fatigue, or his imagination. "Are you certain it is human?"

"Yes, sir. Upper torso, ribs, spine, shoulders, rotting flesh. Looks female. I thought it might be the missing top half to the legs we found this morning, but she's awfully decayed."

"And the head?" Dien asked.

Lars reached for the pommel of his saddle. "No, no head."